ELLERY QUEEN'S CRIME WAVE

Novels by Ellery Queen

The Roman Hat Mystery
The French Powder Mystery
The Dutch Shoe Mystery
The Greek Coffin Mystery
The Egyptian Cross Mystery
The American Gun Mystery
The Siamese Twin Mystery
The Chinese Orange Mystery
The Spanish Cape Mystery
Halfway House
The Door Between
The Devil to Pay
The Four of Hearts
The Dragon's Teeth
Calamity Town
There Was an Old Woman
The Murderer Is a Fox
Ten Days' Wonder

Cat of Many Tails
Double, Double
The Origin of Evil
The Kind Is Dead
The Scarlet Letters
The Glass Village
Inspector Queen's Own Case
The Finishing Stroke
The Player on the Other Side
And on the Eighth Day
The Fourth Side of the Triangle
A Study in Terror
Face to Face
The House of Brass
Cop Out
The Last Woman in His Life
A Fine and Private Place

Books of Short Stories by Ellery Queen

The Adventures of Ellery Queen
The *New* Adventures of Ellery Queen
The Casebook of Ellery Queen
Calendar of Crime

q.b.i.; queen's Bureau of Investigation
Queen's Full
Q.E.D.: Queen's Experiments in Detection

Edited by Ellery Queen

Challenge to the Reader
101 Years' Entertainment
Sporting Blood
The Female of the Species
The Misadventures of Sherlock Holmes
Rogues' Gallery
Best Stories from EQMM
To the Queen's Taste
The Queen's Awards, 1946–1953
Murder by Experts
20th Century Detective Stories
Ellery Queen's Awards, 1954–1957
The Literature of Crime
Ellery Queen's Mystery Annuals: 13th–16th
Ellery Queen's Anthologies: 1960–1976
The Quintessence of Queen (*Edited by Anthony Boucher*)

To Be Read Before Midnight
Ellery Queen's Mystery Mix
Ellery Queen's Double Dozen
Ellery Queen's 20th Anniversary Annual
Ellery Queen's Crime Carousel
Ellery Queen's All-Star Lineup
Poetic Justice
Ellery Queen's Mystery Parade
Ellery Queen's Murder Menu
Ellery Queen's Minimysteries
Ellery Queen's Grand Slam
Ellery Queen's The Golden 13
Ellery Queen's Headliners
Ellery Queen's Mystery Bag
Ellery Queen's Crookbook
Ellery Queen's Murdercade
Ellery Queen's Crime Wave

Ellery Queen's Mystery Magazine (36th Year)

True Crime by Ellery Queen

Ellery Queen's International Case Book   The Woman in the Case

Critical Works by Ellery Queen

The Detective Short Story   Queen's Quorum   In the Queens' Parlor

Under the Pseudonym of Barnaby Ross

The Tragedy of X
The Tragedy of Y

The Tragedy of Z
Drury Lane's Last Case

30th *Mystery Annual*

ELLERY QUEEN'S CRIME WAVE

24 STORIES FROM
Ellery Queen's Mystery Magazine

EDITED BY
ELLERY QUEEN

G. P. Putnam's Sons, New York

SBN: 399-11737-7

Library of Congress Cataloging in Publication Data
Main entry under title:

Ellery Queen's crime wave.

(Mystery annual; 30)
CONTENTS: Hoch, E. D. The case of the lapidated man.—Harrington,
J. My neighbor, ay.—Gilbert, A. The invisible witness. [*etc.*]
1. Detective and mystery stories, American. 2. Detective and mystery
stories, English. I. Queen, Ellery, pseud. II. Ellery Queen's mystery
magazine. III. Series: EQMM annual; 30.
PZ1.A1E4   vol. 30   [PS648.D4]   823'.0872   75–43963

PRINTED IN THE UNITED STATES OF AMERICA

ACKNOWLEDGMENTS

The Editor hereby makes grateful acknowledgment to the following authors and authors' representatives for giving permission to reprint the material in this volume:

Mary Amlaw for *Farewell, Beloved,* © 1974 by Mary Amlaw.

Isaac Asimov for *All in the Way You Read It,* © 1974 by Isaac Asimov.

Georges Borchardt, Inc. for *The Fallen Curtain* by Ruth Rendell, © 1974 by Ruth Rendell.

Collins-Knowlton-Wing, Inc. for *The Raffles Special* by Barry Perowne, © 1974 by Philip Atkey.

John Cushman Associates, Inc. for *The Invisible Witness* by Anthony Gilbert, © 1973 by Anthony Gilbert; and *Who Has Seen the Wind?* by Michael Gilbert, © 1956 by Michael Gilbert.

Elsin Ann Gardner for *A Night Out with the Boys,* © 1973 by Elsin Ann Gardner.

Blanche C. Gregory, Inc. for *Screams and Echoes* by Donald Olson, © 1974 by Donald Olson.

Joyce Harrington for *The Cabin in the Hollow,* © 1974 by Joyce Harrington; and *My Neighbor, Ay,* © 1974 by Joyce Harrington.

Edward D. Hoch for *Interpol: The Case of the Lapidated Man,* © 1974 by Edward D. Hoch; and *The Problem of the Covered Bridge,* © 1974 by Edward D. Hoch.

The Sterling Lord Agency, Inc. for *The Big Story* by Dick Francis, © 1973.

CONTENTS

INTRODUCTION

Dear Reader:

It was Aristotle who said that a good plot goes from *possibility* to *probability* to *necessity*. Obviously, Aristotle was not referring to the plot of a detective story—the tale of detection, as we know it today, was not invented until 3000 years after Aristotle formulated his dictum.

But, with one variation, Aristotle could have been predicting the stage-by-stage plot development of the modern detective story. All we have to do is change the order of the steps.

The detective story starts rather than ends with necessity. "When in the Course of human events" one person is so compellingly motivated that he or she kills another, that action can be deemed *necessity*. Official or amateur investigation then interrogates, examines, observes, sifts, and deduces until a theory emerges, and that theory of the crime and of the culprit's identity goes from *possibility* to *probability*, and in the end to *certainty*—which, when one stops to think of it, is really another facet of necessity. So, full circle, in principle and essence, Aristotle was right, and he did predict the inevitable course of human events. It can be said that we hold these detective truths to be self-evident.

This collection of twenty-four stories marks a vintage year, celebrating the 30th anniversary of hardcover anthologies that have derived from *Ellery Queen's Mystery Magazine.* The

11

24 stories offer you detection of all types—detective, intuitive, and procedural—and a calendar of crime ranging from theft and kidnapping to adultery, blackmail, and murder, including crimes and misdemeanors of high diplomacy. As in previous years you will find humor and horror, ghosts and gumshoes, impossible crimes and miracle problems—minutes of excitement and derring-do, hours of suspense and suspension of disbelief, days of escape and entertainment. . . .

Now then . . . turn the page, gently, gently, and open the door to a different world—rather, to the same world but seen through different eyes.

ELLERY QUEEN

INTERPOL: THE CASE OF THE LAPIDATED MAN

by Edward D. Hoch

Edward D. Hoch's five long-running series in Ellery Queen's Mystery Magazine *are remarkably different in appeal and category. The Nick Velvet stories concern a unique felon who, for a minimum fee of $20,000, steals only the worthless—no jewels, gold, objets d'art—and has to be a topnotch 'tec in order to be a topnotch thief. Rand is a code-and-cipher expert and counterspy. Captain Leopold is a straightforward procedural cop who has a knack for solving baffling, sometimes "impossible" cases. Ulysses S. Byrd is a con man with a gift for spotting gulls and devising nets to trap them. Sebastian Blue and his associate Laura Charme, who work for Interpol, the International Criminal Police Organization, investigate airline crimes, especially when they are bizarre.*

And this Interpol story is bizarre indeed—about an ancient method of murder in a modern setting. . . .

THE MAN's name was Romeo Hyde—or at least that was the name which appeared on television screens throughout England each week at the beginning of *The Thriller Hour*. Once an actor, he was now the highly respected producer of one of the most popular televised entertainments of recent years.

Seeing him, especially against a backdrop of the North Tiverton slag heap, one did not think instantly of acting or television or the theater. He might have been a country

13

squire or a mine owner, climbing over the rocks for a better view of his holdings. At first glance he seemed alone on the slag heap, a graying man of uncertain middle age, carrying a furled umbrella which he used as a walking stick to guide him over the rough spots.

The sky was leaden with the threat of rain, and an occasional gust of wind blew at the flaps of his coat. Somewhere behind him a rock was dislodged, and he turned quickly at the sound. He saw them then, a line of figures silhouetted against the gray of the sky. They had materialized all at once over the edge of the hill, and now they formed a rough semicircle in front of him. He opened his mouth as if to speak, but then the first rock struck him on the shoulder.

Romeo Hyde turned to run, perhaps realizing it was already too late, as more rocks pelted down on him. A single smooth stone struck him on the forehead, and then another hit his temple. He staggered and went down as the stones kept coming with deadly accuracy.

After a time, when the man on the ground no longer moved, the stoning ceased. The line of figures drew back, slowly, and vanished over the hill the way they had come.

The rain which had threatened all morning began to fall, covering the hillside with a misty curtain.

Sebastian Blue was quite pleased with himself. After little more than a year with Interpol, he'd just learned that his special field of investigation, airline crime, had been designated as a new Group H in the International Police Coordinating Division. Sitting in the Secretary General's office on the top floor of Interpol headquarters in Saint-Cloud, outside Paris, Sebastian surveyed the framed photographs and mementos that covered the walls and reflected once more on the vagaries of life. It was personal tragedy, a broken marriage, that had caused him to leave Scotland Yard and seek employment with Interpol. At his age, nearing 50, it could have deepened the tragedy. Instead it had opened up a whole new life, a new career.

"So you see," the Secretary General was saying, "national attitude toward airline crime is changing. You might remember it was not too many years ago when Interpol could not even act in cases of airliner hijacking, because of the political implications in many instances. Today the nations of the world—those that belong to the International Criminal Police Organization—realize that we can serve their national interests while still remaining aloof from politics. The terrorist who hijacks an airliner or mails a letter-bomb is no politician. He is a criminal, and must be treated as such."

"How much of a staff will I have in Group H?" Sebastian asked, anxious to get on with the business at hand.

"I am assigning Laura Charme to work with you, since she has assisted you many times in the past. Our budget is limited, but we will give you what help we can." He motioned toward the organization chart for the Coordinating Division which hung on one wall. Until yesterday there had been only seven groups—now there were eight:

Group A—Files
Group B—Fingerprint Identification
Group C—Murder and Theft, Missing Persons
Group D—Bank Fraud, Smuggling
Group E—Drugs, Morals Offenses, Traffic in Women
Group F—Counterfeiting
Group G—Economic and Financial Crimes
Group H—Airline Crimes

"Naturally your work will overlap the activities of other groups," the Secretary General continued. "A crime like gold smuggling, for example, could involve Group D, Group G, and your group. If the gold is used in payment for narcotics, Group E would also be interested."

"I understand."

"You look pleased, Sebastian. But perhaps the news today is not all good. How would you like to return to England?"

"What?"

"A man named Romeo Hyde has been murdered there. He was a television producer of some renown. *The Thriller Hour* was his creation, I believe."

"And he's been killed?"

The Secretary General nodded. "They found his body yesterday. He'd been lapidated—stoned to death."

Sebastian Blue grunted. "A ritual killing? Something Biblical?"

"We don't know. He was in the north of England, scouting locations for the television series, when it happened. I want you to go there."

"How does Romeo Hyde's death concern Group H?"

"In a most peculiar manner. *The Thriller Hour* did a television show in England a few weeks ago concerning the crash of an airliner. The script caused quite a lot of interest among law-enforcement agencies. His killing may be linked to that script, and to a number of recent plane crashes on international routes. This dossier contains the information you need, plus a copy of the script in question."

"I'll fly to London tomorrow," Sebastian said.

"Take Miss Charme with you. She may be of some use around those television people. And, Sebastian—"

"Yes, sir?"

"When you get back to England, remember—it's not Scotland Yard any longer. You have no powers of arrest with Interpol. Your assignment is simply to gather and supply information."

"I understand," Sebastian Blue said.

It was Laura Charme's first visit to London in years, and she was delighted with the city at its midsummer best. "You never told me it could be this lovely, Sebastian," she said as they strolled along Bishops Bridge Road toward the building where Romeo Hyde's studios were located. "Every time I've been here before it's been rainy and cold, even in July."

"You must have hit it bad, though I'll grant you this is something of a heat wave for London. The temperature rarely climbs above eighty."

"Did you live near here when you were married?"

"No, no, quite far away, really."

"Do you want to go see her—your ex-wife?"

Sebastian snorted. "Not likely. She's married again, and I suppose she's happy. It happens all the time, these days."

"I was glad to hear about Group H. You deserve that."

"We'll see how much I deserve it after this case. The Secretary General warned me not to behave as if I were still with

Scotland Yard, but I must admit I have the feeling already. It's like the old days, being back here."

They went up in the elevator to the offices of Hyde Productions, Ltd., and soon found themselves in the office of the vice president, a nervous little man named Thomas Piggett. "We're still quite confused around here," he told Sebastian. "Forgive me if I have to answer a few telephone calls while we talk. The network is anxious to know about future shows, and there has been a deal pending in the United States."

"Go right ahead," Sebastian said. "But perhaps between calls you can fill me in on a bit of the background. Interpol is especially interested in *The Thriller Hour* episode of a few weeks back—'A Sky to Plunder' was the title, I believe."

"Yes, yes, the one about the airliner crashes. It attracted a good deal of mail."

"Correct me if I'm wrong. Naturally I didn't see the episode in Paris, but in reading the script it seems to me that it was built around a method of poisoning the pilot and copilot with cyanide. The author's gimmick seems to have been that cyanide is often present in the bloodstreams of plane-crash victims because they inhale toxic fumes from burning seat cushions before they die."

Thomas Piggett nodded. "Polyurethane and polystyrene foams give off cyanide gas when burned. It was a pretty good gimmick for the show, actually. The cyanide in the pilot's bloodstream was never questioned because of this known effect of the burning foam. Thus the sabotage of the planes wasn't immediately detected."

"The author's name is given as J. J. Cromwell, with an address of a post-office box in North Tiverton. Mr. Hyde was murdered there, wasn't he?"

"Yes," Piggett said shortly, reaching to answer a ringing telephone. He talked for a few minutes to someone at the network, then hung up. "Yes, North Tiverton. Mr. Hyde told me he was driving up there to scout for locations."

"And to visit J. J. Cromwell?"

"I don't know about that."

"Have you met Cromwell?"

"No. Mr. Hyde dealt with him directly. I don't believe any of us ever met him. Or her."

"Her?"

Piggett smiled. "Women writers sometimes use initials to disguise the fact of their sex."

"Surely not in this era of women's liberation!" Laura said, joining the conversation for the first time.

The nervous little man shifted his gaze toward her. "We are quite aware of the position of women. If you had ever viewed our show, you would know that one of the leading roles is played by a highly liberated young woman. But come, let me show you the sound stage. We're shooting some interiors today for a future episode."

"In the middle of summer?"

"We must get an early jump on fall. Follow me."

Sebastian and Laura tagged along, though he had the feeling the tour of the sound stage was merely an excuse for getting them off the subject of J. J. Cromwell's identity. They descended to the first floor and entered a soundproofed door to find themselves in a high-ceilinged barn of a place strung with cables and wires and hanging flats of scenery. Sebastian avoided a moving microphone boom and found himself face to face with a gorgeous redhead in a black leather jumpsuit.

"Hello there," he said.

Piggett stepped between them. "This is our star, Dusty Summers. Dusty, I want you to meet Sebastian Blue and Laura Charme, from Interpol in Paris. They're investigating Romeo's murder."

"Not exactly the murder," Sebastian started to correct him, but Piggett hurried on, disregarding him.

"Dusty worked very closely with Mr. Hyde."

The redhead seemed to welcome the break in the filming routine. "His death is a great tragedy," she said, shaking her head sadly. "I hope you get the ones who did it."

"Is this your costume for the show?" Laura asked, examining the leather jumpsuit.

"For this episode. *The Thriller Hour* goes in for hand-to-hand combat a great deal—like *The Avengers* some years back, or *Kung Fu* on American television. I have to use karate and judo."

Sebastian saw that Laura was interested. "I'm into that myself. Are you any good?" she asked.

The redhead laughed. "Not really. It's all show business. We fake it pretty well."

"We're especially interested in a show you did a few weeks ago—about the airliner crashes."

"That was the last of the season. We filmed it months ago." She gestured toward the camera dolly. "Now we're starting next season."

"Do you know the author of that episode, J. J. Cromwell?"

"Hardly. We discourage authors on the sets as much as possible. They always want to make changes—or else they don't like the changes we make."

"He lives in North Tiverton, where Romeo Hyde was killed."

"Fancy that. Maybe he didn't like the show."

"Did you receive any personal mail about the show, Miss Summers?" Laura asked.

"Dear, I get personal mail after *every* show! You wouldn't believe some of the letters. They see me in this leather suit or some of my other costumes and it gives them all sorts of kinky ideas."

"We're shooting, Dusty," the director called to her.

"All right! Pardon me now. I have to go deliver a few judo chops in this next scene."

"Karate chops," Laura corrected sweetly.

"What?"

"Karate chops. There's no such thing as a judo chop."

"Sure, if you say so."

They watched her run through the scene, disposing of two cooperative stunt men who took their falls well. "I could do better than that," Laura scoffed. On the way back upstairs she asked, "Do you think Dusty Summers is her real name?"

"In show business hardly anyone uses his or her real name. I imagine some press agent thought it up for her. For that matter, can you imagine anyone named Romeo Hyde? That's from his acting days."

Back in Piggett's office they heard more details of the production company. "It was Mr. Hyde's creation from the beginning," Piggett told them. "He furnished the money, hired the actors, bought the scripts. Despite its popularity, the show was beginning to sag lately. He was worried about its future."

"You said he was scouting locations when he was killed."

"*He* said so. In truth, he drove up to North Tiverton every weekend to relax and get away from business."

"Then he was known to the townspeople?"

"Oh, yes, quite well, I'd imagine."

"Might they have caused his death?"

"For what reason? Romeo Hyde always seemed quite a likable chap to me."

Sebastian flipped over the pages of his little notebook. "I should talk to Scotland Yard about the case. As I understand it, they were already in contact with Hyde about the content of that *Thriller* episode before he was killed."

"That's right. An inspector was in to see him only last week."

"Could the Yard's interest in the show have led to his drive up to North Tiverton? Perhaps to see the author, this J. J. Cromwell?"

"Possibly," Piggett replied through reluctant lips. He didn't like to talk about it. "But as I said, he went every weekend."

"You'd better give me this inspector's name so I can contact him."

"Certainly. Inspector Claude Jennings."

Sebastian didn't bother to write it down.

On the way back to the hotel Laura said, "Sebastian, your face went absolutely white when he gave you that Scotland Yard man's name. Do you know him?"

He stared out the taxi window at the passing street scene. He kept staring out for a long time before he answered her question. "I used to work with Jennings. He's the man who married my ex-wife."

In the morning he visited the building on Victoria Embankment that housed New Scotland Yard. He went alone because he did not want Laura to see him with Claude Jennings. Even after all this time he wasn't certain what his own reactions would be.

Jennings was a handsome man who seemed never to notice women. He'd been a good friend of Sebastian's for many years, and it was partly this memory of friendship that forced Sebastian to leave his job—and his country—when Elizabeth divorced him to marry Claude.

"How are you, old man?" Claude greeted him now, coming to the door to shake his hand.

Sebastian, who was only three years older than Jennings, replied coolly, "I've been fine."

"We hear great things about your work with Interpol. It's a whole new career for you. Got you out of this rut, anyway."

Sebastian grunted and sat down. Jennings had changed little, but his office was larger and it was obvious he was doing well at the Yard. "You seem to be flourishing in the same rut."

"You know me, Sebastian. I was always a plodder."

"How is Elizabeth these days?"

Jennings shifted his eyes. "Very well, thanks. If you're going to be in town long perhaps we could have you out to dinner."

"I'll be leaving this afternoon," Sebastian said, and saw the obvious relief on the other's face. "At least I will be if you can give me some information on this Romeo Hyde business."

"Certainly, certainly!" He shifted some files on his desk. "Bizarre sort of crime, don't you think? People don't get themselves stoned to death these days."

"Hyde managed it, somehow. I understand you were already investigating the television series before the murder occurred."

"Just one episode really—'A Sky to Plunder.' You know, since you left I've been doing some of your old work out at Heathrow. A plane crashed near there a few months back, just about the time they were filming this *Thriller* episode. The pilot had cyanide in his bloodstream."

"As I understand it that's not unusual, especially if the plane burns and the victim inhales toxic fumes."

"Exactly. Which makes cyanide a perfect airborne murder

weapon. Fortunately, if the coroner knows what he's looking for, he can determine whether the cyanide entered the bloodstream through the stomach or lungs by studying the residue in both places. It was too late to do this in the Heathrow crash, because the pilot's body was cremated after the initial autopsy. But we found other evidence."

"What, precisely?"

"Potassium cyanide mixed with the sugar in the little packets for the pilot's coffee—exactly as in *The Thriller Hour* episode. When we checked some unburned packets recovered from the plane's cabin, we found poison in one of them."

"You checked this after the television drama was aired?"

Jennings nodded. "Just last week, as a matter of fact. And there'd been nothing in the press until that time hinting at sabotage." He consulted his notes. "The crash was on March 28th, two weeks before that episode was filmed."

"Coincidence?" Sebastian asked. "Stranger things have happened."

But Claude Jennings shook his head. "The details were too similar. No, this Cromwell chap had to have inside knowledge to write that script."

"Any luck tracing Cromwell?"

"None. A post-office box in North Tiverton. And now Hyde's been killed there. But what's Interpol's interest in all this?"

"There have been other crashes," Sebastian replied. "Probably no connection, but we wanted to check."

"There's something else," Jennings said, his voice a bit hesitant. "Romeo Hyde received special permission to inspect the plane's wreckage."

"When was that?"

"Just before they started filming. He said he wanted to shoot a scene of the show in the hangar where they were assembling the bits and pieces. He looked it all over, but decided against filming there."

"Isn't that proof the crash inspired the script, rather than the other way around?"

"You'd think so, wouldn't you? But the script was written and accepted prior to the March 28th crash."

Sebastian Blue grunted. "I believe a visit to North Tiverton is indicated."

"Wish I could go with you. If you need any help up there, just let me know."

"Certainly." Sebastian got to his feet. He couldn't quite bring himself to shake hands again. "Give my best to Elizabeth."

"I will, old man. Good to see you again."

Laura Charme was waiting for him back at the hotel overlooking Green Park. "How did it go, Sebastian?"

"All right. He was always a gentleman, if nothing else. He invited me to dinner."

"You're not going?"

"No." He smiled at her concern. They'd become very close these past months, even though she was young enough to be his daughter. "But I've got to crack this case, Laura, because Jennings thinks I can't."

"Which case? He's interested in Hyde's murder, and we're interested in the plane crash. Maybe they're not even connected."

"We'll see," Sebastian said.

He rented a car and drove up to North Tiverton that afternoon, leaving Laura in London to check further on the cast of *The Thriller Hour.* The town was about 100 miles to the north, in an area still considered good farming country. Even the coal mines had not completely spoiled the pastoral beauty of the land, or the simple ways of the people.

A few of them, standing at the crossroads, eyed him with natural suspicion as he drove into town. For a moment, remembering the stoning of Romeo Hyde, he wished he'd worn his pistol. But this was England, and though he was no longer a part of Scotland Yard he honored their custom of going about unarmed.

"Welcome to North Tiverton!" a voice said as he left the car in front of a little white church near the center of town. Sebastian saw a young Anglican priest in street clothes coming to greet him.

"Thank you, Reverend. It seems a friendly town."

"No more than a village really. I'm Dr. Crouthers, the pastor."

"Sebastian Blue. I'm with Interpol."

The priest smiled. "Since the tragedy everyone who comes here is either police or press." He studied Sebastian's face. "I suppose you'll want to see the hill where it happened."

"Later. Just now I want to talk to you."

"Why me? Our constable could tell you more."

"Isn't there something Biblical about a man being stoned to death? It's not the usual twentieth-century crime, certainly."

Dr. Crouthers shrugged. "A gang killing, perhaps. The rural areas have their youth gangs just like the cities."

"A youth gang would more likely use knives or razors."

"The method of murder interests you?"

"It interests me because it is ancient, and the case I'm working on—involving airline sabotage—is quite modern. The two don't go together."

"Must they?"

"If they don't, then why was Romeo Hyde killed?"

Dr. Crouthers sighed. "I'm a young man, maybe too young for the people of North Tiverton. They don't always listen to me. Come on, we'll drive out to the hill and I'll show you where it happened."

Laura Charme was waiting for Thomas Piggett when he left the Hyde Productions building for a late lunch hour. The little man seemed startled to see her again, and his nervous mannerisms returned at once. "Miss Charme, isn't it? Do you have more questions?"

"I do," Laura said, falling into step beside him. "We didn't really meet the rest of the cast yesterday."

"It changes each week. Dusty Summers is the only continuing character this season."

"I understand the script of 'A Sky to Plunder' was purchased before that March 28th plane crash. How many people would have seen it before that date?"

"Oh, any number—we have casting and set design and a great deal of preparation before filming begins."

"Mr. Hyde purchased the script himself?"

"Yes."

"Have you used anything else by the mysterious J. J. Cromwell?"

"Yes, two or three. I could check for you."

Laura smiled. "Perhaps I'll come by your office later."

"You're welcome any time."

But after they had parted, Laura knew she wouldn't wait till later. She wanted a look at the files of Hyde Productions, and the lunch hour seemed the best time to do it. The office was open when she returned to it, with only a single secretary working in the outer room. She waited until the girl's back was turned, then made her way quickly to Piggett's empty office. The filing cabinets she had observed earlier were unlocked, with several thick folders containing each of last season's shows.

The files for "A Sky to Plunder" were in the back, and she pulled out the script. The author's name on the first page was Julie J. Cromwell. Piggett had lied about not knowing whether it was a man or a woman, and she wondered why. Flipping through the pages, she saw the interleaved blue and pink sheets that showed revisions had been made. Many revisions.

And most of them were on pages detailing the plane crash and its aftermath.

"Well," a voice said behind her, "it's the girl who never heard of a judo chop!"

She whirled, facing Dusty Summers. The actress still wore her leather jumpsuit, and she crouched slightly as she moved toward Laura. "I was—" Laura began.

"I know what you were doing—snooping!"

Her right hand shot out. Laura turned just in time as the hard edge hit her shoulder instead of her throat. She felt the stab of pain and reacted, catching Dusty's arm before the redhead could get clear. The actress screamed in pain as Laura toppled her to the floor.

"*This* is judo," Laura told her. "Now suppose you start talking. Tell me about Julie Cromwell."

"What about her?" Dusty gasped from the floor.

"Why the big secret about who wrote that script? What's going on in North Tiverton?"

"I don't know."

"Sebastian Blue has gone there this afternoon. He'll find out the truth anyway."

There was something like fright in Dusty's eyes. "They don't like outsiders. They'll kill him too, just as they killed Romeo."

"Who? Did Julie Cromwell cause his death?"

But the redhead had started to sob. Laura wondered what she could do, how she could help Sebastian. Finally she reached for the telephone.

Dr. Crouthers pointed up the hill toward an old slag heap now overgrown with weeds. "This is where it happened," he told Sebastian. "They found him at the bottom of this hill."

"Who found him?"

"The village constable. Someone called him."

Sebastian strolled up a short distance and stooped to pick up a smooth round stone. "You know who killed him, don't you, Reverend?"

Dr. Crouthers sighed. "North Tiverton is a very old village, untouched by city ways. As I said, perhaps I am too young myself to reach these people."

"I saw television antennas on some houses. It's not old enough that they don't watch *The Thriller Hour*. In fact, one of the scriptwriters lives here—J. J. Cromwell."

"Yes," Dr. Crouthers answered. "Julie Cromwell."

"A woman? Could you take me to her?"

"She no longer lives in North Tiverton."

"But you knew her?"

"Yes, I saw her occasionally."

"Did Romeo Hyde come here to visit her?"

"He came every weekend, I think."

"Could you show me where she lived?"

Dr. Crouthers gazed at him. "Would that do any good?"

"Yes, I believe it would."

He brushed back his sandy hair. "Very well. It's a short drive from here."

They returned to the car and drove about a mile down the road, to a little cottage almost hidden from view by an ancient stand of evergreens. "This is where Julie Cromwell lived?" Sebastian asked.

"Yes, off and on. I believe Mr. Hyde purchased the cottage for her some months back." He spoke the words with obvious reluctance. "I believe she came here occasionally to write."

"And Romeo Hyde came here, too?"

Dr. Crouthers dropped his eyes. "Yes."

"Can we get in?"

"I want no part of an illegal entry."

Sebastian smiled at him. "It's hardly as serious as murder. But you're right, of course. Leave me here for a time by myself. I'll walk back to the village."

The priest's lip tightened. "Be careful. The people hereabouts—"

"I know," Sebastian said, as if an unspoken message had passed between them. He waited until the priest's car had vanished down the road toward the village, then began checking the doors and windows of the little cottage. At the rear he found a door held shut by a simple latch, and it took him only a few moments to open it with a plastic credit card slid between the door and jamb.

The interior of the cottage was dark, with shades drawn against the hazy sunlight. As he moved from one room to the next he became aware of signs of a masculine presence— men's shoes under the bed, standing in mute testimony beside a pair of women's fancy slippers. He moved on to the closet and found more of a mixture—his clothes and hers. A desk drawer yielded a first draft of "A Sky to Plunder," written in a firm masculine hand.

But Sebastian was puzzled. If Julie Cromwell had moved away as Dr. Crouthers said, why had she left all these expensive clothes behind?

Something thumped against the cottage roof, interrupting his thoughts. He moved to the door and peered out cautiously. There was nothing to see, but then the sound was repeated, as if a rock had landed on the roof. He opened the door wide and stepped out.

He saw the first man at once, stepping from the shelter of the trees across the road. He was dressed in faded pants and shirt, and Sebastian knew he was one of the villagers who'd watched his arrival earlier. Then he saw the second one, off to the side, and the third coming around the cottage. A rock landed in the dirt a few feet away and he reached instinctively for his gun, remembering too late that he wasn't carrying it.

They formed a rough circle around him, the nearest some 50 feet away, and he saw the stones they were carrying. "What do you want?" he asked.

Another man hurled a stone, and Sebastian ducked his head to avoid it. "What are you trying to—?"

"You're a friend of his, aren't you?" the nearest man taunted. "You're one of them!"

A stone from behind hit him on the leg. He turned, dodged another, and lost his balance, falling to the ground. In that moment he realized for the first time that they might kill him.

Then there was the sharp crack of a revolver from somewhere down the road and the men in the circle paused. They looked in the direction of the shot, their faces uncertain, and saw a small car speeding toward them. Sebastian recognized Dr. Crouthers' car—the one that had brought him out here—but now the young priest was not alone. As the car pulled to a stop Laura jumped out, followed by Inspector Claude Jennings waving a snub-nosed .32 revolver.

The circle of men tried to scatter, running back toward the wooded area, but Jennings fired another shot into the air. "Stay where you are!" he shouted. "I'm a police officer!"

"Thank God we arrived in time," Laura gasped. "The priest told us where you were. When Dusty Summers said your life might be in danger, I had to call Jennings. He was the only Scotland Yard man whose name I knew."

"Looks as if I saved your life, old man," Jennings said.

Sebastian gazed at him distastefully. "And since when did Scotland Yard men start carrying guns?"

Jennings looked embarrassed. "Matter of fact, I had to borrow the weapon—from the young lady here."

Sebastian took them through the cottage, showing them what he'd found. Then, as Jennings made arrangements with the local constable for the men to be taken into town for further questioning, Laura said, "We had to come, Sebastian, because I discovered you were all wrong about Romeo Hyde. He didn't poison that pilot or sabotage that plane. It was all a publicity stunt!"

"Stunt?" Sebastian protested. "But there was poison in the pilot's sugar!"

"Poison that Hyde placed in a packet and then managed to leave with the remains from the plane's cabin. I thought it odd those packets didn't burn. Remember, Jennings told you Hyde received permission to view the wreckage. If he was really responsible for the crash—or if Julie Cromwell was—he'd have removed that poisoned packet. If Scotland Yard hadn't noticed the similarity of the show to the real crash, I'm certain Hyde would have sent them an anonymous letter pointing it out."

Claude Jennings had joined them now. "All for publicity? That's difficult to believe."

"Not so difficult," Sebastian mused, "when we remember that the show was in trouble. It was Hyde's money behind it, and he needed a burst of publicity to keep the show in the public eye for another season."

Laura nodded. "The original script was written before the crash, but when I inspected it this afternoon I found that many changes were made later—changes involving the accident itself. The original script was doctored by Hyde to duplicate the events of the real tragedy and make it appear that life was imitating art. I think Hyde wrote the script himself and put Julie Cromwell's name on it."

"I'm sure of it," Sebastian said. "I found an early draft in a man's handwriting."

"What sort of man could he have been?" Jennings said.

"The sort that gets himself stoned to death in a remote village," Sebastian replied.

The Scotland Yard man blinked. "By these fellows? The townspeople? But why?"

Sebastian turned to Dr. Crouthers. "I think you can answer that."

"I—" He seemed at a loss for words. "I'd rather not."

"Hyde purchased this cottage some months back," Sebastian said. "He drove up here on weekends to relax and write. I suppose Dusty Summers knew about it, as did others on the show. But it wasn't the sort of thing one spoke of, even after he was dead. You see, these simple village people would have none of it. After a time they took the law of God into their own hands. They imposed an ancient punishment for what they considered an ancient evil."

"I tried to reason with them," Dr. Crouthers said, his voice bleak with despair.

"I still don't understand," Jennings said. "Are you saying the people killed him because he loved this Julie Cromwell?"

"No, no," Sebastian grumbled. "You still don't see it, do you, Claude? Even after I've shown you the clothes and the shoes? She wouldn't have left them if she'd moved away. Julie was Juliet, to his Romeo. And perhaps her middle initial stood for Jekyll to his Hyde. He wasn't killed because he came here on weekends to love Julie Cromwell. He was killed because he came here to *be* Julie Cromwell!"

Young Guttierez masterfully non-replied and stared absolutely without blinking for a year-long minute before I tried again. This was really a job for Brenda who used to boast of having read *El Cid* in the original during her Hunter College days. I sighed and spoke again.

"Um, hi there. Is your father home?"

Reinforcements arrived in the shape of an even smaller and more solemn Guttierez sporting a T-shirt lettered *Puerto Rico Encanta*. Double-barreled silence for another minute, then the curtain twitched again. I was about to leave, defeated by this one-sided confrontation, when the two small brown bodies erupted into noise and action. They pounded way back into their lair squealing, "*Mama, Mama venga! Mira, Mama, un hombre!*"

The squeals receded into a distant interior chattering, and stood with my nose pressed to the iron grille, trying to decide whether it was worthwhile waiting around for someone the age of five to come to the door. My whole attention riveted through those open inner doors, listening to the incomprehensible chatter, breathing in the fumes of something cooking vaguely connected in my sensory apparatus with Brenda's superb *paella*, and hoping for the sound of footsteps to head in my direction.

My concentration on the Guttierez interior was such that I didn't notice the adult footsteps coming up behind me. I heard the sound of the voice and almost fell into the lidless garbage can beside the door.

"Hello. What you wan' here?"

I suspected Guttierez of being slightly deaf. He always spoke in a modified roar. In the circumstances it was a bit unnerving and I felt like the notorious neighborhood mailbox thief caught in the act. Add to this the fact that although he and I were about the same height, I was standing down in the entrance to his castle. He towered over me with a six-pack of beer in each hand. It was difficult to recall that Guttierez always roared, he always glowered when playing stick ball with his kids, and I had no debate with the *cerveza fria*.

"Um, I was just looking for you. Nice day,

MY NEIGHBOR, AY

by Joyce Harrington

Joyce Harrington's first published story, "The Purple Shroud" in the September 1972 issue of Ellery Queen's Mystery Magazine, *achieved the highest possible honor that can be won by a mystery short story. It was awarded the coveted Edgar by MWA (Mystery Writers of America) as the best short story in the mystery field published in American magazines and books during 1972. We were not surprised: we had greeted Joyce Harrington as "a new and impressive talent," and had called her story's appearance "an exceptional debut in print."*

Her second story, "The Plastic Jungle," was published in EQMM *three months after her first. Since it was still 1972, the second story also qualified for Edgar consideration; but MWA awarded the laurel wreath to the first story. Personally, we thought "The Plastic Jungle" an "even better, even more impressive" story than "The Purple Shroud," and again we praised the author's talent.*

Now we give you Joyce Harrington's third story, and once more she has produced a "sensitively written study in crime, as contemporary, as modern as tonight's late news." To quote the author herself, the third story deals with "cultural conflicts and the perils of not understanding one's neighbor."

Things grow in Brooklyn besides trees. . . .

* * *

31

IT ALL STARTED the day the old man on the top floor next door emptied his spittoon out the window and the wind was blowing from the east. It wasn't what you might call an elegant antique of a spittoon. More like an old coffee can, and I caught the flash of tin up there in the fifth-floor walkup out of the corner of my eye as I was crouched over my tenderly cherished Christian Dior rosebush inspecting for aphids with a banana peel at the ready.

My wife, Brenda, who was flaked out on the garden chaise in her green bikini promoting a city suntan, caught more than a flash of tin.

"Rats! It's raining," she muttered before she opened her eyes. When she finally did get them open and adjusted to bright blue sky and dazzling August sunshine and a case of instant full-length freckles, she screamed.

"What is it? Damn, what is it? Who did that?"

She scrambled off the chaise and the freckles began to slither in streaky rivulets toward her belly button and down her incredibly long and slender legs. A few dripped off her chin and fell into her well-proportioned cleavage.

"It's not tea leaves, honey."

I must confess that the sight of lissome, fastidious Brenda spattered from head to toe with second-hand chewing tobacco brought out the snide side of my character, and I had difficulty gulping down a fit of guffaws. For my pains I was rewarded with a fit of hiccups.

"Will you stop that stupid noise and *DO SOMETHING!*" she shrieked. Have you ever seen anyone turn red with rage all over? That was Brenda. Bright pink actually, overlaid with lengthening stripes and scattered specks of mahogany, the whole girl trembling and angrier than I'd ever seen her.

I turned away, ostensibly to deposit my banana peel at the foot of Christian Dior, and managed to subdue the grin that was quirking at the corners of my mouth. It crossed my mind that someone had once told me tobacco, like banana peel, was good for roses, but I couldn't remember why. It definitely wasn't good for Brenda.

"A shower, perhaps?" I hiccupped. "I'll scrub your back."

"A shower! A disinfecting is what I need! Don't just stand there. Call the police!"

"What'll I tell them? My wife has been spat on whole[...] I'll get you some paper towels." I started for the ki[...] door.

"Don't leave me here like this. Do something! If y[...] call the police, I will. I will, I will, I will!" Tears we[...] ning to add to the mess on Brenda's face and th[...] rigidity was leaving her outflung arms. She was [...] awful lot of noise.

"Do you want to stay like that so the police c[...] dence?" I grabbed the real-estate section [...] *Times* and began tentative mopping-up op[...] same time trying to steer her indoors.

"Stop that, you nit! You're just making i[...]

She was right. Heads were beginning t[...] windows of the surrounding brownsto[...] her senses long enough to realize that [...] backyard melodrama, and then fled[...] room.

"I'll speak to Guttierez," I called a[...]

When the shower had been dr[...] least five minutes and I had sub[...] clean shirt and a stern manner[...] tierez owned this next-door h[...] tical twin of ours, and lived [...] his silent, round-faced, br[...] silent young sons. Upsta[...] house was a mini-U.N[...] through the open wind[...] ple living loudly in Sp[...] ed English, with an c[...] Chinese. It was mic[...] brownstone genera[...]

I rang the bell[...] there was instant[...] ered plastic cur[...] I hit the buzz[...] outer door r[...] inside the ir[...]

"Hi," I said [...]

I'm ashamed to say that my voice came out somewhat higher than its normal range, and suspicion flamed all over Guttierez's face. He took a firmer grip on his six-packs.

"You lookin' for me? What you wan'?"

"Well, Mr. Guttierez, I'm Jack Rollins. I live next door, you know?"

I got my voice back down into its normal range, but I was having difficulty getting to the point. I scrambled up out of the entryway and felt a little better facing Guttierez at eye level.

"*Si*, I know. What you wan'?"

He was obviously impatient to get inside to whatever was cooking that smelled so good. Whispers and giggles came from behind the twitching curtain, and I caught an occasional "Americano" between the giggles.

"Well, Mr. Guttierez, the old man on the top floor, you know?"

"*Si?*"

"Well, he throws things out the window."

"*Si?*"

"Well, he empties his spittoon out the window."

"*Si?* What is this 'spittoon'?"

I sighed, inaudibly I hoped, and tried again.

"Well, he chews tobacco, you know? And he spits it in a can. And then he throws it out the window."

"Oh, *si!* He is one filthy old man, him."

I squared my shoulders and prepared to do battle for my wife's honor. The guy's machismo was beginning to rub off on me.

"Well, see here, Guttierez. It's got to stop. It landed on my wife today."

"Oh, *lastima!* You wife! She with the bathing suit? In the backyard?"

It was the first time I had ever seen Guttierez smile. He was grinning. He was positively leering.

"That's right. My wife. And I want something done about it." I hoped I was scowling at least as fiercely as Guttierez normally did.

"What you wan' to do? You wan' to fight him? He is *muy viejo*, very old. An' he have one leg. You wan' to fight him?"

"No, I don't want to fight him! He's your tenant. You should speak to him. Tell him it's against the law to throw things out the window. Tell him I'll call the police."

"You called police?" Guttierez was beginning to bristle and his grin vanished.

"No, not yet. But if he does it one more time I will. You tell him that."

"Okay. I tell him. No more out the window."

A young Guttierez, who had been lurking just inside the gate throughout our exchange, now opened the gate and took the beer from his father's hands. Guttierez went through the gate, and as he turned to close it he grinned once more.

"Tell you wife she is verry pretty."

The gate slammed and the chatter and giggles reached a crescendo.

Back in my own renovated townhouse, I settled into my black-leather Eames chair and sought solace with the Sunday *Times* crossword puzzle. The shower was still splashing, so I was safe from vengeance until Brenda got her hair dry. Before attacking square one across I sat back and admired for perhaps the hundredth time the restored beauty of my front parlor.

Brenda and I had scraped and Red Deviled and polished the woodwork, plastered and spackled and painted, replaced missing bits of molding. We had labored mightily and with love, and the result was a gleaming, pristine Victorian mansion with all mod cons, a duplex apartment upstairs which rented at a price that paid the mortgage, and our own lower duplex with garden. Our piece of the city.

I shook my head over Brenda's rage, decided it was justified, and clicked my ballpoint pen into action. The air conditioner hummed gently, producing just the right amount of refrigeration, and I lost myself in the wiles of the puzzle which bore the theme of "The Last Resort." I puzzled away for perhaps twenty minutes and was somewhat nearer sleeping than waking when Brenda stalked into the room.

"Well?" she demanded. The shower had cleaned her up but had not cooled her off.

"Ah, what's a ten-letter word for African animal ending in 'u'?"

"Lesser Kudu. What happened?" Brenda was always very good at natural history.

"Thanks. Aren't you cold?" She had exchanged her spattered green bikini for a pair of shocking-pink short shorts and a purple scarf intricately tied to allow maximum bare skin and freedom of motion.

"No, I'm not cold. It's ninety-two degrees outside. Did you call the police?"

"Well, no. It's very cool in here. The air conditioner is on high." I settled deeper into my chair to give the impression of extreme comfort and immovability.

"If you didn't call the police, what did you do?"

"Well, I spoke to Guttierez. You aren't going outside again, are you? Like that?" I knew I was doing this all wrong. Brenda wasn't the sort of girl you could safely practise machismo on.

"Oh course I am. It's my backyard, isn't it? What did Guttierez say?"

"He said you were verry pretty. He asked if I wanted to fight the old guy."

"Oh, damn, you're impossible!" She dropped onto the blue-velvet Victorian chaise longue which was her pride and joy, and she almost laughed. "Did you ever get to the point?"

"Oh, yes. Point Number One, Guttierez will speak to the old guy. And Point Number Two, your sunbathing gives great visual pleasure to the surrounding natives. Does Mrs. G. ever sunbathe?"

"Of course not. She's always pregnant. There's a steak for the barbecue. Shall I light the fire now?"

During the week following "L'Affaire Tabac" the heat wave was still melting Madison Avenue. Brenda and I shuttled between our air-conditioned jobs and our air-conditioned bedroom, ducking in and out of air-conditioned restaurants along the way. Neither one of us felt much like cooking or even eating with the thermometer pushing 100 day after day, and the humidity making my best Brooks Brothers young-executive-on-the-rise wash-and-wear blue-

and-white stripe look like a much worn and seldom washed suit of the latest in limp dishrag.

The management of the aggressive young ad agency where Brenda wrote copy had considered going on a four-day week for the summer, but had decided that there were too many Goliaths abroad on the Avenue to leave the sling-shots unmanned (or unwomanned) for even one day. So Brenda hammered away at producing bright, clever words designed to sell bras and all-in-ones to the overfed female population of the nation, while I sweltered and accounted for the bookkeeping vagaries of an endless roster of small-business clients of the mammoth accounting firm where I C.P.A.'d. We both regretted our decision to save our vacation time for a January ski tour of Europe.

If we noticed Guttierez and company at all it was only in passing on the evening drag from subway to cool haven. A clutter of brown humanity, stoop-sitting, hoping for a breeze from the bay or even from the Gowanus Canal, and tossing Malta Hatvey cans languidly toward the garbage cans and just missing. Occasionally we heard a guitar and plaintive is-land songs, and saw the kids trundling secondhand plastic tricycles up and down the sidewalk. Mrs. Guttierez had tried to brighten the small front yard with a few marigolds, but the heat and pounding children's feet had left only a few yellow tatters among the Popsicle wrappers on the packed earth.

We passed without acknowledgment, either of overtures toward mutual understanding or mutual hostility. It was too darned hot.

One night, though, we were forced to take notice.

The heat had lifted slightly and the air was electric with premonitions of a storm. Despite the threat of rain Brenda and I decided to take a chance on Shakespeare in the Park. We did it in style: Brasserie box lunches (pâté, *ratatouille,* cold chicken) and chilled champagne (New York State) while waiting in line; a rather fine *Macbeth* with distant thunder obligingly produced on cue by the great Stage Manager in the Catskills; and afterward a taxi home across the Brooklyn Bridge with the lights of our town, ships in the Narrows, the Verrazano Bridge crowning the evening with the spectacle which never palled.

We pulled up outside our house and paid off the driver, adding a generous happy-time tip. A gale-force wind was blowing off the bay and up our street, bending the newly planted plane trees into fragile arcs. Above the clatter of the frantic leaves and the din of the wind playing Frisbee with the garbage-can lids, the roar of Guttierez was heard. The stoop-sitters were energized, plugged in to the crackling atmosphere. The children, not yet in bed, huddled smear-faced and wide-eyed on the top step.

Mrs. Guttierez wept loudly in the arms of a broad full-bellied Indian-faced woman who shrieked imprecations to the tops of houses. Armed with a saw-toothed bread knife, Guttierez bellowed and stabbed the air. The opposition, small, thin, dark, and very drunk, whirled a baseball bat above his head with both hands. The two men circled each other on the sidewalk, slowfooted, eyes aglint with the adrenalin of battle, searching for the deadly opportunity and shouting macho insults at each other.

Brenda stared, breath held, her body stiff with shock and rooted to the pavement.

"Inside!" I shouted. "Get inside!"

She didn't move. She didn't hear. She was hypnotized.

"My God!" she breathed at last. "They'll kill each other."

The wind plastered her long hair across her face, and a single fat raindrop fell on my hand as I tried to drag her away.

"Get into the house, Brenda." I spoke as calmly as I could. "The rain will stop it."

Her fascination broke abruptly, and she whirled on me, her eyes wild with near-hysteria.

"Police!" she screamed. "They'll kill each other! Call the police! I'll do it!"

She bolted for the entrance to our fortress and began scrabbling in her purse for keys. I had mine ready, but the seconds necessary for manipulating the double locks seemed like hours with Brenda shivering impatiently behind me and the shouts and weeping continuing unabated on the sidewalk.

I flung the gate open and Brenda charged through, rattling the double doors and racing down the hall to the telephone. I went back for another look at the combatants. They were still circling, still brandishing their weapons, still shouting. There was not another soul to be seen on the block—no late dog-walkers, no midnight loiterers at the corner bodega, no curious heads at windows.

Lightning flashed somewhere over Staten Island, coming closer, and raindrops spattered the sidewalk. I felt fairly sure that Guttierez and enemy would continue their Mexican stand-off until the deluge, then put down their armaments and go inside for another beer. But you never could tell. When the thunder rolled I went inside and relocked the double locks.

Brenda, at the kitchen phone, was just concluding her conversation with 911. In a tight, edgy voice she gave her name and address.

"Please hurry," she added. "I'm afraid they'll kill each other."

I could imagine the laconic voice on the other end of the wire giving assurance that law and order were on the way, lady. Brenda hung up the phone and dug a cigarette out of her bag, lighting it at the gas range.

"Jack." She slumped in the telephone chair and surveyed the chrome and terra cotta tile, electronic oven and massive freezer, the ranks of custom-built walnut cabinets.

"Jack, we've done all this, and it's beautiful. I love it." She dragged deeply on her cigarette. "But I want out. I don't want to live next door to *THAT* any more."

"Where do you want to go, honey?" I began to massage her tight shoulders, her rigid neck. But she pulled away.

"How do I know? The damn suburbs. Westchester! Nyack! Bloody Australia! The farther the better."

"Brennie, you know you'd hate the suburbs. Those guys are just showing off for their women. They're enjoying every minute of it, and nobody's going to get hurt."

I had some small faith in my words and the flamboyant nature of our neighbors. Still, it was unnerving and not very neighborly to come home to brandished bread knives and baseball bats.

Brenda brooded unhappily.

"Come on, honey." I took her hand. "Let's go be spectators and see how long it takes the police to get here."

We took up stations at the darkened front-parlor window to find that one patrol car had already arrived, while another was flashing its way up the street.

"Well," I commented. "Nobody can say the fuzz doesn't respond in this neighborhood."

Guttierez, leaning indolently against the front fender of the police car, was answering the young officer's questions with expressions of sublime innocence and gestures of incredulity.

"Who, me?!!!" seemed to be the substance of his replies.

Mrs. Guttierez and the bread knife had disappeared. One child remained on the sidewalk, idly swinging the baseball bat. The small thin man and the Indian-looking woman leaned against the railing sipping from cans of liquid clothed in brown paper bags.

The wind had died. The trees stood expectantly, their leaves hanging limp and exhausted. A flash of lightning lit the scene in blue-white relief, and the rain crashed down.

The young policeman ducked inside his car with a final admonition to Guttierez, who nodded, tried to shake hands, then dashed for his house, picking up the boy and the baseball bat on the run. He was joined by the paper-bag drinkers, the woman laughing widely from her round jiggling belly and raising her face to the downpour. I could see her gold teeth.

After a few moments the police cars drove away, undoubtedly to respond to another crisis on another block. We watched the rain punish the empty street.

"Come on, Brennie." I hugged her. "It's bedtime."

We never found out what the argument had been about, but the next evening when we came home from work we found our backyard thoroughly inundated with garbage. There seemed to be about a ton of assorted chicken bones with fragments of yellow rice clinging stickily, dozens of the ubiquitous Malta Hatvey cans, watermelon rind and orange peel, coffee grounds, tea bags, and, yes, even the tobacco chewer of the fifth floor was represented.

"They must have taken up a collection." I tried to laugh, but it didn't come off very well. "What do you think, Brenda? The police again?"

Brenda seemed to have shrunk. Her eyes glazed over as she viewed the unexpected landfill.

"No, Jack," she said quietly. "I think the shovel and hose."

Our neighbors remained invisible and inaudible during the cleanup operation. Brenda remained silent and tight-lipped, wielding her shovel with a tense energy which augured ill for the dispensers of the odiferous revenge. Side by side we shoveled and hosed. All my attempts to point up the ridiculous side of the great kitchen-midden caper fell decidedly flat.

"You should maybe get her recipe for *arroz con pollo.*"

Brenda shoveled.

"We could toss it all back with a little contribution of our own. Make it a real classy garbage war. *Coq au vin* bones, congealed quiche, rind of brie, and shell of clam. Just think how we could expand their horizons."

Brenda swept, and looked determined.

"This may be the answer to the city's disposal problem. Just keep tossing it back and forth. You keep it one day, I'll keep it the next."

"Just shut up and shovel!"

Brenda had the hose in her hand. I shut up and shoveled.

An hour and many plastic bags later Brenda was once again showering away rage and refuse. The refuse would go down the drain. The rage I was not too sure about. Brenda's usual form was an explosion of mildly profane wrath, followed by tremulous laughter or at the very least a self-conscious smirk. This was different. This was cold fury, silent and calculating. Brenda was up to something. And I didn't like it.

I made her a drink, gin and tonic in equal proportions with two wedges of lime, and took it into the bathroom.

"Hey, Bren. Here's a drink."

"Thanks." Steam billowed out of the shower and frosted the mahogany-framed mirror over the sink. I wrote *Bren & Jack 4ever* inside a lopsided heart.

"How about dinner at Gage and Tollner's?"

"No, thanks."

"How about dinner at Peter Luger's?"

"No."

"How about dinner?"

"I've lost my appetite."

Brenda without an appetite was like bagels without cream cheese. Unnatural. And for her to turn down a Peter Luger steak was worse than unnatural.

The shower shut off abruptly and Brenda emerged dripping, a pale bikini shape outlined against rosy sunburn.

"Dry you off, lady?"

"Just hand me that towel."

She snatched the towel from the rack before I could reach it, dried off in a frenzy of flapping terrycloth, and slid into her no-nonsense button-to-the-chin nightgown.

"If you can bear to think about food, there must be something in the fridge. I'm going to bed."

Sweating drink in hand, she long-legged it into the bedroom. I followed.

"Great idea. I could use a little nap myself. And then we can go to Peter Luger's."

Brenda whirled on me, sloshing her drink all over herself and the red shag bedroom rug.

"Beat it, Jack. Just bug off. I'm getting in that bed. And I'm going to drink this drink. Or what's left of it. And then I'm going to sleep, sleep sleep! And I hope I never wake up! I want to be alone. Understand?"

"Okay, Garbo. Okay. All right. Pleasant dreams."

I slouched downstairs to the kitchen where I found sufficient material for a hero sandwich which, along with a couple of beers and my newest old Teddy Wilson records, induced a state of hopeful nirvana. Tomorrow would be better.

When I tiptoed into the bedroom around midnight, Brenda was asleep, asleep, asleep.

Tomorrow came right on schedule, and Brenda woke up. But refused to get out of bed. I brought her coffee, but she still refused to budge.

"Call the office around 9:30, Jack. Tell them I'm sick. I *am* sick." She buried her face in the pillow and moaned, unconvincingly.

"It's Friday. You can't call in sick on Friday."

"Oh, yes, I can. Anyway you're going to do it for me. Tell

them I've got scurvy, beri-beri, jungle rot, anything. Garbage poisoning, that's what I've really got. Please, Jack. I really need a day off to pull myself together after last night. I'll be all right. I promise. Tell them I have a bad case of hives."

"Look, Brenda, you'd be better off to go to work and forget all about last night. It's over. Let it end."

"Hives, dear. In fact, I think I feel one blossoming on my left kneecap right now."

She sat up and scratched energetically and then piled all the pillows together into a cosy sickbed nest. Smiling and sipping coffee, she seemed altogether more like a normal Brenda. Last night's cold and silent fury must have been dissipated by ten hours of sleep on an empty stomach.

"Well," I wavered. "I hate to leave you like this."

"Don't worry. I just want to spend the day in bed with a good book. Haven't done that in a long time."

She settled in more snugly and pulled the covers up to her chin. She looked helpless and vulnerable, even though I knew better, and I really did hate to leave her.

"Shall I bring you something to eat?"

"No, thanks. I'll get up and boil an egg in a little while."

I guess that's what convinced me that all would be well. Soft-boiled eggs were convalescent food for Brenda. Whenever she was recovering from any kind of upset, physical or emotional, soft-boiled eggs appeared on the menu, and disappeared as soon as things were back to normal.

"Well." I knotted my tie. "I guess I'd better be going."

"All right, dear. Don't forget to call in for me. And don't worry." She was already thumbing through a magazine.

"You won't—uh—I mean, you'll stay away from—" I still was not entirely convinced that Brenda's intentions ran solely to bed rest and literature. "You won't start anything with Guttierez, will you?"

"No, dear. I won't start anything. I promise."

I left.

I spent a usual kind of Friday closing out the previous month's books in the super mod offices of a team of graphic designers. The bookkeeper, a minuscule and meticulous Japanese girl, drew graphically perfect numbers and persistently covered up her errors by adding or subtracting a totally fictitious petty-cash amount at the end of each month. Each month Sumi and I engaged in a polite skirmish in which errors were routed, the books balanced, and I laid down anew the simple rules of double entry. Each month Sumi accepted my edicts with apologetic and suitably flattering awe, and I felt like a samurai of the statistics. Until the next month.

I tried to reach Brenda several times during the day but each time the line was busy.

By midafternoon I had settled Sumi's accounts and decided to knock off the rest of the day. It was one of those rare summer days in New York. The unsmogged sky was actually blue and gentle breezes meandered along the cross streets. The storm of the night before had washed away heat, humidity, and dog droppings and as I walked the six blocks to the Grand Central subway station, the city and its people gleamed as dwellers in an iridescent and fantastic mirage.

The subway put an end to fantasy with its congealed heat and the smell of generations of doomed hot dogs sweating out their grease on eternally rotating grills. On the train, sparsely populated with Alexander's shopping bags and noisy groups of day-camp kids, I welcomed the dank wind that swirled through the cars and wondered if this might not be a good weekend to take advantage of an open invitation to visit friends on Fire Island. There was plenty of time to catch an evening ferry, and two days of beachratting in congenial company would bring Brenda out of the garbage dumps.

She met me at the door suppressing manic laughter. Her eyes gave her away. Wild and triumphant, they sparkled with discharged venom. She grabbed my arm and before I could unload my attaché case or broach my Fire Island plan she dragged me to the window.

"Look, Jack." She was almost incoherent. "The gas company. It's the gas company."

"Well, sure. It's the gas company." It was not unusual to see a blue and yellow gas-company truck parked outside. I failed to comprehend Brenda's elation over this one.

"Oh, Jack! You don't get it. It's too fantastic! I reported a gas leak!"

I turned to sniff the air.

"Where is it? In the kitchen?" I headed for the stairs. "Did they find it yet?"

"No, dummy. You still don't get it. Next door. I reported a gas leak next door. And exposed wiring. And fire hazards in the halls. The fire inspectors have already been there. I'm still waiting for the housing department. You know, illegal rooming house. He doesn't have a license. Overcrowding and rats. Plumbing violations, sewer smells. Rent gouging. Everything. Everything I could think of. I even called the Mayor's office, but he was off inspecting snowplows."

"In August?" I was stupefied. No adequate comment came to mind, and I stared out the window as two purposeful men in gas-company uniforms emerged from next door. "They're leaving now."

"Okay. Now what's next?" Brenda paced excitedly up and down the living room. "Child abuse! That's it. I'm sure he beats his kids. Where do you report child abuse?"

"Brenda! Knock it off. That's harassment. It's illegal. He could sue you, for God's sake."

"Harassment! What do you call garbage in our back yard? I'll sue *him*. I'll put him out of business. I'll close down that rat trap. Where's the phone book?"

Brenda's erratic pacing and arm waving came dangerously close to putting my blue Tiffany tablelamp out of business. I pulled her onto the sofa and held both her hands. She squirmed and fidgeted.

"Look, kid. You've done enough for one day. What do you say we call Jenny and Charley and spend the weekend on Fire Island?"

"Oh, no, Jack. We can't do that. We have an appointment tomorrow morning to look at houses in Westchester."

On Saturday we took an early train to wild and woolly Westchester to view real estate. We saw cathedral ceilings and three-car garages, pseudo-saltboxes and split-level bathrooms, cosy cottages nestled into careful foliage allowed to grow just so wild and no wilder, rambling ranches designed from the same general all-purpose scheme for storing a standard quota of children in standard-sized boxes with a standard number of windows.

Mrs. Handiford, the real-estate saleswoman, efficient and motherly, graciously hauled us around winding tree-lined roads in her late-model battleship-on-wheels station wagon, pointing out local amenities and landmarks: stables here, swim club there, home of notable this and pillar of the community that.

"And of course the public school system is one of the finest in the state, although if you prefer private—"

"We haven't any children." Brenda was terse, bordering on rude, but Mrs. Handiford patted her neatly waved silver-gray coiffure and bravely pressed on.

"Ah, well, you're young and there's no place better for starting a family. I'm sure you'll find many activities here to interest you. There's the Arts and Crafts Guild. They have exhibits twice a year. And a very active chapter of the League of Women Voters. We have the Garden Club. They've done those very lovely plantings we saw in the village. Do you play bridge? We have several informal bridge groups, always looking for new members. Tennis and golf, of course. Oh, I'm sure you'll find lots to do, Mrs. Rollins."

"Yes. Well, I have a job. In the city." Brenda was obviously hating every minute of this grand tour of suburban glories.

Dammit, I thought. This was your idea. Let the poor woman get on with her spiel. And glared at her behind Mrs. Handiford's neat and businesslike navy-blue back.

Only momentarily dampened, Mrs. Handiford rallied swiftly and tried another tack.

"Well, if you're both going to be commuting, perhaps you'd like something closer to the station. I have a sweet little place, walking distance. Not much land, so it's easy to maintain."

The sweet little place near the station materialized as a Swiss chalet, replete with kitsch, cuckoo clock, and a grotto in the rear where recirculated water trickled over imitation moss on plastic rocks. Miraculously there were no gnomes. But I fully expected Shirley Temple as Heidi, or at the very least a nanny goat, to come bounding out of the garage-cum-cowshed exuding Alpine charm and the fragrance of edelweiss or Emmenthaler, take your pick. A tour of the interior offered us eaves to bump our heads on, which Brenda did, bottle glass windows reducing the entrance of daylight to a minimum, low beamed ceilings, and endless square feet of dark and intricately carved woodwork.

Brenda was breathing hard by this time, not saying much. Just breathing. And nursing the bump on her head. It was the bathroom that really finished her off. She opened the door, quickly closed it, and tried to choke back a despairing "Oh, God, no!"

She was not to be let off so easily. Mrs. Handiford bustled through the door, taking Brenda's arm as she went. I followed in horrified fascination. There were the gnomes. Frolicking on the vinyl wallpaper, in a landscape featuring distant cows and Matterhorns.

"Of course, it's all custom designed," stated Mrs. Handiford, eyeing Brenda with grim satisfaction.

Indeed it was. The usual facilities were all encased in as much wood carving as possible without interfering with function. The tub-shower enclosure resembled a confessional box and the toilet paper roll, when activated, tinkled *The Sound of Music.*

Revenge must be sweet to real-estate ladies spending unprofitable Saturdays with obviously unsuitable clients.

"Sweet," gasped Brenda. "Utterly too sweet. But not my—" She broke off, headed for the front door at an ungainly gallop, and narrowly missed impaling herself on the staghorn doing duty as a coat rack in the tiny foyer.

Regrouped on the sidewalk, we all three tried to conceal our eagerness to split.

"We've seen so much . . . it's hard to decide."

"It's been a pleasure taking you around."

"We'll have to think it all over."

"If something new comes in. . . ."

"Yes, please do give us a call."

"I'll drive you to the station."

"Oh, thanks. We'd like to walk. It's so close."

"Good-bye then. If I can be of help, don't hesitate—"

"Thanks again. Yes, we can find the station."

"Good-bye."

"Good grief!" snorted Brenda as Mrs. Handiford piloted her dreadnought off to whatever suburban utopia she called her own, which I devoutly hoped included a well-earned double Scotch on the rocks.

"You were right, Jack. Absolutely right. I could never hack this. Not in a million years. Where's that train schedule?"

By the time the train reached 125th Street, Brenda was enthusiastically discussing plans for the erection of a ten-foot-high solid redwood fence to take the place of the post and wire affair currently separating our turf from Guttierez's.

Back home again, the late Saturday afternoon Brooklyn streets basked in a golden glow. We bought Good Humors from Maxie outside the subway station and walked home munching and kicking prickle balls fallen from the huge old chestnut tree at the corner.

"It's okay, isn't it, Jack?" Brenda mouthed around a chunk of chocolate-chip ice cream.

"Sure it is," I replied from the midst of my toasted almond.

"I don't really want to leave," she went on. "And I'm sorry I made all those stupid phone calls. Maybe I should try to talk to Mrs. Guttierez."

"Maybe you should just leave the whole thing alone."

We let ourselves into the house, dim and cool and quiet. Quiet, except for the muffled sound of a radio voice—the unmistakable voice of the WHOM announcer blasting out an Hispanic hard sell, exhorting his listeners to buy Vitarroz. Suddenly the penetrating commercial message was drowned, obliterated by a frantic frightened animal squealing. The squeals continued rising in pitch interrupted only by an inhuman snuffling, a snorting attempt to breathe. In the next moment this hair-raising noise was overridden by cheers and laughter, quite definitely arising from human throats.

"Jack, what's going on?" Brenda whispered. Her words were normal, but her eyes had gone unfocused as she listened intently. "It's them again. I know it. What are they doing?"

"Stay here, Bren. I think it's coming from the yard. I'll go take a look."

I strode off toward the back door, hoping Brenda would not follow. I didn't like the way she looked. Anything could set her off again.

The cheers and squeals had subsided, and WHOM had taken over with a burst of Latino music when I opened the door and stepped out into my garden. The first thing I saw was people. The neighboring yard was full of people. Young, old, and in-between, sitting on kitchen chairs and boxes, lying on blankets, leaning against the fence. One enormous old matriarch sat enthroned on a plastic-covered armchair. Guttierez was having a party.

All conversation stopped and thirty pairs of piercing black eyes turned full on me as I advanced to the center of my yard. Inquiry into the source of the frightful squealing was clearly unthinkable. A quick and furtive survey of Guttierez's yard disclosed a shallow trench filled with charcoal and a young man seated in a corner industriously whittling the end of a long wooden pole. The other end had already been shaped to a tapered point.

I turned to my rosebushes; Christian Dior was definitely drooping and I knelt for a closer look. Across the fence chatter and laughter resumed.

I didn't hear Brenda come out. I heard her gasp.

"My God! It's a pig!"

I turned. A pig it was. A small pig, not quite a suckling but not yet fully grown. I had missed it, lying under the hedge at the back of the yard, eyes closed and panting. A boy wandered over and began poking it with a stick. The pig gave a half-hearted squeal of protest, rose clumsily to its feet and trotted around the perimeter of the yard to escape its tormentor.

The boy trotted after the pig, and other children joined him. Several of the men rose and stationed themselves attentively around the yard. An anticipatory hush fell among the people; the radio was the only sound. The children stalked the pig; the men waited; we watched.

Guttierez marched out of his house, a gleaming, finely honed machete held lovingly in both hands. The waiting circle of guests tensed for the moment of truth. The children began to run. The pig scrabbled and galloped, turning to one side and then the other, seeking escape where there was none. And then the squealing began again.

The pig ricocheted off chair legs and people legs; the children shrieked and tumbled in the dust. The waiting stone-eyed man lunged and missed and lunged again. Guttierez stood motionless at the hub of the pig chase, the machete held ritually across his body. His moment would come. And rising above the shrieks and laughter of the children, the grunts and muttered comments of the men, the pig squealed its mortal terror.

In the corner of the yard the stake sharpener laid down his whittling knife. On light feet he moved, a thin sensitive-faced young man. Slowly and quietly, almost casually, he moved to a position some six feet behind the exhausted animal.

The pig stood at bay, its small wary eyes fixed on Guttierez and his shining blade. It did not sense the danger creeping up from behind. Suddenly the young man tensed, sprang, and soared across the intervening space. The full weight of his falling body flattened the protesting pig, splaying its slender dainty legs in four directions and cutting off its lament in mid-squeal.

A cheer rose from the spectators and the men and children crowded around the pair wrestling in the dusty arena. Guttierez flexed his sword arm and thumbed the edge of the blade. Two men struggled out of the writhing group on the ground, carrying the pig belly up. Its eyes rolled frantically as the men deposited it at Guttierez's feet, holding it immobile, throat exposed.

Guttierez imperiously motioned all others to stay behind him. The seated women drew in their feet and prepared to cover their eyes. The stroke, when it came, was almost anticlimactic. The machete swung upward, flashed once in the sun, and swung down. The hot pig blood spurted in a perfect arc and formed a puddle on the dried earth.

The women forgot to cover their eyes, but groaned instead in a kind of communal sensual satisfaction. The children capered around the carcass whose wound pumped a few smaller and smaller ribbons of blood, which finally subsided to a trickle. The smallest boy explored the puddle and squished his toes in the reddish mud.

The execution of the entire pigsticking must have taken no more than five minutes, but I felt as if I had been holding my breath for an hour. I sucked in a lungful of air, still heavy with the smell of fear and blood, and muttered to Brenda, "I wonder who's going to be awarded the pig's ear."

There was no reply. At some time during the slaughter Brenda must have fled indoors, unnoticed. I thought I'd better do the same.

I found her, tears streaming down her face, hysterically mouthing into the telephone.

". . . killing a pig . . . oh, God, the blood . . . all over the yard . . . come quick, he's got a machete."

I grabbed the phone from her hand and slammed it down.

"What have you done?" I demanded. "Not the police again?"

She was shaking uncontrollably, and now her head began a rhythmic nodding while the tears welled and splattered.

"Brenda. Brenda, they're having a barbecue. That's all it is. Brenda, snap out of it. Where do you think pork chops come from?"

I couldn't reach her. She would not be comforted. But while I was trying, thinking of calling a doctor, the sirens came. We stood at the center of a storm of sirens, more sirens than I thought existed coming from every direction. In moments the doorbell shrilled, fists pounded at the door, voices demanded that we open up.

I ran to the door and opened it to a surge of blue uniforms with guns drawn, emitting a staccato battery of questions.

"Where is it? Where's the body?"

"Next door? Which side?"

"Is he armed? Is he still there?"

"How many are there?"

"You reported the cop killing?"

"One side. Let us through."

Cop killing! I ran after them, trying to explain. They raced through the kitchen out into the yard.

"It was a pig! Only a pig!" I shouted after them. Brenda, in the kitchen, was trying to stop one of them, held onto his arm, and was swept out into the yard. I followed, still hoping to explain the colossal mistake.

In his yard Guttierez stood facing the pig now strung head down from a low-hanging ailanthus branch. The blood-

streaked machete was still in his hand; he was preparing to
disembowel. The charcoal in the trench was flaming and the
double-pointed stake stood ready to impale its victim.

Scores of policemen were swarming into all the neighboring gardens up and down the block, vaulting the fences, con-
verging on the big party. Cop killing is not taken lightly in
this town.

Brenda had not loosened her grip on the arm of the law.
She clung, and with her free arm pointed to the hung pig;
she chattered, gasped, and shook. Her words tumbled out in
an incoherent stream. The policeman looked stunned; all the
policemen looked blank and chagrined, their drawn pistols
hung superfluous and obscenely naked at their sides. They
had come to do battle for a brother and found only a barbecue.

In that momentary hiatus before explanations and re-
criminations must be made, in the silence before the full
weight of embarrassment descended, understanding came to
Guttierez. And with it fury. It swelled his chest and added
inches to his height. His narrowed eyes sought Brenda, and
the fury erupted from his throat.

"A-a-y-y! *PIG!*" he screamed.

And the machete flashed in the sun once more. It left his
hand in a graceful arc, crossed the fence and seemed suspended in the still evening air for endless ages before it came
to rest.

At almost the same instant a policeman standing near Guttierez fired once. He later said he was aiming for the up-
swung arm but was too close and a split second too late. Guttierez lay beneath the hanging pig, the wreckage caused by a
bullet in the brain mingling with the slow drip from the
draining carcass.

Brenda sprawled at the foot of Christian Dior, the machete
still quivering in her chest. The slowly spreading stain on her
blouse matched the roses that drooped over her.

Somebody turned the radio off. And then the screaming
began.

THE INVISIBLE WITNESS
by Anthony Gilbert

Once again we marvel at Anthony Gilbert's grasp of and affinity for a certain type of character. She knew it so well. . . . The world is full of "invisible witnesses"—but "if you're shut off from the world, the world is equally shut off from you."

I SUPPOSE I originally noticed the old woman because she always occupied the same seat in the park. It had a copper plate on the back which read:

In Memory of
Mrs. CHARLOTTE RACE
Who loved this place

A good many of the benches in Phillimore Park have similar inscriptions to commemorate the army of old people who came here for a few hours in the sun during their declining years. The seats were full of them—the old people, I mean. This one looked much like the rest; she wore a black and white tweed coat and a felt basin of a hat over her white hair and a long dark red scarf—the scarf the gift of a dead-and-gone nephew, she told me.

She carried a solid black leather bag that probably contained most of her worldly treasures, and she differed from the rest in that she never had a newspaper or a bit of knitting to occupy her time. She sat with her hands in her lap; nothing moved but her eyes.

One afternoon when she was the sole occupant of the

bench I took a place at the farther end, shaking out my morning paper. On fine days I often walked through the park to my subway station; being a freelance journalist I could choose my own hours. That afternoon, I remember, a wave of pigeons had settled on the asphalt, strutting, and preening their shining breasts. One of them, even plumper than the rest, reminded me of my Aunt Selina who used to attend church in a purple marabout and shawl. The Old Indestructible, they called her.

I hadn't been seated more than a minute or two when the old woman leaned toward me.

"Can you tell me the time, sir?"

I told her it was 3:30.

She leaned back, smiling.

"Then I can stay a little longer," she said.

I supposed her appointment, whatever it might be, was for four o'clock. I wondered whom she was expecting to meet, other than, of course, Death in due course.

After a moment she spoke again. "They're such greedy birds, aren't they?" and she pointed to the pigeons. "Bring a little bit of bread for the sparrows or the ducks and it's always the pigeons that get it."

"Not the gulls?" I murmured. I don't know why I let myself be drawn into a conversation. But it was a pleasant afternoon and I had a few minutes to spare. I liked to watch the gulls flying—like a ballet they were, swooping, diving, soaring again with their prey.

"Only if you throw it up into the air," said the old woman seriously. "And I never do that. Mind you," she added, "it's not much I bring. I'm against wasting food, but a bit of crust sometimes—it doesn't run to more than that when you're living on a small pension."

"I don't know how anyone does. Unless they have friends or something." I meant children; she had a wedding ring worn deep into her finger. It didn't occur to me she might be going to beg. She didn't look the type.

"The Old Age Pension helps," she told me. "Of course, I never taste meat. It's out of the question, the price the way it is. If only people would take a stand and refuse to buy, prices would come down."

I suppose she thought I looked restive, for she rapidly changed the subject, saying how fortunate Londoners were to have these lovely parks.

"I go up to the pond sometimes," she said. "Last year's cygnets are as big as their parents now, such beautiful birds. And did you know the Chinese geese had a family last year? If it wasn't for the parks we should have to go to China to see a thing like that."

A few minutes later she said she must be getting home. "I make myself a cup of tea at four o'clock," she confided. "I find if you don't keep regular hours, that's when you start going downhill. When you've only yourself to keep house for, you get all hugger-mugger if you're not careful."

As she picked up her gloves I saw that her fingernails were beautifully tended and painted a deep coral pink, and her hair under her indifferent hat was carefully arranged.

You'll never let yourself go to pieces, I thought. And then I put her out of my mind. She was just one of a host of elderly women sitting in the sun in the evening of her days. I didn't even know her name.

I saw her again a few days later, still alone on her bench. She smiled and said she'd been watching a baby poodle trying to play with a swan.

"It didn't understand," she said. "Well, they don't at that age. A swan could drown a little dog like that. And the owner was not even noticing. I screamed and the swan went away and then the man came up. I think he thought I was mad, I think they all did."

I murmured something about it being the breeding season, so you had to be careful.

"It's cruel how they have to learn, isn't it?" she agreed. "It just wanted to play." A man went past and she chuckled slyly.

"See that one?" she said. "I call him Mr. Drake. The way he puts his feet down—see?"

I wouldn't have noticed it myself, but she was quite right. He walked exactly in a duck's splay-footed fashion.

"You're very noticing," I congratulated her.

"You might say it's my hobby. He comes here three or four times a week. It's their little habits that turn people into in-

dividuals, you see. Some of them would be surprised to realize how much I know about them."

I saw her quite often after that. Sometimes she shared the
seat with some other old biddy and then she'd just glance up
and smile. At other times she was alone, but she never gave
the impression of being solitary. She felt herself part of the
pattern, I suppose. I wondered what stories she made up
about the other passersby.

I got into the habit of stopping for a few minutes if she was
alone, though I didn't learn much more about her—just that
she had a single room in a big apartment house near the
park, had her own gas-ring but shared domestic facilities. It
was the history of hundreds of thousands of elderly folk with
no home ties. She never complained. Once she said it would
be nice to have a meal out now and again, but of course the
small pension would never permit that.

As I got to know her better a few more facts emerged. She
was a widow, had married a man who had a little neighborhood store business, but he'd gone bankrupt and died soon
after. She'd gone back to work in a shop, selling behind a
counter. She'd enjoyed that—all the different people, see?
Now at 70 she enjoyed her leisure, and there was always
someone nice to talk to. She never spoke of a child; usually if
there have been any, some whisper creeps in.

Once I offered her a newspaper but though she took it, she
laid it on the seat. The passersby were her newspaper—"and
then I have my little radio. That keeps me in touch." Now
and again she went to the public library, but it was a bit of a
walk—"and anyway," she added, "it's people I mind about. I
mean, there's nothing you can do about strikes and rising
prices, but people are always real. You get to recognize them
after a time, though my sight's not quite what it was. But I've
good hearing still. Some of the bits of conversation you pick
up—it makes you wonder. And some of them have a child or
a dog. There's one woman limps on a big stick with a dog's
head for the handle. I think to myself sometimes, you've
probably never noticed me, but say you were in trouble with
the police—couldn't show where you were at such and such a

time—out walking you might say, on your own; well, I might be able to give you an alibi. But no one would think of asking me—the invisible witness."

She laughed. She had a pretty tinkling laugh.

Another visitor and one frequently occupying a seat near my old girl was an old tramp in a tattered black coat and a black hat that no self-respecting bird would have accepted for a nest. He was always laden with a huge haversack packed with parcels, food, debris—that he'd unpack and lay out along the seat—presumably to prevent anyone else from sharing it. My old friend spoke of him once.

"I don't want you to think I'm a vain old woman," she said, "but I'm sometimes terrified he'll come and settle along of me. He gives me such funny looks—it wouldn't do, no, it wouldn't do at all."

"He wouldn't do any harm," I assured her. "There are people all about."

"If he was to ask me for money, what could I say? I don't have any, and that's the truth, but if you keep yourself looking respectable no one believes you. And you do read such awful things. There was that old woman not so far from Harrods, attacked in broad daylight just for the few pounds in her purse. She'd come up to buy blankets, been saving months. And they never got the man who did it."

I insisted she was working herself up over nothing, though I didn't much care for the look of the old tramp myself.

"If you're really nervous you could sit on a seat that was already occupied," I suggested. But she looked startled.

"Oh, I couldn't do that. I like to think of this as my place. Sometimes I wonder if I ever saw her—Charlotte Race, I mean. I could even have spoken to her. There wouldn't have been a plaque on the seat in those days, of course. And you never exchange names. Well, you like to keep yourself to yourself, you know. But I think she'd be a widow like me—a married woman wouldn't have the time to sit around. I daresay she liked the trees and the birds, the same as I do, and a bit of company. I can almost feel her here sometimes. It gives you a sense of belonging."

If her seat was occupied I might find her up by the pond,

where the children sailed their boats and the elderly gentlemen flew their kites. That made her laugh.

"So serious," she said. "You'd think it was the Grand Prix. There's one has a kite shaped like a falcon, ever so realistic. I like to watch out for that. Might have been a gamekeeper's, I think."

The days I didn't go to the park I didn't think about her at all; that was where she belonged and, so far as I was concerned, outside the park she had no existence. I liked her courage, and sometimes wished I could help her; but I had my own troubles—as haven't we all—and they took up a lot of my time.

It was a blustery summer; she still wore the black and white tweed coat and tied the red scarf round her throat.

"Odd," she said, "to think that Humphrey who gave me this has been gone these many years, and I linger on."

It was during that wet July it happened, an event that set the whole neighborhood ablaze, though it didn't rate much above a paragraph in the national press. After all, the news was full of wars and rumors of wars, strikes and violence everywhere, death falling out of the skies—so the death of one little trollop was pretty small beer. Only not in the place where it happened. As my old lady said, there's always the personal element. It might have been me, she said, and that was the general feeling.

The young woman's body was found in a little private garden designed a century earlier for a royal princess, within the precincts of the park. In spring and summer, when the weather was fine, this was a favorite spot, especially for visitors, from both home and overseas. There was a stretch of water, covered with rose-colored lilies whose like I have seen nowhere else, and each season a white duck brought forth her brood and exercised them among the lilies' broad umbrella leaves.

The whole garden was roofed by thick vinery and surrounded by a paved walk within a box hedge; and there were seats at intervals round three sides of the garden. It was on one of the seats, the farthest one from the entrance, that the body was found. The previous afternoon had been cloudy with storm, breaking into thundery rain, and at such times there was something sinister about the little garden—it became a place of shadows and pattering raindrops.

One such afternoon I had dived into the shelter of the vinery during a sudden storm and found my old friend on one of the seats there. She was wrapped in a huge gray raincoat with sleeves like the flukes of a whale.

"You're very brave to be out in such weather," I told her. "Brave and rash."

"It was better when I started out," she said. "I haven't seen you this last day or so."

"I'm not the regular you are," I reminded her. "I go by bus or subway if the weather's unpromising."

"You get tired of your own company," she explained. "And, of course, you can't have even a bird where I live. I like to think Charlotte Race wouldn't let a little bit of bad weather defeat her."

That had been one week ago. And now, not a hundred yards from where we'd been sitting, a woman had been murdered, strangled by her own scarf pulled tight round her throat—garroting, they called it. The body was found huddled in a corner of the seat in the early morning by one of the park keepers. He'd given his usual cry—"All out, all out!"— the previous night, and no one, so far as he could recall, had left the garden. The whole park, in fact, was nearly empty thanks to the thunder and the sudden onslaught of rain, and he hadn't gone round the little garden; he had other duties. And, of course, murder isn't what you come to look for in a Royal Park.

The papers nosed out quite a lot of information about the murdered woman: Thelma Hughes, married, but believed to be living apart from her husband, aged 29, living in a flat in Marylebone. She had a job in a Bayswater Hotel. The previous day she'd been off duty since three o'clock. She'd been leaving the hotel a bit later, presumably to keep an appointment. The weather of the early afternoon had been fresh and a little cloudy, but the ensuing storm had taken everyone by surprise. Great black clouds had scudded across the sky, the wind had risen, thunder had pealed; later had come the rain, but the girl's clothes weren't wet. She must have met her fate, as they used to say, before the storm broke.

On such an afternoon it would be a sort of twilight in the little garden, and she'd been found lying back against the seat, as though resting or asleep. No one would have tried to speak to her or disturb her. Whatever had been the motive of the crime, it wasn't theft, for her bag containing ten pounds in notes hadn't been touched, and there were rings on her fingers and a brooch and necklace at her throat. Nor, we were assured, had there been any attempt at assault. She would have chosen this place thinking it was secret and safe. But if you're shut off from the world, the world is equally shut off from you.

The hotel where she was employed couldn't supply much information; she'd been working for them for a little more than a year, having come from a reputable hotel on the west coast. They knew of no particular men friends, and she had confided in no one. It wasn't even certain that her husband was still alive, or, if alive, was still a resident in England. She'd never spoken of him to anyone. The police advertised for him, of course, but no one came forward. Taken by and large, she was a woman of mystery, and, until now, of no particular interest to anyone.

A day or so after the news broke I was hurrying through the park in the late afternoon; the sky looked ominous and I wanted to escape a wetting. My old lady wasn't on her usual seat, but to my surprise I found her up by the pond. The shelter cut off a lot of the wind, she explained. When she saw me, for the first time she jumped up and came toward me.

"I hoped I'd see you," she said. "You weren't here yesterday."

"I wasn't in this part of London," I explained. "We've had a bit of a rush on. You know, you'll catch your death of cold."

"I wanted to see you," she said. "I want some advice and there's no one else to ask."

She spoke more loudly than usual, and I looked round, but people had packed up with the threatened break in the weather and we had this part of the park to ourselves. The few ducks that were about were blown clownishly by the wind, and all the kite flyers had gone.

"I couldn't ask them," she repeated.

I knew she meant her fellow boarders.

"Ask them what?" I said.

"What I ought to do. About that poor girl."

"What poor girl?" For a moment I hadn't got the drift of her meaning.

"The one they found in the garden, of course. You must have heard—it was on the radio—being a royal garden, I mean."

"That one," I said a bit blankly. "But I don't understand where you come in. If you're afraid you might be next you've only got to keep away from the spot and—"

She was almost shaking me in her agitation. "You don't understand. I saw him!"

That staggered me. "You saw . . . ? Think what you're saying. Whom did you see?"

"I don't know. But he must have been the one." She calmed a little, and became more coherent. "You remember how the weather broke that afternoon. I'd been up here by the pond, all the cygnets were out and the parent birds, a lovely show, and then suddenly it got dark and I thought the storm might break before I got back, so I made for the garden as being the nearest shelter."

"Yes," I encouraged her.

"And I saw them."

"Get this straight," I said. "You saw—what? Two people in the garden. There were probably others."

"No. Only those two. I was walking round looking at the flowers and as I turned the corner there they were, sitting in the farthest seat. I thought at first they were a pair of lovers having a tiff, the way young people do, goodness knows, it's natural enough, and I was going to move away because no one wants eavesdroppers at a time like that when I heard her. . . ."

She paused, drawing a deep breath.

"You mean you heard her speak?" I said.

"Yes. I couldn't help it. Anyone near me would have heard

her, too. She said, 'It's no use, Gerald. I've got you like *that*.' I thought at first it might be—" She hesitated.

"You thought—?"

"I did think she might be telling him she was going to have a baby and he'd have to marry her. You read about that kind of thing."

"But there was nothing in the paper about her being pregnant," I said.

"Yes. I noticed that. But—oh, sir"—she had never called me sir and she had never held onto my sleeve as she was holding onto it now—"there was no love there. I know the voice of love, even when you're quarreling, but this was something different. She was dangerous to him."

"Since he presumably murdered her—" I began and then I stopped. "Did you see him?" I asked.

She shook her head. "I told you, I went back."

"Then how can you be sure it was the same couple? I daresay there were plenty of people in the garden that afternoon?"

"There was a flash of lightning. I saw that little gold cap she was wearing—the papers made a point of that, they thought someone might remember seeing it. Oh, she was the one, I'm sure. What I wanted to ask you was what should I do now? I mean, should I tell the police? My husband always said, 'Keep away from the police, Alice.' They don't do any good, being mixed up with them, I mean."

"If you have any idea who he is—" I said doubtfully.

"I do have a feeling I've seen him somewhere, but of course I see so many, and they all look so very much alike. If they've a dog or a child, that's different, or if they're like that old tramp—didn't someone say once it was depressing how alike old women become? But I do know they say that when anything sensational happens, there are always people coming forward to get the limelight."

"You don't want the limelight," I said.

"I want to do what's right. It must be someone who knows the neighborhood or he'd never have suggested the garden."

"Unless she suggested it."

"I hadn't thought of that," she admitted. "I hoped I'd see

you yesterday—if I was to ask any of them at the house, even mention the police, I'd find my room was wanted. Oh, I daresay it's against the law turning people out for no real reason, but there's ways of getting round the law. They can say you're not fit to look after yourself or something."

I imagined her at the police station, and some ambitious young constable listening to her and perhaps writing her off as one of those old sensation-mongers, just as she'd said. There'd be the newspapers, too.

"Do you think you really saw enough of him?" I wondered. "You didn't hear him speak."

"I've been trying to remember. But I didn't stop," she went on quickly, "the thunder had started and the lightning and I wanted to get home. I thought, it's nothing to do with me, people are always quarreling, and they don't thank you to interfere. I mean, I couldn't have done anything, could I? I couldn't guess how it would end, but I do think now if they'd known I was there, it might not have come to this."

"You can't torture yourself like that," I said roughly. We had moved away from the pond, toward her gate. The thunder that had been growling softly burst into a sudden roar. I felt her shudder.

"I've always hated thunder," she said. "My mother used to tell me it was the angels quarreling. And I shouldn't have troubled you. I ought to be able to make up my own mind. That's what William would have said—William was my husband. I won't do anything tonight, I want to get back before the rain breaks, but I'll sleep on it. My mother always said things are clearer in the dawn, before your ideas have had a chance to get muddled. I'll think about it"—I felt oddly sure she meant she would also pray about it—"and in the morning I'll know what to do."

In the distance I heard the anonymous voice calling, "All out, all out!" I looked round. We virtually had the park to ourselves.

"We don't want to get locked in," said Alice. "I'll take the short cut through the trees."

"Mind how you go," I said.

I saw her feet slipping on the wet grass.

"I'll be all right," she called. "You don't have to worry about me."

She was like some strange spirit dodging among the tree trunks.

I reached the gate in the north wall just before it was locked. The rain was coming down hard by then, and there was no hope of a taxi and the buses were crammed. I remembered my old lady's voice.

Things are clearer in the dawn.

Next morning I woke to what might have been a different world. The sun shone, the whole world sparkled. I took my short cut through the park, but there was no Alice—what was her other name? We never exchange names, she had said. You like to keep yourself to yourself. Charlotte Race's seat was occupied, though, by the villainous old tramp, who was busy spreading his flotsam and jetsam. He was grinning evilly to himself.

I strode past without meeting his eye. She wasn't up by the pond, either, though the children were coming along with their mothers or *au pair* girls, and the first kite flyers were gathering. Someone went past whistling. I recognized the tune. It had been old when I was a child. How did it go? Something like—*Alice, where are you?* I remembered I still didn't know her second name.

I learned it, though, that night. It had been one of those busy days and the evening rush was accumulating round the subway station where people were stopping to buy copies of the evening editions. There was no paper seller there—there never was; people just threw down their money and helped themselves. I never saw anyone take a paper without paying for it or saw anyone help himself to the loose change lying around. It's one of the odd quirks of honesty in a society that isn't particularly thin-skinned.

The man in front of me threw down his money and picked up a paper. For a moment the staring black headlines almost hit me in the face.

> *Second Park Murder*
> *Another Woman*
> *Found Strangled*

it ran, and I put my money down and grabbed a paper.

"An elderly woman who has been identified as Mrs. Alice Calcraft, a pensioner living in an apartment house in W. 8., was found in the early hours of this morning among the trees near the North Gate of Phillimore Park. She had been strangled by a scarf she was wearing. This is the second case of a woman being found garroted in the park during the past 48 hours. The police are examining a theory that a maniacal killer has escaped from some mental home or hospital and is roaming at large."

There was even a warning that unaccompanied women shouldn't roam in the park after dusk.

I stood there like a man riven in stone. People went past and the pile of papers rapidly reduced.

Alice Calcraft, I thought. So that was her full name. A harmless innocent old woman—but that wasn't true any more. Not harmless, not innocent. She'd heard a blackmailing little trollop threaten a man's life—that was what it amounted to, years of dependence winding up in ruin—oh, there are some chances a man can't take. And just because of those few words she'd had to forfeit her life.

A hand fell on my arm. I almost jumped out of my skin.

"What's up, Gerald?" said a voice. I looked up and it was a chap I knew in Fleet Street.

"You're as white as a sheet. Burning the candle . . . ?"

"She called him Gerald," insisted a ghostly voice.

It's no use, Gerald. I've got you like *that*.

"You look as though you could do with a strengthener at The Bull before you join the rush-hour crowd," the chap went on. "Join me."

I looked round. There was no one else with us.

So I folded my paper under my arm and followed him to The Bull.

THE CERULIANA CAPER
by Jacob Hay

Another adventure in high diplomacy in which Sir Vyvyan Bultivant, near the twilight of his brilliant service to the remnants of Empire, becomes the Governor General of a Paradise on Earth and is faced with the delicate task of preserving that Paradise. But then he had the help of King Walilolo IV, a most ingenious Polynesian. . . . Jacob Hay's stories of the British Foreign Service are tales of beauty—there's nothing quite like them under the sun that never sets on the mystery Empire. . . .

IT IS POSSIBLE to suggest that Her Britannic Majesty's Foreign Office was moved more by ancestral instinct than by its computers in selecting Sir Vyvyan Bultivant to be the Governor General of the Pacific island kingdom of Ceruliana, which just might be the closest thing to a Paradise on this Earth. He was just the man for the job.

For nearly two decades prior to his appointment Sir Vyvyan had assisted materially in the dissolution of his nation's once-mighty Empire. Did a newly emergent former Colony need advice on how to establish a Parliament? Did it need words of wisdom on how to set up its own equivalent of New Scotland Yard? Bultivant was there with the answers. He was the Queen's recognized expert in the demanding and tricky job of insuring that one fine evening the sun would indeed set on the British Empire.

It was a wearying task, especially for one whose ancestor, Lord Horatio Bultivant, known to his intimates as "Dashing Horry," had subdued large areas of various segments of Africa with Bultivant's Light Horse, supported by two field batteries and an Anglican chaplain versed in Swahili. On his mother's side Admiral Sir Makepeace Upsham, notable for his skill with frigates and a slightly less adept hand with sloops-of-war, had sailed up practically every bay and river in Asia to maintain the Queen's sovereignty.

"Bultivant is looking a bit peaky," Her Majesty's Foreign Secretary remarked shortly after Sir Vyvyan had returned from making the quondam British Protectorate of Sonnava Gon, in the Indian Ocean, safe for democracy. "He deserves a change of pace, something restful for a change."

"May I suggest Ceruliana, sir," said the Permanent Undersecretary cautiously.

"Sound thinking, Carruthers! Deuced sound," replied the Foreign Secretary heartily. "For the first time in twenty years he won't be hauling down the flag."

It was true; Bultivant was looking peaky. His tour in Sonnava Gon had not been an easy one, and it had not been a simple task to convince the reigning Emir that it was better to debate the issues with his loyal opposition than to have them all beheaded, a point taken with some difficulty by many Indian Ocean rulers. With the departure of British garrisons and the immediate presence of benign British justice, decapitation had become something of a hobby. The tall lean Bultivant frame had acquired a slight stoop, and there was more gray hair on his head than his 50-odd years deserved. Happily, so far as this brief narrative is concerned, there remained steadfast the whimsical gleam in his bright blue eyes.

The Governor Generalship of Ceruliana was, and continues to be, regarded as one of the rare plums of the British Foreign Service. Ceruliana wants no part of independence. It emerged—to use the currently fashionable diplomatic expression—as far as it wanted to emerge in the spring of 1891, when its monarch, the late King Walilolo, asked for and got the protection of the British flag in return for the rights to maintain a coaling station on the island that would have been strategically useful only in the event that the British planned to attack New Zealand.

As of Bultivant's appointment, Ceruliana was ruled by His Majesty, King Walilolo IV, M.A., Oxon., plus a string of initials signifying his membership in a number of British orders. He had won his M.C. at El Alamein in command of the Royal Ceruliana Rifles; his D.S.C. had come later, in Italy. Most importantly, so far as the events of this account are involved, he had been up at New College, Oxford, on the same staircase as Bultivant, and the tall slender Englishman and the somewhat stockier but equally handsome Polynesian had become fast friends, the more as Bultivant agreed fully with the young future King's determination to keep his beautiful island kingdom as unspoiled as the world would permit.

In this aim Walilolo IV had succeeded far better than even he had dared to hope. The exposure of the men of the Royal Ceruliana Rifles to the wiles of Africa and Europe had made them all the more eager to return as quickly as possible to their homes and their simple way of life.

The royal palace was merely a large version of the bungalows in which most of the kingdom's inhabitants lived, situated in the center of the small town of Cerula, on the Bay of Palms, which was the capital. It was some unknown official of the British Foreign Office who, it must be assumed, figured that the name Cerula sounded vaguely Finnish and so, to ward off the snows and icy winds of that northern clime, had decreed that the Governor General's house should take the well-tested form of a Scottish castle, and thus it had been built, to become the largest, most improbable edifice in all Ceruliana. However, so benign was the island's climate that it was entirely livable, and those Governors General who had occupied it remembered it fondly.

Sir Vyvyan Bultivant took the news of his new appointment joyously. Increasingly in recent years he had had the feeling that if he had to throw away one more island or one more chunk of desert, he would go out of his mind. In consequence, the reunion, when Bultivant stepped from the Royal New Zealand Air Force plane which had brought him to Cerula's minuscule airstrip, was a touching one as King Walilolo IV stepped out to greet him.

"Vyv," cried His Majesty, with feeling. "Good show!"

"Wally," replied Bultivant cheerily. "You haven't changed a bit. Come have a drink at Government House."

"Done and done," said His Majesty heartily.

It took Bultivant only a day or two to realize that all the many good things he'd read and heard about Ceruliana were absolutely true, even understated. To begin with, the natives fully lived up to their advance notices as the most cheerful and naturally courteous Polynesians in all the Pacific Ocean. The fish that swam in their island waters were the most succulent; the vegetables they grew in their gardens were the juiciest and most flavorful.

At Government House, Bultivant, who was a bachelor, found that his ever-solicitous staff made him feel as if he had married not one but a dozen wives. His morning tea was always steaming on its impeccably arranged tray, along with a freshly ironed copy of *The Cerula Daily Mail.* His solar topee was kept dazzling white; his shoes gleamed; he could have shaved with his trouser creases. His cook, Lakani, formerly Mess Sergeant of the Royal Ceruliana Rifles, could roast pig as well as Claridge's could roast beef, and his baked taro on palm leaves was nothing short of superb.

And for good company and conversation there was always Walilolo IV and his cousin and Prime Minister, Prince Omeamunu, who was a very decent chap for all that he had been up at Cambridge.

So this happy situation continued for the first six months of Bultivant's appointment. Then a cloud no larger than a man's hand appeared on the horizon in the form of a personal note from an old friend in London.

"Dear Vyvyan," Bultivant read, "would you be good enough to extend your courtesy to Mr. Leonard Midderley, who is chairman of the board of Midderley International Hotels & Motor Inns, Ltd., and who plans to arrive in Cerula shortly to discuss a matter of considerable importance with you and His Majesty, the King. He will be arriving early next month by the regular weekly flight of South Pacific Airways. Will notify you by radio as to exact date. Cannot overemphasize the importance of this visit as to the kingdom's economic well-being. Yours, etc."

Oh, Lord, Bultivant thought unhappily. All England and large parts of the outside world knew of Leonard Midderley and his meteoric rise from simple publican to hotel magnate, a rise initiated when he and Mrs. Midderley had visited their married daughter in the United States and had stopped overnight at a Howard Johnson's Motel. Immediately on his return to the United Kingdom, Mr. Midderley had borrowed and scraped up sufficient pounds to add a hideous modern bedroom wing to the thatched-roof, half-timbered charm of his XVth Century Boar's Head, on the main Southampton-London road.

American tourists, in their rented cars and gasping at the quaintness of it all, nonetheless were delighted to discover, as they neared the end of the long and exhausting drive to London—on the wrong side of the road!—the equivalent of an American motel in the English countryside. "Children Under 12 Free! TV in Every Room!" The Boar's Head prospered beyond Leonard Midderley's most fantastic dreams, and Midderley Motels was on its way, first throughout the United Kingdom, then on the French Riviera, on to the Greek and Turkish coasts, to North Africa, to the Costa del Sol—so it inexorably went.

And now it seemed, Bultivant reflected, Ceruliana was next on that greedy list. Further, he thought angrily, what the devil was wrong with Ceruliana's economic well-being to begin with? Its annual crop of the finest copra produced in the Pacific and its milky coconuts always fetched top prices and more than sufficed the kingdom's modest needs. What Ceruliana definitely did not need was one of those horrible Midderley International Hotels and a concomitant "tourist industry."

It was a matter for immediate and decisive discussion with King Walilolo IV.

"Come over for a sundowner and we'll talk about it," His Majesty said affably in response to Bultivant's telephone call.

"It's damnable, Wally, and you know it," Bultivant declared bitterly, as he sat with the king on the veranda of the royal palace, sipping a pink gin that sat like vinegar on his tongue. "How could it happen?"

"Easy, Vyv. How could it happen? I suspect this Midderley chap has his eye on the old duPlessis plantation. French family that came out here in the eighteen-sixties and hoodwinked my great grandfather into a land grant.

"They've always been absentee landlords and, all things considered, good ones, but they've died off over the years, and as I understand it, their fortunes in France were ruined during the war. So what's left of the family is probably only too glad to sell off a plantation none of them has ever seen— there hadn't been a duPlessis on the island since the nineteen-twenties. It's a superb area, near Luvala on the northern coast, with at least three miles of virgin beach."

"Oh, God," moaned Bultivant. "But isn't there anything we can do to stop this man? Can't you issue a royal decree, or something? Revoke the grant? Anything?"

"Not a damned thing, Vyv. At least, not under the legal code you British drew up for us. My royal powers are, to say the least, limited. However, there are other solutions. I have been giving the problem some thought."

"Such as?" Bultivant asked, brightening. "I confess I haven't an idea in the world."

"A reversion to primitive savagery," King Walilolo suggested gravely. "Doubtless, this Midderley will have been briefed on Ceruliana in London to the effect that we are a Pacific paradise. But London could be wrong—which, I'm afraid, would be nothing new. When Midderley arrives, he could find an island in turmoil."

"Savagery? Turmoil?" Bultivant asked in bewilderment. "But both are utterly foreign to Ceruliana, Wally."

"Then we'll have to invent some, right? It shouldn't be too difficult. Let's see." The King mused briefly. "Omeamunu here shall organize a revolt among the northern head-hunters—"

"But there are no headhunters in the north," Bultivant protested, "or anywhere on the island."

"But Midderley can't be sure of that. Perhaps London was misleading him. Perhaps, too, London hasn't told him that I am plotting to liberate Ceruliana."

"You are?" Bultivant stared.

"And drive out the foreign devils, as well," His Majesty continued calmly. "With, naturally, the customary expropriation of property and the concomitant land reforms."

"Damned shame Ceruliana isn't ripe for rebellion, old

boy," murmured Prince Omeamunu, grinning at his cousin. "You'd be a natural."

"Further," His Majesty added imperturbably, "in the interest of reviving our Cerulianian national pride, I may well reestablish some of our ancient customs. I rather fancy the ritual sacrifice of a virgin thrown into the sea from the top of Kowlinga Head to appease the gods of the waters. A small roasted boy might make an appropriate offering to the gods who rule our copra crop—I feel quite certain that Mr. Midderley will, in the frame of mind I hope to produce in him, be unable to differentiate between a small roasted boy and a small roasted pig."

"About this revolt I'm supposed to lead—?" Prince Omeamunu asked dubiously.

"Simple, my dear cousin. Take a platoon of the Rifles into the hills above Akoaka and try a bit of target practice. Every afternoon. And don't spare the ammunition. Come to think of it, it's just about time for their annual field exercises anyway."

"And who am I supposed to be?" Omeamunu persisted.

"The Accursed Usurper, who has vowed to fight on until every last one of my loyalist followers has been slain, to fight on for years if necessary," replied the King. "I, of course, have vowed eternal resistance. Not a bad scenario, though I say it myself."

"Positively brilliant," Bultivant agreed. "We shall have to bring the Bishop in on the scheme, of course." He grinned. "Terrorized by your reversion to primitive ways, he shall find sanctuary in Government House where, naturally, the radio, our sole means of communication with London, will, regrettably, have broken down."

The Right Reverend David Hanaloa, the Anglican Bishop of Ceruliana, when advised of the scheme, was more than delighted to become a part of it. "I shall look as abject as an early Christian martyr," he declared cheerfully, and Bultivant reflected that, as the founding father and prime mover of the Cerula Amateur Theatrical Club, the Bishop could undoubtedly pull it off.

As to his own role in the affair, Bultivant rather fancied

himself in one of the late Sir C. Aubrey Smith's old parts, a
garrison commander on India's Northwest Frontier, belea-
guered and outnumbered by a mad Khan, as played by the
late Basil Rathbone.

Two days after this scheme was hatched, a radiogram
advised Bultivant that Mr. Leonard Midderley would arrive
in Cerula in precisely two weeks. So there was ample time. As
of that radiogram's arrival, Bultivant gave up his refreshing
morning shave and gave orders to his astonished household
staff that henceforward his clothing was to be left unpressed,
his shoes unshined. Further, morning tea would be served
lukewarm, as would all meals.

"It's just a temporary measure, my dear fellow," he assured Daniel Urnamoa, the Government House majordomo
and late Sergeant Major of the Royal Ceruliana Rifles. "Purely a tactical move, nothing more. But for the time being I
should like you to reduce this place to something of a shambles, and I leave it to you to convince our most excellent staff
to provide only the most slovenly and surly of services. Be a
good chap, and do what you can."

In on the scheme from the beginning had been Bultivant's
aide-de-camp, Captain the Hon. Peter fitz-ttench, a most
amiable and efficient young man as well as a most enthusias-
tic member of the Cerula Amateur Theatrical Club, and noted for his excellent imitations of Sir Noel Coward. He was
scheduled to go under house arrest for drunkenness on
duty, and spent much of his spare time in his room polishing
his alcoholic lispings and slurrings and unsteady gait.

Prince Omeamunu and the First Platoon of the Royal Ceruliana Rifles had marched jauntily off to the hills above the
village of Akoaka, courteously pausing en route to advise the
village residents that they were out for a bit of harmless target practice and that things might become a bit noisy at
times.

The King himself was far from idle. With the aid of his valet and former batman in the Rifles he devised a means of
strapping a pillow over his abdomen and under his taku-
taku, the Cerulianian version of the sarong, which left his
torso bare.

The effect was to give him the absurdly gross gut of a Japanese sumo wrestler. Put aside for the nonce were the exquisitely cut suits he'd had custom-tailored in Hong Kong and London. Gone were the London shoes that usually adorned his now bare feet. But his greatest personal sacrifice came when he ordered his valet to shave his head absolutely bald. He looked simply awful, but the barbaric effect was much enhanced.

Probably not since the Relief of Lucknow had such a seedy greeting party met an arriving dignitary as met Mr. Leonard Midderley when he stepped off the elderly South Pacific Airways D-C 3 onto the Cerula airstrip. There was Bultivant, with a two-day stubble of beard on his cheeks, his solar topee as stained and battered as his once white suit was rumpled. There was Captain fitz-ttench, weaving ever so slightly, his ADC's usually immaculate uniform creased and conspicuously grease-spotted, his boots dulled with purposeful neglect.

"I've brought the Land Rover instead of the limousine, Mr. Midderley," Bultivant explained in what he hoped sounded like a hoarse croak. "Captain fitz-ttench thinks it's best we get back to Government House as inconspicuously and as quickly as possible. There's been a spot of trouble."

"Thash the bloody trufe," confirmed the Captain, and unsuccessfully suppressed a belch. "Lesh get the hell out of here." (fitz-ttench was much pleased with his belch; it had had just the right stifled resonance.)

It was a badly shaken Leonard Midderley whom Bultivant escorted into Government House. The Governor General was clearly close to a nervous breakdown, and his ADC was all too obviously sloshed to the ears, undoubtedly from fright. Shaken, but not panic-stricken, for Leonard Midderley had not risen from pubkeeper to hotel tycoon on the strength of no guts. Years of mounting success and good living had put a paunch on the lean young former Corporal of Royal Marines who had come out of the commandos to marry the daughter of the owner of The Boar's Head, and pouches and jowls had fleshed out the face; but Leonard Midderley still knew how to take charge in a tight situation.

"Just what the hell is going on around here?" he demanded to know of Bultivant as Majordomo Daniel Urnamoa shambled into the library, his usually spotless white jacket flapping unbuttoned, with a tray of drinks.

"It's been hell, sir. Everything's come unstuck. Let me explain the situation as best I can," Bultivant replied.

"Thash a laugh," Captain fitz-ttench giggled. "How'n hell can anybody exshplain anything about this damn island?"

"Captain fitz-ttench," Bultivant appeared to explode, "you will retire to your quarters and consider yourself under arrest for conduct unbecoming an officer!"

'Shokay with me, surr, your Guvnorship." With which, Captain fitz-ttench weaved uncertainly out of the room.

"Been a bit of a strain on him, I'm afraid," Bultivant explained apologetically. "Only two days ago he was nearly ambushed by Omeamunu's headhunters. Bit of a near thing, that."

"Did you say headhunters?" Mr. Midderley asked incredulously. "I did hear you say headhunters?"

At this point in the conversation the Anglican Bishop entered, his shoulders stooped, his face a picture of purest anguish. "What good," he asked dramatically, "is the sanctuary of Government House, what good is the protection of the Crown if Omeamunu's people can, with impunity, burn down the Chapel of All-Saints-in-the-Woods, along with the Sunday School building?"

"It might have been Walilolo's own troops, Bishop," Bultivant said. "They've been restive lately. No telling where their loyalty really lies. Quite possibly with Wa Ching." He turned courteously to the now thoroughly bemused Midderley. "Wa Ching, I should explain, is one of our local Chinese merchants who, I have reason to believe, may be an agent of the Red Chinese government. But he is only another of our worries here in Ceruliana, I can assure you. First and foremost, there is King Walilolo, a strange, moody man, utterly unpredictable."

"How do you mean—unpredictable?"

"You will see during the audience I have arranged for you with His Majesty tomorrow morning. But perhaps now we can turn from our own tangled problems to a happier subject, your visit. I understand from London that you attach considerable importance to it. I'd be most interested to learn more. . . ." Bultivant let the question hang unspoken.

So Mr. Midderley, with many references to the contents of his gleaming alligator-hide attaché case, told him in considerable, and appalling, detail.

"Wally?" Bultivant spoke into his telephone in guarded tones from his private office after Midderley had gone to his rooms to freshen up for dinner (Bultivant had thoughtfully selected the North Guest Suite so that the Great Man should be certain to hear, through Government House's ever-open windows, the sound of gunfire). "It's much worse than we imagined. He's planning a twelve-story hotel, with six hundred rooms, plus fifty guest cottages—" Bultivant heard the King's low whistle. "Wait," he went on, "there's more to it, much more. There'll be two swimming pools, a gambling casino, a sauna bath—"

"A sauna bath!" His Majesty interrupted in astonishment. "In this climate! Vyv, you've got to be kidding."

"The tourists will expect it. All Midderley International hotels have sauna baths, and this one will be no exception."

"But where will all these tourists come from?"

"He plans charter flights for tour groups. From Australia, New Zealand, Japan, from all over," Bultivant replied glumly. "A hell of a lot depends on your performance tomorrow, and I warn you, the man doesn't scare easily."

"Wait," said the King, and his tone was grim.

Following a miserable breakfast of cool porridge, preceded by an even worse cup of tea, a scowling Leonard Midderley set out with Bultivant for the royal audience in the black Humber limousine which was the Governor General's official transport.

"Quite safe to drive it in Cerula itself; it's just the countryside that's a trifle dicey," Bultivant began cheerfully as they passed through the gates of the Government House.

Midderley ignored the overture. "Bultivant," he said bluntly, "if I were in your shoes I'd shake up that bloody staff of yours until their back teeth rattled."

"Easier said than done, my dear fellow. I'm afraid the natives are rather an indolent lot, and highly sensitive. Rebuke them, and like as not they'll quit on the spot."

"Oh?" Midderley looked thoughtful. The putative Midderley Ceruliana would need one hell of a lot of staff. "That means I'll have to import Japs."

"Quite impossible, I'm afraid. Ceruliana for the Cerulianians, as the King phrases it. No, Japanese are definitely out of the question."

Midderley spent the rest of the brief drive to the Palace sulking in silence.

Bultivant barely repressed a gasp when he escorted Midderley into the royal presence. Walilolo IV had really done it up brown. He was sprawled obscenely on the royal throne, a fan-backed, rattan affair that tended to creak with age, clad only in his *taku-taku* which, along with the shell bracelets encircling his wrists and ankles, Bultivant recognized as treasures from the Royal Museum. The Governor General promptly prostrated himself.

Midderley gasped in disbelief. "Dammit, sir!" he exploded, ignoring the royal presence. "You're an officer of the Crown!"

"Do as I do, for God's sake," Bultivant whispered fearfully.

Unwillingly and much against his better judgment Mr. Midderley sank slowly to his knees and then stretched his not inconsiderable bulk on the floor. There was absolute silence apart from the hotel tycoon's stertorous breathing.

"Uwana kula," His Majesty barked contemptuously.

Bultivant hauled himself to his feet and Midderley followed suit. So far, Bultivant thought, the charade was going precisely as planned.

"We will now speak in the English tongue," the King declared in the stilted language of a British missionary school. "Please to proceed. I trust your first night in our island was a pleasant one, Mr. Midderley?"

"I kept hearing rifle fire all night," the ex-Marine, who recognized rifle fire when he heard it, replied sullenly. The King's brows darkened.

"The northern savages, led by my accursed cousin, Prince Omeamunu. We have sworn to destroy each other, though it take the rest of our lives. I fear there may be years of fighting before he is overcome." Midderley's face fell. "But now to business," the King continued, dismissing his blood feud lightly.

It was a subdued, even hesitant Leonard Midderley who proceeded to outline his tentative project. He seemed to lack his customary enthusiasm.

"Most interesting," the King murmured at the conclusion of the presentation. He turned to Bultivant to conceal an irrepressible smile. "Mr. Midderley understands, of course, that after our independence and our nationalization program the kingdom would own seventy-five percent of his proposed hotel properties and profits."

"Independence! Nationalization! Seventy-five percent!" Mr. Midderley was not only dumfounded, he was outraged. He turned on Bultivant. "Why the bloody hell wasn't I told these things in London?"

"I'm afraid our information officers do tend to be somewhat lax in these matters," Her Majesty's Governor General replied ruefully. "Perhaps my reports were somehow overlooked. Perhaps you did not phrase your inquiries with sufficient clarity."

"On top of everything else, a civil war," Mr. Midderley continued bitterly. "Plus a labor force that won't work. It's just too damned much, Bultivant. I'm getting back to London as fast as I can. Can Government House radio Auckland and charter me a flight?"

"I think that can be arranged," Bultivant answered smoothly.

In this wise Mr. Leonard Midderley was enabled to depart from Ceruliana the following morning after spending the remainder of that wretched day in the sympathetic but less than cheering company of the Governor General, the miserable Anglican Bishop of Ceruliana, who greeted them at Government House with the dismal news that Prince Omeamunu's rebels had just sacked and burned the Mission School at Loamoa, and Captain fitz-ttench, who had seemingly been released from durance vile to enjoy what he made to appear one of the world's more monumental hangovers.

If possible, dinner was worse than lunch. As what Bultivant described as "a special treat, an old native dish," the Government House kitchen staff, exercising their combined ingenuity, had produced a turgid stew, on the surface of which floated objects that Mr. Midderley could not identify, nor wanted to. It tasted like a poor grade of fish glue. Mr. Midderley did not even touch his breakfast; there were bound to be emergency rations on his chartered aircraft, perhaps even a thermos of honest-to-God hot tea.

It was a splendid celebration that evening in Government House, and Chief Chef Lakani's roast pig had never been better. King Walilolo IV was back in his elegant Hong Kong dinner jacket, as was Prince Omeamunu, who had returned in cheery triumph from his rebellion. The Anglican Bishop was once more impeccable, and for the occasion Bultivant and Captain fitz-ttench had donned evening dress uniform, with decorations. The threat to Ceruliana's peace and serenity was gone away over the horizon.

"I'm rather glad we didn't have to bring up the virgin sacrifice and the roasted small boy," Walilolo IV said thoughtfully after they had risen for the Loyal Toast. "That might have been laying it on a bit thick, even for Midderley."

Bultivant raised his glass of finest Government House champagne (the kind *not* served at Government House receptions). "Gentlemen, I give you the Leonard Midderleys of the world. They keep us on our toes."

"Amen," said the Anglican Bishop of Ceruliana.

"Hear, hear," came the response.

THE HAUNTED MAN

by *Henry Slesar*

Martin Gannet was a haunted man, and he had good reason to be. He saw "ghosts from the past"—terrifying ghosts . . . a strong story, perhaps more comfortably read before the ghostly stroke of midnight. . . .

GANNET knew that Kitty would want him to look his best at dinner, so he wore his blue serge suit, a shirt with a white collar and broad red stripes (not too flashy), a conservative gray tie, and no gun.

The last sartorial decision was the toughest he had to make. But it couldn't be helped; he no longer had suits tailored to accommodate the bulge of a shoulder holster. That hadn't mattered for the past week; he had worn one anyway. On the day he saw the terrifying apparition in the apartment house elevator he had dug up the Smith & Wesson .38 that had lain idle in his bedroom closet for almost four years. He thought he was done with the need for armor; the padrones had quietly approved his retirement at the age of 60; he had left no enemies behind (except those in their expensive coffins); and proper businessmen didn't carry pieces, they carried attaché cases.

He looked the part when he left the duplex on East Sixty-third Street. His pewter-colored hair neatly brushed, his slight paunch softening the still-muscular slope of his neck and shoulders, Gannet looked like the executive the world

81

believed him to be (Kitty mostly; but then, Kitty *was* his world). But he was jumpy. When he pushed the elevator button he held his breath until the door slid open and he saw that the car was unoccupied.

Kitty Russo's place was on the west side, a couple of big drab rooms that her twenty-three-year-old enthusiasm had converted into page 56 of *House & Garden*. It was a co-op, and Gannet had bought it for her, as a college graduation present. She had refused it at first. He said it was for her father; that if Joe Russo hadn't been so dumb about life insurance he would have left her the kind of money it took to buy the place.

Kitty had cried a lot, and Gannet had cried a little, and in the end she had thrown her arms around him and thanked him and called him Uncle Marty the way she used to when she was a kid, not a college graduate with a job, her own apartment, and now, a serious boyfriend.

"Dr. Ira Hammel," Kitty said, introducing him, with a little proud emphasis on the "doctor."

Hammel looked too young to be a physician. He was good-looking but too plump in the center for Gannet to think of him as mature. But he shook Hammel's hand and smiled and refused his offer of a drink.

"Booze and me don't get along," Gannet said cheerfully.

"I told Ira about your colitis," Kitty said.

"Oh, oh," Gannet chuckled, "here comes the bill, right?"

"Does it still bother you?" the doctor said. "Kitty says you had it pretty bad a couple of years back, but you seem to have it licked now. Low-residue diet, I suppose?"

"Hey, what is this? I came here for dinner, not an examination!"

"Right!" Kitty laughed. "One low-residue dinner coming up."

It wasn't bad. Kitty kept the menu simple, so she didn't make any big mistakes. The doctor-boyfriend was quiet, respectful; obviously Kitty had filled him in on the second father role that Gannet played in her life. And Gannet didn't stay late, which they both obviously appreciated.

But when he emerged from the apartment building into

the misty rain that was slicking down the sidewalks of West End Avenue he saw another one of *them.*

The man was wearing a raincoat, as if he had anticipated the weather that the forecasters hadn't predicted. He wore a felt hat pulled well over his eyes. He stood on the corner as if waiting to signal a cab, but his hands were thrust deep into his pockets.

Then he turned, and Gannet saw that he had no mouth.

His frightened reaction was audible, but the man simply stared at him relentlessly. Gannet whirled, running back toward Kitty's apartment house door. He didn't know if the man without a mouth was following him, but it didn't matter; he made a frantic effort to open the door, then realized it was locked.

He fumbled for the button that would sound a signal in the apartment upstairs, but by the time he found it his panic had subsided. Nobody had followed him. The man without a mouth was no longer in sight.

He went home and debated whether to break his year-long abstinence and have a drink. Even the fact that he was considering it shook him badly.

"Cracking up," he said to himself. "If I'm seeing things *without* drinking, who knows what the booze will do?"

The phone rang at 11:30, and it was Kitty.

"Well, what did you think?"

"Of the boyfriend? He's okay. Doesn't talk much, does he?"

Kitty laughed. "You had him awed. I told him what a big shot you were—all those shoe-repair stores you own. I told him, 'Wait until you see his duplex tomorrow'."

"Tomorrow?" Gannet said. "We made a date for you to come here tomorrow?"

"I'm making it now," Kitty said. "He wants to do this right, Uncle Marty. I told him you were the only family I had, and he's got this old-fashioned thing about it."

"What old-fashioned thing?"

Kitty giggled. "He's going to ask you for my hand in marriage. I'm just calling to make sure you give him the right answer. A simple 'Yes, my boy,' will do. Is that understood?"

When he didn't reply, she said soberly, "Uncle Marty, are you okay? I didn't poison your colon or something tonight?"

"I'm fine," Gannet said. "A little surprised, maybe. Boyfriend, okay. But marriage?"

"Would you rather we just lived together? It's the Now thing, you know."

"Never mind that Now stuff!" Gannet growled, which seemed to please Kitty. It's exactly what her father would have said, Gannet realized, and he remembered with a feeling deeper than sadness how much the girl had adored Joe Russo.

Kitty said, "No food," so all Gannet prepared for their visit the next evening was a wheel-shaped tray of hors d'oeuvres that cost $60, thanks mainly to the preponderance of caviar. He also ordered whiskey. When the doorbell rang at 6:30 he thought it was the kid from the liquor store, but it was a tall silent man who had no mouth.

Gannet dropped the wallet he was holding and began to scream. His vision blurred, or maybe the figure itself evaporated back into the mysterious limbo from which it had come; but by the time he came to his senses there was nobody in the doorway, and Kitty's new boyfriend was poking him all over, and Kitty herself seemed to be crying a hundred miles away.

"It's all right," Ira Hammel said. "It's not his heart. He's had some kind of shock, but he's coming out of it."

Gannet was thinking: the kid sounds like a doctor now, he even *looks* older. But then Gannet was himself again, which meant that he blustered out half a dozen excuses for what had happened, none of which seemed to convince Hammel or satisfy Kitty.

"All right," Gannet said finally. "I'll tell you what it was, but you've got to promise not to send for the men in the white coats. Is it a deal?"

Then he told them about the first man in the elevator.

"He wasn't a big guy. About my height, not so meaty. He was wearing a gray suit, ordinary. He was in the corner of the elevator, reading a newspaper. He didn't even look up when I got into the car. But then I turned around and saw him looking at me. Don't ask me about his eyes or his nose. I don't remember anything that he *did* have, only what he *didn't*."

"What do you mean?" Kitty said.

"I mean he didn't have any mouth. Nothing there at all. Just skin covering everything from nose to chin. It was something to see—something I didn't want to see again."

"A deformity," Hammel suggested.

Kitty said, "Could there *be* such a thing, Ira?"

"I suppose," the doctor shrugged. "I'll have to look it up in my *Anomalies and Curiosities of Medicine.*"

"Wait. Listen," Gannet said. "I saw it again—I mean in the elevator—a man without a mouth. The next day."

"He probably lives in the building," Kitty said.

"No. You don't get it. It was the same thing all over again, no mouth, nothing. *Only it wasn't the same man!*"

Hammel looked at the girl, and Gannet knew what the unspoken message was. But he went on.

"I saw another one yesterday, when I came over to your place for dinner. Going home, on the corner, a man in a raincoat, hailing a cab, I guess. He turned around and so help me God he didn't have a mouth, Kitty! Don't tell me it was the same guy, because it wasn't. He was somebody else, but no mouth."

Hammel asked the obvious question.

"Yeah," Gannet answered. "That's right. Just before you two got here. I ordered some stuff from the liquor store—I don't keep any booze in the place since I stopped drinking—and I thought it was the kid making the delivery. But it was another one of *them.*"

"A man without a mouth."

"Yeah."

"Oh, Uncle Marty," Kitty said unhappily. "You must have been seeing things, that's all. Maybe you're working too hard. Maybe there's something wrong with your vision, some kind of blind spot in your eyes." She turned to Hammel hopefully. "Couldn't that be it, Ira? Just a spot in his eyes that blurs his vision?"

"Could be," he said, his tone noncommittal.

"It just got to me," Gannet said. "You understand? Once, twice, I could chalk it off. To fatigue. Old age."

"You're not old!" the girl said.

"But I'm not tired, either," Gannet said. "Working too hard? I put in two, three hours a day at most. Other times I'm just hanging around, visiting the track, stuff like that. No, it's something else. Freaks walking around. Martians maybe. Hey, you think it's Martians, Doc?" He gave him a feeble smile.

"Why pick on you?" Hammel said.

"Yeah," Gannet nodded. "That's right. I never had anything to do with Martians, so why pick on me?" He looked at the young doctor gravely. "What you really want to say, Doc, is that the trouble is up here." He touched his head.

Ira Hammel smiled.

"Eye, ear, nose, and throat," he said. "That's all I know about, Mr. Gannet."

They never got around to the main event of the evening: marriage talk. But Hammel, unaccompanied by Kitty, came around the following day. He had phoned an hour earlier, and Gannet had agreed to see him; but by the time he arrived, Gannet seemed to have changed his mind. He opened the door only the space of four inches, and said, "Look, Doc, do you mind if we talk later? I'm not feeling so hot this afternoon. I got a headache."

"Maybe I can help."

"Sure you can help—by being a nice boy and going away."

"I won't stay long. I just wanted to talk to you for a while."

"About marriage?" Gannet said. "Look, you don't need my blessing, just treat my little girl right."

"Not about marriage," Hammel said gravely. "About you. And the Syndicate."

Gannet's hold on the door loosened. The young doctor took advantage of it and gave it the slightest push, enough to give Gannet a view of his sober expression. Then he was inside, and Gannet was telling him to sit down. There was a hard edge to Gannet's voice, but it didn't scare Hammel. Gannet decided Kitty's boyfriend wasn't as soft as he looked.

"Okay," Gannet said. "What do you know about me?"

"I know you were called up before the State Crime Commission back in the 'fifties."

"You weren't old enough to blow your own nose back in the 'fifties."

"That's right. I remember only what I've read in the magazines or seen in television documentaries. But this man I saw yesterday, this psychiatrist, he was just getting his medical degree during the hearings, and he remembered all about it. He remembered you, too."

"Psychiatrist?" Gannet said. "You were talking to a shrink about me?"

"Kitty asked me to," Hammel said. "I figured it wouldn't hurt to get an opinion. This psychiatrist wasn't much help as far as making any kind of diagnosis—he said he wouldn't even try with such slim evidence. But when I mentioned your name—well, he remembered the rumors about your involvement with the mob. If I'm talking out of turn, tell me to shut up."

"Shut up," Gannet growled. Then he went to the front door and opened it. "Now get out of here and stop worrying about things that aren't any of your business. And you better not say one word of this bull to Kitty, or I'll *really* be a Papa to her and tell her that her boyfriend stinks. Who knows? She might even turn you down, buster, and you can find yourself another girl."

Hammel looked at him steadily.

"This friend of mine," he said. "This psychiatrist. He said he had an idea about these apparitions you've been seeing. It sounded valid to me." He paused. Gannet knew his price for continuing was a closed door. He cursed, and slammed it shut.

"All right. What did the shrink say?"

"He said there was no doubt they were hallucinations. But the pattern of hallucination was fairly clear, given the patient's background. Hope you don't mind me referring to you as the 'patient,' Mr. Gannet."

"I still don't know what you're talking about."

"My friend said that seeing a lot of men without mouths might be an indication of a deep-rooted guilt feeling, pertaining to some symbolic representations. I mean, what does it bring to mind, the idea of a man without a mouth?"

"You tell me, Doc."

"Someone who can't talk," Hammel said. "Isn't that obvious? That a man without a mouth is silenced. Mouthless men tell no tales, my friend said." He hesitated. "Just like dead men."

Anger pumped blood into Gannet's face.

"What the hell kind of talk is that? What the hell are you trying to say, buster? You calling me a murderer?"

"Please," Hammel said softly. "I'm reporting a conversation now, not a personal opinion. You asked me, I'm telling you. This psychiatrist says that your past associations may have left you with strong guilt feelings relating to—well, to informers, or would-be informers. That's not an accusation, it's merely an analysis."

Hammel stood up. "Look, I'm trying to help you. And the only reason I'm trying is because of Kitty. Because I'd jump off the George Washington Bridge if Kitty said, please jump, Ira. Now I'll go away and do exactly what you told me to do—stop worrying about things that aren't any of my business."

He walked to the door and this time opened it himself. Gannet said, "There's something else you don't do. You don't say one blessed word about this to Kitty or I'll wrap your diploma around your neck."

"I wasn't going to tell her," Hammel said.

He went out quickly. Gannet, still angry, thought of something else to tell him and again flung the door open. Hammel had caught a Down elevator, and the doors were closing. But a man had got out on Gannet's floor and was coming toward him.

When Gannet saw the man's face, the blank stare of his eyes, the terrible pink mass of flesh where his mouth should have been, he let out an involuntary howl of fear and slammed the door shut, locked it, bolted it, and whimpered as he tried to keep the specter from entering, certain that he was about to try. But nothing happened.

"Oh, God, God," Gannet whispered. "When does it quit? When?"

That night, damning his insides, he took his first drink in a year.

He took a bottle of Scotch into his library and filled half a glass with it.

He sipped it slowly, and evoked phantoms.

Who was the first one? Chaudry, of course. Who could forget the first? Chaudry, who sweated himself half to death before Gannet fired the gun that finished the job. They hadn't even told him what Chaudry had done to inspire their wrath, and Gannet had made a mark for himself by not asking. That was the professional way, they told him, and he had swelled up with pride, and never confessed that he had been afraid to ask what Chaudry had done.

They gave him a reason for killing Vic Santione: Santione was stooling, Santione's big mouth had to be shut with graveyard dirt, and Gannet was the boy to do it. Gannet hadn't done the job too well; Santione died in the hospital, not in the street. But he hadn't talked. One of Gannet's slugs had got him in the throat. Not a precaution: luck. But Gannet was lucky—then, and half a dozen hits later, always lucky. Never booked. Never indicted. He did good clean work.

But had he?

Had he really succeeded in silencing them all? Had he failed to put them away forever, because there *wasn't* any forever? Were there ways for them to come back, ways for them to haunt him?

"Ghosts," he whispered aloud, feeling the effect of the alcohol. . . .

He dropped in to see Kitty's doctor-boyfriend at his office. He came as a friend, he said, not as a patient, just to check out the business address of the man his Kitty was engaged to marry.

"You got a nice office, Doc," he said.

Hammel said, "Have you seen another one?"

Gannet knew what he meant. He felt the embarrassing sting of tears in his eyes.

"I couldn't take going to a shrink," he told him. "I'm not the type, you know? But you, you got a head on you for stuff like this, I can tell."

"I'm not a psychiatrist," Hammel said.

"You can help me," Gannet said stubbornly. "I got ghosts haunting me, that's how I figure it. I never believed in ghosts before, maybe I have to change my mind."

"I'm not a spiritualist, either."

"I figured two ways," Gannet said. "I could go to a doctor. Or I could go to a church and talk to a priest or somebody."

"Both might help," Hammel said carefully. "That's one thing psychiatrists and the church have in common—they know confession is good for the soul.

"It's the root of the problem, isn't it? Guilt feelings build up pressure in the mind. Sometimes the pressure becomes unbearable, then there's some kind of explosion."

"In the brain, you mean."

"You might have been right when you used the word 'ghosts.' The ghosts of the past may be haunting you because you haven't told the truth about them—not to yourself, not to anyone."

Gannet stood up, angry again.

"I knew I was wasting my time," he said, and went to the door.

Hammel stopped him by saying, "Kitty and I are having an engagement party in a week. We'd like you to come, Mr. Gannet."

"I don't like parties," Gannet growled, and left the office.

On the way out of the doctor's building he bumped into a man without a mouth. He almost blacked out at the sight of him, but managed to make it to the nearby hack stand. He was sick in the taxi, dry-retching, to the alarm of the cabbie. He was still sick when he got home.

Then he remembered the tape recorder.

Kitty had bought him the thing for Christmas, and he had lied and said it was just what he wanted. Actually, he hadn't touched it since. It was still nestling in its styrofoam bed, its sample reel of tape untouched by sound.

He took it out of the closet and put it on top of his library desk. He stared at the switches that said, ON, OFF, RECORD, STOP, REWIND, PLAY.

He didn't understand gadgets, but he turned on the power

of this one, picked up the small microphone attached, and plugged it into the receptacle labeled MIC.

Then he pressed RECORD and saw the reel begin to turn. That was all there was to it.

But the next step was more difficult.

Into the MIC he said, "My name is Martin Gannet. In 1945—no, '46—I shot and killed a man named Rick Chaudry in North Bergen, New Jersey."

Alarmed at what he had just said aloud, he pushed the button marked STOP.

Then he played it back.

My name is Martin Gannet. In 1945—no, '46—I shot and killed a man named Rick Chaudry . . .

He closed his eyes.

This was the way, he thought. This was the only way. If the ghosts wanted a confession, this would be it. The only ears that would hear it would be the electronic ones in the guts of this little toy. Then he'd take the tape and seal it in an envelope. He'd put the envelope into his desk, alongside his Smith & Wesson .38, and write on it something like: *To be opened after my death.* Maybe then the ghosts would stop haunting him.

He rewound the tape all the way and started the machine again, placing the microphone close to his dry lips.

"My name is Martin Gannet," he said.

The engagement party was noisy. Kitty seemed to have invited no one but girl friends, and Hammel no one but colleagues. Maybe that accounted for the party's shrillness; they all seemed eager to pair off with each other; maybe another engagement party would stem from this one.

Gannet felt uncomfortably isolated, at least until Kitty herself paid some attention to him. She was fixing things to eat, so she asked him to come into the kitchen.

When she saw him in the bright light, she said, "Uncle Marty, you look *wonderful!* A hundred percent better!"

He grinned. "Feeling pretty good," he said.

"No more—trouble?"

"Nah, that's all over with," he said. "All over and done

with. I think you were right, you know, about that little blind spot. I think maybe I need glasses or something, that's all."

"And you haven't seen—anything—for a while?"

"Nothing," he said, and chuckled. Then Dr. Hammel came in, looking for Kitty, and she turned to him happily.

"Ira, isn't it wonderful? Uncle Marty says he's feeling much better. No more of those silly hallucinations!"

She picked up a tray of cheese and crackers and kicked open the swinging door to the swinging party outside. The two men didn't follow her.

Ira looked thoughtfully at Gannet, who said, "Look, I said some things to you, Doc. I hope you can forget them."

"I didn't take any offense."

"Well, that's good, on account of you marrying Kitty, that means you'll be stuck with me, too."

Hammel said, "Is it true what she said? That you're all right? No more hallucinations?"

"Not a one," Gannet answered. "Maybe they were ghosts from the past, like you said. But they've gone back where they came from." He smiled and dug into his pocket. "Oh, I got a little something for you and Kitty. Engagement present." He handed him the white envelope with its gift certificate. "I figured you knew what you needed more than I did," Gannet said, and heard Hammel whistle at seeing the amount.

Gannet left the apartment half an hour later, enjoying a sense of well-being. The night was clear, so he decided to walk a while before hailing a cab. At a stop light he stood beside a young woman in a light cloth coat. She had a nice, trim figure, and he wasn't too old to admire it. But then she turned—and she had no mouth.

Gannet made a strangled noise and stepped off the curb without looking. The driver of the sedan braked quickly, but not soon enough.

Kitty was his first visitor at the hospital, of course. She was accompanied by Hammel.

"You're a lucky man, Marty," the doctor said, calling him by his first name for the first time. "You must have good strong bones, because you didn't break one of them."

"I'm okay," Gannet said, his voice unconvincingly weak. "I just got the wind knocked out of me, nothing else. The guy barely touched me. Look, pull some strings, Doc, get me out of this place."

"There's no hurry," Kitty said. "They want you here for observation, at least for a couple of days. I'll get you a toothbrush and some things."

"And my Blue Cross card," Hammel grinned. "Don't forget that, honey. No use adding insult to injury."

Gannet knew it would be useless to protest—Kitty had that determined look. He gave her his apartment key, and she kissed him on the forehead and left. He was glad for the moment alone with Hammel. With some bitterness he said, "You were wrong, Doc."

"What do you mean?"

"You and your theories! Those men without mouths. You thought I was being haunted by a lot of ghosts from the past, but you were wrong!"

"Why do you think so?"

"Because I saw another one—tonight! And it wasn't a man—this was a woman!"

"What?"

"You heard me," Gannet said, his voice stronger now. "I saw a woman without a mouth. And there isn't a woman in my whole life I ever—I mean, I ever felt guilty about. So your whole idea goes up the flue! They aren't ghosts of the past!"

Hammel shrugged. "I told you I wasn't a psychiatrist. Maybe my diagnosis was wrong, or maybe it was incomplete. Anxieties aren't always that simple to understand."

After Hammel had left, Gannet stared at the white ceiling of his hospital room and wondered about it. He knew he had to be right, and the doctor wrong. There hadn't been any need for that tape-recorded confession after all.

Then he remembered where the tape was, and where he kept his important documents—like Blue Cross cards.

Alarmed, he threw back the covers of his bed and put his feet on the floor. A moment of dizziness, then he was all right again. He went to the locker on the opposite wall and saw that the emergency-room orderly had simply hung his street clothes inside. He dressed as quickly as his physical condition allowed and left the room, trying to look like a visitor instead of a patient.

When he opened his front door, he knew that what he feared had come true.

Kitty had looked in the top drawer of his desk and seen its contents. The gun might not have disturbed her; she knew he owned a gun, and understood his fear of the jungle city. But she had also seen the envelope, and its mysterious instructions, and he knew that Kitty would be too curious to leave the tape unplayed. She had always been as nosy as a kitten, hence her nickname; her given name was Mary, not Katherine.

From the moment he stepped inside he could hear the drone of his own voice on the tape, talking about Chaudry, talking about Santione, talking about all the others. He felt a cold sickening clutch at his heart. *All* the others, dear God in heaven!

He pushed open the closed library doors and saw her at his desk. He hardly recognized her. Her face was bleached of color, and shock had done something strange to the angle of her eyes and the line of her jaw. She looked at him and snapped off the tape machine. She said, "Second time."

"What?" Gannet said.

"It's the second time I played it. I heard it the first time, but I didn't believe it. I didn't!"

"You shouldn't have listened! Didn't you read what it said on the envelope? Didn't you?"

"Daddy," Kitty was moaning. "Oh, Daddy." He knew she didn't mean him. He was "Uncle" to her, never Daddy.

"Oh, God, honey, listen to me," Gannet pleaded. "You don't know about these things. You don't know how a man gets pushed and shoved in this world until he has to be like an animal. That's the only reason, Kitty, try to understand!"

She was rewinding the tape.

"No, no, Kitty, don't, honey," he begged. "Don't torture us any more, don't."

But she rewound the tape and started it near the end of his guilty recitation.

"*. . . Phil Bolduc,*" his voice said. "*Cerritos, California. He* *was a junk dealer, narcotics, not scrap iron. That was, let's see, 1965, February. Yeah, I remember February, because it was cold, freezing in New York and I was glad to get a job out west."*

"Stop it, Kitty!" Gannet cried, feeling his soul shredding.

"Tom Wykoff," his voice went on inexorably. *"Same year, same state, I think it was in November. That was almost the last one. Except for . . ."* He remembered how he had hesitated. *"Except for Joe Russo. Joe had this daughter in college. They called her Kitty. He was worried about her finding out what he was doing, he never stopped worrying about that. Only then they needed a fall guy for a payroll job that went sour and they picked Joe and he refused. He said he wouldn't take a rap, he said he'd spill first, so that made him a hit case. I told them I didn't want to do the job, Joe was my friend, he was like family, but they didn't care about that. It was like a test of my loyalty, they said, I had to do the job."* Silence. The tape was over.

Kitty didn't bother to switch it off. She looked at Gannet and said, "Is that why you took such good care of me, Uncle Marty, is that why?"

"You heard what I said, honey! Joe was like family, and you, too. But orders were orders. You think it wouldn't have worked the same way for your Daddy if he was told to hit me?"

"Is this the gun you did it with?"

She reached into the drawer.

"Is it, Uncle Marty? Is this the gun?"

"Put it down, honey, that thing is loaded."

"Tell me how you killed my father! Your best friend! Why don't you tell me how?"

"Put it down, please," Gannet said.

He walked quietly up to the desk, and she fired. The bullet had only inches to travel, and the force of it knocked him halfway across the room. But he had time enough to see Kitty's face, and knew that she was as surprised as he was that her finger had squeezed the trigger.

He thought, sometimes we're haunted by the past, sometimes by the future . . . and then he was unconscious.

The room was full of misty rain. But the rain was white, blindingly white, and without moisture. The sky had the rounded look of a silvery bowl, and Gannet blinked at it and wondered if it was day or night.

He thought about the possibility of being dead, but there was something pressing underneath him that seemed too tangible; death wouldn't feel this way, he was sure of that. But where was he, and why?

Then his vision cleared somewhat, and he saw the man without a mouth.

He wanted to scream, but couldn't; something had deprived him of the power to make any sound, even though the terrible apparition was standing above him, looking down with piercing eyes, and he had no mouth.

Then there was another one beside the first, and then still another, all with no mouths. Then there was a woman, her mouthless face swimming into focus over his head, and again Gannet tried to make his terror vocal, but he failed.

Then he heard one of them speak, even without a mouth, able to form words.

"Eyelids moving. What's taking the anesthesia so long?"

"Fighting it," another voice said.

"Pulse dropping," the woman said.

"We're losing him, Ed!"

"Past tense, Phil," the first one said, the first man without a mouth, and Gannet closed his eyes and entered the welcoming dark. The surgeon named Phil removed his mask and wiped the sweat off his lips as he turned to leave the Operating Room.

B AS IN BLUDGEON

by Lawrence Treat

It started with the dangers of lead poisoning and ended with the brutal murder of Marlie Pratt. No, it really ended, as all homicides should end, with the arrest and conviction of the murderer. . . .

Inspector Mitch Taylor had his usual run of luck, good, bad, and indifferent, with the emphasis on—but find out for yourself. . . .

ON HIS day off Inspector Mitch Taylor should have had more sense than to stay home. Because, right after Amy had gone out shopping and left him alone, the phone rang. And it had to be the dispatcher telling him something had turned up and they wanted him down at headquarters.

Only it wasn't the dispatcher. It was some dame all the way from Dallas, Texas, telling him he didn't have to worry about the shampoo soap in that tube, it couldn't hurt anybody, and besides, the company was giving up on lead and using aluminum.

Mitch said yeah a few times and figured either it was some crank or else the wires had got twisted, and he hung up. Then about five minutes later some other dame was calling from L.A. to tell the Taylor family pretty much the same stuff. This time Mitch managed to interrupt long enough to ask what it was all about, and it seemed that Amy had wanted to know whether you could get poisoned from using tooth-paste out of a lead tube.

It was all news to Mitch, but it seemed Amy had got the big companies all het up about lead poisoning, because right af-ter the L.A. dame, somebody called from Boston with pretty much the same pitch. Only this one, her voice was a little higher and she said there wasn't enough lead in a tube of ointment to kill a mouse.

That made three in a row and Mitch was thinking up a wisecrack or so for the next time around, and he had a pretty good one ready. He was going to ask why they were changing from lead if lead was okay. He figured that would shut them up, only he never got the chance to sound off. Because the next call was from the dispatcher telling him signal two-nine, which meant a homicide. It was up in the Short Hills section and a squad car would be waiting downstairs, so get going.

The cop who drove him, it was Malone from up in the Eighth Precinct, and it seemed he knew all about lead poi-soning. He had a brother-in-law who was a house painter, and after twenty years the white lead finally got to him. He ended up with brain damage that left his hands so weak he could hardly hold a spoon. And he had a gray line along his gums. You ought to see him.

After that they got to talking about hospitals. Malone had just come out of one—he'd caught his hand in a car door on account he'd forgot to take it away when he'd slammed the thing shut. But the point was, the nurses weren't like they used to be. Now twenty years ago—

Mitch let him rattle on until they got to Short Hills, which was on the outskirts of the city and looked like real country except for that stucco apartment house. It was kind of like a concrete block in a bird bath—too big, and it didn't belong there.

The usual bunch of cars were there in front of it, precinct and headquarters and press cars, along with an ambulance and Jub Freeman's traveling laboratory truck. Upstairs on the second floor the place was jammed and they were all talk-ing about what a beating this Marlie Pratt had taken before she'd died. Mitch managed not to get a look at the body—it would have left him seeing it every time he stopped talking.

He didn't get much in the way of details, because as soon as Lieutenant Decker spotted him, the Lieutenant told him to check the neighborhood and see what he could dig up. The sort of woman Marlie had been, who her friends were, what they thought of her around here. And whether people had noticed anything yesterday afternoon, which was when the homicide had been committed. Any strangers, anything unusual—Mitch would know what to look for.

He was glad to get free of the mob, but before he left the place he got hold of Balenky who had been one of the first ones here and had the dope. It seemed that the dispatcher had got an anonymous call that there was a body in Marlie Pratt's apartment. The super, his name was Kutch and he had the apartment underneath Marlie's, had a key, so he unlocked the door for the police. Perkins was questioning him right now, and Balenky said it was even money Kutch had done it and that he'd confess before lunch.

"With all that blood around," Mitch said, "all you got to do is find the murderer's clothes, and you got him."

"Where?" Balenky said. "Where do you find 'em?" And when Mitch didn't answer, Balenky grinned and let the light hit that gold tooth of his. "Besides," he said, "the killer washed and scrubbed up, but good. Water's all over the bathroom and even leaked downstairs."

"Well," Mitch said, "I wish we could get this business over with. It's my day off and I want to get on back home."

"What were you doing?" Balenky asked.

"Loafing around, and thinking I ought to paint the ceiling." Mitch grunted, and added, "So maybe I'm lucky after all. You paint the ceiling and breathe in all that lead, and it's no good."

"Maybe," Balenky said. "But a lot of ceilings get painted. Matter of fact, I paint my own every couple of years."

"Gets you in the head," Mitch said, tapping his forehead and looking solemn, so Balenky wouldn't know he was being kidded. "I been noticing you. You want to watch yourself." And Mitch went off.

He had to shake loose from a couple of reporters on the way out, and he walked a block or so before he saw the shabby little store with a big awning that covered the newsstand

and a soft-drink machine. The sign read JESSE'S, and a little guy with a long nose was standing or sitting at an open serving window. You could tell right off by the way he looked that he knew most of the neighborhood gossip and he'd tell you all about everything, and maybe he'd know what he was talking about and maybe he wouldn't.

Mitch fingered a paper, like he was a customer, before he started the conversation. "You heard about what happened?" he said.

The little guy cranked himself up in a nasal voice. "You kidding? All those cops and the TV truck, and then they had it on the radio. Marlie Pratt."

"You knew her?"

"Was talking to her yesterday, and a nicer dame you don't want to meet. Except she had those way-out ideas."

"What kind of ideas?"

"You know. Screwball stuff. Can't eat anything unless it's organic. Can't buy anything unless it's got some kind of a seal of approval. Won't use a spray can on account you breathe the stuff and maybe it's poison. Same thing with that you buy in tubes. 'They're lead tubes,' she says, 'and lead's a poison.'"

"Where do you suppose she picked up an idea like that?" Mitch said, thinking mostly of Amy.

"I wouldn't know," Jesse said, "but I can tell you this—she don't know what she's talking about. And believe me, I got more sense than a lot of doctors do. You ask anybody around here and they'll tell you they come to Jesse's first, and then afterwards go to the doctor. Now the way I look at it, if you got something wrong with you, you got to have confidence that you're going to get better, and that's what I give them. Confidence. The body heals itself, so what can a doctor do that I can't, huh? Tell me that, Mister."

"You got something there," Mitch said, to kind of shove the guy along.

"You're a cop," Jesse said. "That's right, isn't it?"

"Sure."

"I like cops. A couple of months ago a cop came in here with his family. They'd been out in the fields near here and his kid had got in some poison ivy. Been playing in it, so the cop asks me if I got something for poison ivy, and you know what I told him?" Mitch didn't answer because he didn't have to. "I told him to go home and wash the kid with brown soap and hot water. Hot as he could stand it. That, and a tube of anti-itch, for a quarter."

"About Marlie," Mitch began, but Jesse wasn't ready to get around to her.

"I could have sold him anything I wanted to," Jesse said. "I could have sold him a bottle of something for a dollar, because I got a cure for anything. Take a look back there in the shop."

Mitch stared into the shadows behind Jesse and saw long rows of shelves stocked with cans and bottles and packages. Mitch couldn't read any of the labels, but he got the idea that all that stuff had been there for a long time and it wasn't selling so fast. Meanwhile Jesse kept right on talking. "I got things you can't buy anywhere else in town," he said. "Good old-fashioned items that I only sell to my regular customers."

"Like Marlie?"

"Sure. Like Marlie. Maybe she didn't think the same way as me, but we got along."

"You say you saw her yesterday. Was she alone?"

"No. She was with this guy, he comes to see her maybe once a month, and they stop in here for a paper."

"Know his name?"

"She calls him Corny."

"Cornelius," Mitch said. "Must be Cornelius."

"That's it," Jesse said. "That's what she called him. They'd been scrapping about something and they were so mad they wouldn't hardly talk to each other. He dropped his dime and when he bent down to pick it up, and he was having trouble getting it, she tried to step on his hand. What do you think of a dame who'd do that, huh?"

Mitch kind of muttered something and let the guy jabber on, but it was mostly a waste of time. Still, you had to listen, because you never knew when somebody was liable to come up with what you were really after.

After a while, though, Jesse ran out of steam, so Mitch paid for his paper and left. After that he spoke to a couple of kids and to a dame who took in washing, but he got nowheres.

By afternoon the homicide squad had about all they could find, so they turned things over to the guys in the Eighth and went back to headquarters. There, like always, they sat down in the squad room to see what they could figure out.

Decker led off. "Let me sum up where we stand," he said. "The M.E. tells us Marlie was killed late yesterday afternoon or evening, and she was beaten with a wooden instrument similar to the cricket bats that were hanging up on the wall and are now missing. Anybody here play cricket?"

It seemed nobody did, so the boss explained that a cricket bat was something like a baseball bat with the fat part flattened out, so you could hit a home run every shot. Only Marlie, she'd been hit with the thin edge and it had broken her skull, and she'd been out cold right from the beginning.

"If she hadn't been," Decker said, "she'd have screamed her head off. And brother, that would have been fine for us, because somebody would have heard her and called us. And that would have been that."

The Lieutenant wrinkled up his puss and took a deep breath, like he was thinking of Marlie and didn't want to blame her for not yelling. Then he pulled at the corners of his mouth and got back to his facts.

"The killer," he said, "then washed up thoroughly. His clothes must have been badly stained with blood, and he either took them with him or else dropped them down the incinerator. And then he left, probably wearing Marlie's white shirt and blue jeans.

"Next, about that anonymous call. The super, name of Kutch, admitted he made it. It seems that the water leaked down into the Kutch kitchen, so this morning he went upstairs to see what the trouble was. He opened the apartment with his passkey, but he wanted none of what he saw, so he put in that call. You talked to him, Perk. Anything else there?"

"Nothing more that I got," Perkins said, "but I wouldn't cross him off the list. He claims he didn't hear anything because he was listening to a football game and he had the volume on high, but I've heard that one before."

"The rest of you," Decker said, "checked up on the other tenants in the building. A couple of them say that late yesterday afternoon they saw a guy in a white shirt and blue jeans walking down the street towards the bus stop. The bus drivers whose routes took them in the area around that time don't remember any such passenger."

Decker looked at some notes. "Marlie's married, but she's been separated from her husband for about two years. After the break-up she resumed her maiden name of Pratt. Her husband lives in Philadelphia, but we haven't been able to get in touch with him. Name's Cornelius Talbot. And that's where we stand now. Any ideas? Anything else we ought to know?"

Mitch piped up with what Jesse had told him, so it seemed Marlie had seen her husband yesterday afternoon and they'd had a scrap. But whatever else, the first order of business was to get hold of him.

The Lieutenant told Mitch to get in touch with Philadelphia and find out what he could, so Mitch was at the phone on and off for the next couple of hours. He was lucky, too, on account he got hold of a Philadelphia cop named Epstein, and this Epstein was a wow. He checked up on Talbot and where he lived and what the neighbors knew about him and where he was, and it all added up.

It seemed that Talbot was in a hole, on account Marlie wanted dough and he didn't have it, so he'd gone to see her and talk it over. He was the kind of a guy who never had much anyhow. Give him a buck and it went to the first panhandler with an honest mug on him, or else to the first kid who looked like he wanted an ice-cream cone. Which made Talbot a real softie, right down to the holes in his socks. Except everybody said he had a temper, and when he got sore you'd better watch yourself.

With that information Mitch called the airlines and found out that Talbot had taken a nine A.M. plane out of Philadelphia yesterday morning, and he had a reservation to come back at ten P.M. the same day, only he never showed up. So where was he?

With the case shaping up like that, it looked like it was just a matter of locating Talbot. Still, the Lieutenant had to go full steam ahead on all the other angles. It seemed that Jub Freeman had come up with a collection of hairs and assorted fibers. He had hair from two males and two females. One of the females was Marlie, the other one was a dame with light-brown hair that she was dyeing black. As for the males, they both had brownish hair, and from the descriptions of Talbot, that fitted him perfect.

On account Mitch ought to have had the day off and here he'd turned in a pretty good job, Decker told him to go on home. If they got hold of Talbot, they'd let Mitch know.

He got back a little after five and naturally the big companies were calling long distance and trying to explain about lead in their toothpaste tubes.

"I'm sorry you were bothered," Amy said, "and maybe I shouldn't have sent those letters, but I did it because of a woman named Selma Cameron."

"Who's she?"

"I don't know, but she got my name from some list and she phoned me and asked me to write those letters. She kept calling me every day and nagging me, and I finally wrote the letters. Then she phoned again yesterday to make sure I'd sent them. She's so persistent, and I don't know what to do about her."

"If she calls again," Mitch said, "get hold of her number and then hang up. After that I'll handle her, I'll get her off your back."

"I know you will," Amy said, "and I have her phone number right here."

What with getting to the bottom of those long-distance calls this morning and feeling he'd got Amy settled down, Mitch felt pretty good. He slept fine and woke up with the feeling that the Marlie Pratt case was going to get wound up today. And when it was, he and Amy were going out and celebrate.

In the morning, though, things didn't look as good as Mitch had expected. Talbot hadn't gone back to Philadelphia and hadn't been located here. It looked more and more as if he was the guy they were after, because he'd been with Marlie and he had the motive and there was a half-empty bottle of bourbon with the label of a Philadelphia store that they'd found in her apartment. Then to pin it down, this Kutch who was the super, he said Marlie often went around in blue jeans and a white shirt. Which, Decker said, were no longer in her closet.

So the perpetrator must have left wearing her stuff instead of his own bloodstained clothes, and it all pointed to Talbot.

Still, they didn't have him in custody, not yet, and until they did they had to keep chasing down every clue they could get hold of. Which was why Decker started reading off the names in Marlie's address book and assigning them to the men to check up. But when he came to Selma Cameron, Mitch spoke up.

"I heard of her," he said. "She's a nut on food poisoning and stuff like that. Let me tackle her."

Decker nodded that it was okay, and at the end of the briefing session Mitch got his car, Number Four, and headed out for Jefferson Avenue, where the Cameron female lived.

She wasn't particularly tall, but she was the kind of a dame you don't tangle with unless you have to. The way she opened the door, she was ready to slam it back in your face and maybe throw you downstairs if she felt like it. Still, when Mitch showed his identification, she backed off and let him into her apartment.

The hallway where you came in, there wasn't too much light, but there was enough to show a bunch of photographs hanging on the walls. The pictures, they were teams, maybe women's soft ball and stuff like that. Then when Mitch stepped into the living room, the first thing he noticed was the pair of crossed cricket bats mounted over the fake fireplace. Then he took a good look at this female and he noticed she had black hair but you could see she'd dyed it because the roots were brownish and much lighter.

Mitch started easy, the way he always did. First off, he asked her whether she knew what had happened to Marlie and whether Marlie had been a friend of hers and when was the last time they'd seen each other. The Cameron answered straight out, nothing nervous about her. She said she hadn't seen Marlie for a week or so, although they usually saw each other pretty regular.

Along about then Mitch began to get the feeling that the Cameron dame was in this a lot deeper than she wanted him to think. So he fished around for a while, a little of this and a little of that, kind of trying to get the feel of things and wondering whether to bring up the Amy business. Only the Cameron dame did it for him.

"I think I've spoken to your wife," she said.

"That's right, and you been pestering her for quite a while."

"I talked to her about some consumer problems."

"Look," Mitch said. "You been nagging her, but from now on you're going to lay off. Understand?"

"Don't threaten me with your Gestapo methods," Cameron said.

Mitch figured she was just trying to get off the subject, so he came right back on. "You and Marlie were pretty thick, weren't you?" he said.

"We were lovers," Cameron answered. And the way she said it, kind of proud and daring him to fault her, it made him admire her.

"Sure," he said. "That's why you were so jealous of this guy she was going around with. That's what the fight was about." And he waited to see how she'd react. Because he had nothing particular in mind except to hope he could rile her. Only what happened was, she burst out laughing.

"Jealous of a *man*?" she said. "Me?"

Mitch let that one go, and he pointed to the cricket bats. "Where'd you get those?" he asked.

"I'm president of the American Women's Cricket Association. Since cricket bats cost so much, I import them wholesale and sell them here at cost, but I gave Marlie a pair free."

"These?" Mitch said, pointing.

"Of course not. Do you mean to say—"

Mitch interrupted. "I just want to know whether you hit her with these."

"Me?" Cameron yelled. And Mitch had the feeling he was finally getting somewheres, so he kept pushing.

"Did you?" he demanded.

She practically spat out her answer. "No!" she yelled. "No—no—no!"

"Just take it easy and tell me where you were Sunday afternoon around five or six."

"I was in the mayor's office, knitting him a pair of woolen pajamas."

"Look," Mitch said. "Either you answer straight or you're going down to headquarters in a patrol car."

Her eyes, they'd been kind of brown and about normal in size, but now they narrowed and went black with gold dots in them. Mitch told himself that maybe that was the last thing Marlie ever saw, when Cameron was standing over her and beating her to a pulp.

With that he turned away and pointed to the bats. "She was killed with one of these," he said. "What did you do it for?"

He was still fishing. He figured he'd opened up a brand-new angle and right now he wasn't sure if it was Cameron or Talbot. But whatever he expected, what she did next just about knocked him for a loop. Because she crossed the room like she had a swarm of bees chasing her, and she grabbed the knob of the bedroom door and slapped it open.

"There!" she screamed. "There's your murderer—Cornelius Talbot, and just look at him!"

The guy lying there on the bed kind of lifted up his head and then let out a sigh, like he'd done all he could to escape and he hadn't made it, so now he was giving up.

"Talbot?" Mitch said. "Are you Cornelius Talbot?" And the guy nodded weakly. Which was a break if there ever was one.

Still, Mitch wasn't any too sure who'd killed Marlie. Maybe it was Talbot and maybe it was Cameron. But whichever it was, Mitch was certain of one thing: Cameron had knowingly harbored a fugitive from justice, and if she kept bothering Amy, Mitch would slap down, hard. And with that much settled, Mitch got down to the business in front of him, which was the kind of chance he didn't get any too often.

With the whole city looking for Talbot, Mitch had him along with a second suspect who was in this as deep as anybody. And while you usually don't let two suspects talk in front of each other, on account you don't want them to find out anything they didn't know before, still, with the pair of them here and all het up, this was the time to get them talking.

"How'd you get here?" Mitch asked Talbot.

"I hardly know. Marlie and I had an argument on Sunday, and after I left her I walked around. But then I decided we had to talk things over a little more quietly, so I went back. She was lying there in blood—blood—"

Talbot stuck his hands in front of his face and kind of wagged his head, like he was still looking at Marlie and couldn't believe it. Which either was true, or else made him a damn good actor.

"So after you killed her, then what?" Mitch asked.

"I didn't kill her. I don't know who did. I can't even remember what I did after I saw her lying there, except that somehow I came here. Marlie had talked about Cameron, they were friends and I wanted to be with somebody who'd known her and loved her."

"You lost your head and killed her," Mitch said, still pushing it. "Remember now?"

"I didn't—I couldn't. Even if we were separated and I wasn't in love with her any more, she was still my wife. We'd had some good years together, so how could I hurt her?"

"Then what did you run away for?"

"I don't know. It was a shock, and I was exhausted. I don't know where I went, but I must have been walking all night long. For hours and hours. I didn't eat. I just walked. I don't know where. I don't even remember getting here."

"He killed her," Cameron said flatly. "I'm sure of it."

Talbot shook his head, and his jaw dropped. "I couldn't kill her. I couldn't kill anybody, even if I wanted to. My hands—they have no strength. I couldn't grip a bat no matter how hard I tried. Look!"

"How do I know—" Mitch began, but Talbot interrupted.

"Lead poisoning," he said, "from all the years I painted toys. The manufacturers bragged about them—expensive, hand-painted toys. Sure, with my hands! Let any doctor examine them."

"We'll do just that," Mitch said. "We'll go down to headquarters and have a doctor look you over." Then he turned to Cameron. "And you better come along, too."

"What for?"

"Harboring a fugitive from justice," Mitch said. "You knew we were looking for Talbot, didn't you?"

"Yes. I thought he'd killed her, but I couldn't make him admit it. I wasn't going to let him go until he confessed. Then *you* came along and had to stick your nose in my business."

"Not your business," Mitch said. "Ours."

About a half hour later he got back to headquarters with Talbot and the Cameron dame. He figured there ought to be brass bands playing and a citation waiting for him, but it didn't exactly work out that way. Instead, as he came down the corridor to the door marked *Homicide Squad,* Lieutenant Decker happened to step out.

"Oh, Taylor," he said casually. "Glad you're back. We got a confession out of Jesse after a couple of witnesses showed up and said they'd seen him leave the apartment Sunday afternoon wearing a white shirt and blue jeans. Which explains why our guy in blue jeans never got to the bus station. It was Jesse, and he only had to go as far as his shop."

"Why did he do it?" Mitch asked quietly.

"Marlie was ruining his business, with her talk about consumer education and how nobody should buy old stock, some of which had been condemned. That was about all that Jesse had—junk he'd bought cheap because it had been banned by the food and drug people. So he went to see her on Sunday afternoon to ask her to lay off. They had an argument and he lost his head and beat her up. We found the cricket bat in the back of his store." Decker frowned and glanced at Mitch's two prisoners. "Who are they?"

"Cornelius Talbot," Mitch said. "And Miss Cameron, who was a friend of Marlie's."

The Lieutenant nodded like this was pretty much what he'd expected. "Mr. Talbot," he said. "We've been looking for you, and we'll want a statement from you in a little while." Then he turned to the Cameron dame, who let fly.

"This man," she said. "This dim-witted, misguided policeman who arrested me under false pretenses and—"

Mitch kind of edged behind her, and as soon as he caught the Lieutenant's eye he gave him a wink. The Lieutenant nodded, okay, he'd cut her down to size, which he was good at. Only Cameron swung around and started after Mitch like she wasn't going to let him off so easy. So Mitch did the one thing that would get her off his back. He went on into the Men's Room.

THE ADVENTURE OF THE GREAT TRAIN ROBBERY

by Robert L. Fish

Once again the game is afoot, and Schlock Homes, the Master Defective—oops, the Master Detective—walks in relentless pursuit of archvillains and secret agents. Secret indeed! Two of them followed Homes and Watney like shadows, leaving their footprints in the otherwise unblemished snow; but close as the prints were to our hero and his colleague-chronicler—close enough for the perpetrators to be apprehended—even the brilliant, analytical Homes could not catch the nefarious pursuers. And that, dear readers, takes some doing! . . .

IT WAS RARE, indeed, for my good friend Mr. Schlock Homes and myself to disagree as to the merits of his ability in resolving a case, yet such a situation arose in regard to an affair which I find reference to in my notebook as *The Adventure of the Great Train Robbery*. In my estimation, the case allowed Homes as great a use of his exceptional powers as any I can recall, but the fact was that Homes himself was far from satisfied with his performance in the matter. I can but leave it to the reader to judge for himself.

It was upon a Wednesday, February 31st, that we first heard of Sir Lionel Train. Homes had been exceptionally busy those early months of '68, first with the problem of the championship kittens stolen just hours prior to an international show, a case I find referred to as *The Adventure of the*

Purloined Litter, following which my friend went on to resolve the curious puzzle of a punch-drunk prize-fighter, a case I later chronicled as *The Adventure of the Rapped Expression.* It was not, therefore, until the final day of February that the matter of Sir Lionel came to our attention.

This particular Wednesday the weather had turned quite poor, with a night of fierce snow followed by dismal skies and a sharp drop in temperature. Homes, therefore, had given the day over to relaxation and was bent over his laboratory bench with me in sharp attendance, studying some putty-like material called "Plastique" he had received without comment just that morning from his old friend M'sieu C. Septembre Duping, in Paris. We had already noted its colour and odour, as well as its rubber-like consistency, and Homes was about to strike it with a hammer to test the resilience of the strange material, when there came a sudden disturbance on the stairway, and a moment later Homes' brother Criscroft had burst in upon our scientific experiments.

It was extremely odd for Criscroft to appear at our quarters at 221 B Bagel Street without prior notice, and even more unusual to see that normally most controlled of gentlemen gasping for breath. His clothing was awry, his gaiters unbuckled, and there was an urgency about him which communicated itself at once to Homes's razor-sharp instincts. Homes immediately replaced the putty-like substance in its wrapping, returned the hammer to its proper place in the tool rack, washed and dried his hands carefully, and, wasting no time, faced his brother.

"Well, Criscroft," said he, lighting a Vulgarian, "this is indeed a pleasure! But you appear disturbed—or have I misinterpreted the signs?"

Criscroft fell into a chair, still fighting for his composure.

"As usual you are correct, Schlock!" he exclaimed. "We may well be in deep trouble, indeed! I fear some grave misfortune may have befallen Sir Lionel Train."

Homes nodded in instant understanding. "Who?" he inquired.

"Sir Lionel Train, head of Q6-JB45-VX-2DD-T3, the most secret of our secret services. Other than the Yard and Special Services, no one has ever heard of the man."

"Ah! *That* Sir Lionel Train!" Homes said, and nodded. "Pray favour us with the details."

"Very well," Criscroft said. He sat a bit more erect, obviously relieved to have his brother's aid with the dire problem. "Well, then, the facts are these! Sir Lionel has his country estate at Much-Binding-in-the-Groyne, a typical English village near Tydin, Notts, where he spends his mid-weeks with his famous diamond collection. In any event, early this morning a neighbour of his, out to check the weather, happened to notice Sir Lionel struggling in hand-to-hand combat with an assailant in his bedroom. Not wishing to be hasty, this neighbour returned to his house and took up a pair of binoculars, with which he verified the sight he had seen. Satisfied he had not been incorrect—for through the binoculars he could see this unrecognizable assailant's hands around Sir Lionel's neck—he immediately sent his butler off to Scotland Yard with the information."

"He did not interfere directly?"

"Of course not. They had never been introduced."

"I understand. But he continued to watch?"

"He had come out without his slippers. No, once his butler had been sent off, this neighbour repaired to his basement where he is building a bottle-in-a-ship."

"I see. And Scotland Yard—?"

"Aware of Sir Lionel's true status, the Yard instantly communicated with the Home Office, who in turn sent a messenger to advise me. When my man could not locate a cab, I hastily dressed and ran all the way. Schlock, you must go to Much-Binding-in-the-Groyne immediately and do everything in your power to save Sir Lionel!"

Homes considered his brother steadily behind tented fingers.

"At what hour did this neighbour note Sir Lionel struggling?"

"A bit before seven this morning."

"It is just after noontime. It is possible, of course, that I may arrive too late. However, we can but try. Tell me, where was Lady Train during all this?"

"Lady Train is visiting relatives."

"Sir Lionel has no staff?"

"Just a new maid he employed only yesterday, right after Lady Train left. Sir Lionel has an aversion to butlers."

"I see. But regarding your fears, surely Sir Lionel does not keep State secrets in his country home?"

Criscroft shook his head decisively.

"Sir Lionel commits nothing to paper. Still, under the duress of torture, who knows what secrets he might divulge?" Criscroft came to his feet. "It is in your hands, Schlock," he said. With an abrupt nod in our direction he stepped on a gaiter buckle and stumbled heavily down the stairs.

"Ah, well, Watney," said Homes with a sigh, "a pity our afternoon is to be compromised. They are playing the Hayden Go Seek concerto at Albert Hall and I had hoped to attend. However, duty before pleasure. You might bring along your medical bag, as it seems it might be useful. And you might also bring along Duping's gift. Studying it might help us while away an hour or so on the train."

The Nottingham Express dropped us off in Tydin, and a rented trap was easily arranged with the station-master. He also furnished us with directions to Sir Lionel's estate, and moments later we were driving smartly along the newly-cleared road to Much-Binding-in-the-Groyne.

Here in Nottinghamshire the sun had wormed its way through the heavy overcast, a blanket of glistening snow stretched across the endless fields, and ice glittered on wires that hung between each house and a line of poles inexplicably planted in a row along the highway. Had our mission not been of such serious intent, we might well have enjoyed the brisk air and lovely scenery.

Sir Lionel's home lay around a curve beyond the quaint village. We passed the village green, crossed a small burn lightly crusted with ice, and slowed down as we approached the house. I was about to direct our trap down the carriage-way when Homes suddenly placed a hand upon my arm. I pulled our panting horse to a stop and looked at my friend inquiringly.

"From here on it would be best if we proceeded by foot," said he, his eyes sparkling with the excitement of the chase. "Note the unbroken expanse of snow. It would not do to disturb it without first seeing if it can answer any of our questions."

"True," I admitted, and looked about for a weight to throw down, but it seems our station-master had overlooked putting one into the carriage. Homes noted my search and shook his head.

"Block the wheels with Duping's package," said he impatiently. "Time may be of the essence."

Shamed at not having thought of the simple solution myself, I dropped from the trap, propped the wheel against the horse's wandering, and turned to Homes, medical bag in hand. But Homes's attention was already directed towards the smooth snow that stretched on all sides of the manor house. A frown appeared on my friend's lean face, to be replaced almost at once by a look of determination.

"Come!" said he, and started off on a large circuit of the grounds with me close upon his heels. The snow lay unblemished in all directions. We passed the stables at the rear and the coach-house to one side, and at last came about our huge circle to our starting point. Suddenly my companion froze in his tracks.

"Homes!" I cried in alarm, since the temperature was not that low. "What is it?"

"Later," said he fiercely, and dropped to one knee to study intently two pairs of footprints beside our trap which I swear had not been there upon our arrival. I waited in silence as my companion checked them thoroughly, and then watched as he slowly rose to his feet with a frown, brushing the snow from his trousers.

"Two men," said he slowly. "One tall and thin, and from the angle of his prints, of rather intense nature. The other is short and walks with a slight limp. I should say without a doubt that the shorter of the two is a medical man by profession, and a bit absent-minded in the bargain."

"Really, Homes!" I exclaimed reproachfully. "I can understand that you might arrive at the relative heights of the men by the lengths of their stride, but surely you are pulling my leg when you claim one of them to be a medical man—and an absent-minded one, at that!"

"At times I wonder at you, Watney," said Homes impatiently. "You have forgotten that today is Wednesday, the traditional day for doctors to leave their practise to their nurse and take to the open air. You have also failed to properly examine the tracks this man left; had you done so you would have noted that the shorter of the two is wearing golfing shoes. Since the snow is too deep for playing the game, one can only assume he put them on automatically before leaving the house, an action which not only clearly indicates his absent-mindedness, but also serves as further proof of his profession, since on Wednesdays doctors don them from force of habit."

"He might have been a dentist," I hazarded a bit sullenly, although in truth I did not doubt the accuracy of Homes's masterful analysis.

"No, Watney," said he. "Dentists, from constant standing, develop much larger feet. But we are wasting time. The two men undoubtedly passed as we were in the rear near the stables. However, since their spoor does not approach the house, it is evident they have gone off about their business and have nothing to do with the case. Come!"

He turned and moved off towards the house, breaking trail through the snow, while I followed as quickly as my shorter legs would permit. A moment later and Homes was stamping the loose snow from his boots on the porch, while examining the lock on the main door with narrowed eyes.

"Homes!" I exclaimed as a sudden thought struck me. "I should have also brought my revolver! Surely if there are no footprints in the snow, the assailant must still be within the house, for there is no other exit."

"You forget the overhead wires leading to those poles in the road," he said, reaching into his pocket for his set of picklocks. "They have obviously been placed on each house to afford an auxiliary means of exit from the upper stories in case of emergencies; otherwise what purpose would be served by the spikes in the poles, forming a ladder? No, Watney, our assailant would have no problem leaving the house without leaving footprints, especially if he were small."

I nodded in admiration for Homes's analysis, and then followed my friend into the silent house as the door quickly succumbed to the magic of his touch. We made our way through the main hall and up the steps of the grand stairway. At its head an open door leading to the library revealed a large safe standing ajar. Homes shook his head pityingly.

"Had the miscreant known, as we do, that Sir Lionel commits nothing to paper, he might have saved himself the trouble of struggling with that heavy safe," said he. "But let us continue our search."

We moved from the library, making our way along the balcony that fronted the floor below across an ornate railing. As we reached the corner, a sudden guttural sound brought us up short, and a moment later Homes was dashing down a hallway in the direction of the strangled noises. I followed in all haste, my medical bag banging against my thigh. Homes threw open a door and paused abruptly.

"It is Sir Lionel himself!" he said, turning to me. "Pray God we are not too late. It is in your hands now, Watney."

I hastened to the side of the bed and bent over the man. He lay on his back, one arm dangling helplessly over the side of the large mussed bed. Sir Lionel was wearing his pajama bottoms, but his chest was bare and even as I watched, it rose and fell, accompanied by his stentorian breathing.

"Homes," I said in a low voice. "The poor man has been badly treated, indeed. Note the scratches on his shoulders; note the puckered red blotches on his cheeks and lips; smell the sweet odour, similar to Chanel Number Five, doubtless one of the new perfumed anaesthetics."

"But he put up a brave struggle from the appearance of the bedclothes," Homes commented.

"Which probably saved his life," said I, and reached down and shook the man gently. "Sir Lionel!"

"Not right now, darling," he muttered, and opened his eyes sleepily. They widened incredulously at sight of my face. "Eh, what? Who? What, what? What? Who? What, what?" He turned and saw my companion. "Schlock Homes! How much did my wife pay—"

"The poor chap is completely incoherent, Homes," said I, and plunged the needle of my hypodermic into his bare arm. "The shock of sudden rescue often does this to people."

Sir Lionel's head fell back onto the pillow. I pulled his arm up to fold it across his chest and then paused.

"Homes!" I ejaculated.

"Yes?" said he.

"Look here," I said, and pointed to a tattoo that ran across the biceps, and which had been revealed as I drew up his arm. "What do you make of this?"

Homes moved swiftly to my side and read the tattoo over my shoulder.

"'Left 36, Right 21, Left twice to 15, Right 9'." My friend straightened up, staring at the mysterious symbols with a bitter look in his eyes. "Criscroft stated that Sir Lionel never committed secrets to paper, but he said nothing of a tattoo!"

"But surely those numbers can have but little significance, Homes," I said, hoping to soothe him. "They are probably merely the result of a boyish prank from his University days."

"I doubt it is that simple," Homes replied heavily. "They are obviously references to the political left and right. Undoubtedly the numbers delineate the code name of our secret agents in certain countries of both persuasions." He shook his head. "Come, Watney. If Sir Lionel is settled for the moment, let us continue our search of the house for more clues."

I hastily tucked a cover to Sir Lionel's chin and followed Homes as he moved from the room. Our search was more thorough this time, starting in the cellars, including the kitchens, and returning to the upper stories. At the far end of the final corridor we came upon narrow steps leading to the attic rooms, and Homes took them evenly, with me upon his heels.

At the top a small landing beneath the eaves revealed a door set between dormers and partially open. Homes peered cautiously around the jamb and then stepped swiftly back, drawing me into the shadows. From my new vantage point I could see into the room; a young lady was bending over a small attaché case, tucking a chamois bag into its depths. Homes gripped my arm painfully.

"Do you see that young lady?" he demanded in a taut whisper. "That, Watney, is none other than Miss Irene Addled, international jewel thief, and the only woman who ever bested me! And yet, see to what sad end she has come. Despite the proceeds of years of crime, see where she has ended—a maid of all work in a small country manor house! There is a lesson here for all of us, I am sure, but unfortunately, there is no time to explore it. Come!"

He pushed his way into the small room. The young lady looked up from closing her small case and then shrank back against the wall, aghast at sight of my companion.

"Mr. Schlock Homes!" she cried in terror. "What are you doing here?"

"It is all right, Miss Addled," Homes said gallantly. "I am not here in respect to you, nor am I one to bear a grudge, especially against one upon whom evil days have so obviously fallen. Still, I fear I have some bad news for you. Your master has been viciously attacked. However, thanks to Dr. Watney, he is resting comfortably. I suggest you go down and sit by his bedside. It will comfort him to see a friendly face upon awakening."

"And then may I leave?"

"As soon as the ambulance arrives. Dr. Watney and I shall go for one at once. I realize this means the end of your new-found employment, but if you stop by our quarters I shall do my best to see if I can arrange suitable employment in some other ménage."

"Some day, somehow, I shall find some means of thanking you!" she cried, and flung her arms about his neck, still holding her attaché case. Homes reeled back, blushing, while Miss Addled hurried down the steps. Homes and I followed and watched as the thankful young lady moved towards the master bedroom with a remarkable sense of direction considering her few hours in the house. With the matter settled, Homes and I descended the main staircase and walked out onto the porch. Suddenly Homes stopped so abruptly that I ran into him from behind.

"Homes!" I said in a muffled voice. "What is it?"

"I am a fool!" he cried.

"But why?" I insisted.

His thin finger pointed dramatically. "We have been followed!"

I came from behind him and stared. It was true! The same two sets of footprints that had so mysteriously appeared beside our trap were now facing us again, leading directly to the house. There was no mistaking the long stride of the taller man, nor the spike-marks of the shorter.

"I am an idiot!" Homes cried. "I should have realized the only reason Sir Lionel was left alive was precisely because he had *not* revealed the secret of that tattoo, despite the terrible torture. Obviously, the smaller man left the house by means of the overhead wires for the purpose of bringing an accomplice, a larger person to exert greater pressure on Sir Lionel. And, locating the accomplice, the two returned to the house."

"But where are they now, Homes?" I cried.

"Obviously, they heard our sounds of search and have gone away. But these footprints are still quite fresh, Watney! They cannot have gotten very far. Come! After them!"

With a bound from the porch we dashed through the snow to our trap and scrambled inside, not even wasting time to unblock the wheels. I cracked the whip close beside our horse's ear, and with a convulsive leap he sprang forward. My last conscious memory as we rose in the air under the force of an explosion was of Homes's voice tinged with a bitterness I had seldom heard before.

"I am a *double* fool!" he cried. "Allowing them to booby-trap us!"

It was several weeks before we were released from St. Barts and allowed to return to the ministrations of Mrs. Essex. Sir Lionel Train, obviously unnerved by events, had gone off to the continent on a protracted holiday with a young nurse, and we had had no word from poor Miss Addled. But despite what I consider one of Homes's most brilliant successes, he continued to consider it a failure, and to brood heavily upon it.

"Look, Homes," I said at breakfast the first day we were able to be up and about, "after all, Sir Lionel suffered no permanent harm, and that was your major assignment. Nor was the secret of the code numbers ever revealed, since the explosion apparently frightened the villains away. And as for poor Miss Addled, I am sure your paths will cross again one day. So how can you possibly consider this case a failure?"

"You do not understand, Watney," said he bitterly, reaching for a curried curry. "It is the fact that we had those nefarious criminals within our grasp and allowed them to escape! And not only to escape but to hamper our pursuit by planting an explosive practically under our noses. How does one live down an insult of such dimensions? How, in addition, does one advise an old friend like M'sieu C. Septembre Duping that, due to my idiocy, his gift to me was destroyed? No, Watney, I shall not rest until I lay those two rascals by the heels!"

There being no arguing with Homes when he was in this mood, I turned to the morning *Times*, hoping to discover some interesting case which might take my friend's mind from his obsession. Suddenly, a new feature, imported from the American colonies, struck my eye.

"Homes!" I cried. "I do believe you will find this of interest."

He reached over and removed the journal from my hand. I watched his eyes narrow as he noted the design I had been studying. Suddenly he struck his fist upon the table, causing the chived chives to jump.

"There can be no doubt, Watney—it is they!" said he with deep satisfaction. "Note the silk topper worn by the shorter of the two—surely the sign of Harley Street affluence. And note the rather stupid expression on the face of his taller accomplice, for had he not been stupid he would never have crossed swords with Schlock Homes. A pity we should find them by pure chance, but better this way than not at all." He reached for his magnifying glass. "What are their names again?"

I came to read over his shoulder. "Mutt and Jeff."

"Precisely! A letter to the editor of the *Times* at once, Watney, if you will!"

MRS. MURKETT'S LODGERS
by Helen Hudson

Helen Hudson's "Mrs. Murkett's Lodgers" is the kind of short story that doesn't come along too often. So welcome it— savor its strangeness, relish its oddness. It is what might be called an "old wine" story—it has body and bouquet. . . .

"What, exactly, is your occupation, Mrs. Murkett?" Meg asked.

"I just try to help people, dear. That's all. Nothing very mysterious or dreadful about that, is there?"

IT WAS an odd house with most of its windows tucked up under the roof and a garden that looked as if it had been dumped out of a passing lorry. There was no bell but the door opened before she could lift the heavy brass knocker.

"Come in, dear," Mrs. Murkett said. She was a tiny woman dressed in brown with a pile of dyed brown hair as if she'd been dipped in gravy. A cozy, homey little woman, the girl thought, ready with hot-water bottles and tea and advice— and two kinds of potatoes at dinner.

"You've come about the rooms," Mrs. Murkett said. The estate agent must have phoned, the girl thought.

Mrs. Murkett hung her coat on a clothes tree covered with coats of all kinds that looked as if they'd walked in from the nineteenth-century: opera capes and military capes and an academic gown. All far too big for Mrs. Murkett.

"I expect you'll be wanting your tea after that long cold

journey," Mrs. Murkett said, opening the door to the sitting room. It was a small room almost completely filled by a round table holding a huge brass tray and a half dozen chairs drawn up to the table as if permanently ready for a party. The rest of the room was cluttered with photographs and brass: candlesticks and andirons and pots full of ferns and tall tubs with plants growing out of them and urns holding nothing at all. Unless it was somebody's ashes, the girl thought.

"Sit here, dear," Mrs. Murkett said, pointing to the chair on her right. "I like to keep my left side free. No sugar, I believe. But you do take macaroons."

The girl, who had a passion for them, blushed. Mrs. Murkett smiled encouragingly. "Now that we're all tickety poo, you must tell me about America, dear."

The girl opened her mouth and closed it again. It must be my clothes, she thought, though she was wearing standard Anglo-American gear: sweater and skirt and flat-heeled shoes. Unless Mrs. Murkett could hear her thoughts and detect the accent.

"I haven't been in America for ages," Mrs. Murkett went on. "Not since my last trip with Lady Jocelyn. She always takes me with her when she goes. Her mother died there, you know."

The girl put her cup down. Mrs. Murkett, she decided, was definitely odd, staring at her with the dull brown eyes like splashes of gravy. The phone rang but Mrs. Murkett made no move. "That'll be the Bishop of Ely, poor dear, wanting to get through to Sir Thomas More. But we won't let him interrupt us for theological discussions now, will we?"

She tilted her head to the left and sat smiling silently for a moment. Then she looked at Meg. "I expect America's too cold this time of year for your poor dear father," she went on. "Takes the heart right out of you, doesn't it?"

Leave my father out of this, Meg thought savagely. He was lying in a cold bed-and-breakfast place on the other side of town, getting far too excited over Sir Walter Scott's *Old Mortality*, with his black suit and black bowler carefully brushed for the day when his heart would realize he was home again and could slow down to its old relaxed pace.

"Let's go home, Meg," he had said in New York after his wife died. He hated America. There was no dignity in it. In America he had sat in a cage for eight hours a day with the roar of the subways rushing past him, swathed in dank air that smelled of sweat and juicy fruit gum.

In England he had been a porter at Bedford College, Cambridge, dressed formally in a black suit and black bowler. He had walked through quiet courts delivering the mail and important messages, talking to dons and famous professors and undergraduates on their way to Parliament or a peerage. "Good morning, Mr. Tuke," they said. Everyone knew him. And he knew everyone, by name and estate and family lineage. In his free time he copied down the titles of the books in the college and got them out of the public library. He had become an educated man. But in America it didn't matter what he knew as long as he could make change. Or what he wore. He might have been a deaf mute sitting in his underwear taking in and pushing out coins. All because of those church brasses.

"Too bad about the brasses, dear," Mrs. Murkett said.

Meg jumped. "I beg your pardon?"

"Your mother's passion for brasses, dear. She would love it here, wouldn't she?" Mrs. Murkett looked around the room at the huge brass tray and the candlesticks and andirons. "I rather fancy them myself," she said. "So bright. And so durable."

It was true, Meg thought. It was the brasses that had kept her mother in England and the brasses that had finally driven her out. She had come as a young girl just out of high school from the hills of Vermont to nurse poor Aunt Martha dying in Cambridge. And had fallen in love with church brasses, escaping when she could to rub away at knights and ladies with little dogs at their feet. She stayed on and was trapped by the war and a tall young man in a bowler, leaning against the font.

"That's a lovely bit of work you've got there," he said, admiring her raised rump. Extraordinary in such a small person. Powerful arms, too. He imagined her with her sleeves rolled up, rubbing away at his lumbago. "That's the first

Master of Bedford you've got there," he said, "Sir Roger de Pugh. 1301–1375."

She looked up, impressed. By the time she discovered he was a porter and not a don, she was too much in love with his long lean body and trim speech to care. For a while she was happy, wandering around Cambridge and cycling out into the flat countryside, rubbing vigorously in village churches and listening to William's talk at home—all about lords and Honorables and the young duke who flew to Paris whenever he wanted fresh croissants for breakfast.

But after a while the brasses had disappeared from the churches because of the hordes of American women who came every summer. They were rubbing right down to the stone, the vergers complained, and dousing their cigarettes in the fonts. She got lonely sitting in a four-room cottage in Histon, waiting for William to come home. When he did, his conversation annoyed and bored her. The young duke had gone long ago and she was no longer charmed by the Honorables who arrived in Bentleys and Rolls-Royces while William cycled miles each day on a push bike. His pictures of the Queen and the College Master, hanging over the fireplace, made those of her parents look permanently ashamed.

"He's a great man, the Master," Mr. Tuke would say. "Was even vice-chancellor of the University. But he came by the Porter's Lodge every day just the same. 'Good morning, Mr. Tuke,' he always said."

"It's a miracle you didn't levitate right through the roof."

"I held onto the desk," he said.

He insisted on reading bits out of his library books to her in the evening, always by titled authors such as Lord Byron and Lord Tennyson. She yawned and longed for a telly.

"They're having *Faison Sauté aux Champignons* at High Table tonight," he would say. Not to mention the five other courses, she thought, and the sherry and the wines going round and round at dessert. High Table and low wages, she thought, drinking up more in one night than William made in a month.

"We're having Glazed Peacock *aux* Candied Tailfeathers," she said. "And it's getting cold."

He laughed and sat down to his pork and mash. No pride, she thought angrily. No pride at all. Never a Christmas off since she'd known him and he often worked late into the night, making special deliveries of this and that. As if they couldn't wait till morning, or pick up their mail themselves. They even left their letters for him to stamp. "It isn't decent," she said, scouring the pot.

"What isn't?"

"Licking other men's stamps like that. You might as well lick their boots."

"They're gentlemen," he said. "They wouldn't expect it."

"They're snobs," she said. "You should stand up to them." She was always standing up. Even during tea she stood at the kitchen sink doing the washing while he ate.

He put down his knife and fork. He could not understand her. He felt rich just walking about the colleges. He could enjoy the gardens and the fine old buildings like any peer of the realm. It excited him to think that he was walking the same stones as the greatest men of England—Newton had lived in Trinity and Milton in Jesus and Cromwell in Sidney Sussex. He could go on all night while she yawned in his face. She had never heard of any of them. "Lincoln lived in a log cabin," she said. "And he was the biggest of the lot."

The colleges were merely huge stone buildings to her and so dirty, like the county courthouse back home, only colder inside with stern stone figures watching from the walls to make sure she didn't walk on the grass. Even the Halls seemed dark and gloomy with yards of paneling to be polished and plain wooden tables and benches with no backs. Only the chapels interested her, and she went to a different one every Sunday.

But they were a disappointment, too. For the services were all in English and there was no mystery in them. It seemed strange to hear it said straight out like that, as if they were all talking to each other instead of God. She gave it up and spent Sundays polishing the linoleum and washing her hair. Cleanliness being next to godliness, she felt closer to Him that way. She sat before the fire with her wet hair spread on her shoulders and let William rub it dry. Prices went up but William's wages stayed down.

She took a job cleaning offices. But rubbing the brass on doorknobs and knockers and name plates did not satisfy her, even though she could do it standing up. "Let's go home," she said. She didn't want her only daughter talking like a foreigner. In America she could make money selling her rubbings and work in a factory with other girls, eating sandwiches together and discussing movie stars whose faces she knew and whose private lives, far more interesting than dons' or undergraduates', she could follow in detail in the magazines. At home everyone had washing machines and television sets by now. She was tired of the endless succession of gray days and the early morning fog covering the fields like cream in a saucer. And the unbroken flatness. She longed for hills she could go up and down. . . .

"She missed the challenge, dear," Mrs. Murkett said, stirring her tea. "Americans are like that. Climbers."

Meg shivered. "Could I see the rooms now, please?" she said.

"Oh, you'll like them, dear," Mrs. Murkett said. "Quite suitable. And so handy."

"Handy to what?"

"Why, the library, dear. Such a nice occupation, I always think. Working in a library. Passing out information to people in need. Rather like me, I should say."

Meg wanted to shout at her. She was dripping all over Meg's skirt. How could she possibly live in the same house with a woman who did not have the decency to stay inside her own life? "What, exactly, *is* your occupation, Mrs. Murkett?" she said.

"I just try to help people, dear. That's all. Nothing very mysterious or dreadful about that, is there? Though there are some who want to make it sound wicked or just plain silly."

Meg went through the motions of looking at the flat. It was distressingly neat and clean and comfortable. And two flights away from Mrs. Murkett's round table. "I'll let you know," she said reaching for her coat from among the old-fashioned cloaks and capes in the hall.

"Gifts from the bereaved," Mrs. Murkett said. "So kind. This one"—she fondled the academic gown—"belonged to a vice-chancellor of the University. A most imposing man. This was his house, you know, when he first came to Cambridge. He's still here but ever so discreet. Indeed, he has never so much as exposed the tip of his toe. Such a privilege to share my little things with him."

Meg opened the door quickly. "I'll let you know," she said again.

"I'll expect you tomorrow," Mrs. Murkett said. "Around seven." And Meg knew that she was right again.

After she left, Mrs. Murkett sat down in her sitting room and smiled. Soon she would have new lodgers in her empty flat, complete with a new spirit, giving her a new scope for her talents. They would drive the others out, the sullen souls who manifested at odd hours whenever the house was empty. Like Gillian Glegg whose parents had been Mrs. Murkett's last tenants. Gillian was their only daughter, a petulant girl, killed in a fire in the Birmingham Arms Hotel along with fifty RAF Cadets.

"What was she doing in Birmingham?" Mr. Glegg said.

"You can ask her yourself," Mrs. Murkett said.

But he never did. For his daughter seemed reluctant to come over, reluctant to leave all those RAF Cadets, no doubt. The Gleggs had been on their way to Birmingham to find out by themselves when their car crashed. Mrs. Glegg had died instantly but Mr. Glegg lingered on. Long enough to accuse Mrs. Murkett. "I *had* to swerve," he said. "She was standing there, right in the middle of the road. What did you want to bring her *there* for?" He glared at Mrs. Murkett with blood-shot eyes before closing them forever.

Since then his daughter had taken to roaming Mrs. Murkett's house, looking for her lost parents. Mrs. Murkett could hear her now, snuffling in the hall on her way up to the empty flat. They're not here, she longed to shout. They left long ago. Which was Gillian's fault after all, wasn't it?

Mrs. Murkett closed her eyes, not caring to remember. And heard the vice-chancellor's step overhead, his slippers slapping the floor. He had never materialized, never even come into her sitting room which had once been his study. As if he resented her being there with her little things on the shelves where his books had been and her round table in the place of his desk. She had hoped for long cozy conversations about Leslie Howard and the Duke of Windsor and the late Cyril Murkett who had passed in Mauritius with his face towards England and his mirror to the wall. She wondered how he had managed the journey, unprepared as he was. He had merely packed his bag for Mauritius. But the vice-chancellor was an arrogant man who refused even to come downstairs.

The Tukes would be different—a timid girl and a dying man and a woman who had enjoyed rubbing. They were certain to cooperate. Mrs. Murkett folded her hands and listened resignedly to the moaning in the hall and the slap of slippers overhead.

"Ever know anyone named Murkett, Dad?" Meg asked as soon as she got home. He was sitting up in bed, reading, with the Queen and the Master looking over his shoulder. He glanced up for a moment.

"No. There's a garage named Murkett but I never had anything to do with them. Never owned a car." He bent his head to Lord Chesterfield again.

"Dad, listen. Please. It's important."

"What is?"

"That name."

"What name?"

"Murkett."

"Why must we discuss a garage at this time of night?"

"Because it's *her* name, too. And she seems to know all about us."

"Who does?"

"Mrs. Murkett. The woman with the flat."

"Nice flat, is it?"

"Lovely. But she's impossible."

"Well, she won't be living in it, will she?" He began to read again.

"Dad, please."

"I must finish this tonight if you're to take it back tomorrow. Terrible the way they make one gobble up books."

"Dad!"

"Well, then. What's the matter with her?"

"She's peculiar."

"I expect it's change of life. Takes some women that way. Your mother, for instance. Used to get up five times a night to check the stove and douse all the used matches. Had to give up my pipe. Wanted me to take up chewing gum instead. Terrified of fire, she was."

But she had died a terrible death anyway, though not from fire. She had been crushed getting off the Lexington Avenue express one evening, coming to meet him at work. Squeezed to death by the hordes trying to get on and off the train at the same time. Her powerful arms hadn't helped her then. She had been squashed like a paper bag right opposite his window. Nice little rump and all. That was technology and efficiency and progress for you. That was America. "Let's go home, Meg," he had said right after the funeral. . . .

Meg avoided Mrs. Murkett as much as possible after they moved in. But one evening Mrs. Murkett stopped her at the stairs. "How's your father, dear?" she said, looking up at Meg with her huge dull eyes.

"As well as can be expected, thanks."

"No, dear. I'm afraid not. He's fretting, you know, poor man. Takes most of us that way near the end, imagining it will be just a great empty place with nothing but air and angels flying around. Perfect strangers staring and playing their harps and waving their bare feet in your face. But, of course, it's not really like that at all. Tell your father I'm here to help whenever he's ready, will you? A very distinguished-looking man, your father. A bishop, I should imagine. Sent back for cheating on the tithes. He'll be wanting some assistance when the time comes. So he can have someone ready to welcome him over there. Tell him I'm here to help, won't you, dear?"

Meg nodded vaguely and ran quickly up the stairs. Her father looked up from Sir Edward Bulwer-Lytton. "Very comfortable, this place Meg," he said. "And so quiet. No cars. No people. And the phone hardly ever rings. But odd. The water in the taps, for instance. Starts to gush suddenly for no reason at all."

"Just something in the pipes, Dad."

"And there's something odd about that woman, too." She had been up that afternoon asking him did he want to make contact. "Extraordinary question, wasn't it? I told her there was no one but my cousin in a nursing home in Royston and he had three wives and six children and wouldn't even recognize me. Why should I want to make contact with poor old Ernie?"

"She didn't mean Cousin Ernie, Dad."

"Who then?"

Meg sat down on the bed and took his hand. "She's a medium, Dad."

"Good Lord! I'd rather she was a garage."

But she had admired his picture of the Master with his face laid out like a place setting where no one would ever care to eat. He was clutching the lapels of his gown and looked as if he were about to say something lengthy in Latin.

"Do I detect a faint family resemblance, Mr. Tuke?" Mrs. Murkett had said.

"I hardly think so. That is Sir Herbert Pennyfeather."

"My vice-chancellor," Mrs. Murkett cried.

"My Master," Mr. Tuke said.

"Ah, dear Mr. Tuke. I sensed immediately you were a kindred spirit. That you belonged to this house and its inhabitants. For you realize, of course, that Sir Herbert himself was once a resident here. In fact, he still is. In the rooms he loved."

"I hardly think so, Mrs. Murkett. He is, in fact, in Great St. Mary's. Unless," Mr. Tuke smiled, "he's in the Lodge of Bedford College, sitting down to his five o'clock sherry."

Mrs. Murkett sat up very late that night, unnerved by the sight of the picture. Sir Herbert had never had a face before. Would he materialize now, she wondered, at some awkward time—when she was in her bath or entertaining the vicar? She switched her thoughts to Mrs. Tuke.

The next evening she stopped Meg again. "I'm sorry to have to say this, dear, but I can't help feeling that things are not as they should be."

"Oh? My father and I are quite happy here."

"Yes, dear. Why shouldn't you be? But what about the others? That's the point, isn't it? So many of *them* and only two of you. I myself have been hounded to death since you moved in."

"Hounded?"

"By a very persistent, I might say, bullying voice. Someone is trying to get through, dear. And *not*, as your father tried to pretend, some person named Ernest in Royston. I am being subjected to the most frightful nagging, even abuse. And constant interruptions. I am letting them all down as a consequence."

She dropped her voice. "Yesterday she unzipped poor Mr. Dipple's trousers right in the middle of a most important message from Sir Winston. Lady Churchill was that upset. Something must be done."

"What are you suggesting, Mrs. Murkett?"

"You must help me to identify that poor troubled spirit, Miss Tuke, so we can make proper contact. It's no more than common humanity, dear."

Meg sat down on the steps thinking wildly. "I don't really know, Mrs. Murkett. Unless it's young Raskolnikov. He was always in a terribly overwrought state."

"Sounds foreign, dear."

"He's Russian."

"Oh. I don't think that can be right, dear. Ever since the Revolution they've been afraid to come over. Can't blame them, can you, poor dears?" The phone began to ring. "That'll be the Duchess of Devonshire. She's feeling terribly neglected over there. So many duchesses, after all, not to mention crowned heads. She'll be wanting a booking for tomorrow. Always lets it go too late. And her people have so far to come. The problem of coordination in this profession is perfectly dreadful. I shall have to computerize."

The phone stopped ringing. "Yes, dear, I'm coming," she called. "But I can't possibly fit her in tomorrow. I have a haunting at three." She began to move toward the sitting room. "You be thinking about that voice, won't you, dear?" she called over her right shoulder. "Someone who speaks English. In a *woman's* voice."

Upstairs, Mr. Tuke was lying in bed with a book by Lord Beaconsfield on his chest and his eyes closed. "How are you, Dad?" Meg said. He looked terrible. All this talk of making contact was having its effect.

"Been thinking of Nellie," he said, opening his eyes. "I never should have taken her back there, you know. Killed her, didn't it?"

"But she wanted it, Dad."

"Still, I should have been firm. That's always been my trouble, you know. She's as much as told me so many times. I didn't stand up enough, she always said. At the right time. In the right place. For the right reason. Even to *her*. And she should have sat down more. That woman was up here again. She said someone wanted to come over. Your wife, she said. I told her it couldn't be Nellie. Nellie's in America. She would never want to come back here. She hated it here." He closed his eyes. "Besides, she never liked the Master. She'd never move in with *him* here."

"Pay no attention, Dad. She's mad."

"Do you think there could be something in it?" he said. He had opened his eyes again and was staring at her. "Maybe that's Nellie in the bathroom, turning on the taps. She was always one for a good wash, whenever she was bored or upset."

"Forgotten about English drains, Dad? You can't blame *them* on Mother."

He was silent for a moment. "What do you think she wants then? That woman downstairs?"

"Clients, probably. Or someone to polish her brasses."

The next morning Mrs. Murkett met her right outside the door of the flat. "I sensed you might be leaving," she said.

"I'm leaving for work as always, Mrs. Murkett. I'm sorry but I can't stop now."

"Oh, I shan't keep you long. I'm used to being quick. My profession demands it. My spirits hate dawdling. I've got Queen Victoria on the sofa right now. Still looking for Albert, poor dear. I've promised to do my best though it's something entirely new in the field. Something . . ."

"Please don't let me interfere, Mrs. Murkett."

"But you are, dear. That is exactly what you *are* doing. Interfering. Setting up wicked vibrations. My voices have been complaining. They are reluctant to come over."

"I don't understand you, Mrs. Murkett."

"I think you do. It is not pleasant to house scoffers and cynics in one's own bosom. Even from ignorance. And that voice is driving us all mad. Interrupting constantly and in such a vulgar accent. And such language! Really, quite shocking."

"That is certainly *not* my mother," Meg said.

"Right in my sitting room. I cannot tolerate it any longer."
She bent her head to the left. "She's coming over now. Really, such vulgarity! Something must be done, Miss Tuke. Immediately!"

Mr. Tuke lay listening to the voices in the hall and thinking about Nellie. He had been getting more worried all week. The library books lay unread beside him and he took more and more sleeping pills to keep from thinking. He didn't like to imagine Nellie wandering around Mrs. Murkett's sitting room, and what was left of her could hardly be more than a sprinkle of dust on the table. And he doubted she would have enough voice left even for a whisper.

It was all nonsense. He was an educated man—if self-educated. A man of reason. It was his *heart* that was weak, not his head. But Mrs. Murkett frightened him. At one time she would have been burned for a witch. Not so long ago she would have been collecting pennies from children at fairs. Now people like her were written up in books and interviewed on television. He had seen a whole section in Heffer's Bookstore labelled OCCULT.

It was all because of the war, he thought, bombing people's minds worse than their cities. After that they could believe anything. Even the smart young undergraduates who never wore gowns any more and looked like the "desert rats" he had seen in American films, men who left civilization to prospect for gold. Perhaps they wouldn't want him to wear his black suit and black bowler any more. Or be Mr. Tuke any more. Just Bill or Pop, as he was called in America.

He fell asleep and dreamed that Nellie was sitting at Mrs. Murkett's round table, waiting for him, with her hair spread over her shoulders and her enormous rubbings spread out in front of her. "They don't want them in America," she was saying through sobs. "They're not big enough for America. But I can't do them any bigger. My arms are too short."

Mr. Tuke got out of bed and stood up for a moment to show Nellie he still could. Then he put on his black porter's suit and his black bowler. Would she recognize him, he wondered. He felt quite fit. Ready to take the mail round the college or Nellie for a punt on the river. For his arms were long, and powerful, too.

He walked slowly out into the hall, feeling weak but excited. His heart was beating quickly as it had in the old days when he was hurrying to meet Nellie in some college chapel, hurrying to admire her rump and her rubbings.

He turned the corner of the hall and saw her standing at the top of the stairs with her hair hanging loose and her face shining. She stretched out her arms and he walked into them. And felt himself lifted up, high up, above Mrs. Murkett's house and the courts and gardens of Bedford College and the spires of King's. Up to the magnificent Porter's Lodge with the Head Porter himself waiting to welcome him in. And the Master holding out a hand, ready to say, "Good morning." And to call him Mr. Tuke again.

Mrs. Murkett sat in her sitting room waiting for another prospective lodger. For the third-floor flat was vacant again. Poor Mr. Tuke had passed quite suddenly and with no help from her. And his daughter had moved out right after the funeral. Mrs. Tuke had never come at all. But Mrs. Murkett had the vice-chancellor hanging over her mantel. "You keep it," Miss Tuke had said. "It belongs here." But the house seemed terribly empty just the same.

Mrs. Murkett waited but there was no knock. It grew later and later. She continued to wait and hope. And then the sounds began: Gillian Glegg moaning in the hall on her way upstairs. And, overhead, the vice-chancellor moving restlessly, looking for his lost books. And his missing picture? For tonight he seemed more impatient than usual, like a man at the end of his tether. Suddenly she heard his step on the stair. Tonight, for the first time, he was coming *down!*

"*My Master,*" Mr. Tuke had said.

Come to take possession at last.

Suddenly she heard someone at the door. The new lodger, thank God. But no knock came. Just a faint, persistent sound moving closer—from the knocker on the door to the big brass knob in the hall to the kettle in the kitchen; closer and closer—to the andirons and the candlesticks and the trays in the sitting room; rubbing, rubbing, rubbing. She clutched the arms of her chair. Mrs. Tuke had come at last.

THE CORRECTOR OF DESTINIES

by Edward Wellen

It doesn't seem possible, after more than a century and a quarter of detective-story writing, after literally hundreds of thousands, perhaps millions, of novels, novelettes, and short stories have been written about imagined detectives, that someone could come up with a new type of crimebuster. But Edward Wellen has—that is, to the best of our fallible memory, we have never previously read a story about this particular species of sleuth.

Historically speaking, Mr. Wellen's detective is "The Corrector of Destinies" rather than "The Man of Last Resort"; but generically speaking, he is both. . . .

And now we will let you discover the new 'tec type for yourself. . . .

I stuck my finger in the law book to hold my place and raised my head and then an eyebrow. It was Number 10805. He still had the polished politeness of outside, still carried his station in life with him.

"I hope I'm not interrupting you, but this is the first chance—"

I sighed inside but worked up a smile and said, "Not at all. Sit down, sit down." I had to get over that habit of repeating myself. Unless the man bounced on sitting down, one "sit down" was enough. "What's on your mind?"

His case was on his mind, of course. Every prisoner always

had his own case on his mind. He leaned forward and told me about it.

"I managed a branch of a big brokerage firm. This night I was staying late at the office, catching up on paperwork. About eight o'clock a man wearing some kind of bank messenger's uniform came in and pointed a gun at me." He smiled. "My wife had me on the phone at the time, complaining about my not coming home and when I saw that gun pointing at me the phone fell from between my cheek and my shoulder. I remember the receiver swinging back and forth and her voice fading in and out saying, 'Lamont, are you listening? Lamont, what's wrong?'

"The man waved me away from my desk and picked up the dangling phone and said, 'Sorry, honey. He's busy right now.' And he hung up. He was wearing gloves, so I figured him for a professional. He certainly knew what he was after. He had me unlock the cage and we went in and he helped himself to $2,000,000 worth of bearer bonds. He taped my hands together behind my back, sat me down on the floor, then taped my feet together.

"That's how they found me an hour later when my wife got worried enough or mad enough to phone the cops after getting no answer to her calls. They never found the man and they never got the bonds back."

He leaned nearer. "Now here's the thing that gets me." He looked more bewildered than bitter, as though he still didn't know what had hit him. "The man got past the building's night-security man by showing a note from me on one of my noteheads that said to let him in. The note was in my handwriting, which is distinctive enough for Pat, the building's night-security man, to recognize, but the trouble is I never wrote it."

I took that in, then shook my head. "No, the trouble is the note was in your handwriting."

His mouth was a twist of lemon. "Yes, the note was in my handwriting, though I tell you again I didn't write it. Pat had kept it and they had that as evidence against me. They said the note was just a cover. They said the whole thing was an inside job, that I was in with the Mob."

"Were you?"

He didn't get mad. "Hell, no. I admit I liked to gamble now and then—and what's the stock market but the biggest gamble of all?—and I did lose some money in Las Vegas, though not as much as they said I did."

"They brought that out at your trial?"

"If they could've, they would've brought out a candy bar I stole when I was six." Now he looked more bitter than bewildered. "The prosecutor tried to make all kinds of deals with me. But I had nothing to bargain with. I had never seen the stickup man before, still don't know who he was. I couldn't return all or any of the two million dollars. The bonding company didn't believe me. My firm didn't believe me. They leaned on the prosecutor, but I don't think they had to lean hard. He threw the book at me. And the jury bound it in leather and the judge stamped it in gold."

I decided I liked the man. Whether or not he was conning me, he still held onto his sense of humor about himself and the fix he was in. But the first hundred years were the hardest, and he had a long way yet to go. Unless I could help him.

"That's it then? You got a bum rap and you want to get out?"

"Of course I want to get out. I hate having to pay for someone else's crime. True, I don't have much to go back to—my wife left me—but I do have my name to clear."

I looked at him. Was that true? Or did he have his share of $2,000,000 to go back to? I guess I stared, but his eyes met mine without wavering.

But that doesn't mean a thing. A good con man can out-stare and out-honest-countenance a saint.

I liked what I saw of him, but the one thing I can't stand is to have someone con me. But I could judge him only on the basis of my instincts. My deliberation was brief: I quickly brought in my verdict: the man was sincere.

He seemed to sense that I had committed myself, for he relaxed a bit. But the sweat of the brow was just beginning for me.

If he hadn't been in on the pulling of the job, how explain the note? The court had bought it as a stupid and clumsy way of getting the accomplice in. But Number 10805 seemed neither stupid nor clumsy.

He seemed bright, and bright people make the best subjects. I took my finger out of the law book and wagged it like
a metronome.

"Now look here, follow this closely, I want you to concen-
trate, this is a very heavy matter we're dealing with. . . ."

He followed my finger with growing puzzlement as I in-
toned slowly and soothingly. Then he snapped his gaze from
my finger and laughed. He shook his head.

"You want to see if someone could've hypnotized me into
writing that note. The answer's no." He took a deep breath
and elaborated on it. "A few years ago I went to a dentist who
specializes in using hypnosis to calm patients with an unrea-
sonable but real fear of the dentist's chair. He tried to put me
under. He just couldn't. Something in me puts up too much
resistance to going under. So I had to go back to the Nov-
ocain injections which leave my gums sore and puff up my
face."

"So you didn't write the note consciously or unconsciously.
But you say the note's genuine. How genuine?"

"The prosecution brought in handwriting experts to prove
under great magnification that the note was in my handwriting."

"Come on now, don't tell me you didn't have your own
handwriting expert."

"I did. And he got on the stand and said pretty smugly that
the note wasn't in my handwriting. But he crumpled under
cross-examination. I could tell the jury didn't believe him.
Even I didn't believe him. He only made my case worse."

I felt his eyes on me as I looked around at the shelves and
shelves of law volumes. In my time I had thumbed through
them all. Something in them should offer Number 10805 an
out. No; legal ploys would have to wait till we had sorted out
the truth about that note. There was no way of getting
around it. We had to face it.

The whole thing of the note smelled fishy. I swiveled to
meet his gaze and shot the question at him as it surfaced in
my mind.

"Why didn't the building's night-security man—Pat?—
phone up to you to confirm the note?"

"Pat said he tried to, but couldn't get me. As I told you, my wife was on the line at the time. The office switchboard was off and only my phone was working. So Pat gave up, shrugged at the irregularity, and let the man in. He was certain it was my handwriting—or at least my signature."

I struck quickly at the opening. "What do you mean by that?"

"It's been puzzling me where anyone could have got samples of my handwriting. Of my signature yes, but not of my handwriting. I dictate—dictated—all my correspondence, and typed whatever notes I made—I can hunt and peck with the best."

I frowned. Then I smoothed my brow, making it a *tabula rasa* for the new thought I felt coming. "What did the note say? Can you remember the exact wording?"

"Can I?" He smiled grimly. "It's burned into my brain. The exact words were, 'Pat, Let delivery man in,' and then my signature."

I turned my pad to a fresh sheet and printed: Pat, Let delivery man in.

"That right?"

He craned to see, and nodded.

"Good," I said. "Now let's alphabetize it."

I put the letters into alphabetical order.

a a d e e e i i L l m n n P r t t y

I looked at Number 10805. "What's your full name?"

For a moment Number 10805 gave the appearance of having forgotten it. Then he got it out. "Lamont van der Pleyster."

I set that down and he nodded that I had it right. "Good," I said. "Now let's alphabetize that." I put the letters of his name into alphabetical order.

a a d e e e L l m n n o P r r s t t v y

"See the likeness? Except for the 'i' there's not a letter in the note, capitalized or uncapitalized, that isn't in your signature. All a guy'd need are two samples of your signature. One he'd use as is, to sign the note. The other, which would be necessary to get the slight variety that's natural, he'd snip into separate letters. Then he'd juggle the snippets to form the note, Scotch-tape them in place, put a blank piece of your notehead on top, and trace the words, using either a light box or a window on a bright day. Result, an almost perfect forgery."

He hammered his fist on the library table. I turned quickly to shake my head at the guard standing by the door and the guard went back to doing nothing.

"Sorry," Lamont van der Pleyster said. "But it hit me how right you are. Something about the wording always bothered me. Now I know what it is. If I had written the note, I wouldn't've said 'delivery man.' I would've said 'bank messenger.' But there is no 'b' or 'k' or 'g' in my name, and I guess an 'i' is the easiest letter to imitate."

"True, true," I said, suddenly weary for no reason. I spoke briskly to wind it up. "Tomorrow or the next day I'll fix you up with a writ of *coram nobis*—a writ of review based on an alleged error of fact. When the handwriting experts take another and closer look at those 'i's' in the note placed in evidence, the fact of forgery should become plain. And you'll have your chance to show the court how someone framed you and got you sent up."

His face had taken on a look of release. I tried to hide my pity. I had a hunch about the someone who framed him.

His wife and the "delivery man" had to be in it together. Two things pointed to it: her well-timed phone call that prevented Pat from confirming the note and her easy access to his signature and notehead.

His former wife, I should say. She'd left him. And that should help the case resolve itself. His lawyer through private investigators, or the law on its own, would either find his former wife and the delivery man living together somewhere or find that the pair had split up. If the man was still with her, he should be a cinch for Pat to identify. If he had tired of her in the meanwhile and ditched her, she might be more than willing to finger the man when they caught up with her.

All that went through my head while he heaped me with thanks. "Sure, sure," I said casually, because all the expressions of gratitude and the promises to remember me that have bent my ear over the years add up to a garden full of withered forget-me-nots.

I glanced at the wall clock and got up, saying, "Time to get back to my gardening. See you later." I shelved the law volume and made for the door. While nodding at the guard I glanced caressingly at the books lining the walls of the prison law library and told myself for the ten-thousandth time that one day I would find the key to my own case—the key that would get me out.

I nodded left and right to the cons in the yard as I crossed to my rosebushes in the shop building's L. All but one or two, and they were new fish, gave me a nod back or a good word.

But I knew what they said about me—that the old lifer could help everyone but himself, that deep down he really didn't want out, that he had become too institutionalized to face the outside world as a free man.

I smiled at the cons but I was really smiling to myself. They did not know that, no matter how my own case turned out in the end, they, by coming to me to resolve their legal problems, were in a way helping me escape.

RIGHT ON, CHICK!
by S. S. Rafferty

*Chick Kelly, the medium-time nightclub comic with a slan-
guage all his own, was finding show biz tough. Out-of-town
bookings were as scarce as roosters' eggs, so Chick opened up
a small Third Avenue club to keep doing his act.*
   Kelly's calling card might read:

Chick the Dick

Comedy Schticks and 'Tec Tricks

A refreshing change of reading pace—right on, Chick!

WHEN I quit the road and opened up a small Third Avenue
night club, I thought I'd left all my troubles behind me. I
overlooked two important details. One, that the national
economy was going to opt for instant poverty; two, that my
sister would now have my phone number. She sometimes
uses it instead of 911, Manhattan's police emergency number.

Lila was born with a silver panic button in her hand, so I
have learned to divide everything she dreams up by seven.
That's not a bad rating on the Chick Kelly Reality Index. I
know some guys—most of them producers and press

143

agents—who are divisible by forty-eight before you get to the truth.

It's about 6:00 p.m. and I am at the joint having a business breakfast with Barry Kantrowitz, my former agent and present partner. Barry was as successful an agent as I was a comic, so we were made for each other. Barry is divisible by three.

Of course, having breakfast with Barry is no great culinary experience. How any guy can eat shredded wheat with milk is beyond me. It's like eating a wet mattress. I go for the Brisbane Special—a rare strip sirloin, eggs over easy, hash browns, and plenty of mayonnaise.

I'm halfway through the first egg when Ling, my headwaiter, comes over and tells me that Lila is on the phone to inform me that my niece and nephew have been kidnapped.

I might as well have been talking to a farmer in Outer Mongolia for all the sense I got out of her. The children had been missing for five hours, and since they were the only witnesses to the D.A.'s killing, it had to be a snatch. And if I ever loved her, I would start negotiations with the underworld for their safe return.

This is some breakfast conversation! I told her to put Arthur, her husband, on, but she said he was at police headquarters. I told her I would be over pronto, hung up, and started dividing by seven.

My nephew and niece are 14 and 9 respectively. Flip is a big kid. To spirit him away would require all seven of the Santini Brothers and a large van. His sister, McCawber, is a human eel, and it would take fancy footwork just to shake her hand.

At this point, folks, you're probably asking yourself what's with the names? I can take credit only for Flip. McCawber was her father's idea. Arthur McQuade (pronounce that AH-thur, as in AHdvertising agency) is more in love with his ancestors than the Dalai Lama. The girl is named after James Petny McCawber, who invented the inkwell or something. Flip's real name is Foster Chapin McQuade, and God help him. Arthur did not take it kindly when I suggested that a kid named Foster sounded like he was being raised by someone else for pay. How could I introduce him? Meet my Foster nephew? So I call him Flip. Mostly because he's all mouth ("like someone else I know," my mother would add).

Normally I would write the whole thing off as two kids being late for dinner, but the D.A. killing got to me. It's time to get on the think, which I do.

I tell Ling to get me a copy of the *Post*, which, when you think of it, is like asking Walter Cronkite to tune in NBC for the latest news report. Ling reads more newspapers than a presidential adviser.

"What do you want to know, boss?" he says with a hurt look on his face. I had really wounded the guy.

"What's with the D.A. being murdered?"

"Not the D.A. An assistant. He was the prosecutor in the Siepi case. They found his body behind a soda-pop machine in the East 14th Street IRT subway station this afternoon."

Ling goes on to give me the picture, spitting out data like a teletype. Miles Corbett was an ambitious Assistant District Attorney, and the Siepi case was his first big shot at the headlines. I was already familiar with the Siepi hassle. They had nailed old Gino with a Murder One for knocking off Sally Bond. In my book it was a draw.

Gino Siepi was a hood and Sally was an ex-tramp who made her bread by blackmail. Good old Gino the Sappy was the last person seen leaving Sally's apartment on the night she got it. The boys in blue played tag and Gino lost.

So where does this leave me? *Did* the kids see Corbett get it? This Ling cannot answer, so it's back to Ma Bell for me.

Believe it or not, there are a few cops who like me. Not love me, mind you, but like me. One of them is Steve Kozak. Steve is a sergeant on the Vice Squad and we have mutual friends.

Steve tells me that he doesn't know too much about the case except that the cops didn't want to take Siepi to trial. The evidence was full of holes, but Corbett, being top man while the D.A. was out of town, insisted. For three days he's getting his pants beaten off in court, and it looks like Siepi will soon be walking the streets again. Then on Wednesday, Corbett makes a grandstand play for the TV cameras and announces he will bring in vital evidence the next day.

"We told him it was a dumb thing to do," Steve tells me, "but a guy who wants to be Governor someday has to create cliffhangers for the public. As for the snatch, I'm empty. Sorry about the kids. Give me ten minutes and I'll dig around."

Now I'm getting scared. It's the gut response when trouble decides to sit on your porch instead of someone else's.

The phone ringing was as startling as a clang out of hell. It was Kozak with a spadeful.

Corbett had left his apartment on East 86th Street yesterday morning at 8:45. According to his wife, he was carrying an envelope in his briefcase which he had picked up at Kennedy Airport the night before around midnight.

At this point the police theory was that Sally Bond, being the bright girl she was, had salted away her blackmail dope with someone out of town. It was the old "If something happens to me, open this envelope and spill the beans." That someone got in touch with Corbett and flew in with the goods.

"So how do the kids figure in?" I asked him.

"Your niece and nephew were on the same subway as Corbett. The little girl recognized him on television when they announced his murder. She said he had been sitting across from her all the way from 77th Street, and just before the train pulled into the 14th Street station he bolted into the next car. She remembered that he had been carrying an unusual-looking briefcase—Corbett's was made of ostrich skin. Lieutenant Jaffee thinks that Corbett saw his killer and was trying to get away. He also thinks your niece may have seen the killer, too."

"*Jaffee!* Is Jaffee on the case?"

"Yeah, Chick, so I'd stay clean if I were you."

Early on I said a few cops like me. Jaffee hates me. He has never forgiven me for getting out of a murder rap when a lady was found dead in my apartment.

"Does he know the kids are relatives of mine?"

"I don't know, but what's the difference? He'll do a good job anyway."

That I had to give him. I have seen Jaffee in action and he's good. Believe me, I respect my enemies.

"The thing that gets me, Steve, is how you guys got a line on the kids."

"Their father called in Thursday night after the little girl recognized Corbett's picture on a TV newscast about his murder."

Good old AH-thur, the civic-minded goon. If he had kept his mouth shut, the kids would now be safe. I made a mental memo to break AH-thur's neck when all this was over.

"Didn't Jaffee put a guard on the kids? He drops them into this mess, makes them a target, then doesn't guard them?"

"That's what's odd about this, Chick. He had three men outside their apartment building, one in the rear and two in the lobby. All good eye men. They never saw the kids leave. Jaffee's had the building searched twice."

"Why didn't he put someone right outside the door?"

"Mrs. McQuade wouldn't allow it."

Oh, yes, the old Kelly family bugaboo—what will the neighbors think?

"So what's happening, Steve? Was it one of Siepi's morons?"

"That's the party line at the moment, but they've all gone beddy-bye. But you can't discount anyone who was in the Bond dame's little black book. We estimate that crowd to be about a hundred, so take your pick."

Sweet sufferin' Saint Sebastian! My palms are beginning to sweat. I have loved very few things in my life, even an ex-wife or two, but those two kids really ring the gong with me. Right now I want to get a machine gun and knock off every hood in town until I find them. But that's Nutsville.

"Tell me straight, Steve, do you think they'll knock them off?" My throat is getting very tight, and I'm fighting back a crybaby bit.

"Straight, Chick, I really don't know. If it was Siepi's boys, I don't think so. Hoods don't usually kill kids. They'd probably just hold them until their hit man gets out of the country. But if it was someone else, one of the people being blackmailed, you can't tell. But take it easy. You sound shaky. Jaffee has every available man on the street. He's set up a command post at the 19th Precinct, so you know where not to show up."

I hung up, went back to my table, and near got sick looking at the steak and eggs. Ling had gone out and bought the bulldog edition of the *News*, which had pictures of the kids. I have the same ones on my dresser. Ling is reading the recap, but I am hardly paying attention. Then a sentence hits me and I ask Ling for a repeat.

"Police are asking anyone who saw a person carrying an ostrich-skin briefcase in the vicinity of the Union Square station of the IRT around 8:45 Friday morning to come forward."

Now that strikes me as funny. That's the hazard of being a comic. You see and hear the oddball things in life. The sight of a guy who has just murdered someone in a crowd walking around with his victim's briefcase—in ostrich yet—is just inviting attention. Yet, if he took the blackmail dope out of the case, he would surely dump the case, wouldn't he? Anywhere, just to get rid of it. Now, in little old New York, an expensive briefcase left sitting somewhere does not go homeless for long. In fact, out at Kennedy, it is the basis for an entire industry.

I don't know what Jaffee is thinking right now, but that briefcase intrigues me. If he has a command post, I can have one too, so I go into action. First, I tell Ling to call Mario Puccini, who runs a small limousine service out of 76th Street. When he shows up, I give him a sack of money and tell him to start hitting the hack stands and hangouts like the Belmore at 23rd and Lex and Kaye's at 78th and Lex. There are more cabs in New York than patrol cars, so right away I'm ahead of Jaffee on surveillance. Since the kids' pictures are in the *News* and cabbies wouldn't be caught dead without a copy, they knew what faces to look for.

Now I have to find out where Siepi's boys have dived for the mattresses. Jaffee, I know, is pulling in every stoolie in town, but he's kidding himself. No stoolie is going to sing a medley that ends up with "Old Man River." Okay, I've got an angle. Ziggy Klein fronts the five-man combo that plays my joint on weekends. If you want to find out what's going on under the scalp of New York, get a bunch of musicians together and have them ask questions. They're into the scene. Ziggy and his boys get busy with their contracts.

I get these pots simmering and reach for another. Who was on Sally Bond's Hit Parade of Secret Sins? Ten years ago this would have been an easier task. But since the unions have decided there were too many newspapers in New York and buried all but two, there aren't too many gossip scribes around with that kind of info. So I turn to Tish Loman, whom I don't particularly like, but she digs me and I'm kind of a rat with women. Tish tosses parties for a living. Yes, folks, there are people so anxious to get into society that they hire people to throw a party for them. Tish knows every celebrity in the city and all the dirt besides. However, I do not feel like being charming at the moment, so I send Barry Kantrowitz to her place as my emissary. I have other fish to fry.

On my way up to 86th Street I ask the driver if he's on my payroll and he says he is. He also gives me his theory of the whole affair. If there are 2000 hacks on the street, there have got to be 3000 different theories. It is an occupational disease with these guys.

I was surprised, but relieved, to find that Jaffee had not planted one of his boys outside the Corbetts' apartment door.

The guy who answered the buzzer was a tall good-looking kid who told me that his sister, Mrs. Corbett, could not be disturbed. The death of her husband had floored her and the doctor had her under sedation. He was about to give me the heave-ho when I told him who I was.

"Chick Kelly. The comedian! Well, how are you? I'm in the business myself in a way. I'm a drama student at Columbia."

He said his name was Ted Saunders and that he lived with his sister and brother-in-law when school wasn't in session, which it wasn't. Come to think of it, the McQuade kids were on vacation, too.

Saunders invites me in and I can tell he is trying to build a show-business contact. I should have told him that I had to open my own club to keep doing my act, but why spoil it? I needed information. Saunders is full of information because he has already done the audition for the police.

It seems his brother-in-law left the apartment around 11:30 p.m. on Wednesday to go to Kennedy Airport and didn't get back until about 3:00 a.m., then went straight to his den where he stayed until 5:00 or 5:30 a.m. He got some sleep and left for court around 8:45.

"Yes," Saunders said, "the briefcase was unique. My sister had it made in Mexico last year. Miles was very proud of—"

He stopped short when a woman in a wrapper walked into

the living room. She was probably a stunner under normal conditions, but right now she looked like hell.

"More police questions?" she asked with a weary kind of exasperation.

"No, Stella, Mr. Kelly isn't from the police. He's Chick Kelly—you know, the comedian. Mr. Kelly, my sister, Mrs. Corbett."

"Oh, Lord, what next? Police, Chinese orphans, and now a comedian! Are you a friend of Ted's, Mr. Kelly?"

I didn't get a chance to answer because Saunders had already shot a question.

"Chinese orphans? Stella, maybe you should cut back on that sedative, honey. You sound a little delirious."

"Ted, stop treating me like a child. There were two Chinese orphans here when you were out this afternoon. Collecting for war orphans. I gave them a dollar just to get rid of them."

The conversation went on between brother and sister and I know it's time to do a dissolve. I fast-talk my way out of there with a story about knowing the late Mr. Corbett and dropping by to pay my respects.

It took three tries before I found a phone that worked, which is a remarkable feat in itself, the odds usually being five to one. I plunk in a dime and when Lila's voice comes on, I tell her to shut up and listen.

"Last Halloween the kids went to that school dance as Chinese, didn't they?" She gives me a yes and I tell her to check the closets. Lila is confused but obedient, and when she comes back with the news that the costumes are missing, I shout hallelujah and tell her that her children are no more kidnapped than I am and that when we turn them up I want first licks.

Back at the club, things are really humming. The cabbies haven't turned up anything, but Ziggy's boys are firing on all sixes. Siepi's boys have holed up in a private house on Staten Island. That's a trade card for my eventual confrontation with Jaffee. I also put out the word to the cabbies that we are no longer looking for the charming McQuade tots, but to keep the brights on for Lum Foo and his panhandling sister.

I was beginning to think that Barry Kantrowitz had eloped

with Tish Loman, but he turns up finally, and has he got some nuggets. Now I'm ready for Jaffee and I'm enjoying myself immensely. Of course, my original concern was to find the kids, but now I had Jaffee to show up. Maybe it's my nature to be an SOB, maybe not. But Jaffee had worked me over once, and I wanted to get even. As Rodney Dangerfield, a fellow comic, says, "I don't get no respect," and I wanted some respect from that hard-nosed Lieutenant.

The 19th Precinct is on East 67th Street. You can always tell a cop from the 19th—they have a built-in bored look from standing guard outside foreign Embassies all day and night. They ought to float the UN over to Hoboken and save the city a lot of money. The move wouldn't hurt Hoboken any, either.

Lieutenant Jaffee is a rough piece of work. He's built like a tank and has a shiny dome. The men in the Division call him Bullethead. They tell me he got a law degree going to NYU nights, which gives me a great line about his studying in the dark.

I wasn't two feet into the squadroom when he spots me and lowers the boom.

"What the hell do you want, Kelly?" my old pal greets me with a snarl. "Beat it."

"Hello, Lieutenant, nice to see you again." As you may have guessed, I can be very charming.

"Look, Jokeboy, I don't need you around here. Scram."

"Whoa, Lieutenant, just a sec. I have an interest in this case you're on."

"Your niece and nephew. I know. But I won't hold that against the McQuades. I haven't any news, and if I did, I'd tell your sister, not you."

"That's proper. No argument from me. But I have some news, and I thought I'd give it to you rather than the newspapers. You see, Lieutenant, I have an affection for you. I want in every way to—"

"Cut the trimmings, will you, Kelly? If you have some information, dish it out. I'm not that vain."

I'm thinking "a guy with a bullethead should be vain?" If Jaffee was a heckler in an audience, I would really take him apart. You know, like, "Well, I see the Fifth Artillery is in town," or "Aren't you glad the war is over so you can get parts for your head?" But I know Jaffee has a low boiling point beyond which he is not adverse to using his hands in the clenched position, so I stow the wisecracks and get down to business.

When I tell him about the kids wandering around dressed like Orientals, he first doesn't believe me. Then he does believe me and almost cannonades himself through the ceiling. It's beautiful. Then he tells a flunky to put the word out to the patrols and chews another one out for being a wall-eyed idiot. I assumed he was one of the great eye men at my sister's apartment.

After he gets that done, Jaffee gives me a piece of his mind about my probably being a bad influence on the kids and that if he were my brother-in-law he would make sure they never saw me. Bullethead as my brother-in-law! The one I've got is no peach, but Jaffee! My God, I'd commit sororicide, and even nephewcide and nieceacide.

"I know you feel very jubilant, Kelly, but don't take any comfort from it. I almost wish Siepi's guys did have them. At least they'd be safe."

"What are you talking about, Jaffee? Safe?"

"Those kids are out there somewhere playing amateur detective, and you can bet someone is gunning for them. That's not funny."

You know, he was right. I hadn't thought of that. If the entire police force couldn't find them and a thousand cabbies couldn't spot them, how could a lone killer do it? But still and all, it was a fact that wouldn't go away.

Okay, enough of jaffing at Jaffee. I gave him the five names Tish had come up with and he grins.

"You can forget about Jeb Farrell the decorator and Phil Morgan the fight promoter. They're accounted for at the time of the murder. Why look so surprised, Kelly? We sift through dirt, too. As for McIlroy, we have a possible. He's been known to toss some weird parties and could be a blackmail victim, although he denies it. He says he was walking in Central Park at the time of the killing. Hah! The other two are new to me. We'll check it out, but this Phyllis Court doesn't fit into the picture. This was a man's job, I'm sure of it. The last one, Calvin West, who's he?"

"My sources say he's a painter with a past. No one knows too much about him."

"Your source is Tish Loman, so stop being coy. You just can't leave the ladies alone, can you, Kelly?"

Someday I am going to devote a whole day trying to analyze why Jaffee dislikes me. I am getting a sneaking suspicion it has to do with women. With his looks Jaffee couldn't attract Tugboat Annie. When we have time I'll do a whole number for you on my approach to women. It's cool, man, cool.

Jaffee is busy sending out his underlings to check on the names and is ignoring me.

"What are you going to do about the kids, Lieutenant?"

"What the hell do you think I'm going to do? Only now it won't be so difficult. I think I know where they are."

"Yeah? Where do you think?"

"Two kids dressed up like Orientals stand out in a crowd, and if this nephew of yours is half as smart as his mother thinks, then there's only one place they'd head for. Chinatown."

"But they don't know anyone in Chinatown."

"They don't have to know anyone. It's the Chinese New Year and there'll be dancing in the streets all night. Hanragan," he said to one of his plainclothesmen, "get Mrs. McQuade on the phone and find out if either child has a Chinese classmate. They could be holing up there."

I started to leave when Jaffee barked at me, "Kelly, you stay the hell out of Chinatown, do you hear me? I've got experts in that district and they can comb it clean without your help. By the way, you may care to know they're celebrating the Year of the Rat."

So Jaffee wants to play zap. He's a creampuff.

"Oh, by the way, Lieutenant, I've been so busy digging up names for you to check and finding out about the kids that I didn't have time to rush out to 241 Elizabeth Street in Tottenville. That's in Staten Island, you know. You take the ferry over the waves. That's where you'll find Siepi's brood. Out in Tottenville at 241 Elizabeth Street they are celebrating the Year of the Dope."

I am out of there like a shot, flag a cab, and head back for the club. I've just got time to do the eleven o'clock show. I quiz the driver and he tells me he's been clued in on the Chinese switch. I start wondering how much this is all costing me. Then I start planning just how I am going to punish my nephew. There is that season pass to the Knicks that I could lift. No, that's capital punishment and that's been outlawed. But why plan? He won't be able to see after AH-thur gets hold of him.

It was a wild night. The eleven o'clock show went over good, but the two o'clock brought in a bunch of drunks, which is par. I stayed at the club all night so I could act on any calls from cabbies—I didn't completely cotton to the Chinatown theory. We got a nibble about seven o'clock in the morning, but it turned out to be two real Chinese kids in the Bronx. It was the first time I had seen the sun come up in seven years. It hadn't changed much.

Then, at 10:30, we got a hot tip. A driver spotted two Chinese kids in the 300 block on Jay Street in Brooklyn, then lost them. He thinks they might have ducked into one of the buildings, so he's standing watch. I tell him to keep the meter running, then I make a jump for Mario's waiting limo, and barrel out there.

We cruised up and down the 300 block, but no kids. Then it hit me. Why would they come all the way over to Brooklyn, I'm asking myself, when bango! There it is in front of me. The Transit Authority Building. The whole thing started on the subway, didn't it? What a dummy I am. Flip is a smart little son of a gun.

The guy behind the Lost and Found counter did a double take when I asked him.

"What's with the ostrich briefcases?" he says, giving a silent *oy veh* with the hands. I'm the third to ask that question this morning. First it was the guy with the mustache, and then it was the two kids, Chinese kids, and now me. More silent *oy vehs* and then he says the kids were there about twenty minutes ago. He can't tell me much about the first guy, just that he had a mustache and a scar on his cheek.

Back in the parked limo, I am trying to focus in on the faces on Tish's list, but no luck. No guy with a mustache and scar.

"Why would Flip come down here anyway?" Mario asks me. "If someone found it they would give it to the cops."

"The kid was on the right track, Mario. Because the other

guy came down here, too. Now that guy's got two problems. He has two kids running around loose who might be able to identify him, and the blackmail papers are also floating around somewhere. I'm trying to visualize what Corbett must have done on that subway. He spots this dude and knows he's going to get it, so he tries to beat him into the next car. Now he couldn't have stashed the briefcase in the 14th Street station because the cops have pulled it apart and found zero."

"Hey, Chick, I ain't been on a subway for years," Mario says from the front seat, "but why didn't that D.A. get off at 18th Street if he spotted the guy at 23rd?"

"Mostly because there isn't an 18th Street station, Mario."

"Hell, there ain't. I used to date a bimbo on East 19th Street years ago and always got off at that station."

I didn't bother to mention it to Mario, but I think we knew the same bimbo because I remember getting off at 18th Street too, on the same mission. I'm out of the car and back into the Transit Authority lickety-split. I ask the guy at the Lost and Found what happened to the IRT 18th Street station, and do you know what I get? "Did someone lose it?" he asks. Everyone wants to be a comic.

"Look, you're breaking me up, pal. Just give me a straight answer."

"Yeah, they closed it down about ten, fifteen years ago. It was some kind of economy drive. I forgot it was there, to be honest with you."

"Maybe it was demolished. You know, sealed up or something?"

"Maybe the entrance, but not the station. Why bother?"

When I got back to the car and asked Mario for the gun, he gave me the Alice in Wonderland routine.

"Come on, Mario, you've hauled iron around in this heap for years. Give. Please?"

"But, Chick, you don't have no license."

"Neither do you, buddy. Is it sterile?"

He gives me a nod, hands me the gun, and I slip it into my pocket. I've got an idea in my head that's going to make Jaffee the joke of the Department. I tell Mario to get back to the club. I can get where I'm going faster by the rattler.

At the Jay Street station I grab the IND and get off at Sixth and Fourteenth. I probably could have figured a route to take me directly to the 14th Street station at Union Square, but I really didn't have five years to spend. Besides, the best way to go is the way you know. I came up on Sixth (okay, Avenue of the Americas) and headed east, stopping at one of the rag shops where I bought a genuine Japanese flashlight. With all the Jap goods flooding the country, I'm beginning to think they really did win World War II.

I flagged a cab and had him take me to 18th and Park and found just what I expected. No entrance. I then hoofed down to the 14th Street station, went through the turnstile, and pushed my way to the downtown local track.

There is one criticism leveled at New Yorkers that is unfair. People, mostly tourists, think that local citizens are indifferent and cold. They're just minding their own bloody business, folks! Now if I were in Cleveland, and Cleveland had a subway, someone would wonder what a guy was doing entering a dark subway tunnel and report it. Not in New York, baby. If you want to go for a stroll up the tracks, you can go right ahead and nobody will make a peep.

I waited till a downtown local train had cleared the station, then slipped down the narrow stairs to the track and ran like hell toward 18th Street. Up ahead of me I could see the headlights of another train, probably as far up as 33rd Street. I have read that if you lie down in the center of the tracks, a train will roll over you without touching you, but I wasn't about to prove the theory. Old Fleetfoot Kelly made it in plenty of time in the half light of the tunnel.

The 18th Street station was something out of a Fellini movie. It was a complete station with its tiled walls, muted change booth, and stairs that led nowhere. It was something dead. A tomb.

I came up on the platform on all fours. The station had about four dirty 40-watt bulbs burning a dull illumination that created a bevy of shadows. A painter broad I used to know would call it chiaroscuro, and the chiaroscuro was scaring the devil out of me. I heard a scurrying in the corner and reeled with the gun ready to find a rat or something, when I found two rats in Chinese clothing.

"Uncle Chick, baby," that young punk says to me with his

sister hanging on his arm. Man, I wanted to bust him one in the chops.

"Boy, you two are beautiful, really beautiful. What are you trying to do, give your mother a heart attack?"

"Chick, we solved it, man, don't you dig it?" he says, holding up the ostrich briefcase. His father sends him to one of the best schools in the city, and he talks like a hipped sideman.

"Yeah, I dig, Foster."

"What's with the Foster bit, Chick?"

"Uncle Charles to you, buster. How are you doing, McCawber?"

The light of my life says she's okay, but I know she's scared. She comes to me and I give her a hug. That's the chimpanzee syndrome. And she's part monkey anyway. I had put the gun in my pocket and was holding her when I heard him.

"Bring the case over here, kid," the voice said from the dark end of the platform. "Don't move, Kelly."

Flip walked into the shadow, then came back without the briefcase and stood next to me. I would jam the bloody gun in my jacket pocket where I couldn't get it out easily!

"Look, pal," I said to the voice, "I can't see who you are, so let's call it even. You scamper out of here and we'll forget the whole thing. You're as free as a big beaked bird. We'll wait here for ten minutes—an hour if you like."

He didn't answer and I knew his silence was going to be killing *us*. I couldn't see him, but my ears are like sonar webs. He hadn't moved since he had last said his piece, so I had a blind fix on him. I have played soldier with the kids since they were old enough to hate Pablum, so I hoped they'd remember the script.

I yelled as loud as I could, "Hit the deck!" and dove into the dark at the voice.

I was almost on him when I felt the burn in my arm. I had one hand on him and we both went down. There was no scuffle—he was motionless. Jaffee's shot had gone through Ted Saunders, Corbett's wife's brother, and plinked me in the arm . . .

Jaffee was, of course, full of threats; there was my carrying iron, trespassing on subway tracks, interfering with a police investigation, and contributing to the delinquency of minors. The last was AH-thur's two cents.

What really ticked Bullethead off was the interview I gave to the media. I told them I knew it was Ted Saunders all along. He could easily have had a peek at the papers Corbett brought back from the airport, and he could have known the kids were in Oriental dress. My theory was that Teddy-boy had seen a lucrative future in the papers Corbett had gotten, and went after them. I also added that Columbia's Drama School should beef up its course on makeup. Ted's phony mustache and scar were from hunger. I had him on voice anyway; that's why I tried to fake him out with the escape bit.

One TV newsman went bananas over my heroics and called my leap at Saunders Kierkegaardian. And we all know what a fine acrobat he was.

Anyway, I got the headlines and the club is jammed with tourists who want to meet the great comic-detective. No, that's not right—the great detective-comic.

Just before I went on for the eleven o'clock show, McCawber calls me to tell me they are grounded for six weekends. And I tell her that's cruel and inhuman punishment and that she should get herself a lawyer. Before I hang up, she wants to know if she and Flip really have to call me "Uncle Charles." She doesn't like "Uncle Charles."

I'm about to say okay, but I can never resist an opening. "Maybe, if you're really good for a while. But for the time being you can call me 'Uncle Rocco.'" That ought to drive AH-thur up the wall a few times.

Right on, Chick!

SCREAMS AND ECHOES
by Donald Olson

At first this story may strike you as strange, perhaps as the strangest story you have read in years. But there is nothing strange about it—not really. It is a story of our times, and it has a great deal to tell us—of the way it was, of the way it is. . . .

After that first invasion they came every day, and it was frightening. . . .

LAST MONTH I called someone from the State Conservation Department to come over and look at the maples, having noticed how the leaves on the lower branches were turning brown and shriveling up; when I examined one of them I found a black larva wrapped in a sticky web within the folded leaf. I don't suppose the man will come now—not that it matters any more—and even if I wanted to I couldn't call him again: the phone has been removed and now there's no link at all with what lies out there beyond that ragged line of hills—no radio, no TV, no phone.

Not that it can last, of course, nor do I expect it to, even if my daughter Margaret does. "Progress" moves much faster than human life; its hideous tide will engulf us long before any disease has had time to settle within my organs, like that dry black worm in the folded leaf.

Louise was appalled the one and only time she was here.

"A cynic's Eden," she dubbed it sourly. The necessity of

leaving her car on the other side of the ridge and taking the footpath the rest of the way had outraged her comfort-conscious body, dulled her appreciation of the sublimity of the view, and horrified her exalted sense of the social proprieties—she couldn't believe we had neither friends nor acquaintances out here. The recent death of her husband Larry had given her a less remote view of mortality and put the sort of scare into her for which fifty years of perfect health and pampering had left her unprepared. My sister Louise is neither devious nor tactful; even in childhood I had recoiled from the abrasiveness of her manner, and that jarring encounter with death had rendered her even less inclined to diplomacy.

"I want you both to come—at least for a while," she had said, less than an hour after her arrival. "I'm all by myself in that mausoleum. It's horrid. You've no idea."

Her expression amused me. "Be honest, Lou. How many days have you been alone since Larry died?"

"I'm not talking about the *days*. Of course there are people during the day. I'm not like you, Philip. I'm not a recluse. Thank God I have friends. It's the *nights,* my dear. They're endless and—lonely. Oh, why must you always be so obstinate!"

"Margaret and I are happy here, Lou."

"But I'm not happy *there.*"

"Then it's obvious what you must do. You must come and stay with us here."

I knew how unthinkable this would be to her, otherwise I shouldn't have dreamed of suggesting it. It was merely one of those dismal alternatives which, even as a child, she had always rejected.

"That's preposterous, and you know it."

"We've plenty of room. And all the conveniences. And just smell that air, Lou."

She sniffed. "I don't smell anything."

"That's what I mean."

"But it's all so—empty."

She'd soon realized she was getting nowhere with me and turned to what I'm sure had been her original intention: what she wanted, of course, was Margaret.

"It's dreadful for her being stuck out here in the wilderness. It's unnatural."

"Unnatural? Ah, Louise, what a sad commentary on your life that you should find trees and flowers unnatural."

"Oh, stop it, Philip. You know what I mean. I'm talking about Margaret. It's unnatural for her."

"Nonsense. She's quite happy here. And safe."

"Because she doesn't know any better. It's not fair, Philip. *She's* not a tree—and she won't be a flower forever. She deserves a chance to lead a normal life."

"A life like yours, you mean."

"And what's wrong with that?"

"If you don't know I can't very well tell you."

"But do you really think this is what Rachel would have wanted?"

"Rachel was like you, Louise. Blindly trustful. Your lethal world out there is what killed her. It won't have Margaret, too."

"Don't be dramatic. Germany in '39 was not the *world.*"

"Maybe not. But the world has become the Germany of '39."

"You do sometimes spout the most insipid journalese. Even your poetry is tainted with it. That's the trouble with you people. You spend your lives reporting violence. It warps your judgment. You think that's all there is."

"And how often do you take a walk—alone—through Central Park?"

She fussed with her rings. "I'm not saying there's no violence. I'm not that stupid. But hiding from it—that's hardly the answer."

"It's my answer, Lou."

"But must it be Margaret's?"

"You sound as if I'm forcing her to stay here. If you want her to come with you you're quite welcome to ask her."

Margaret had put on her prettiest dress for the occasion of her aunt's visit; although there was not a trace of slyness in the girl's nature her instincts were infallible: Louise's face was frankly approving. My daughter was seventeen at the time. She had her mother's dark hair and eyes, as well as her strong, pure features. Her character, however, was her own.

She had none of Rachel's melancholy, and Margaret's zest for life was immediately visible.

Rachel and her entire family had been slaughtered by the Nazis. Louise, by the way, had grossly exaggerated the extent of my career as a journalist. Berlin had been only my second assignment—and my last. During those months I'd become a bridegroom, father, and widower, and had seen enough violence to last me a lifetime. As soon as I could get Rachel's money released from the Swiss bank I'd come home with Margaret and settled here in this wooded, sparsely populated corner of the state close to the peaceful little village where I'd been born. I bought up all the surrounding land so that we should be assured of complete privacy. Here I finished my first book of poems, *Screams and Echoes,* and most of *Night-Pieces.*

We had our books and our music and each other, and the task of making the farm self-sufficient was a joyous one. Our gardens and our animals kept us always busy. It was a good life and I knew Margaret would have no desire to follow her aunt back into that arid wasteland where existence is nothing but an aimless flight from boredom or a bitter contest among malcontents.

I was right. Politely but firmly she declined Lou's invitation, and later that evening when she was reading aloud to us I was secretly delighted with the poems she chose.

For thus I live remote from evil-speaking; rancor,
Never sought, comes to me not; malignant truth, or lie.

Speaking from memory, she looked up from the book as she spoke these lines and gave me a secret, blissful smile, and happiness flashed through me like a sudden burst of warmth. I didn't dare glance at Louise; I think the visible expression of such perfect joy would have seemed to her shocking, indecent.

My sister never visited us again, and since she was an indifferent letter writer we never heard from her except during the holidays. The next dozen years brought no change to our way of life, except that both Margaret and the farm grew more beautiful with each passing season. Some witling once wrote that failure in life is to form habits. He was wrong. Happiness in life is to form habits; they are the bar lines that mark off the measures in life's music.

Yet if we remained the same, things around us did not: the ulcer of society was making its cancerous advance upon us. On our more distant rambles we would come across ominous signs; empty beer cans, trampled cigarettes, spent cartridges. In the hunting season the air was filled with the crack and ping of shotgun and rifle.

Stupidly I ignored these omens—until it was too late.

I'll never forget the day they first came. Margaret and I were on the veranda, and I turned to her and said, "Listen . . . is that thunder?"

Even as I spoke I knew it wasn't, for it was already reaching a crescendo that drowned out the strains of the *Pathetique* coming from inside the house. (I often played it at sundown, timing it so that the *adagio lamentoso* coincided with the decline of the sun below the ridge.)

And then we saw them.

"Look, Father!"

They came one by one bounding over the ridge, hunched low on their roaring motorcycles, silhouetted briefly against the pink-orange sunset, then spinning down the slope— there must have been a dozen of them. The noise was shattering.

Margaret's arm shot out as though in warning. A narrow suspension bridge, a really charming bit of engineering, crossed the river at the foot of the slope; before reaching it the path curved rather sharply, and though I was quite sure the bridge itself could support the weight of the machines, they were approaching it so fast I was sure they would miss the curve and plunge, one after the other, into the rock-filled stream below.

I underestimated them. With the flawless instinct of birds they swept down the path, veered smoothly to the left, and shot over the swaying, bucketing bridge with whoops of glee, turned to the left once more, and raced along the path that borders this side of the river.

When the dust had settled behind them I took Margaret's hand. We were like two mute survivors of an earthquake. "Come up and lie down. I'll call the Sheriff."

"Shouldn't you wait?"

"For what?"

"To see if it happens again."

"Once was too often. There are plenty of signs. They knew this was private property."

Even so, I was unaccountably glad that she continued to urge me to do nothing, and I tried to forget the incident, which wasn't easy since it had a special, unpleasant significance for me. To Margaret they were no more than men on motorcycles. To me men on motorcycles suggested too many grim memories; during those months in Germany I'd seen too many men on motorcycles.

That was the first of what soon became a daily invasion. They came always at the same sunset hour, flying noisily over the ridge and swooping down the slope and across the bridge with their wild, lusty cries. The second time it happened I did call the Sheriff, which accomplished nothing. From the first sound of his gravelly, officious, boozy voice I disliked the man intensely, and when he asked that inane question, "Did they do any damage?" I knew I was dealing with an imbecile.

"They're *tres*passing," I replied with iciest precision of tone, to which he merely grunted and said, "Pretty hard to move cross country round here, Mister, without trespassin' on your property, ain't it?"

Every afternoon was shattered now by the roar of their engines and the scream of their lungs, while my hopeless attempt at a confrontation was a farce. I had stationed myself at this end of the bridge and when they appeared made a melodramatic signal for them to stop as they came hurtling down the slope. They pulled up smartly on the other side of the bridge and sat stiffly astride their purring machines waiting for me to make a move. They were all young and suntanned, and though I suppose they couldn't actually have been identically built and featured, they gave this impression because of their common uniform of tight pants, black boots, studded belts, helmets, and gleaming black leather jackets labeled BLACK DOVES.

"This is private property!"

No one moved or spoke.

"All clearly posted. You saw the signs. You're trespassing."

The leader of the pack folded his arms across his chest and laughed. "Hell, mister, we ain't trespassin'. We're just exercisin' our rights of passage."

"Call it what you like, it's still trespassing and it's illegal."

The youth pointed to a flock of sparrows pecking at crumbs Margaret had thrown them. "So's them there birds, if you wanta make somethin' out of it. How come you don't call the Sheriff, man, and have him bust them there birds?"

One of the others giggled. "Hell, he's got enough jailbirds. He ain't fixin' to bust no sparrows. Nor Doves, neither."

The leader stopped smiling. "Move aside, old man, if you know what's good for you."

I moved aside.

When I got back to the veranda where Margaret stood watching I detected on her face a look too gentle to be termed reproof, yet betraying certainly a note of displeasure with my performance. I felt it necessary to answer that look. "What else could I do? They're barbarians."

"Those boys?"

What did she know of boys—or barbarians? "You should have stayed out of sight. You must have seen how they looked at you."

"*Hide* from them?" Something in the innocent-defiant way she said this reminded me of Rachel.

After that I tried to ignore the daily intrusions, shutting myself in the house and turning the record player up higher, angry at Margaret for refusing to come inside, and disturbed because the feeling of anxiety this gave me was totally devoid of emotional shape. I thought of her standing out there and I imagined it was Rachel standing at the window of our apartment near the Tiergarten watching the Storm Troopers roar into the street on their motorcycles; and yet I knew I was merely using this fantasy to screen from my mind something more immediate and frightening.

What finally caused me to break my silence was the sight of that brash leader of the pack as he swerved away from the others one afternoon, motioning them to go on, and then executed a long, sweeping, rather beautiful maneuver which carried him to a spot just below where Margaret stood. From the window I saw his white teeth flashing, his cocky mannerisms, the sculptural elegance of his body.

Margaret had grown to womanhood in a state of pure innocence in an environment of total peace; but innocence is like a bird without wings if a predator should steal into the garden.

At dinner that evening I remarked that I'd noticed her talking to one of the interlopers.

"Did you, Father?" Her smile treated the subject with thoughtless indifference. "Why didn't you chase him away? He was alone at the time."

"That wouldn't have solved anything."

"I suppose not." She reached for the carrots. We ate for a while in silence, then I said, "I don't mean that we should appease them. I'm not saying that."

"Oh?"

"There are just the two of us. We haven't even the protection of the law."

"Aren't you making a fuss over nothing, Father?"

"You don't know what people are like," I said. "But don't worry. I'll find a way to deal with them."

"How?" Her tone was still playful. "By shutting yourself in the house and pretending you don't hear them?"

"It's safer than displaying yourself to them. If you knew anything at all about the viciousness of the human animal—"

"I'm sorry, Father. I just can't get used to the idea of hiding from anything. I've never had to."

For some reason this gave me a very guilty feeling, and at the same time it made me all the more determined to have it out with the Sheriff, much as I hated the thought of going into the village. If a community can be said to have a hang-dog look, that one does.

His only reply to my complaint was that the cyclists were "good lads" and not the hooligans I seemed to think they were. I got the impression that he recognized only three serious infractions of the law—murder, robbery, and rape—and his detestation of the third was not convincing. He declared that he couldn't be expected to neglect his duty to the electorate by wasting time baby-sitting with a bunch of fun-loving youngsters. That, he took care to emphasize, would be in the nature of extraordinary duties for which he could not expect the taxpayers to defray the cost.

For so thick-skinned a creature he managed to convey the

message of his venality with unexpected subtlety; one could only assume he'd had considerable practice.

"Before I'd bribe you to do your duty," I said frigidly, "I'd take a rifle and defend my property myself."

His face darkened. "You just better mind your own p's and q's, mister. Anything happens to them boys—" He looked at me with a deeper, more furtive hostility. "These are simple folks around here. Decent folks. They don't hold with no funny business. Take my advice. You and your girl clear out of these parts."

"I didn't come here for your advice."

"Folks around here, they figger there's a reason when somebody's standoffish. Figger it ain't natural, a man holing up with his own daughter, year after year, all to themselves."

So intense was my loathing for the man that I couldn't bear to look at him again, couldn't get out of his sight soon enough.

That night I asked Margaret what she thought of the idea of moving away.

"Leave the farm, you mean?"

"Yes, Go away. To the Caribbean, perhaps."

"I don't know, Father. I like it here."

"Still, we might think about it."

She didn't answer.

Later, unable to sleep, I got up and walked out past the barn and the chicken house and stood on the bridge looking down at the narrow rushing stream and listening to it bubble over the smooth round rocks which the moonlight made oddly black and head-shaped. With a shudder I crossed to the other side and passed up the slope to the ridge, careful not to turn my ankle in the deep ruts worn by the cyclists' spinning wheels.

Up there I stood looking out across the hills to the invisible horizon, and then quickly, as if lost in that dark landscape of infinity, back toward the farm, reshaped by shadows and strangely unfamiliar on the side of the moonlit hill. I thought of Margaret asleep in there, and alone, and I was aware of a vague mounting dread on her behalf. Something *had* to be done. Something . . .

The very next afternoon the *adagio* of the *Pathetique* was pierced by a sudden sharp scream from Margaret, and at the same time I heard the rending crash of metal on stone and the loud startled cries of the young men.

From the veranda I saw how the bridge dangled loosely from its posts on the farther bank. A welter of black figures moved confusedly in a cloud of dust, and the two injured, or dead—at the moment I had no way of knowing—were being lifted out of the rock-filled river.

Margaret stood rigid and alone halfway between the house and the river. She looked safe to me for the first time in weeks. I was glad it had happened.

To be kept locked up, incommunicado, in that dismal hole of a cell in that filthy jail was bad enough, God knows, but to be vilified and terrorized by that wretched excuse for a Sheriff and his ape-like deputy, neither of whom had evidently ever heard of due process, nearly drove me mad. That the two riders were expected to die of their injuries was only one of the vicious lies they told to torture me; another was that Margaret had made no request to see me. The situation was so grotesque I nearly forgot at times where I was, fully expecting to be roughly awakened in the middle of the night and dragged out to be shot or lynched.

What saved my sanity was one of the Sheriff's most flagrant lies: he said that Margaret confessed to seeing me tamper with the bridge the night before the accident. I knew better than that. Margaret would never have done such a thing.

In the end it was not my threats of legal recourse that won my release, but the financial "compensation" I was forced to pay. Only when I was free did I learn that neither of the two men had been badly hurt.

As I hurried back to the farm I decided it had all been from the start an elaborate scheme for extorting money from me. Now, I hoped, we would be left in peace. From the ridge it looked as if nothing at all had happened. Under the hot white glow of the summer sun even the bridge looked as it always had. I wondered who had repaired it. But then as I moved down the slope and crossed the river I saw the first signs of devastation.

The chicken house had been destroyed—what I'd seen from the ridge was only a burned-out shell. The barn was intact but the livestock were missing. More alarming than any of this was the condition of the grounds—deep ruts crisscrossing the whole area, including what was left of the flower and vegetable gardens.

After seeing this I was mortally afraid of going into the house, it was so threateningly silent—a graveyard stillness mocked by the leering impertinent sun.

Outside the door I called Margaret's name. Flies buzzed out of the humid interior, which was dark, as if all the blinds had been shut against the sun, the stale, flannelly heat so palpable you could almost touch it. The room was a shambles of broken furniture and window glass. From the muddy tracks they must have driven their machines throughout the house.

In my study I waded across a carpet of shattered records—not one was left unbroken, nor would I ever again be able to play the *Pathetique* on that machine.

I think I must have aged twenty years in the time it took me to move from the study to the bedroom upstairs. Slowly, slowly, I opened the door.

Margaret, sitting on the edge of the bed, was alive and smiling.

Suddenly dizzy, I put out my hand to grasp the door frame.

She wore a slip which had been torn diagonally from shoulder to hip and was now held together by a pin. Her hair was tangled and had an unwashed look totally unlike Margaret. There were bruises on her upper arms and her lips were swollen.

But it was the smile! That fixed yet curiously unfocused smile that made me break down and weep as I'd never wept in my life, not even when I'd watched them drag Rachel down those endless stairs, her feet bumping horribly on each step.

We should never have stayed; we should have gone away when it first started. "We'll go now," I promised. "Far away. Oh, Margaret, Margaret!"

"Don't be silly, Father," she said, her voice uncannily serene. "We don't have to go now. It's over. We're safe again."

"Safe. Here? Never. We'll go—"

"Here, Father. We'll have more privacy now right here than on any—island! We've paid for it. They won't bother us again."

"Brutes! Liars! They said I did it. But I didn't, Margaret. I swear to you I didn't. The bridge was old and weak. It couldn't take the constant stress of those machines. But they wouldn't believe me. They even said you'd signed a statement that you'd seen me tampering with it. What did those animals do to you, Margaret?"

"Nothing, Father. Not then. I did tell them I saw you do it."

Mad, mad, I kept thinking. "You—"

"Told them, Father. Yes. Well, I couldn't tell them the truth—that I was the one who did it."

My lips shaped words I hadn't the strength to speak.

"I did it the night before it happened. Something had to be done, and I knew you would do nothing. Except run away. All these years, Father, the way we've lived. Did you think we would never have to pay for it?"

And I thought it was *her* innocence I'd been protecting. What a fool, what a fool.

The smile on her face softened, became tender, compassionate. Her arms reached out for me. "Come. We must both pretend it never happened. Nothing has changed, you see. Everything is just the way it was . . ."

EDITORIAL POSTSCRIPT

The story you have just read was nominated by MWA (Mystery Writers of America) as one of the six best new mystery short stories published in American magazines and books during 1974.

A NIGHT OUT WITH THE BOYS

by *Elsin Ann Gardner*

It was the annual meeting of the Brierwood Men's Club. . . .

THE LIGHTS were dim, so low I could hardly make out who was in the room with me. Annoyed, I picked my way to the center where the chairs were. The smoky air was as thick as my wife's perfume, and about as breathable.

I pulled a metal folding chair out and sat next to a man I didn't know. Squinting, I looked at every face in the room. Not one was familiar. Damn that Russell! I didn't belong in the gathering, and he had to have known it.

Adjusting my tie, the wide garish tie Georgia had given me for Christmas, I stared at the glass ashtray in the hand of the man next to me. The low-wattage lights were reflected in it, making, I thought, a rather interesting pattern. At least, it was more interesting than anything that had happened yet that evening.

I was a fool to have come, I thought, angry. When the letter came the week before, my wife had opened it. As always.

"Look," she'd said, handing me my opened mail. It was a small rectangle of neatly printed white paper.

"It's from that nice man down the block. It's an invitation to a meeting of some sort. You'll have to go."

"Go? Meeting?" I asked, taking off my overcoat and reaching for the letter.

171

You are invited, the paper read, *to the Annual Meeting of the Brierwood Men's Club, to be held at the Ram's Room at Twink's Restaurant on Monday Evening, January 8, at eight o'clock.*

It was signed, *Yours in brotherhood, Glenn Russell.*

"Oh, I don't know," I said, "I hardly know the guy. And I've never heard of the club."

"You're going," Georgia rasped. "It's your chance to get in good with the new neighbors. We've lived here two whole months and not a soul has dropped in to see us."

No wonder, I thought. They've heard enough of your whining and complaining the times they've run into you at the supermarket.

"Maybe," I said aloud, "people here are just reserved."

"Maybe people in the east just aren't as *friendly* as the people you knew back home," she said, sneering.

"Oh, Georgia, don't start that up again! We left, didn't we? I pulled up a lifetime of roots for you, didn't I?"

"Are you trying to tell me it was my fault? Because if you *are,* Mr. Forty-and-Foolish, you've got another think coming! It was entirely your fault, and you're just lucky I didn't leave you over it."

"All right, Georgia."

"Where would you be without Daddy's money, Mr. Fathead? Where would you be without me?"

"I'm sorry, Georgia. I'm just tired, that's all."

She gave a smug little smile and continued. "You *are* going," she nodded, making her dyed orange hair shake like an old mop. "Yes, indeed. You can wear your good dark brown suit and that new tie I gave you and—"

And she went on and on, planning my wardrobe, just as she'd planned every minute of my last fourteen years.

So the night of January eighth I was at the Annual Meeting of the Brierwood Men's Club. What crazy kind of club had a meeting *annually?* A service club? Fraternal organization?

It was almost eight when the men stopped filing into the room. They were, with hardly an exception, a sad-looking lot. I mean, they looked depressed. A gathering of funeral directors? A club for people who had failed at suicide and were contemplating it again?

"I think this is all of us, men," Russell said, standing on the dais. "Yes. We can begin. Alphabetical order, as always. One minute each, no more."

Alphabetical order? One minute?

A sad tired-looking man in his fifties stood up and went to the platform.

"Harry Adams. She, she—"

He wiped his brow nervously, then went on.

"This year has been the worst ever for me. You've seen her. She's so beautiful. I know you think I'm lucky. But I'm not, oh, no. She's been after me every minute to buy her this, buy her that, so she can impress all the neighbors. I don't make enough money to be able to do this! But she threatened to leave me and take all I've got, which isn't that much any longer, if I don't give in.

"So I took out a loan at the bank, told them it was for a new roof, bought her everything she wanted with the money. But it wasn't enough. She wants more. A full-length mink coat, a two-carat diamond ring. I'll have to go to another bank and get another loan for my roof. I'm running out of money, I'm running out of roofs—"

"One minute, Harry."

Dejected, the little man left the platform and another man took his place.

"Joe Browning. She invited her mother to live with us. The old dame moved in last April. I can hardly stand my wife, but now I've got two of them. Whining, nagging, in stereo, yet. You can't imagine how it is, guys! You think you've got troubles? You should have the troubles I've got. I get home from work five minutes late, I've got two of them on my back. I forget my wife's birthday, my mother-in-law lets me have it. I forget my mother-in-law's birthday, my wife lets me have it."

He looked over at Russell, sitting on the platform.

"More?"

"Ten seconds, Joe."

"I just want to say I can't stand it at home any longer! I'm not a young man any longer. I—"

"Minute, Joe."

And then it was another's turn. I sat there rigid with fascination. What a great idea! Once a year to get together and complain about the wife! Get it out of the system, let it all out. And to think I hadn't wanted to come!

Some guy named Dorsey spoke next. His wife had eaten herself up to 280 pounds. And Flynn, his wife had gone to thirty doctors for her imagined ills. Herter, his wife refused to wear her false teeth around the house unless they had guests, and Hurd, his wife wouldn't let him go out with the boys, and Klutz, his wife had wrecked his brand-new sports car three times during the year, and Lemming, his wife gave all his comfortable old clothes to charity, and Morgan, his wife kept going through the house, finding his liquor bottles and pouring them down the sink.

And then it was my turn.

And the whole time I was listening to these men I was thinking, they think they have it bad? Really? Because none of them had a wife as rotten as mine. Oh, I guess we all think now and then that we've picked a lemon off the tree of love, to get poetic for a moment, but compared to those men with their crummy complaints I really did have the all-time booby prize.

I'd figured when Morgan got up to speak it would be my turn next, so I rehearsed what to say. It wasn't, you understand, that I wanted to impress anybody. But to be actually able to say it out loud, to tell the world what she'd done to me—pure heaven!

I took my place on the dais and looked at Russell.

"You can begin now," he said kindly.

"Fred Norton. Her name was Annie and she was my secretary and she was twenty-three years old and I loved her more than anyone else on earth and I knew I always would and my wife who is cold like you wouldn't believe found out and told everyone on the west coast what I'd done and said we'd have to move a thousand miles away from 'that tramp,' only Annie wasn't a tramp and I'll never in my life see her again and I still love her so much and my wife keeps bringing the whole thing up and I try to forget her because it hurts so much, but I know I'll never be able to, especially with my wife reminding me all the time."

"One minute, Fred."

"I can't stand my wife!" I yelled into the microphone as I left the platform.

Never in my thirty-nine and three-quarter years had I felt

so good. Almost laughing from the deep pleasure of getting it all out of my system, I took my seat and half listened to the others. Owens, with his wife who told his kids he was a dummy, and Quenton, whose wife had gone back to college and now thought she was smarter than he was, and Smith, whose wife slept until noon and made him do the housework, all the way down to Zugay, whose wife made all his clothes so that he went out looking like a holdover from the Big Depression. Which he certainly did.

One guy, who hadn't spoken, interested me. He was smiling. Actually sitting there with a big grin on his face. I was staring at him, wondering if his face was familiar, when Russell spoke.

"All right, men. Time to vote. George, hand out the paper and pencils, okay?"

Vote?

"Vote?" I asked the man sitting next to me, whose wife hid his toupee when she didn't want him to go out.

"Sure. Vote for the one who has the lousiest wife."

I scribbled down the name Fred Norton. After all, I did have the lousiest wife.

Glenn Russell collected the slips of paper and sorted them. In a few minutes he turned to face the men.

"For the first time, men," he said, "a new member has won. Fred Norton. The one with the wife, you remember, who called his nice girl friend a tramp."

Then he smiled. "Congratulations, Fred!"

I half rose, feeling somewhat foolish and yet proud. It was indeed an honor.

And then all of them, all the sad-faced, beaten-down men, gathered around me and shook my hand. Some of them actually had tears in their eyes as they patted me on the back.

Later, as we all went to the lounge to have a drink before going home, I found Glenn Russell at the end of the bar and went over to him with my drink.

"This is some deal," I said. "It really, really felt good to get it out of my system. Whose idea was this club?"

"Mine," he said. "We've met once a year for the last six years. I control the membership and I wanted you to be included this year. That wife of yours is really something, isn't she?"

"Yes," I agreed. "She sure is. How come you didn't speak? Because it's your club?"

"Oh. No, my wife passed away a few years ago."

"I'm sorry," I said, feeling suddenly awkward. "That guy sitting over there, the one who's had the big smile on his face all evening, who the heck is he?"

"Gary McClellan? He's the vet in our fair city."

"Oh, sure, now I remember. Say, didn't my wife tell me that McClellan's wife died last year in some sort of horrible accident?"

Russell smiled broadly and patted me on the arm.

"Of course, old man! McClellan was last year's winner!"

EDITORIAL POSTSCRIPT

The story you have just read was nominated by MWA (Mystery Writers of America) as one of the six best new mystery short stories published in American magazines and books during 1974.

THE RAFFLES SPECIAL

by Barry Perowne

Perhaps the most distinctive quality of E. W. Hornung's original Raffles stories was the aura of decadent charm that emanated from the writing and the characterizations. Well, that is exactly the appeal Barry Perowne has infused into his new stories about A. J. Raffles, amateur cracksman-and-cricketeer—into the writing, the characters, and the authentic turn-of-the-century background and color. And this Raffles exploit has an extra and special charm—as you will learn. . . .

"Shh!" said A. J. Raffles suddenly. "Listen, Bunny!"

Tense beside him in the concealment of a thicket of wait-a-bit thorn, I held my breath.

Far off on the veldt, desolate and illimitable in the moonlight, a jackal howled. Twenty paces from us, a water tank elevated on iron supports cast a long shadow across the glinting tracks of a single-line railway.

I heard a faint humming from the rails.

"A train," I said

"At last!" said Raffles.

His gray eyes gleamed. His keen face was beard-stubbled. Any resemblance which either of us bore now to gentlemen, in this war which many people were predicting would be the last of the gentleman's wars, was purely coincidental.

177

Our uniforms as subalterns, the rank in which we had been called up from the Reserve for active service with a Yeomanry regiment, were in tatters. We had had the bad luck to get captured, but had escaped from the crowded P.O.W. camp, and for many days now we had been on the run.

The humming from the rails was growing louder.

"A goods train, probably," said Raffles.

I swallowed with a parched throat. We still were deep inside Boer territory.

"What if it's a troop train," I said, "crammed with Oom Paul's sharpshooters?"

I had developed a considerable respect for grim old President Kruger and his fighting farmers.

"We'll soon know," said Raffles. "There's the smoke!"

Distant puffs of it, flame-tinted, billowed up against the vast sky limpid with stars. The locomotive came into view, the respirations from its smoke-stack becoming less frequent as it approached.

"Slowing down," said Raffles. "Yes, they're going to take on water here, Bunny."

I could make out now the gleam of the locomotive's piston rods. They were beginning to idle. It was a train of half-a-dozen goods trucks, tarpaulin-covered, with the guard's small van at the rear. The rails of the track vibrated, a jet of exhaust-steam hissed out between the wheels, and I felt the slight tremor of the earth under my feet as the locomotive came to a standstill abreast of the water tower.

From the firelit interior of the cab a man jumped down, evidently the fireman, for his face, overalls, and railwayman's cap were black with coal dust. He had in his hand a long rod of iron with a hook at the end. The driver, an older, bearded man in overalls and peaked cap, with a short clay pipe in his mouth, clambered down after the fireman.

"And here comes the guard," Raffles whispered.

The guard's shadow, with widebrimmed hat, bandolier, and slung rifle, flickered over the sides of the goods trucks as he approached from the rear of the train.

Raffles breathed, "Ignore the old driver, Bunny. Keep the

fireman occupied while I get that guard's rifle. Right? Off we go!"

We darted out from the shadow of the bush, Raffles making for the guard, myself for the fireman, who was reaching up with the rod, his back to me, to unhook the cumbersome hose of the water tank.

The driver, lighting his pipe, saw me and shouted a warning as I raced past him. The fireman turned quickly. I was almost upon him. He aimed an almighty sideswipe at me with the iron rod. I heard it whistle over my head as I butted him in the belly and we went down together, locked and wrestling, rolling over and over in the dust.

The man was all muscle and sinew, from stoking engines. I never had felt anything like it. I could not hold him. He got on top. His knee drove into my chest. His hands clamped on my throat. His eyes glared down at me from his mask of coal dust. I clutched at his arms. They were like iron bars, but suddenly, blindingly, a solid deluge of water descended upon the pair of us. It was as though the heavens had opened. We rolled apart, gasping and spluttering, from the shock of it.

As I staggered to my feet, I saw that in our fight we had rolled right under the hose, from which the deluge was coming. Raffles had started it. He had one hand on the small wheel of the water cock. In the other he held the rifle, menacing the driver and guard with it. They had their hands up, and the fireman, drenched like myself, his face washed almost white, also put up his hands rather sullenly.

"Now then," said Raffles, as he turned off the downpour. "This train is from Pretoria, of course, and is bound for Beira, in neutral Portuguese territory. It just so happens that my friend and I are going that way ourselves, so we'll gladly take the train there for you. There's just one small point. When we steam across the frontier, we shall need to look less like a pair of tramps and more like a driver and fireman. So I'm afraid we must trouble you for your overalls and caps."

Mutely glowering, the driver and fireman surrendered the garments, and Raffles and I, taking turns holding the rifle, put them on. Raffles found a clasp knife in the pocket of his overalls. He told me to cut lengths from the rope that held down the tarpaulin on the nearest of the goods trucks. With the lengths of rope I bound the men's wrists behind them and hobbled their ankles, not too tightly.

"You'll soon be able to free yourselves," Raffles told the captives. "It's a pity trains are so rare on this line. You have a long walk ahead of you. But my friend and I have already done our share of walking, as you can see from the state our boots are in. Ah, well, fortunes of war! Ready, Bunny? Then come on!"

In overalls, mine soaking wet, and railwaymen's caps, we clambered up into the locomotive cab.

"Can you drive this thing?" I asked anxiously, as Raffles examined the controls.

"I begged many a ride on the footplate when I was a kid, Bunny. I was train mad," said Raffles. "This is an old London and South-Western Railway locomotive—'Brockenhurst' class. I recognized it as soon as I saw it."

He manipulated various levers. Steam hissed, and with a chugging and rumbling, and a clank of couplings from the goods trucks, the locomotive began to move.

"Get busy with that shovel!" Raffles shouted to me, above the din. "D'you want to find us back in Pretoria, behind barbed wire again? Stoke up! Give me a head of steam!"

A wild exhilaration filled me as, with the shovel, I opened the door to the red glare and hellish heat of the firebox.

"Steam for the Raffles Special!" I shouted, and went to work shoveling coals from the bunker as the first train we had ever stolen began to gather speed.

The veldt was streaking past at a great rate when at last dawn broke over the endless expanse. My overalls had long since dried, my face and hands were black, my muscles ached.

As the crystalline early light gave way to a shimmer of heat currents, I glimpsed an isolated Boer farmhouse or two, and once we passed a distant wagon drawn by a plodding line of yoked oxen.

Hunger gnawing as the day wore on, I foraged in the loco-motive toolbox, where I found the driver's and fireman's lunch cans. As we gratefully munched black bread and biltong, and washed it down with good Dutch beer, I asked Raffles what he thought was in the goods trucks.

"Nothing of much value, Bunny," he said, his face as black and oily as my own, "or there'd have been more than one guard on the train."

Only once, in the great loneliness under the sun, did we see armed men—a group of horsemen, with bandoliers and slung rifles, who were near enough for me to see their stern, heavily bearded faces.

"A Boer *kommando*," said Raffles.

He pulled the dangling cord of the steam whistle to give them a cheery salute, but they made no acknowledgment, not so much as a wave.

"I'm afraid we'll find more of those fellows when we get to the Boer frontier station," Raffles said.

"So we crash through at speed?" I suggested.

"And get fired at?" said Raffles. "No, Bunny. Firing would alert the Portuguese over on their side, make them wonder what was wrong, and try to stop us to find out."

"But they're neutral, Raffles!"

"Would they take a neutral view of train robbers, Bunny? We can't be sure, and I don't much like the possibility of internment in Portuguese East for the duration."

"Oh, dear God!" I said.

Repeatedly, after that, I stopped shoveling coal, wiped sweat from my eyes with a bit of cotton waste, and peered ahead anxiously through one of the two small round windows of the locomotive cab.

When at last I spotted, far ahead along the rails, a cluster of sheds come into view, my throat went dry. I saw the small figures of men, some of them on horseback. There seemed quite a lot of them—most of them armed, I noted, as Raffles slowed down our rate of approach and pulled the steam whistle cord, loosing off three short blasts of greeting.

"Behave naturally!" Raffles shouted to me. "Stick your black face out with an affable smile, and wave as we pass through!"

"*If* we pass through!" I shouted back.

My heart thumped as I peered ahead through the round

window. There was no barrier across the line. It stretched straight ahead, between the sheds and the waiting men, into no-man's-land, as the locomotive chugged slowly, hissing exhaust steam, into the little station—and kept moving.

I leaned out from the footplate, with a smile and a wave to the men as they watched the locomotive steam slowly past them, followed by the clanking goods trucks. I could see that the men were expecting the train to stop, but it was not until the guard's little van at the rear was gliding past them that I heard from one of the men a shout of surprised inquiry.

"They're shouting," I called to Raffles.

"Acknowledge," he called back.

I leaned out, looking back at the men, and nodding as though with vigorous understanding, at the same time waving to them in reassurance—and farewell.

None of them moved. They just seemed surprised. Their figures dwindled as Raffles opened the throttle a little and our speed discreetly increased.

"Now for the Portuguese, Bunny!"

Again our speed decreased, as we steamed, chugging sturdily, towards a cluster of small buildings with whitewashed walls, typically Portuguese. Raffles sounded our whistle, and I saw men emerging from the buildings—short, dark men in dusty green uniforms, with white cross-belts and slung rifles.

As we steamed slowly past the soldiers, Raffles and I, from our respective sides of the locomotive cab, protruded our grimy faces, showing our teeth affably as we waved our greetings. One or two of the men waved back, amiably enough. But as the goods trucks went on clanking slowly past them, and the guard's little van followed, I was dreading an outburst of shouts—and, possibly, of shots.

Nothing of the kind happened. I could hardly believe my eyes as I looked back at the soldiers gazing after us in mild surprise as they receded behind us. I gave them a final wave and turned to Raffles.

"By God," I shouted, exultant, "we're through! We've done it!"

"Now for Beira," said Raffles, with a grin, "We'll take no risks of internment. When we get near town, we'll abandon this train for someone else to find and take in. We'll sneak down to the dock area under cover of night and try smuggling ourselves aboard some ship, outward bound. Come on, now, stoke up! Give me steam!"

"Farewell to Oom Paul!" I yelled, as I seized the shovel again and the locomotive began to pound along, with quickening respirations and blasts of the whistle, on our journey to freedom.

When we finally reached London, after many delays, difficulties, and enforced wanderings, we learned that the hostilities in South Africa were virtually over. Pausing only long enough to report at the Yeomanry depot, and to visit our civilian tailor in Savile Row, we went north at the invitation of a chap we had been at school with, a young Argyllshire laird called Kenneth Mackail, for a week's fishing.

"Ye bonnie banks and braes," Raffles remarked, as, his dark hair crisp, his tweeds immaculate, a pearl in his cravat, he leaned with me beside him on the rail of the little sidewheeler steamer plying up Loch Long from Glasgow to Dunoon, where Ken was to meet us. "How do they look to you, Bunny?"

"After all we've been through," I said, contemplating the northern sunshine mellow over the tranquil waters of the loch, and breathing the air redolent of the heather on the distant moors, "they look enchantingly peaceful to me."

"They'll be ringing with gunfire soon," Raffles reminded me. "It'll be the twelfth of August in a few days—the 'Glorious Twelfth,' when everybody comes north for the opening of grouse-shooting."

"I'm glad Ken Mackail doesn't own a moor," I said. "My war-worn nerves are only equal to a little quiet fishing."

Ken was waiting for us on the jetty at Dunoon. A slightly built, wiry chap with sandy hair, he wore the kilt, with a dirk in his stocking. He had brought his dogcart, and the cob in the shafts trotted off with us sturdily on the long, jolting ride to Mackail Lodge, which was up among the moors.

"There's one thing," Ken said presently, as we clattered along, "which I feel I should mention. You chaps are just back from active service in South Africa, whereas I was out there—as you know—as correspondent for a newspaper with a strongly antiwar policy."

"Different people, different views," said Raffles, tolerantly.

"In the main, Bunny Manders and I go through shot and shell with judiciously open minds."

"Absolutely," I said.

"I'm relieved to hear that," Ken said, in his rather serious way. "The fact is, I'm involved in a bye-election, down in Glasgow. I'm standing for Parliament on a platform of generous peace terms for the Boers. Polling will be on the fourteenth, so I'm afraid I shall be busy on the hustings, down in Glasgow, most of the time you're here. My ghillie Macpherson and his wife, my housekeeper, will look after you very well."

"We have no fears on that score, Ken," said Raffles.

"Absolutely not," I said. The road, a rutted track corkscrewing up over the moors, was traversing now the edge of a gorge where, deep down on our left, a stream out of the highlands tumbled merrily over falls, foamed among rocks, and broadened out here and there into fishworthy pools. I was mentally reviewing the salmon and trout lures in my fly case when I saw another dogcart bowling down the track towards us with the horse at a rapid trot.

Narrow as the track was, the oncoming cart showed no sign of slowing down, and Ken said, "Quick! We shall have to get out!"

This we did, and Ken, going to the cob's head, backed his cart up, precariously tilting, on to the steep heather slope on the right, just in time for the other cart to pass. A ramrod, hawk-nosed man in tweeds held the reins, at his side an attractive girl in a tam-o'-shanter.

As they clattered past with a wheel of their cart about an inch from the gorge edge, we all three stood with our hats raised, but, for all the acknowledgment we got, we might just as well have kept them on.

"That was General Finlayson and his daughter Janet," Ken said with a hint of bitterness, as we climbed back into his dogcart. "The General's not long back from South Africa. He's been put on the Retired list, and he's standing against me in this bye-election, on a platform of punitive peace terms to be imposed in Pretoria."

"Bunny and I heard of him, out there," Raffles said. "A real fire-eater!"

"He owns the Castle Crissaig moors, up above my little place," said Ken. "He's on his way now to catch the steamer to Glasgow, with Janet to see him off. He's due to harangue shipyard workers tomorrow, along Clydeside. What did you think of Janet?"

"Conspicuously bonnie," said Raffles.

"I hoped to marry her," Ken said gloomily, "but the war ruined my chances. I wrote critically, in dispatches to the newspaper I represented, about the General's harsh methods in the field. The result is, he regards me as a pacifist traitor, and it's ruined me with Janet. But damn it, a man must stand by his beliefs—or what is he?"

"He's certainly not a Scotsman," Raffles said, "fit to wear the trousers—or, rather, the kilt—in his own house."

Ken Mackail's house was a typical old moorland lodge, hard by the brawling stream, which Raffles and I, next day, Ken having gone off early, to catch the steamer to Glasgow and the hustings, fished in the company of Ken's ghillie, Macpherson, a gaunt man with an old retriever called Shoona perpetually at his heel.

"Well, Macpherson," said Raffles, when, having caught nothing but a couple of small brown trout all morning, we sat in the heather to eat the sandwiches and drink the whisky put up for us by Mrs. Macpherson, "I'm afraid Mr. Manders and I seem to be a bit out of practice."

"Ye canna tak' fish, sir," said Macpherson, "if there's ower few fish in the watter."

"So the fault's not entirely ours?" said Raffles. "You set our minds at rest. But tell us, Macpherson, how d'you fancy Mr. Mackail's chances in this bye-election?"

" 'Deed, sir," said Macpherson gloomily, "wi'out the Lunnon politeecian coming up to support him on the hustings makes awfu' persuasive speeches to yon Glesga folk, I wouldnae gie a bawbee for the young laird's chances. General Finlayson's a dour opponent, an' a gleg one, forbye, which is why there's ower few fish in our watter."

Raffles asked what General Finlayson had to do with the paucity of fish, and Macpherson said grimly that, if we were so minded, he would show us—after dark.

As it turned out, the night was far from dark. In fact, when we reached the high moor after a long, rough trudge alongside the tumbling stream, the moon was almost as bright as we had seen it over the South African veldt.

We now were on the Castle Crissaig grouse moor, General Finlayson's property, and Macpherson, with Shoona at his heel, warned us to watch out for the General's gamekeeper, James Fraser, who, with the Glorious Twelfth not far off, was apt to be on the prowl.

"Wi' a gun for poachers," said Macpherson. "Bluidy James Fraser!"

Near a small corrie of rowan trees, a little old stone bridge cast a humpbacked shadow over the stream, which here flowed deep and fishworthy. Macpherson led us furtively on to the bridge and showed us a small iron wheel secured by a chain and a massive padlock. He explained that the wheel was used to raise and lower a fine-mesh metal grille. When the grille was lowered, as it was now, fish which had spawned in the upper waters of the stream, were unable to return down stream, through Ken's water, to the loch.

"And this is General Finlayson's little pleasantry?" Raffles asked.

"Aye," said Macpherson. "He's awfu' grudgesome against Mr. Mackail."

"Well," said Raffles, examining the padlock, "I happen to have in my pocket a small implement that might, just possibly—"

"Hist!" said Macpherson. "Bluidy James Fraser! Quick, mak' for yon rowans!"

The three of us, with the wise old Shoona at Macpherson's heel, darted off the bridge and into the tree-shadowed corrie. Peering out, I saw in the moonlight a figure on a bicycle, lampless, approaching along the rough track through the heather.

"Och!" whispered Macpherson, incredulous. "'Tis young leddy from Castle Crissaig!"

Reaching the bridge, the girl in the tam-o'-shanter laid down her bicycle, looked quickly around her over the moor, then ran on to the bridge. Taking from her skirt pocket what must have been a key, she unfastened the padlock. Through the chortling of the stream as it flowed fast under the bridge,

I heard the jingle of the padlock chain, then a grinding sound as she began, exerting considerable effort, to turn the iron wheel.

"She's raising the grille," I whispered.

"Letting many a fine fish through into Ken's water," Raffles murmured.

"Gowd help the lassie," Macpherson whispered, "if bluidy James Fraser comes roarin' on her like a wild man an' tells her feyther!"

For an hour Janet Finlayson remained on the bridge, glancing continually about her over the moonlit moor; then she wound the grille down again into the water, refastened the chain and padlock, and pedaled off on her bicycle.

"Now we know where her heart is," said Raffles. "This'll be good news for Ken!"

As we stepped out, elated, into the moonlight, we were all grinning, and I fancied that even Shoona was baring her canines with sly amusement.

Our fishing next day, on Ken's water, was unbelievable. Macpherson was bent under the weight of our creels. And in the evening, just in time for dinner, Ken turned up on a quick visit to see if we were enjoying ourselves. As buxom Mrs. Macpherson set a superb dish of salmon on the table, Raffles and I were waiting for Ken to comment on it, so that we could tell him to whose significant action we owed the noble repast.

But Ken seemed scarcely aware of what he was eating. He looked preoccupied, worried, and Raffles asked him if the election was not going well.

"A specter's arisen for me," Ken admitted, "but I'm not going to depress you chaps with it—you're here to enjoy yourselves."

"We might enjoy a romp with a specter," said Raffles. "Tell us about it."

It was the specter of the written word. In one of his dispatches from South Africa to the antiwar newspaper he had represented, Ken had accused General Finlayson of ordering an entire Boer family, caught sniping from a farmhouse, to be severely flogged with a rhinohide whip, a *sjambok.*

"I'd sent off the dispatch, written in my own hand," Ken

told us, "by a route that bypassed the censor, when I found out that the story, though it seemed quite in character for General Finlayson, wasn't true. Luckily, I was able to stop my dispatch from being published."

"Then what's the trouble?" Raffles asked.

The trouble, Ken explained, was that his manuscript on the *sjambok* atrocity had not been destroyed by his newspaper, but filed; and he had now received a warning from a colleague on the newspaper that the manuscript had vanished from the files and somehow fallen into the hands of a newspaper that supported General Finlayson's candidature.

"According to my colleague," Ken said, "that newspaper's sending one of its staff men up to Glasgow to confer with General Finlayson's election agent. That agent's as crafty as a fox. I wouldn't put it past him to have my story printed in pamphlets that seem to emanate from my own Election H.Q., and flood the constituency with them."

"And plant people at your meetings," Raffles said, "to ask you why, if the story were true, you suppressed it at the time?"

"Exactly! I couldn't deny I'd written the story. They have the evidence—my own manuscript," Ken said. "But it could be make to look that I'd raked it up now—a story I know to be false—to blackguard my political opponent. It could ruin my chances. Lesser things than this, just before a poll, have swung many an election."

"And polling's on the fourteenth?" Raffles said. "H'm! What's this journalist chap's name and when is he expected in Glasgow?"

"I don't know his name," Ken said, "but my colleague's pretty sure the chap'll be coming up tomorrow on the London-Glasgow express."

"The Cock o' the North," Raffles said thoughtfully. "And to-morrow being the tenth, a lot of important Londoners will be on that train, bound for the grouse moors. As I recall, the Cock o' the North steams into Glasgow at eleven p.m. and most of the visitors on it put up for the night at that huge old hotel right alongside the station. H'm!"

He said no more on the matter, but next morning, when I went down to breakfast, Ken had already left to catch the steamer from Dunoon back to Glasgow, and I heard Raffles's voice from the kitchen. I was buttering a bannock hot from the oven when he came into the breakfast room.

"What were you talking to Mrs. Macpherson about?" I asked.

"I was taking a look at her game larder, Bunny."

"Grouse-shooting doesn't start till day after tomorrow, Raffles. There can't be much in the larder yet."

"Only ground game," Raffles said, unfolding his napkin. "After you with the teapot, Bunny."

I was at a loss to divine his intentions when, on the steamer from Dunoon, we arrived that evening in Glasgow and booked in at the hotel adjoining the station. Familiar to every dedicated grouse-shooter, the huge old warren of a hotel was virtually deserted. We had the echoing dining room almost to ourselves. But at eleven o'clock, when we heard the Cock o' the North, dead on time, steam into the station next door, what a change came over the scene!

We were sitting, with our coffee and liqueur whisky, in saddlebag chairs loomed over by a castor-oil plant, in the vast gaslit mausoleum of a hall, when suddenly the rank and fashion of London came streaming in, all talking in loud, confident voices, all tweed-clad, the ladies looking about them through their lorgnettes in search of old friends in the crowd, the men with their guncases and shooting-sticks and their setters, pointers, retrievers, and spaniels, all of which looked as if they had pedigrees at least as long as those of their owners.

"Keep an eye open for anyone who looks like a journalist," Raffles instructed me, through the din that was going on, the barking of dogs, the shrill yapping of a solitary Pekinese, the cries of well-bred delight as ladies kissed each other through their veils, and men with bluff shouts shook one another's hands heartily.

"As a social occasion," Raffles remarked, "only a Buckingham Palace garden party can compare with this, Bunny!"

"You've seen it before," I said, "but it's all new to me."

I was impressed, recognizing many a face familiar to high society.

With trains or steamers to catch at an early hour, bound for the moors further north and the sacred rites of the Glorious Twelfth on the day after, the distinguished Londoners soon started going upstairs in loud converse to their rooms, while venerable pageboys, each with the leashes of half-a-dozen dogs in either hand, hobbled downstairs with them to the basement kennels.

"I didn't notice anyone who looked particularly like a journalist," I said, as peace reigned once more in the hall.

"I'll see what I can find out at the desk, Bunny. Order us a couple of nightcaps."

When Raffles returned to me, there was a gray gleam in his eyes. "He's here, Bunny! There's a journalist in Room Three-o-one. That'll be our man. He's probably arranged to meet with General Finlayson's election agent first thing in the morning."

With a flash of enlightenment, I exclaimed, "But he's going to lose Ken's fatal manuscript during the night?"

"Shh!" said Raffles. "Come on, we'll take these drinks up to my room."

In his room, when he turned up the gaslight, I saw that his valise had been unpacked by the chambermaid, his night-shirt laid out neatly on the bed, a box of Sullivans and his favorite bedtime reading, *The Adventures of Baron Munchausen,* placed conveniently to hand.

"These doors have bolts, Bunny," he said. "People in hotels are apt to bolt their doors, and bolts can be awkward to deal with. So, as conspirators seem to have started a hare in this election, I thought we might as well take a leaf out of their books," He unlocked a small grip he had brought from Mackail Lodge. "This is from Mrs. Macpherson's game larder," he said, and held up, dangling by its ears, a fine hare.

"It's been paunched," he said, "and very well hung. Now, while we finish these drinks, the hotel will be settling down for the night. I'll leave you then for a short while. Wait for me here."

He was gone for about fifteen minutes, returning so suddenly that, with my nerves still on edge from our South African hardships, I sprang to my feet with a racing heart.

"Now then, Bunny," he said, "I've tried the door of Room Three-o-one, and it's bolted, as I thought it would be. So I've laid a good scent of hare on the carpets of all the stairs, landings, and corridors. There's only the night porter on duty, down in the lobby, and he's asleep already. Here's my dressing gown. Put it on over your clothes, slip down to the basement, and release the dogs. When turmoil ensues and people come out of their rooms to find out what's going on, I shall be watching my chance to slip into Room Three-o-one. Off you go, and I'll see you at breakfast—all being well."

"Oh, dear God!" I breathed. On the stairs and in the broad corridors only an occasional gaslight had been left burning, dimly blue, as I stole down to the lobby. Most of the lights there had been turned off. The night porter was sound asleep in one of the saddlebag chairs. I tiptoed across the lobby and down stone stairs to the basement. I opened the kennels door.

Dimly I made out, in faint light filtering down from the lobby, the well-bred heads of setters, pointers, retrievers, and spaniels as they thrust them out between the bars of their cages to sniff at me in friendly inquiry.

"Good dogs, clever dogs," I whispered to them, as I opened cage after cage. "Go find the hare, dogs! Push him out! Hie on! Go seek!"

The Pekinese, waking with a startled snuffle, hurled scandalized yaps at me and, when I released him, immediately attacked my trouser cuffs with sharp teeth and bloodcurdling snarls. But then he spotted the procession of hunting dogs, led by a fine Gordon setter, streaming up the stairs to the lobby, and immediately rushed with indignant yaps to take his rightful place, as oriental royalty, at the head of the exodus.

Normally mute in the chase, the well-trained hunting dogs, excited by their unfamiliar surroundings and the hysterical yapping of the Pekinese, so far forgot themselves, when they picked up the scent of the hare, as to give tongue—especially the Cocker, Springer, and Welsh water spaniels—with a fearful clamor. Through the din I heard the wild shouting of the night porter.

When I reached the lobby, I saw the porter chasing the

pack up the main staircase and whacking vainly at the tail-
end dogs with a rolled-up newspaper. I followed unobtru-
sively.

In the dim-lit corridors, bedroom doors were opening on
all sides. People were coming out in disarray and alarm,
some carrying candlesticks, and all shouting at each other to
know what was happening.

"Keep calm!" I called to them, as I hurried along the corridor. "There's nothing to fear, ladies! You'll be taken care of.
Arrangements are being made!"

"What kind of arrangements?" demanded a man wearing
a nightcap and carrying a candlestick.

"Adequate ones, m'lud, adequate ones," I assured him, recognizing his fine, judicial features as those of a famous
judge at the Old Bailey. "Calm the ladies, m'lud!"

I hurried on up to the next floor, where my own room was
located. On this floor, too, though the shouting and barking
of the main chase was now coming from the floor above, the
third floor, confusion reigned.

Twisting and turning through the seething throng, I
gained the refuge of my own room. I closed and bolted the
door and, holding my breath, stood listening to the uproar
going on all over the hotel, but particularly, it seemed to me,
on the floor above—the third floor.

Shaken and appalled, I wondered if Raffles could have
been trapped, red-handed, in Room 301.

Not until long after the disturbance had died down did I
fall at last into an exhausted slumber. I slept so heavily that,
when I went down to breakfast, the grouse-shooting crowd
had left to catch their trains and steamers northward to the
various moors, and the great dining room seemed deserted.

My heart sank. I feared the worst. But then I saw him. His
tweeds immaculate, a pearl in his cravat, Raffles was break-
fasting at a corner table—in the company, to my surprise, of
Ken Mackail, wearing the kilt and a smiling face. I wondered
uneasily what his presence portended.

"Ah, here's Bunny Manders," Ken said. " 'Morning, Bunny. I'm here at the hotel to meet with a political chap who's
come up from London to speak in my support on the hust-

ings today. I ran into Raffles in the lobby here. He tells me you chaps came down from Mackail Lodge last night to see the Harry Lauder show at the theatre. How was the show?"

"The show?" I said. "Oh—most amusing—pawky, I believe is the word."

"I've just been telling Raffles," Ken said, "I've got great news. General Finlayson called on me last night at the place I'm lodging at during the election campaign. He came to see me in case I'd heard any rumor of a conspiracy to make use against me of a certain war dispatch of mine—a dispatch which, as the General put it, he understood I'd had the decency to suppress when I realized it was untrue. He wanted me to know that, the moment he got wind of the conspiracy, he told his election agent that, unless he stopped the journalist who'd got hold of my manuscript from coming to Glasgow, and make him destroy the unfortunate dispatch, the General would take a horsewhip to the pair of them."

I swallowed with a dry throat. "The journalist—never *came?*" I faltered, with a furtive glance at Raffles. Meditatively buttering a finnan haddie, he did not meet my eyes.

"The fellow didn't dare come," Ken laughed. "God, what a fine man General Finlayson is, at heart! He's so ashamed of his election agent that he's suggested we call a truce to the election campaign just for tomorrow, the Glorious Twelfth, and celebrate the rites on his Castle Crissaig moor. He's invited me to bring my guests, too—that's you chaps. You'll come, of course, and stay over at Mackail Lodge until after the declaration of the poll, on the fourteenth. I insist!"

"We'll be delighted, Ken," Raffles said, "Now, Bunny, if we're to catch the next steamer back to Mackail Lodge and cast a fly or two—"

"Go ahead," said Ken. "Enjoy yourselves. I must wait here for the political chap from London who's come to help me."

I reached for the teapot with a palsied hand. But later my tone was grim when I demanded of Raffles, as we clattered in a hansom along Sauchiehall Street to the steamer dock, what had happened in Room 301.

"Something that gave me food for thought, Bunny," he said, in a strange tone. "I'll tell you about it when I've had time to think over its implications."

His withdrawn manner and knitted brows warned me not to pursue the matter with questions. I felt very uneasy. Even so, and despite the fact that we had not anticipated doing any shooting when we came north, the following day lived—for me—wholly up to its reputation as the Glorious Twelfth.

The sky was cloudless over the high moors of Castle Crissaig, the grouse were plentiful and strong on the wing. As a host, General Finlayson turned out to be surprisingly genial, and I noticed that the charming Janet made a point of acting as gun-loader for Ken Mackail. With Macpherson performing a like office for Raffles, and bluidy James Fraser for myself, while Shoona retrieved faultlessly to hand, I added my quota of bangs to the gunfire resounding all over Scotland, on this great day, from the corries of Ben Lomond to the screes of John o' Groats.

With the thaw that had set in between Mackail Lodge and Castle Crissaig likely to be permanent, and Janet now as good as his, Ken was not noticeably depressed when, on the declaration of the poll on the fourteenth, a third candidate was elected to Parliament over the heads of Ken and General Finlayson.

In fact, it was as happy a young laird as ever wore the kilt whom Raffles and I left waving to us from the jetty at Dunoon when we went off on the steamer to Glasgow to catch the Cock o' the North express back to London.

"So, in any case," I remarked to Raffles, as we paced the deck of the little steamer, "that political chap who came up from London to speak for Ken made no great difference to the election result."

"Evidently not," Raffles agreed. "But something I learned gave me the shock of my life, Bunny!"

He offered me a Sullivan from his cigarette case and, lighting up, we leaned with our arms on the rail, alongside the paddle wheel rumbling and splashing in its housing.

"As you know, Bunny," Raffles said, "they told me at the hotel desk that the man in Room Three-o-one was reputed to be a journalist. Well, when you released the dogs in your clever way, the chap came out in his nightshirt to see what was happening. I was able to slip into his room for a few uninterrupted minutes. There were various documents littered on the bedside table. Ken's manuscript was not among them, so it wasn't the man we were looking for—he was Ken's political chap. But I did find a newspaper article ringed round in blue pencil. I skimmed through it hastily, and realized at once that it was about the occupant of the room himself."

"The occupant?" I said.

Raffles nodded. "He was a journalist, right enough, Bunny. The article said he'd been a war correspondent in South Africa, was captured by the Boers, and, because he also held a cavalry commission, was put in the P.O.W. camp at Pretoria. That's the same camp as we were in, with several thousand others, and he evidently escaped a few days after us. The article said he hid among empty coal sacks in the tarpaulin-covered goods truck of a train on the Pretoria-Beira line."

My heart began to thump.

"He was in dread," said Raffles, "that the train would be stopped and searched for him at the Boer frontier station, but, as he peered from his hiding place, he saw that the train was passing through slowly, first the Boer station, then the Portuguese station, without stopping!"

My scalp tingled. "The Raffles Special!" I breathed.

"The evidence, I think, is conclusive," Raffles said. "We had a clandestine passenger, Bunny, who was on board when we stole that train. Evidently he didn't see what happened at the water tower, but when the train went through into Portuguese East without stopping, he was convinced—according to the newspaper article—that Providence was watching over him, especially as the Boer High Command had offered a reward for his recapture."

"A reward?" I said. "Oom Paul offered a reward?"

"He didn't offer a reward for you and me, Bunny," Raffles said, with a wry smile, "but the Boers offered twenty-five pounds for our passenger's recapture, dead or alive."

"Only twenty-five pounds?" I exclaimed. "He can't have been particularly important!"

"As to that, Bunny, the newspaper article refers to him as a young statesman with a brilliant future before him. One can never tell, of course. Such things are on the knees of the gods."

He dropped his cigarette over the side and looked thoughtfully across the waters of Loch Long at the banks and braes gliding by, bonnie in the mellow northern sunshine.

"Who knows, Bunny?" said A.J. Raffles. "Perhaps you and I will prove to have been on the knees of the gods when we stole, you stoked, and I drove the train that carried young Mr. Winston Spencer Churchill to safety."

THE FALLEN CURTAIN
by Ruth Rendell

The more short stories by Ruth Rendell we read, the more we like her work. It grows on you . . . This is a fascinating story, full of sensitive observation—and chilling to the marrow. It is a story of "tension, as of time stopped," and the memory of it will not, of its own volition, go away and hide. Nor will the disturbing undertones become silent, even though the almost-taboo theme is handled with fine delicacy. . . .

THE INCIDENT happened in the spring after his sixth birthday. His mother always referred to it as "that dreadful evening," and always is no exaggeration. She talked about it a lot, especially when he did well at anything, which was often since he was good at school and at passing exams.

Showing her friends his swimming certificate or the prize he had won for being top at geography: "When I think we might have lost Richard that dreadful evening! You have to believe there's Someone watching over us, don't you?" Clasping him in her arms: "He might have been killed—or worse." (A remarkable statement, this one.) "It doesn't bear thinking about."

Apparently, it did bear talking about. "If I'd told him once, I'd told him fifty times never to talk to strangers or get into cars. But boys will be boys, and he forgot all that when the time came. He was given sweets, of course, and lured into

197

this car." Whispers at this point, meaningful glances in his direction. "Threats and suggestions—persuaded into goodness knows what—I'll never know how we got him back alive."

What Richard couldn't understand was how his mother knew so much about it. She hadn't been there. Only he and the Man had been there, and Richard himself couldn't remember a thing about it. A curtain had fallen over the bit of his memory that held the details of that dreadful evening. He remembered only what had come immediately before it and immediately after.

They were living then in the South London suburb of Upfield, in a little terraced house on Petunia Street, he and his mother and his father. His mother had been over 40 when Richard was born and he had no brothers or sisters. ("That's why we love you so much, Richard.") He wasn't allowed to play in the street with the other kids. ("You want to keep yourself to yourself, dear.") Round the corner in Lupin Street lived his Gran, his father's mother. Gran never came to their house, though he thought his father would have liked it if she had.

"I wish you'd have my mother to tea on Sunday," he once heard his father say.

"If that woman sets foot in this house, Stan, I go out of it."

So Gran never came to tea.

"I hope I know what's right, Stan, and I know better than to keep the boy away from his grandmother. You can have him round once a week with you, so long as I don't have to come in contact with her."

That made three houses Richard was allowed into—his own, his Gran's, and the house next door on Petunia Street where the Wilsons lived with their Brenda and their John. Sometimes he played in their garden with John, though it wasn't much fun as Brenda, who was much older, nearly 16, was always bullying them and stopping them from getting dirty.

He and John were in the same class in school, but his mother wouldn't let him go to school alone with John, although it was only three blocks away. She was very careful and nervous about him, was his mother, waiting outside the gates before school ended to walk him home with his hand tightly clasped in hers.

But once a week he didn't go straight home. He looked forward to Wednesdays because Wednesday evening was the one he spent at Gran's, and because the time between his mother's leaving him and his arrival at Gran's house was the only time he was ever free and by himself.

This was the way it was. His mother would meet him from school and they'd walk down Plumtree Grove to where Petunia Street started. Lupin Street turned off the Grove a bit farther down, so his mother would see him cross the road, waving and smiling encouragingly, till he turned the corner into Lupin Street. Gran's house was about 100 yards down. That 100 yards was his free time, his alone time.

"Mind you run all the way," his mother always called after him.

But round the corner he always stopped running and began to dawdle—stopping to play with the cat that roamed about the bit of waste ground or climbing on the pile of bricks the builders never came to build into anything. Sometimes, if she wasn't bad with arthritis, Gran would be waiting for him at her gate, and he didn't mind having to forgo the cat and the climbing because it was so nice in Gran's house.

Gran had a big TV set—unusually big for those days—and he'd watch it, eating chocolate, until his father came from the factory in time for tea. Tea was lovely, and fish and chips that Gran didn't buy at the shop but cooked herself, and cream meringues and chocolate eclairs, and tinned peaches with evaporated milk, all of it washed down with fizzy lemonade. ("It's a disgrace the way your mother spoils that boy, Stan.")

They were supposed to be home by seven, but every week when it got to seven, Gran would remember there was a cowboy film coming up on TV and there'd be cocoa and biscuits and potato crisps to go with it. They'd be lucky to be home in Petunia Street before nine.

"Don't blame me," said his mother, "if his school work suffers next day."

That dreadful evening his mother left him as usual at the corner and saw him cross the road. He could remember that,

and remember too how he'd looked to see if Gran was at her
gate. When he'd made sure she wasn't, he'd wandered on to
the building site to cajole the cat out of the nest she'd made
for herself in the rubble.

It was late March, a fine afternoon and still broad daylight
at four. He was stroking the cat, thinking how thin and bony
she was and how some of Gran's fish and chips would do her
good, when—what? What next? At this point the curtain
came down. Three hours later it lifted, and he was in Plumtree Grove, walking along quite calmly, ("Running in terror
with that Man after him!") when whom should he meet but
Mrs. Wilson's Brenda out for the evening with her boyfriend.

Brenda had pointed at him, stared and shouted. She ran
up to him and clutched him and squeezed him till he could
hardly breathe. Was that what had frightened him into losing his memory? They said no. They said he'd been frightened before that ("Terrified out of his life!") and that Brenda's grabbing him and the dreadful shriek his mother gave
when she saw him had nothing to do with the curtain coming
down.

Petunia Street was full of police cars and there was a crowd
outside their house. Brenda hustled him in, shouting, "I've
found him, I've found him!"—and there was his father all
white in the face, talking to the policeman, his mother half
dead on the sofa being given brandy, and—wonder of won-
ders—his Gran there, too. That had been one of the strangest things of that whole strange evening, that his Gran had
set foot in their house and his mother hadn't left it.

They all started asking him questions at once. Had he answered them? All that remained in his memory was his mother's scream. That endured, that shattering sound, and the
great open mouth from which it issued as she leaped upon
him. Somehow, although he couldn't have explained why, he
connected that scream and her seizing him as if to swallow
him with the descent of the curtain.

He was never allowed to be alone after that, not even to
play with John in the Wilsons' garden, and he was never
allowed to forget those events he couldn't remember. There

was no question of going to Gran's even under supervision, for Gran's arthritis had got so bad they had put her in the old people's ward at Upfield Hospital. The Man was never found. A couple of years later a little girl from Plumtree Grove got taken away and murdered. They never found that Man either, but his mother was sure it was the same one.

"And it might have been our Richard. It doesn't bear thinking of, that Man roaming the streets like a wild beast."

"What did he do to me, mum?" asked Richard, trying.

"If you don't remember, so much the better. You want to forget all about it, put it right out of your life." If only she'd let him. "What did he *do,* dad?"

"I don't know, Rich. None of us knows, me nor the police nor your mum, for all she says. Women like to set themselves up as knowing all about things, but it's my belief you never told her no more than you told me."

She took him to school and fetched him home until he was twelve. The other kids teased him mercilessly. He wasn't allowed to go to their houses or have any of them to his. ("You never know who they know or what sort of connections they've got.") His mother only stopped going everywhere with him when he got taller than she was, and anyone could see he was too big for any Man to attack.

Growing up brought no elucidation of that dreadful evening but it did bring, with adolescence, the knowledge of what might have happened. And as he came to understand that it wasn't only threats and blows and stories of horror which the Man might have inflicted on him, he felt an alien in his own body or as if his body were covered with a slime which nothing could wash away. For there was no way of knowing how, there was nothing to do about it but wish his mother would leave the subject alone, and to avoid getting friendly with people, and to work hard at school.

He did very well there, for he was naturally intelligent and had no outside diversions. No one was surprised when he got to a good university, not Oxford or Cambridge but nearly as good ("Imagine, all that brainpower might have been wasted if that Man had had his way.") where he began to read for a science degree. He was the first member of his family ever to go to college, and the only cloud in the sky was that his Gran, as his father pointed out, wasn't there to see and share his glory.

She had died in the hospital when he was 14 and she'd left her house to his parents. They'd sold it and theirs and bought a much bigger one with a proper garden and a garage in a suburb some five miles farther out from Upfield. The little bit of money Gran had saved she left to Richard, to come to him when he was 18. It was just enough to buy a secondhand car, and when he came down from university for the Easter holidays, he bought a two-year-old Ford, took his driving test, and passed it.

"That boy," said his mother, "passes every exam that comes his way. It's like as if he couldn't fail if he tried. He's got a guardian angel watching over him, has had ever since he was six." Her husband had admonished her for her too-excellent memory and now she referred only obliquely to that dreadful evening. "When you-know-what happened and he was spared."

She watched him drive expertly round the block, her only regret that he didn't have a nice girl beside him, a sensible, hard-working fiancée—not one of your tarty ones—and saving up for the deposit on a house and furniture. Richard had never had a girl. There was one at college he liked and who, he thought, might like him. But he didn't ask her out. He was never quite sure if he was fit for any girl to know, let alone to love.

The day after he'd passed his test he thought he'd drive over to Upfield and look up John Wilson. There was more in this, he confessed to himself, than a wish to revive an old friendship. John was the only friend he'd really ever had, but he'd always felt inferior to him, for John had been (and had had the chance to be) easy and sociable and had had a girl to go out with when he was only 14. He rather liked the idea of arriving outside the Wilson's house, fresh from his first two terms at the university and in his own car.

It was a Wednesday in early April, a fine, mild afternoon and still, of course, broad daylight at four. He chose a Wednesday because that was early closing day in Upfield and

John wouldn't be in the hardware store where he'd worked ever since he left school three years before.

But as he approached Petunia Street up Plumtree Grove from the southerly direction, it struck him that he'd like to take a look at his Gran's old house and see if they'd ever built anything on that bit of waste ground. For years and years, half of his lifetime, those bricks had lain there, though the thin old cat had disappeared or died long before Richard's parents moved. And the bricks were still there, overgrown now by grass and nettles.

He drove into Lupin Street, moving slowly along the pavement edge until he was within sight of his Gran's house. There was enough of his mother in him to stop him from parking directly outside the house ("Keep yourself to yourself and don't pry into what doesn't concern you."), so he stopped the car some few yards this side of it.

It had been painted a bright pink, the window woodwork picked out in sky-blue. Richard thought he liked it better the way it used to be, cream plaster and brown wood, but he didn't move away. A strange feeling had come over him, stranger than any he could remember having experienced, which kept him where he was, staring at the wilderness of rubble and brick and weeds. Just nostalgia, he thought, just going back to those Wednesdays which had been the high-spots of his weeks.

It was funny the way he kept looking in the rubble for the old cat to appear. If she were alive, she'd be as old as he by now and not many cats live that long. But he kept on looking just the same, and presently, as he was trying to pull himself out of this dreamy, dazed feeling and go off to John's, a living creature did appear behind the high weeds. A boy, about eight. Richard didn't intend to get out of the car. But he found himself out of it, locking the door and then strolling over onto the building site.

You couldn't really see much from a car, not details. That must have been why he'd got out, he thought, to examine more closely this scene of his childhood pleasures. It seemed very small, not the wild expanse of brick hills and grassy gullies he remembered, but a scrubby bit of land 20 feet wide

and perhaps twice as long. Of course it had seemed so much
bigger because he had been so much smaller—smaller even
than this little boy who now sat on a brick mountain, eyeing
him.

He didn't mean to speak to the boy, for Richard wasn't a
child any more but a Man. And if there is an explicit rule that
a child mustn't speak to strangers, there is an implicit, unstat-
ed one that a Man doesn't speak to children. If he had meant
to speak, his words would have been very different, something about having played there himself once, or having
lived nearby. The words he did use came to his lips as if they
had been placed there by some external (or deeply internal)
ruling authority.

"You're trespassing on private land. Did you know that?"

The boy began to ease himself down. "All the kids play
here, mister."

"Maybe, but that's no excuse. Where do you live?"

On Petunia Street, but I'm going to my Gran's . . . No.

"Upfield High Road."

"I think you'd better get in my car," the Man said, "and I'll
take you home."

Doubtfully the boy said, "There won't be no one there. My
mum works late Wednesdays and I haven't got no dad. I'm to
go straight home from school and have my tea and wait for
when my mum comes at seven."

Straight to my Gran's and have my tea and . . .

"But you haven't gone straight home, have you? You've
hung about trespassing on other people's property."

"You a cop, mister?"

"Yes," said the Man.

The boy got into the car quite willingly. "Are we going to
the cop shop?"

"We may go to the police station later. I want to have a talk
to you first. We'll go—" Where should they go? South London has many open spaces, commons they're called—Wands-
worth Common, Tooting Common, Streatham Common
. . . What made him choose Drywood Common, so far away,
a place he'd heard of but hadn't visited, so far as he knew, in
his whole life? The Man had known, and he was the Man
now, wasn't he?

"We'll go to Drywood and have a talk. There's some chocolate on the dashboard shelf. Have a piece if you like." He started the car and they drove off past Gran's old house. "Have it all," he said.

The boy ate it all. He introduced himself as Barry. He was eight and he had no father or brothers or sisters, just his mum who worked to keep them both. His mum had told him never to get into a stranger's car, but a cop was different, wasn't he?

"Quite different," said the Man. "Different altogether."

It wasn't easy finding Drywood Common because the signposting was bad around there. But the stranger thing was that, once there, the whole layout of the common was remarkably familiar to him.

"We'll park," he said, "down by the pond."

He found the pond with ease, driving along the main road that bisected the common, then turning left onto a smaller lane. There were ducks on the pond. It was surrounded by trees, quite a wood of trees, but in the distance you could see houses and a row of shops. He parked the car by the water and switched off the engine.

Barry was very calm and trusting. He listened intelligently to the "policeman's" lecture on behaving himself and not trespassing, and he didn't fidget or seem bored when the Man stopped talking about that and began to talk about himself. The Man had had a lonely life, a bit like being in prison, and he'd never been allowed out alone. Even when he was in his own room doing his homework, he'd been watched ("Leave your door open, dear, we don't want any secrets in this house.") and he hadn't had a single real friend. Would Barry be his friend, just for a few hours, just for this evening? Barry would.

"But you're grown up now," Barry said.

The Man nodded, but as if that didn't make much difference, and then he began to cry. He cried as grownups do, almost tearlessly but with shame and self-disgust.

A small and rather dirty hand touched the Man's hand and held it. No one had ever held his hand like that before. Not possessively or commandingly ("Hold onto me tight, Richard, while we cross the road.") but gently, sympathetically—

lovingly? Their hands remained clasped, the small one covering the large, then the large one enclosing and gripping the small. A tension, as of time stopped, held the two people in the car quiet, motionless. Then the boy broke it, and time moved again.

"I'm getting hungry," the boy said.

"Are you? It's past your teatime. I'll tell you what, we could have some fish and chips. One of those shops over there is a fish and chip shop."

Barry started to get out of the car.

"No, not you," the Man said. "It's better if I go alone. You wait here. Okay?"

"Okay," Barry said.

He was gone only ten minutes—for he knew exactly and from a distance which one of the shops it was—and when he got back Barry was waiting for him. The fish and chips were good, almost as good as those Gran used to cook. By the time they had finished eating and had wiped their greasy fingers on his handkerchief, dusk had come. Lights were going up in those far-off shops and houses but here, down by the pond, the trees made it quite dark.

"What's the time?" said Barry.

"A quarter past six."

"I ought to be getting back."

"How about a game of hide and seek first? Your mum won't be home yet. I can get you back to Upfield in ten minutes."

"I don't know . . . Suppose she gets in early?"

"Please," the Man said. "Please, just for a little while. I used to play hide and seek down here when I was a kid."

"But you said you never played anywhere. You said—"

"Did I? Maybe I didn't. I'm a little confused."

Barry looked at him gravely. "I'll hide first," he said.

He watched Barry disappear among the trees. Grownups who play hide and seek don't keep to the rules; they don't bother with that counting-to-100 bit. But the Man did. He counted slowly and seriously, then he got out of the car and began walking round the pond.

It took him a long time to find Barry, who was more proficient at this game than he, a proficiency which showed when it was his turn to do the seeking. The darkness was deepening, and there was no one else on the common. He and the boy were quite alone.

Barry had gone to hide. In the car the Man sat counting—97, 98, 99, 100. When he stopped he was aware of the silence of the place, alleviated only by the faint, distant hum of traffic on the South Circular Road, just as the darkness was alleviated only by the red blush of the sky radiating the glow of London. Last time round it hadn't been this dark. The boy wasn't behind any of the trees or in the bushes by the waterside.

Where the hell had the stupid kid got to? Richard's anger was irrational, for he had suggested the game himself. Was he angry because the boy had proved better at it than he? Or was it something deeper and fiercer—rage at rejection by this puny and ignorant little savage?

"Where are you, Barry? Come on out. I've had about enough of this."

There was no answer. The wind rustled, and a tiny twig scuttered down out of a treetop to his feet. God, that little devil! What will I do if I can't find him?

When I do find him I'll—I'll kill him.

He shivered. The blood was throbbing in his head. He broke a stick off a bush and began thrashing about with it, infuriated, shouting into the dark silence. "Barry, Barry, come out! Come out at once, d'you hear me?" He doesn't want me, he doesn't care about me, no one will ever want me—

Then he heard a giggle from a treetop, and suddenly there was a crackling of twigs, a slithering sound. Not quite above him—over there. In the giggle, he thought, there was a note of jeering. But where, where? Down by the water's edge. The boy had been up in the tree that almost overhung the pond.

There was a thud as of small feet bouncing onto the ground, and again that maddening, gleeful giggle. For a moment the Man stood still. His hands clenched as around a frail neck, and he held them pressed together, as if crushing out life.

*Run, Barry, run. . . . Run, Richard, to Plumtree Grove and
Brenda, to home and mother who knows what dreadful evenings
are.*

The Man thrust his way through the bushes, making for
the pond. The boy would be away by now, but not far away.
And the Man's legs were long enough to outrun the boy, his
hands strong enough to insure there would be no future of
doubt and fear and curtained memory. . . .

But the boy was nowhere, nowhere. And yet—what was
that sound, as of stealthy, fearful feet creeping away? He
wheeled round, and there was the boy coming toward him,
walking a little timidly between the straight, gray tree trunks
toward him. A thick constriction gripped his throat. There
must have been something in his face, some threatening
gravity made more intense by the half dark, that stopped the
boy in his tracks.

Run, Barry, run, run. . . .

They stared at each other for a moment, for a lifetime, for
twelve long years. Then the boy gave a merry laugh, fearless
and innocent. He ran forward and flung himself into the
Man's arms, and the Man, in a great release of pain and anguish, lifted the boy up, lifted him laughing into his own
laughing face. They laughed with a kind of rapture at
finding each other at last, and in the dark, under the whis-
pering trees, each held the other in a close embrace.

"Come on," Richard said, "I'll take you home. I don't know
what I was doing, bringing you here in the first place."

"To play hide and seek," said Barry. "We had a swell time."

They got back into the car. It was after seven when they
reached Upfield High Road, but not much after.

"I don't reckon my mum's got in yet."

" I'll drop you here. I won't go up to your place. Barry?"

"What is it, mister?"

"Don't ever take a lift from a Man again, will you? Promise
me?"

Barry nodded. "Okay."

"I once took a lift from a stranger, and for years I couldn't
remember what had happened. It sort of came back to me tonight, meeting you. I remember it all now. He was all right,
just a bit lonely like me. We had fish and chips on Drywood

Common and played hide and seek like you and me, and he brought me back nearly to my house—the way I've brought you. But it wouldn't always be like that."

"How do you know?"

Richard looked at his strong young man's hands. "I just know," he said.

He drove away, turning once to see that the boy was safely in his house. Barry told his mother all about it, but she insisted it must have been a nasty experience and called the police. Since Barry didn't know the license number of the car and had no idea of the stranger's name, there was little the police could do. They never found the Man.

Editorial Postscript

The story you have just read won the highest possible honor that can be won by a mystery short story. It was awarded the coveted Edgar by MWA (Mystery Writers of America) as the best new short story in the mystery field published in American magazines and books during 1974.

DEPRECIATION ALLOWANCE
by *Henry T. Parry*

---

*"When would it be recognized that people wear out too, that
old people are also entitled to a depreciation allowance?"*

"How do you plead?"

"Guilty, Your Honor."

"Before sentence is passed, do you have anything to say?"

"Your Honor, I would like it if you would send me to jail
right now, if that's how it's done. If you give me a suspended
sentence, my son-in-law, Bill Jenkins, is only going to try
once again to put me in a home for old folks. Have you ever
visited a home for old folks, Your Honor? Retirement homes
they call them now, and give them names like Valley View
and Sunset Years. Used-people lots is what they ought to call
them, and with no resale value either.

"I went to visit old Dutch Smith at Maple Shade. He was
tied to a chair with a towel to keep him from slipping to the
floor. The place smelled like the hallway outside a public toilet. Half the staff treated them like bad children or as if they
were cases of empties being returned for recycling.

"But worst of all were the cheery ones who joshed and kidded the old people as if they were never to be taken seriously
and weren't of any real account. I'd rather have a person
downright mad at me than to have them say, 'My, we're feeling grumpy today, aren't we?' or 'Watta ya say we step out tonight, Wolf?' All right, I'm old. I can't do anything about

210

that, Your Honor, but I do know that I would rather go to jail than to a home for old folks."

The judge looked at the country man in his town suit, with his neck seamed and weathered in the gaping collar of the new white shirt, his out-of-date broadbrimmed hat hanging from thick fingers which shook almost imperceptibly. Gathering up the probation report, the judge tapped the pages neatly together and said, "John Clemson, attempted armed robbery is a serious offense. I sentence you to three years. Sentence is suspended. Court is adjourned."

The old man stood mutely before the bench, the courtroom around him suddenly brisk with the sounds of people who had places to go. He turned and saw Ella Davis, the girl who worked at the checkout counter of the supermarket, standing behind him, with protruding cylindrical curlers making her head look like a scarf-covered gun turret—Ella, who would have been the chief witness against him if the trial had been held. Her good-natured face worked with the effort to say the right words. On the night of the holdup she had not had that problem.

"Now, Mr. Clemson," she had said, "you must be out of your head. Put that gun away, you're shaking it so. At your time of life to be sticking up a supermarket where most everybody knows you and—"

"Ella, give me the money. I'm not out of my head and I'm not going to hurt anybody. I know exactly what I'm doing."

"There ain't so much here, Mr. Clemson. I just came on duty. Now if you was to hold me up later—say, at nine o'clock—there'd be more money here." Her foot slipped to the alarm. When the manager, a new man who had just been transferred from the city, appeared, Clemson handed him the gun, a World War I automatic pistol, unloaded and with the trigger missing. The manager was unversed in the intricacies of country relationships, and the head office was equally so, so charges were pressed. From then on the due process of law had set in.

"Mr. Clemson," the court attendant said softly, "you're free to go now."

Free, he thought, you bet I'm free. They call me a senior citizen. Well, by Jupiter, I'm a citizen, a free American citizen before I'm a senior anything. I'll starve, I'll walk the highways, I'll die in the snow alongside Interstate 80 before they get me into a home! I'm going to die a free man, even if it would have been in jail. Miserable maybe, and guilty. But free.

"Mr. Clemson." The court attendant placed a kindly hand on the old man's arm. "You can go any time you've a mind to."

The old man glanced briefly at the white-haired attendant. Jim Mulcahy, Harry Mulcahy's boy, he thought. Harry who was with me in the 102nd Engineers, blowing up wire and emplacements and anything else in the Argonne that needed blowing up. We used to take turns, one wiring and placing the charges, the other pushing the plunger. Once I pushed it too soon and when Harry came back to our hole he didn't have any pants, just naked from his puttees up. All he said was: "Kinda impatient, ain't you, John?" Let's see, Harry must be dead now, what, ten years maybe.

"Dangerous old coot, ain't he?" he heard the attendant whisper. "You better watch yourself, Bill, he might have some plans for you next time."

"Come on, old man. Let's get going. You've made enough trouble and you got off mighty lucky."

Bill Jenkins, his son-in-law, stood beside him, burly in his checkered mackinaw, red-faced from working outdoors in the prairie winter. Together they went down the marble steps of the courthouse to the parking lot where the Civil War statue stood sentinel to an encampment of cars.

"Wait here in the car. I got to pick up some things," Bill said.

The old man settled himself in the front seat. Waiting is what old people do the most of, he thought, and they know what they're waiting for. He picked up the reminder list Bill had left on the seat. *Deposit check,* he read. That would be for the sale of the timber. Black walnut and oak that had stood since before the farm was homesteaded by his grandfather, home from Stone's River and Missionary Ridge. He could still hear the snarling of the chain saws when the lumbering crew had taken out the trees, leaving raw stumps. "That land goes into soybeans," Bill had said.

The next item on the list bore out his intention. *Dynamite,* it read. Bill would spend the winter blasting out the stumps and when the frost was out of the ground he would go in there with the big tractor and plow. *Quarter-inch bolts.* He laid the list aside.

But it was his own fault, wasn't it, that he was penniless in his old age? He had deeded the farm to his daughter and when she was killed in a car accident, the terms of her will conveyed the farm to her husband. Within a year Bill had remarried, to Anna Johnson who was the teller at the local bank. Bill was a good farmer, thorough and hard-working, and attentive to detail, but the gossip was that Bill had married Anna to get someone to relieve him of the paperwork. If so, he succeeded for Anna took over with drive and a certain amount of dry zeal, coupled with considerable aggressiveness in dealing with the various agencies of government designed to help farmers.

In the county agent's office it was said that the agent broke out in simulated tears on being told that Mrs. Jenkins was on the phone and would speak to no one but him. Anna had scored a minor triumph, too, in the matter of depreciation allowances on farm equipment, pointing out a method whereby larger amounts could be taken early in the life of new equipment and demonstrating the economics of replacing old equipment with new to obtain higher and faster write-offs against taxes.

It had been Anna's suggestion, well supported by figures, that caused Bill to sell the timber. Something to do with capital gains. How, the old man wondered, had his father and grandfather ever been able to farm without benefit of capital gains and depreciation allowances? When would it be recognized that people wear out too, that old people are also entitled to a depreciation allowance?

Two months after Anna moved into the farm as Bill's wife, Clemson moved out of the house and partitioned off crude living quarters in the corner of the barn where the equipment was stored and repaired. The separation had been, if not amicable, at least quiet and civilized. He had not explained his reasons, and they had asked him for none, happy to accept what they regarded as a windfall. His reason was that he could no longer bear to see a stranger where his grandmother, mother, wife, and daughter had been.

Anna was not the one who first suggested that Clemson would be better off in a retirement home. Anna was for letting nature take its course in the partitioned-off corner, knowing with her actuarial sense that the years remaining to the old man were few. But Bill was sensitive to the talk of neighbors, to the oblique references, and had defensively and heatedly pointed out it was the old man's wish, not his, to live in the barn. He had come into the barn one day when Clemson was working on the tractor engine and handed the old man several envelopes.

"When you get a chance, read these and we'll talk about it. I want you to think seriously about what's in them. And let's think about setting a date."

The envelopes contained illustrated brochures describing several retirement homes—happy, contentment-filled places where young-old men in shorts rode three-wheeled vehicles that gave rise to unintentional but disturbing associations with childhood, and where smiling foursomes sat at bridge, the ladies' hair set as if by precision instrument, with highball glasses discreetly but comfortably sunk in holders at the side of the table; sunny vacation spots where everything, everything, was taken care of.

He compared the literature with what he knew from his experiences in visiting old Dutch Smith at Maple Shade and tossed it into the trash drum. I'm poor, I'm old, he thought, and I'm not wanted here no matter how I stay out of the way, no matter how I try to help where I can. But they will never get me into one of those places. Nor into the county home either. It was then that he decided that the only institution he could honorably enter was prison, and had set about planning the purposefully inept holdup that would send him there. But now the suspended sentence had barred that solution.

Bill Jenkins slammed the trunk compartment shut and squeezed in behind the wheel.

"Got enough dynamite back there to blow us all the way back to the farm."

These were the only words spoken until Bill drove into the

barn and parked, the car looking citified and dandy beside the blunt rural usefulness of the tractor and plows. The old man started for his room when Bill paused in unloading the car, came over to him and stood close, his hard muscular bulk bulging over the old man's thin toughness.

"There's going to be no more cute tricks, old man, making Anna and me look cheap. Making it look like jail was better than staying here with us."

"Bill, that just ain't so. You wanted to put me in a home for old folks. I'd been satisfied to live here in the barn but you don't really want me on the place. So I'd rather go to jail than rot away in a home for old folks. Nobody's going to budge me from that."

"We'll see, old man, we'll see. Tomorrow morning at eight o'clock I want you to be sitting in the front seat of that car. You and me are going out to Maple Shade and that's where you're going to stay. And there ain't nothing you can do about it. Come on now, why do you make me get tough with you? Henry Smith says his father is there and the old folks all have a pretty good time together."

Clemson remembered Dutch Smith, who had once had a tryout with the Cubs, straining helplessly against the towel that kept him from pitching to the floor. It would never happen to him. Never.

"Remember. Eight tomorrow. Get packed tonight and I hope you got the good sense not to make any more trouble. I've stood the last from you I'm going to stand."

He left the old man standing in the gathering darkness, surrounded by the depreciable equipment of modern farming. To be old, Clemson thought, may put you at the mercy of others, but it does not necessarily mean you are helpless.

He cooked his simple supper on the two-plate burner, listened to the news on the radio, and began gathering his clothes for packing. Realizing that he was already wearing his good suit, he picked up his remaining clothes and threw them into the trash drum. He tucked the pictures of his wife and daughter into his pocket. One more thing and he would be ready to go.

He walked out into the darkness of the barn and without turning on the lights picked up the items he would need.

Long forgotten reflexes came to his aid as he worked in the dark. When he had finished, he walked in the early winter night down the lane to the highway.

Two miles along the road he turned into Chubby's Diner where the long-haul truckers stopped, and stood in the gelid light of the neons beside a row of parked trucks. A driver came out of the diner, flipped away his cigarette, and prepared to mount to the cab that loomed over the old man.

"Excuse me, mister," Clemson said, "I wonder could you see your way clear to give me a lift to"—he hesitated, then picked a town 300 miles west on the Interstate—"to Seneca Falls. I won't talk much or make any bother. I—I got some folks waiting there to meet me. They're real anxious to see me and now that I don't drive any more—I know they'd be real glad to see me."

The trucker looked appraisingly at him, a retired farmer in his town clothes, harmless enough, no trouble, weighed the "No Riders" sign against the boredom of the endless Interstate, and helped the old man climb into the cab. The diesel sprang to life, the rig stalked warily to the highway's edge, and roared onto the road. Maybe Anna could figure out how much depreciation allowance an old man was worth: expected remaining life, short; estimated salvage, zero. All he knew was that you had to set your own values, that a man can be free only if he insists on being free, and is willing to sacrifice everything else.

Riding high in the snug dimness of the cab, he watched the darkness fleeing westward before the headlights, and saw the limitless prairie circle slowly away on each side of the road, locked in winter, waiting for spring to soften and open it. With spring Bill, having blasted out the last of the tree stumps, would get ready to plow what had once been the woodlot. When he went to start the tractor's engine, the little bundle wired to the ignition circuit would do its work, just as though the man sitting in the driver's seat were a tree stump.

FAREWELL, BELOVED
by Mary Amlaw

This is the 411th "first story" published by Ellery Queen's Mystery Magazine . . . a beautiful story, poetic and lyrical, but with a dread hearbeat. . . .

The author, Mary Amlaw, is in her mid-thirties "and holding"; single "and husband-hunting"; with a typical "writer's potpourri"—schoolteacher, social worker, public relations work, and "mostly a classical musician."

"In 1974," Miss Amlaw wrote us, "I decided to go for broke"—become a full-time writer. "I got a lot of letters saying, 'We loved your story so much it breaks our heart to have to return it.'" Well, Miss Amlaw's first story broke our heart too—but we did not return it.

Miss Amlaw's hobbies reveal the woman: "writing, reading, concertizing. People. Psychology. Bridge, chess, hiking, bowling, beachcombing, stargazing." We cannot resist one more quotation from her letter: "In all seriousness I'm aiming at becoming a 'compleat' writer. I have to. I've been so hooked on it all my life that if I were stranded on a desert island, I'd write with bone fragments on pieces of tree bark." Oh, how proud we'll all be of her one of these days!

"Shule, shule, shule agra,
Only death can ease my woe.
The love of my heart from me did go,
Cathutheen, mavourneen slaun."

THIS DAY a great shame has come to our house. That is what my papa says. He shouted it at me, and at my mama, and at my brother Sean. "Tell me who it was did it," he roared, shaking his fist in Sean's face. "Who was it met her all summer on the hill?"

My mama wails, "Hush yourself, Paudeen, and don't be lifting your hand in anger this day. My heart is breaking."

I ask her why is her heart breaking? But she only pushes me from her and cries on.

Upstairs Father Robinson sits by my sister Kathleen. He is the only stranger my papa has ever let come under our roof. Sean says my papa is mad. Sean says if we could get away from here, we would find the world much different than things are here. But we will never get away. Sean tried to and had to come back. Kathleen never even tried. I would go if I was old enough to get to a town without being stopped and sent back.

My papa let Father Robinson go upstairs and sit by Kathleen. She is dying from having a baby too soon. My mama says it will be a blessing if the poor blind babe dies with her. My papa swore that Kathleen for shame would have neither priest nor prayers to bury her. He is angry with Sean for bringing Father Robinson here. In spite of my mama's tearful shushings he cannot hold his anger. He backs Sean into the wall, roaring, "Who brought this disgrace on her? Tell me, or you'll be lying in the grave with Kathleen, and it will be my fist put you there!"

But Sean says not a word.

Father Robinson comes slowly down the stairs, such a strangeness about him that even my papa looks as he descends. Mama sniffles into her apron and papa looks and looks, his fist full of Sean's collar.

"The girl is dead," the Father says.

My mama weeps with great noise. My papa glares.

"No," Sean says low. "No, not dead?"

The Father nods. "Gone. Gone in peace. God have mercy on her soul." His bright black eyes move from Sean's face to my papa's fist gripping Sean's collar. My papa turns Sean loose.

"Did she confess herself?" my papa asks. "Did she name the blackguard who shamed herself and us?"

"He cannot tell," Sean says. "It is privileged matter—not one word can he say." He stands spread against the wall under the foxskin my papa nailed there last winter, his eyes cold and bright.

"Who are you to forbid me to ask after my own daughter?" my papa roars. "Is this why I sent you off to your uncle, to have you come back cocky and bold, daring to raise your hand to me now you stand so tall? Fair ruined you are, come back to me sick and unfit for work, and making my daughters heedless as yourself! Where is the fortune you were going to make us if we let you go off to study? Pipedreams! What have I out of it? A son too sickly to work my land and a daughter disgraced and dead!" He shoved Sean hard against the stairwell. "I'll have no defiance in my own house. You'll tell me who it was or go from my roof this night!"

Sean came home because Kathleen sent for him. But my papa doesn't know that. He thinks Sean couldn't find work to keep himself when my uncle died.

"Paud, you'll not turn him out!" my mama cries weakly. "And him with the fever coming and going on him all the winter past."

She says it because Father Robinson is there, watching. She has seen Sean go coughing to the fields at my papa's word, the fever on him and rain coming down thin and cold, and she said nothing to save him. Sean says she has no feeling for us, but Kathleen always said, "No, there you are wrong. She is worn out with work and the old devil's temper. She is not unfeeling, but only weak."

My papa keeps Sean pinned against the stair. He is strong, my papa. Sean laughs short and hard into his face. The Father looks at them both, his mouth pulling down. I wonder how much Kathleen has told him. Enough for him to help me run away?

"How terrible was her sin, Father?" Sean cries out. "More terrible than his who promised her to Mick Farrell come summer, and him with two wives already buried by hard living with him?" He could hardly talk with papa's hand so close to his throat. "What had she to confess? It was I told her she did no wrong to love. And she believed me. She was innocent. She believed me. Let what sin there is be on my head. She was sinless."

Sean's eyes get very bright. The Father puts his hand on Sean's shoulder. Sean's head falls low and lower over the Father's black sleeve. Almost I think he is crying.

"God is merciful, son," the Father murmurs. "Who can say it is not as you tell it?"

"Am I bound then to give her poor secret to this drunken sot that fathered us, for him to spread about making her name a dirty thing, a thing to laugh at and repeat in the taverns and fields with a snicker?"

The Father's fingers move against Sean's thin shoulder. "To lie is forbidden," he says softly to Sean. "Nothing forbids silence."

My papa shouts, "I am the authority in my house!"

Sean doesn't even look at him. But the Father watches. I wonder how much Kathleen has said. She always made me promise to say nothing. "It is our grief, and we will overcome it," she promised me. "We will leave here, you and I and Sean. Then nothing that happened here will matter. But if people learn the old devil is mad, they will be afraid of us, and think we are mad, too."

My papa comes heavily across the bare floor to me. I would run but he would catch me later, alone, when no one would be near to help me. So I stand quietly as his big hands fall on my shoulders.

"You'll tell me what I must know," he says. "You're my fine girleen, Maura! Who was it met with yourselves and Kathleen on the hill last summer, when I wasn't about to see for myself?" His hands grip my shoulders down to the bones. Sean moves fast as fire across the room to me.

"Let her be," he growls. "She knows nothing."

My papa's hands dig harder into my shoulders. I don't dare wriggle away, but Sean sees on my face that those big hands hurt.

"Knows nothing?" my papa says. "Wasn't it yourself told me she knew letters and numbers and writing as well as yourself, and must go to school to learn more?" My papa shook me lightly. "Come now, Maura. Do you know so many things, and not know one face and the name that goes with it?"

"She never saw anyone but ourselves," Sean says for me. "The climb always wore her out, and she slept. She knows nothing." His hands come under my chin and lock around my face. I feel brave with Sean behind me, and look straight at my papa. Silence was not forbidden. Father Robinson had said so.

"So that's the way of it." My papa looks down at me. Sean's hands tremble on my face. The fever is on him and it is like being touched by worms of fire. Like fingers of sun brushing me when I slept on our hill.

I loved the hill. It was always bright and safe and warm, the sun thick and dry in the long grass, and Kathleen singing songs into my hair. Sean would tell us of our uncle's farm and tell us things to laugh at until the sun made me sleepy. Even when I felt him lift me from Kathleen's arms and put me down in the grass in my half sleep I was never afraid. When I woke I stayed where I was, dreaming happy things into the cloud shapes until shadows stretched cold down the afternoon. Then Kathleen would come to me laughing and a murmuring breeze sprang up around her. Twigs and pretty green things littered her hair. I'd brush it clean for her.

"Maura knows nothing," Sean tells my papa. "Nothing."

My papa rubs his chin. I know by the flat look of his eyes what he will do to Sean and me when Father Robinson is gone. Sean knows, too. His hands stay on my face to keep me brave.

"This," says the Father, "is a sorry task to lay on a child."

My papa lets me go. "Keep your secret then." His face is twisted with anger. "I'll learn the name I want from the babe itself. Its own face will tell me its father soon enough."

My papa's face is black. I am glad for the rain rattling the window. If it were quiet, he might hear how fast I am breathing and think I am hiding something from him.

"Run to your room now," Sean whispers. He gets between me and my papa and leans against the wall while I climb the stairs. My papa watches me all the way to the top, squinting his eyes at me and rubbing his whiskery chin, rubbing and rubbing.

"You baptized the babe?" I hear him ask the Father. "By what name?"

"The name the poor girl gave me," the Father said. "Sean."

"Sean, is it?" says my papa in a voice that makes me shiver even with all the stairs behind me. "There's not that many Seans about to hide the one I want."

"Paud, don't disgrace us before the Father," my mama says. "Kathleen is dead. Let her rest in what peace she can find."

"Sean, is it?" my papa says again. "Sean."

"She'd not call the babe by its father's name," my mama says, "for the bad luck it would bring on both."

Then the Father says, "Why has the little girl never come to school? I must speak to her and see what learning she has."

Moving shadows go down the long upstairs hallway to the room where my Kathleen lies. Someone—Sean or the Father or my mama who helped the baby get born—left a long white candle burning by the bed. It throws gold over Kathleen's still face and makes firepoints wink in and out of her black hair.

She was sleeping quietly. I was glad, for most nights she slept little. Often the last winter months I'd wake to find her weeping over me, the moon a ghostly glitter at the window beyond.

"It's the dreams upset me," she confessed. "They say I will soon die. Maura, if the dreams are true and the Dullahan takes me off, will you pray for me?"

I couldn't understand her tears or her urgency. Often she took me from my bed and held me while stars littered the sky. "Second sight is on me," she said unevenly, "and hard are the things it shows me. Sean, choking of a sudden in the mud of a far field, thin as sparrow bones, the blood of his sickness a bright stain on the ground. Flowers spring up there, blood-red flowers. I am in the earth. Over my head stand weeds." She fringed my face with kisses. "And you, Maura, there is no escape for you either. Poor Maura. Poor Maureen." Her voice mourned like the sea.

She told me then how to care for the baby to come, to keep it warm and dry and feed it often with a rag dipped in warm milk. And I must keep it quiet, and not let it cry when the papa could hear, lest it anger him into beating it to death. She made me say it all back to her, time after time, then she rocked back and forth with me in her arms until the moon died in the black night. Sometimes Sean would hear us and wake, and carry me to my bed. Then he would quiet Kathleen as she quieted me until she could sleep a little.

Now she slept with no tossing or evil dreams. A bit of string held most of her hair, and the candle beside the bed threw gold shadows over her face. She seemed to smile in the candle glow.

A thin mewing came from the cradle under the window. I went to it and lifted Kathleen's baby out. He was warm in my arms. I rocked him and he hushed.

His eyes were shut tight. That's why my mama said he was blind, because his eyes didn't open. I sat on the floor by his cradle and tucked his dark head into the base of my neck, and kissed him, and he hushed.

My mama came into the room. She never noticed us, but began to wash Kathleen. She worked fast, my mama. Sean came to the doorway and leaned against the frame. "The Father's gone," he said, "but he's coming tomorrow to see about Maura."

My mama didn't answer. She tugged Kathleen's gray dress over her head and reached for the brown dress on the chair.

"Must she wear rags even in her grave?" Sean growled.

"She has no better," my mama said without looking at him.

"Wait." Sean prowled through Kathleen's things and dragged out a handful of filmy blue stuff. Mama reached out but the stuff, so light, so pretty, floated away from her touch.

"Where did she get such a dress?" my mama asked in a cracked voice.

"I brought her the goods home from Dermott's with me," Sean said. "She made it up nights."

"You brought me nothing," my mama said.

Sean spread the filmy skirt over Kathleen. He took the string from her hair and brushed at the hair with his fingers. Over and over, over and over his fingers sifted the feathery dark weight of Kathleen's hair.

My mama slapped Sean's hand away. "You'll not touch her!"

Sean lifted his head. My mama moved thin as frost to the

window. "I'm not blind as the misbegotten babe," she rasped. "Couldn't I see the look of her after she'd been with you? Only a woman loved looks that way. And now this—the babe, blind, and 'Sean' as well!"

Sean's eyes glittered like blue fire. They seemed to stand out of their sockets. Everything else about him was still.

My mama hugged her thin arms. A bitter smile twisted her face. "Deny it, then!" she said. "Deny it. You cannot!"

Sean's face hardened like the rock floor of the pasture pond. He lifted his hand as if to strike my mama. Blacker and blacker went his face. He was on his feet and coming at my mama. She backed against the window. Her head came up.

"I will not unsay what I have said," she told him spitefully.

Sean didn't hit her. He let his hand fall and swept it towards the door. My mama slithered out and down the stairs. Sean stared after her, his eyes still glittering. Then he knelt on the floor by Kathleen's bed and buried his head next to hers. Hoarse choking sounds came from him that made a hurt inside me. I laid the baby in his cradle and stood by Sean. He didn't know I was there until I touched his shoulder.

"Maura," he whispered. "Were you here all this time?" Gray streaks ran down his face. I was afraid of his face so gray, the eyes so black. I nodded.

"You heard what she thinks of me?" He put his arm around me. Heat came off him like a fireplace.

"Are you crying because Kathleen is dead?"

"No. Because I am not."

This morning Kathleen had stood by the table cutting bread while Sean brought water from the well. The rains had not come but the air was full with the smell of them. My papa squinted at Kathleen standing so pale and quiet at the bread. He rose from his place and dragged her into the square of sunlight on the floor. My mama got up as he pulled Kathleen's skirt tight into his big fist.

The patch of sunlight vanished.

"Paud!" my mama cried as he lifted his heavy hand. "If you touch her you'll kill her, she's too far gone!"

My papa thrust Kathleen from him. She fell against the table. He came after her and pulled her head up by the hair.

"Paud!" my mama shrieked.

My papa lifted Kathleen by her hair and her elbow. He held her against the wall. I ran to the well for Sean. One look at me and he sprinted for the house, cursing my papa as he came.

Kathleen lay crumpled like sand on the floor. Her skirt showed blood. My papa stood rocking over her. "I scarce touched her," he said to the walls. "Scarce put my finger to her!"

Kathleen reached for Sean. "The baby," she sobbed. "Sean!"

Her cry went through me. Sean crouched beside her. "Be quiet," he said. "Save your strength." He pulled her little by little into his arms, pulling gently to keep her from screaming again. Sweat glistened all along her hairline. She closed her eyes and hung gasping against him.

"Kathleen!" I cried, scared. "Kathleen!"

She opened her eyes. "The dreams were true," she panted. Her eyes were glazed, the way fever sometimes does to Sean's. "You remember all I told you, how to take care of my baby?"

I nodded. "Ah, Maureen, poor Maureen," she gasped. "I saw worse for you than for us. God love you, mavourneen." She shuddered and dug her fingers into Sean's shoulder. She screamed.

The house echoes still with the sound of it. Even when the rains started hard and heavy they could not beat out the sound of her screaming.

"You must pray for Kathleen," Sean said. He held me close against him. "Look well at her and learn her face."

Kathleen's long lashes hung like bruises against her cheeks. Bits of hair still damp with her struggling curled against her forehead. But the blue vein in her temple was still, and the pulse beat no longer like a bird in her throat.

"That devil downstairs will give Kathleen neither cross nor stone to comfort her," Sean said.

"Weeds will stand over her," I said from her dream.

"You must find where they put her," Sean said. "Go there sometimes and throw a flower into the grass for her, and say her a prayer so she won't lie forsaken."

I nodded my head. "Won't you come, too?"

"No. I'm leaving, Maura. I would take you but you'd be no better off, there is death in me. Father Robinson will come for you, if not tomorrow then the day after. He will help you. Go with him, Maureen. Do not let him leave this place without you. Say it!"

"Father Robinson will help me," I repeated. "He will come and I must go with him. The Father will help me."

Downstairs I heard the floor creak under my papa's weight.

"Go now," Sean said. "Run to your room and close the door. That devil and I have bitter words to speak between us."

"Sean?"

He kissed the top of my head. "Go. Go, mavourneen."

I went as my papa came lumbering up the stairs. He moved thick and heavy past me, my mama weeping at his heels.

"Don't curse the boy, Paud!" she moaned. "The evil is done. For the love of God don't call down more on this house!"

I hid my head under my pillow but it didn't block out my papa's voice measuring out a slow and terrible fate. That was why Sean would die alone in a muddy field. He was cursed.

Sean and my papa shouted in the room where Kathleen lay sleeping in her narrow white bed. They roared and hurled oaths at each other. Sean began to cough, long racking coughs that kept on and on, and on, and still my papa shouted, "Deny it or give me another's name!"

At last Sean went clattering down the stairs. The door thudded shut behind him.

I ran to the window and leaned out into the rain.

He was splashing through the wide puddles, his head bent to the wind.

"Sean!" I called. He didn't hear.

"Sean!" I cried. "Don't leave me, Sean!"

He paused as if the wind had brought him my voice. I

leaned over the sill, my hair falling black and heavy around me.

"Sean!" I wailed. "Sean, Sean, Sean!"

The keening wind brought my cry back to me. Sean turned and threw me a kiss, and lifted his arm in farewell. Then he wheeled and walked on.

I watched until he was only a blue blur against our hill, running green with the March rain.

The house is full of strange footsteps sent by the Father to carry Kathleen away. I will follow and find where they buried her. I will say her a prayer, and throw her a flower into the grass so she won't lie forsaken.

Tonight, when he sleeps, I will go to my papa. I will take the breadknife Kathleen used this morning with me. I will stand over him and lift my arms high and straight over his heart.

I will plunge the breadknife deep into his chest. Once for Kathleen, once for Sean, once for me.

I will dress the baby and myself and wait until the Father comes. We will put a cross on Kathleen's grave. Papa won't be able to stop us. Then the baby and I will leave and find Sean and never come back.

The Father will help. The Father will help me. Sean said it would be so.

THE $1,000,000 DISAPPEARING ACT

by Harold Q. Masur

Another adventure of Scott Jordan, lawyer-detective, and another fast-paced, hard-hitting, tight-packed yarn of criminal legalities, legal criminalities, and assorted financial shenanigans. . . . We all know, sometimes to our sorrow and frustration, that computers can make mistakes. But is the legend true, really true, that banks never make mistakes? The legend flourished when accounts were kept by human hands. But today, alas, even your friendly neighborhood bank is likely to be computerized. . . .

"Doctors!" Colonel Jaeger said. "Trying to soft-soap me. But I can read the signs. Morphine and cobalt. They might as well put it in writing. So I know the score and it's imperative to get my affairs in order at once. That's why you're here, Counselor."

His nurse had phoned my office, relaying an urgent request for my immediate presence at Manhattan General. I'd been handling various legal chores for Colonel Donald Jaeger ever since he retired from the Corps of Engineers to start his own construction company. But I hadn't seen him in almost a year and his appearance shocked me. He was gray, pitifully dwindled, the bones prominent in his fleshless face.

"What did you have in mind, Colonel?"

"A new will."

"What happened to the old one?"

"Tore it up after Lucille and I separated. That wife of mine!" He made a face. "The one I married two years ago. Senility, myopia—no fool like an old fool. She gave me two years of hell before we split up. Too busy for a divorce, so she's still my wife, and I want to make a new will cutting her off cold."

I shook my head. "You can't do that, Colonel."

He bristled. "Are you telling me what I can or cannot do with my own money?"

"It's in the statutes, Colonel. The law does not permit a man to leave his widow penniless. Unfair to the taxpayers if she has to go on welfare."

He exhaled in disgust. "You're a lawyer. I'm paying you for advice. Let's have it."

"The law provides for a minimum, at least one-third of the estate."

He digested it without pleasure, then shrugged in resignation. "All right, so a man has to pay for his mistakes. So she gets one-third of three million. Not bad for a measly two years of marriage."

"Any charitable bequests?"

"No, sir. I am not an eleemosynary institution. All the rest, residue, whatever you lawyers call it, goes to a niece. Suzy Bemis. Haven't seen much of the girl, but she's the last of our blood line, and I want her to have the money."

"Any instructions about your construction company?"

"It's no longer part of my estate. Sold it a few months ago to one of those conglomerates. In the process of phasing myself out when this abomination hit me. I want you to handle probate, Jordan. No strange lawyers dipping their paws into the till."

"I'll put it in the will. How about an executor?"

"Suzy would be able to handle it with your help. You'll find her in the telephone book."

"How much time have I got?"

"I want that paper signed, sealed, and witnessed this afternoon." He closed his eyes and sank back exhausted. "All right, Counselor, get cracking."

I went back to my office and dictated. My secretary skipped her lunch hour. At two o'clock Donald Jaeger's Last Will and

Testament was neatly stapled into a blue document cover. I took it back to the hospital, enlisting Jaeger's nurse and one of the residents as witnesses. When the formalities were completed, the colonel showed me a double row of false teeth in a bleak grin.

"Any questions," he said, "talk to Sam Blake. Sam is the auditor at Jaeger Construction and knows more about my finances than I do." Suddenly he winced and the doctor leaned over to give him a shot.

He was going under fast when I looked back from the doorway. "Hang in there, Colonel," I said softly and left.

Two days later he was dead.

I attended the funeral services. The widow, Lucille Jaeger, sat in the front row, sleek and brittle, her tearless eyes darting suspiciously around the chapel. I recognized the man at her side, a lawyer named Victor Knebel, and felt what I always feel whenever our paths crossed, instant and total hostility.

People were gathered in the aisles, talking in hushed whispers. I made inquiries and someone pointed out Sam Blake, a slender clerical-looking man with a lined and anxious face. I approached and introduced myself.

"Ah, yes, Mr. Jordan," he said. "The colonel mentioned your name. He said you might need some assistance and would be getting in touch with me. If I can be of any help at all—"

"I'd appreciate it. Could you spare some time tomorrow? I'll be at my office all day."

"Mid-afternoon would be fine."

"I'll expect you. Is Mr. Jaeger's niece here?"

"I was just talking to her. Let me get her for you." He separated a girl from a small group and brought her over. Suzy Bemis had a fine-boned oval face and vivid blue eyes shadowed at the moment with sadness.

I said, "May I offer my condolences, Miss Bemis? My name is Scott Jordan. I was one of your uncle's lawyers."

She nodded gravely. "Poor Uncle Don. I didn't even know he was ill. I didn't know anything until Mr. Blake called and told me about the funeral."

"If it's any comfort, Miss Bemis, he spoke to me about you before he died."

She seemed pleased. "He was always so busy. I didn't think he ever thought of me."

"Oh, he thought of you, all right. In fact, you're the principal legatee and the executrix of his will."

Her eyes widened. "But—but what about Lucille?"

"Didn't you know they had separated? Your uncle disliked the woman intensely. He left her the minimum allowed by law, but he did not want her involved in administering his estate. Incidentally, I'll be handling probate."

"I hardly know what to say. I never expected to be an heiress." She tilted her head and regarded me quizzically. "Are you capable of defending yourself, Mr. Jordan?"

"Now there's a non sequitur, Miss Bemis. How do you mean?"

"I mean, have you ever met Lucille Jaeger?"

"Not socially."

She gave me a pitying look. "Then brace yourself. Lucille is not going to like this. I'm not sure I care to face up to her myself. Would I be allowed to waive my share?"

"Miss Bemis, by working hard all his life your uncle managed to accumulate considerable property. He had the right to distribute that property in any way he liked. Would you frustrate his final testament now?"

She blinked. "Well, no, not if you put it that way."

Organ music floated toward us and a mortuary assistant beckoned everyone to please be seated. "May I call you later in the week?" I asked.

She nodded, smiled fleetingly, and took a seat in the front row as far from Lucille Jaeger as possible. The services were brief and I got out ahead of the mob. I was halfway down the block when Victor Knebel and his client caught up with me.

"You didn't waste much time, did you, Jordan?" he growled. "Filing that phony will before Jaeger was even cold."

"Not phony, Knebel. It meets every testamentary provision required by law. And how long did you want me to wait?"

"A decent time, Jordan, a decent time." Knebel was a

broad-beamed balding man with a voice like a foghorn. "We're going to contest it, you know."

"On what grounds?"

"Undue influence."

"By whom? Neither I nor the only other legatee besides Mrs. Jaeger had seen the deceased in over a year. His nurse will testify that he sent for me and that I spoke to him for less than twenty minutes. When did I have enough time to exert undue influence?"

"The niece," Lucille Jaeger broke in vehemently. "That Suzy Bemis. She's been seeing him secretly. I won't sit by and let her have my husband's money. We'll fight you all the way to the Supreme Court."

Knebel said, "We'll prove a lack of testamentary capacity. The colonel was old, sick, under stress, in pain, unable to think clearly. He was *non compos* and in need of a guardian."

I gave him a horse laugh. "That line won't even get you to first base, Knebel. Jaeger's doctors were in constant attendance. He had nurses around the clock. They will testify that his mind was sharp and logical right up to the very end."

He compressed his lips. "Er, this thing can be settled out of court, you know."

"No way, Knebel. No discussions. No settlement. I owe Jaeger an obligation to see that every provision in his will is carried out to the letter and I intend to do just that."

Lucille Jaeger said acidly, "We're wasting our time, Victor. This little man needs a lesson. Let's go."

She was on her way. Knebel gave me a lingering narrow-lidded look, then went after her.

Sam Blake knew exactly what I needed. He appeared at my office the next afternoon with several lists of prepared figures. He spread them out on my desk and said, "The colonel never believed in maintaining a large cash balance. He was always investing in common stocks, industrials, and utilities, occasionally some high-yielding bonds. As you can see, the estate now comprises a very substantial portfolio. At the current market it is worth somewhere in the neighborhood of three million dollars."

"That's a nice neighborhood. How do we stand on taxes?"

"Unavoidable, Mr. Jordan. With some concessions to the widow." His finger traced the list, pausing to indicate where subscription rights were still pending and should be exercised, where certain bonds were approaching maturity. It was a complicated situation, making Blake's continued advice indispensable.

"If you can spare the time, I'd like to retain you officially as accountant for the estate."

He agreed promptly, a rueful twist to his lips. "I'm available. I can give you all the time you need."

"Are you leaving Jaeger Construction?"

"By request. Now that the colonel is gone, the new parent company is cleaning house. They're putting in their own men."

I made a quick decision. "Sam, I have a spare room temporarily available. It's yours until we close out the Jaeger estate. You'll have a desk, a telephone, and a midtown address for arranging interviews."

He sat for a moment, blinking. "I—I gratefully accept."

"My secretary will give you a key so you can come and go as you please."

Victor Knebel had decided not to contest the will. Whatever his problems, he was not an idiot. He realized the futility of his position and made no attempt to block probate. So in due course the will was admitted to probate and Suzy Bemis received her letters testamentary as executrix for the estate of Donald Jaeger, deceased.

I had seen Suzy half a dozen times, partly business, partly social, always enjoyable. She was employed by an advertising agency, writing copy and television commercials. She was splendid company, bright and light-hearted, and now in my office, expecting her for lunch, I found myself waiting with a high degree of anticipatory pleasure.

At the restaurant she regarded me curiously and said, "You told me to keep the afternoon free. What sort of assignation did you have in mind?"

"No assignation, Suzy. Business. After lunch we have an appointment at the Gotham Trust, lower level, with a state tax representative who is going to record every item in your uncle's safe-deposit box. We will then remove the contents and you will open a checking account as executrix of the estate."

"Using what for money?"

"A balance of fifteen hundred dollars in the colonel's account. From there we proceed to a brokerage firm where you will offer the securities for sale."

"Is it a large estate?"

"Suzy, your uncle left approximately three million dollars, one-third of which goes to Lucille, and the balance, after your share of the taxes, is yours."

She gasped. "I—I had no idea."

"Well, you're rich. Are you having dessert?"

"Just coffee. If I get fat, you won't take me out any more."

The Gotham Trust was around the corner on Fifth Avenue. The state tax man was waiting for us. Half an hour later, my brief case bulging, we went upstairs to the office of Mr. Henry Wharton who examined our documents and opened an estate account on Suzy's signature as executrix. Wharton congratulated her and said he hoped she would become a permanent depositor.

Outside I flagged a taxi and we rode down to a building on Wall Street. We took an elevator to the tenth floor. Zachary Bernard was waiting for us. He took one of Suzy's hands in both of his own and said, "All this and money, too? Miss Bemis, I'm delighted. Will you marry me?"

I said, "Don't get carried away, Zach. Looks aren't everything. She's perverse, illhumored, and quarrelsome."

"That's not true," Suzy said. "I'm an absolute delight."

"I know a place where we don't even need a license."

"Stop poaching, Zach. We have business to transact."

"Business is my life's blood. The conference room is back here." Zachary Bernard, Ph.D. in Economics, was a bear-shaped man with a beatific smile that opened wide when I spilled stock certificates across the table. He shuffled through them.

"Some of this merchandise may be worth holding, Counselor."

"No advice, please. The testator's widow has to be paid off in cash, so liquidate the lot."

"We'll need certain documents—state tax waivers, letters testamentary, death certificates, stock powers."

"You'll have everything by tomorrow afternoon."

"Then I'll study the list and start unloading at once. Just permit me some discretion in timing."

Victor Knebel was on the horn every day demanding a full accounting of the colonel's assets and Xeroxed copies of every brokerage transaction, making sure the widow got her full one-third interest.

The first batch of securities sold brought checks for $1,000,000. I called Suzy and she came over and we brought them to the Gotham Trust for deposit. I told her I would be out of town for at least a week negotiating the purchase of a factory site for a client.

Actually it took ten days.

Less than half an hour after I returned to the office, Victor Knebel marched in, his jaw set at its normally truculent angle. "You were away," he accused, "and your secretary hasn't sent me any additional confirmation slips."

"That's right," I told him. "Because no additional stock has been sold."

"What's holding up the works?"

"Market conditions. We're waiting for an upturn."

"My client is impatient. She wants that estate wound up without delay." He consulted a small notebook. "According to my figures you've already sold one million dollars' worth of securities."

"Your addition is correct."

"What happened to the proceeds?"

"They've been deposited to the estate account."

"May I see the bank statement?"

I have a normally low flashpoint, but this troglodyte was getting to me. I buzzed and asked my secretary for the Jaeger folder. She had filed an envelope mailed from the Gotham Trust while I was out of town. I tossed it over. Knebel opened it. His eyes narrowed stonily as he scanned the statement.

"There's been only one deposit," he said grittily. "Fifteen hundred dollars. What happened to that million bucks?"

He tossed the statement back. I glanced at it and saw only the initial transfer from the colonel's savings account. And the closing date was well after the brokerage checks had been deposited.

"You said the money had been deposited to the estate account," Knebel snapped. "Then show me the duplicate deposit slips. I want—" He reared back. "Where are you going?"

I was on my feet and moving. "To the bank," I said, almost bowling him over.

He was trotting along at my heels, out of breath, when I pushed through the bronze doors of the Gotham Trust and headed for Mr. Henry Wharton's desk. I placed the deposit slips and the monthly statement in front of him. He studied them.

"Seems to be some kind of mistake," he said.

"To say the least. Your statement fails to credit the Jaeger estate with one million dollars. Please note that these deposit slips bear the bank's official stamp."

"If there has been an error, Mr. Jordan, it will be rectified on your next statement."

"No, sir," Knebel broke in. "It will be corrected now. At once. We have a right to know what happened to that money."

Wharton sighed, picked up his phone, and spoke earnestly for a moment. Then he stood up and walked away. Knebel kept pacing the room, his lips tight. After a while Wharton returned. He sat down, looking noncommittal. He coughed once and cleared his throat.

"Gentlemen, we have a problem. Our computers have apparently credited this one million dollars to someone else's account."

"Mr. Wharton," I said, "*we* don't have a problem; *you* have a problem. You will simply charge the other account and credit the money to the estate."

"I'm afraid we can't do that, Mr. Jordan."

"Why the hell not?"

"The money has already been withdrawn."

I stared at him. "Well, damn it, get it back!"

He blinked. "The holder of the account seems to have disappeared."

"What!" Anger reverberated in the sudden high pitch of Knebel's voice. "You listen to me, mister. That money was properly deposited. We have receipts. It was in your custody. If the bank bungled, the bank is responsible."

Wharton gazed expressionlessly at the ceiling. "Well, now, I just spoke to our attorneys and they are not entirely convinced of our liability."

Dark blood suffused Knebel's face. "If those slick Wall Street lawyers think they can get you off the hook they've got a loose connection. We'll sue. We'll expose the bank's shoddy bookkeeping, its defective equipment, its incompetence and irresponsibility, and in the end you'll have to make good."

Incredibly I found myself in complete agreement with Victor Knebel. "Mr. Wharton," I said, "just how did your computers happen to make this mistake?"

"The computers did not make a mistake. They did exactly what they were programmed to do. They correctly credited the money to the account number on your deposit slips."

"I'm afraid you just lost me."

"Those numbers are printed in magnetic ink, scanned by the computer, and automatically credited to the appropriate account."

"Are you saying that the numbers on our deposit slips belonged to someone else's account?"

"Precisely, sir. It is a highly sophisticated system and it does *not* make mistakes."

"Well, damn it, the bank supplied those deposit slips and they bear the number the bank gave us."

"Not so, Mr. Jordan. They bear the number of an account belonging to a man named Edward Sloane."

"Then you printed the wrong number on our slips."

"We printed the correct number," he said firmly. "I have here the slip for your initial deposit of fifteen hundred dollars. Now look at the subsequent slips for your million dollars. The numbers do not coincide."

"Then the error was made by your printer."

"Impossible. Once the type is set, it cannot change by itself. If the first slip off the press is correct, all others would be exactly the same."

Victor Knebel could not contain himself. He glared at me and said in a clogged voice, "Jordan, if you're pulling a fast one, I'll have you disbarred. I'll turn you over to the District Attorney. This is fraud, embezzlement, misappropriation of fiduciary funds. As a matter of fact, I'm going to lay it before the D.A. right now." He wheeled and went storming out.

I sighed and turned back to Wharton. "Who does your printing?"

"Empire Bank Stationery, Incorporated."

"How long have you been using them?"

"As long as I can remember."

"Have you ever investigated their background?"

"They have no underworld connections, Mr. Jordan, believe me. Their integrity is unimpeachable." He sat up and looked me directly in the eye. "I am going to state categorically at this time that we did *not* supply the Jaeger estate with those incorrect deposit slips. And I think you should know that the bank is going to disclaim all responsibility."

"Mr. Wharton, you wrongfully turned that money over to a Mr. Edward Sloane. Now you say you cannot locate him. Why not?"

"Because the moment we realized what happened we tried to block his account. It was too late. The money had been withdrawn. We called his hotel, the Sutton Towers, and were informed that he had given up his suite and left the country."

"When did he open the account?"

"About two months ago. And after his account was credited with those brokerage checks he began making heavy withdrawals."

"And nobody became suspicious?"

"Mr. Jordan, the Gotham Trust is a major bank. We are literally flooded with transactions every day we're open. Deals are frequently consummated in cash. If a man's balance covers the request, we honor his withdrawal. We do not inquire into motives. That is neither our function nor our obligation."

"Can any of your employees describe this Sloane?"

Wharton shrugged. "I doubt it. They see too many faces."

I kept asking questions, but apparently I had milked Mr. Henry Wharton dry and when I left I did not shake his hand because the bank might in the near future be at the other end of a lawsuit.

So by some clever piece of legerdemain $1,000,000 entrusted to my care had seemingly vanished into thin air.

The manager of the Sutton Towers was a fussy little man with an air of perpetual harassment. "I have a rather vague recollection of the man," he told me. "Mr. Sloane had only one distinctive feature, a Mexican-type mustache. He seemed quiet and reserved, and his hair was turning gray. He rented a small suite on a month-to-month basis and paid with checks drawn on the Gotham Trust. After the bank called this morning I spoke to the housekeeper. She tells me that he seldom slept at the hotel."

"How long did he stay?"

"Only two months. Then he phoned to say that he was canceling the suite because he had bought some property on one of the Caribbean islands and was going there to live. His clothes had already been removed."

The Caribbean, I thought, was the last place on God's green footstool that Mr. Edward Sloane would ever be found. I thanked the manager, left, and took a cab down to Hudson Street.

Empire Bank Stationery, Incorporated had a full floor in a solid old building. In an office soundproofed against the constantly clacking presses a Mr. Louis Neiderman squinted through his trifocals at one of my cards. He was a bent and withered old gnome with a quirky smile.

"Attorney-at-Law," he said. "So, Mr. Jordan, somebody is suing me?"

"No, Mr. Neiderman."

"Then what? You're drumming up clients?" He chuckled, advertising an advanced case of emphysema. "More than fifty years ago I started this business, a storefront on Houston Street, one small hand press, and maybe twice in my life I needed a lawyer. So what's on your mind?"

"Mr. Henry Wharton of the Gotham Trust suggested that I speak to you."

"So it must be about those Jaeger deposit slips." He shook his head. "It couldn't happen. Not in this shop. We printed only one batch of those slips, and we pulled proofs, which are still in the file. They are absolutely, positively correct. So once the type was set, Mr. Jordan, how could it turn out with different numbers?"

"Do you supervise all the work yourself, Mr. Neiderman?"

"Me? I'm retired. My son runs the business, with the help of our foreman, Eric Braun."

"May I talk to your son?"

"Next week maybe. He's on vacation, a cruise, somewhere in those Greek islands."

"How about Braun, the foreman?"

"Eric is home sick with the flu, a hundred and two fever. Why do you think I'm here? At my age I need this head-ache?"

"Would you let me have his address?"

"Why not? What can it hurt? He will tell you what I told you. Empire Bank Stationery does only quality work."

"I believe you, Mr. Neiderman. As you say, what can it hurt?"

"It can hurt plenty. The flu is catching. Maybe you should take a flu shot first." He gave me an address. "You want I should call him and tell him you're coming?"

"If you would, please. I should be there in fifteen min-utes."

He was dialing near-sightedly when I left.

It was a converted brownstone in the East Village. But I never got close enough because a police barricade had blocked the area. Three radio cars, flashers rotating, were haphazardly parked. Two patrolmen guarded the entrance.

On the opposite curb a small crowd of onlookers craned their necks. I joined them and spoke to a young man in fad-ed jeans, his eyes alight with excitement. "Somebody knocked off the Dutchman," he told me. "An old geezer named Braun."

"Are you sure?"

"He bought it all right. A neighbor lady found him. I hear

his skull was bashed in. Must've been some junkie looking for
an easy score and didn't know the Dutchman was home. Hey,
look! They're bringing him out now."

Morbid curiosity is not one of my weaknesses. I cleared
out, trying to look casual and inconspicuous. But I felt uneasy and troubled. With Braun dead a primary source of information was gone forever.

I stopped at a phone booth, got through to Suzy Bemis,
and briefed her on the latest developments. She detected the
note of worry in my voice. "Can we be held responsible for all
that money, Scott?"

"It's something that may have to be ironed out in litiga-
tion."

"I really don't care about the money."

"Lucille cares. And the Surrogate cares. Our probate
courts take a very sharp interest in how decedents' estates are
administered. Besides, a man has been murdered and I think
there's a connection."

There was a long silence. She said earnestly, "I'm not worried, Scott. I have confidence in you."

It was nice to hear, but as I left the booth I felt like an ag-
ing Don Quixote with a spear of straw in a palsied fist. I did
not want to be involved in a homicide.

As it turned out, I had no choice. Detective Lieutenant
John Nola rang my bell that evening. He nodded curtly and
waited for me to step aside. In my living room he handed me
a card. It was my own professional business card.

"There was a special price on a print order of one thousand," I told him. "I used to pass them around rather freely."

"Yeah. You passed this one to a Mr. Louis Neiderman of
Empire Bank Stationery. You also made inquiries about the
company foreman, Eric Braun. And you left Empire to visit
Braun."

I sighed. "And now Braun is dead. Neiderman must have
told you that he tried to phone Braun while I was still in his
office and got no response. So Braun was already shelved."

"I'm not accusing you, Counselor. I'm asking for your version."

"I went there, Lieutenant. But the place was crawling with
cops, so I simply turned and split."

Nola sat down and lit one of his thin dappled cigars. "All

right, Counselor. Fill me in. Why did you want to see
Braun?"

I gave it to him, chapter and verse, the whole scenario.

"One million dollars," he said. "Missing."

"Along with a man named Edward Sloane."

"Is it your impression there's some connection between the
missing money and the death of Braun?"

"It seems like a logical conclusion." I looked at him hopefully. "Perhaps your boys found a valise full of money at
Braun's apartment."

"They found a heavy brass candlestick with Braun's blood
on it and a few partials." He looked sour. "When did we ever
solve a case with even a good set of identifiable prints anyway?"

"You queried the other tenants?"

"Yes. One of them saw a stranger on Braun's floor."

"With a Mexican-type mustache?"

He nodded. "Fitting the description you got of Sloane at
the Sutton Towers. My guess is that he's long gone from this
city. Nevertheless, we'll keep looking." He stood up and said
from the door, "I expect you to keep me informed of all
developments as and when they occur."

Victor Knebel rang the next day and said that he was
bringing Lucille Jaeger to my office for a conference on safe-
guarding the balance of her husband's estate. She was convinced that my stewardship would lead to additional disasters
and was insisting on supervision. He hung up before I could
tell him what I thought of the idea.

Ten minutes later I had a visitor, a thin flinty gent who
presented credentials. Mr. Hobart Prime, Frauds Division,
Internal Revenue Service. I was not due for an audit, however. After some preliminary sparring Prime directed his inquiries toward the Jaeger estate. He seemed well informed
about the current status of our account at the Gotham Trust.

Finally he said, "I take it you are acquainted with a lawyer
named Victor Knebel."

"To my great sorrow, yes."

"Would you be willing to help your government?"

"In what way, Mr. Prime?"

"We have a situation, Counselor. The government received a letter informing it that Knebel would be flying to Montreal on Friday. His purpose, to visit the branch office of a Swiss bank in order to open a numbered account and deposit illegal funds in the sum of one million dollars."

I sat erect, my adrenalin pumping. "A letter from whom?"

"Anonymous. Here is a copy." He proffered it, saying, "We often receive tips of this nature. We pursue all leads, regardless of source. Our investigators learned that the only case in Knebel's office involving a sum of that size was the Jaeger estate. Further investigation led to the Gotham Trust and the information that an employee of the bank's printing contractor had been murdered. That brought Lieutenant Nola into the picture. He suggested that I contact you and he promised to meet me here this afternoon."

I barely heard him. I was staring at the letter, feeling a sudden chill. A familiar defect in the type had caught my eye. It had been typed on my own office machine.

"We checked the airlines," Prime said. "And Knebel does have a reservation with Air Canada for Montreal on Friday morning."

I forced myself to pay attention. "Mr. Prime, how would Internal Revenue benefit? Even if you got your hands on that million, it still belongs to the Jaeger estate."

"There will be a sizable inheritance tax, Jordan. The government intends to make sure that all the money is available." He smiled. "Could I see a complete inventory of the estate?"

I buzzed Sam Blake and asked him to gather his files on the colonel's affairs. Prime and Blake were both accountants and the two men juggled figures knowledgeably between them. They bent their heads together, Prime interrogating and Blake answering with numbers.

They were still going strong when my intercom announced the arrival of Victor Knebel and his client. I passed the news to Prime. "Have them join us," he said. "Tell them I am making inquiries about estate taxes."

Lucille Jaeger sailed in ahead of her lawyer. She nodded curtly at Blake and fixed Prime with an imperious eye. "We have an appointment with Jordan. You'll have to come back later." He identified himself and she snapped, "Well, you'll get only a minimal tax from me. A widow is entitled to allowances."

"You may not get much yourself," Knebel told her. "Not if Jordan keeps handling the estate."

Mrs. Jaeger was fissionable material and Knebel's remark touched her off. She cut loose with a shrill and bitter indictment, attacking my competence and my integrity. Then she turned to her lawyer. "I know, Victor, I know. I promised to let you do the talking. Go ahead."

Knebel focused on Prime. "Are you aware, sir, that a huge sum of money is missing from the estate account?"

"I have been so informed."

"Well, our chief concern now is to make sure the rest of Colonel Jaeger's estate remains intact."

"Internal Revenue shares your concern, Mr. Knebel. I would suggest then that you find yourself a good lawyer."

"Me? But I am a lawyer, sir."

"Let me quote an old aphorism: 'The lawyer who represents himself has a fool for a client.'"

"What! What are you talking?"

"I am talking about your prospective flight to Montreal on Friday of this week. Would you care to discuss the purpose of that trip?"

The door behind him opened and I saw Lieutenant Nola slip quietly into the room, encompassing the scene with a quick circular sweep of his eyes.

Prime leveled a finger. "Then please explain why you made a reservation for such a flight on Air Canada."

Knebel stiffened. "I made no such reservation!"

"The company's records prove otherwise."

"Then the company's records are mistaken. Why in God's name would I want to go to Canada?"

"Your intention was to visit the branch of a Swiss bank where you could open a numbered account and deposit one million dollars. Does that sum sound familiar to you?"

Knebel blanched. Sudden anger wrestled him out of his chair. "That's a lie! A damned vicious slanderous lie! I demand to know where you got that information."

"We received a letter."

"From an anonymous source, no doubt. I wouldn't be surprised if Jordan himself mailed it. Trying to take the heat off himself."

"Then how would you explain this little item?" Nola said, stepping forward, holding up his hand, and displaying a stage prop. It was a false mustache with drooping corners.

A touch of spirit gum, powdered hair, and cotton in the cheeks could effectively alter a man's appearance. And it would fit the description of the missing Edward Sloane.

"I don't have to explain it," Knebel said. "It's not mine."

"It was found in the glove compartment of your car."

"Then it's a plant, a frame-up. Ask Jordan."

I said, "I think he's telling the truth, Lieutenant. The letter implicating Knebel was typed here in my office." In the enveloping silence all eyes turned in my direction. Nola moved to peer over my shoulder. "Look at that *W*, John. Slightly off center, with a tiny break in the upper right serif. A unique characteristic of my machine."

"Are you saying *you* wrote the letter?"

"Not me and not my secretary. Which leaves only one other candidate." I looked at Blake. "How about it, Sam?"

He was staring at me, his face suddenly waxy.

"You had access to my typewriter," I said. "And access to my files. You were bitter. You felt that Colonel Jaeger had let you down by selling his company. All those years of work and a new management arbitrarily gives you notice. That rankled, didn't it, Sam? And it started you scheming. You decided to plunder the colonel's estate.

"So you concocted an ingenious plan to deceive the bank's computer system. You approached Eric Braun, made a deal, and one night, alone at the plant, he printed up counterfeit deposit slips for the Jaeger estate, but bearing an account number acquired by you as Edward Sloane. You substituted those slips for the real ones in Jaeger's file and the computer credited our deposits to Sloane's account. Then, before we received the bank's statement you withdrew the money and Edward Sloane ceased to exist."

"You're making a terrible mistake," he said in a rusty voice.

"Then you should have no trouble convincing a jury. How much did you pay Eric Braun?"

"Ten thousand dollars cash," Nola broke in. "We found the money hidden in Braun's apartment."

"How about it, Sam? Will they find an equivalent sum drawn from your own bank account?"

"It—it had nothing to do with Braun."

"Then he died for nothing. He was putting the bite on you for more, wasn't he, Sam? And you knew it would never stop. So Braun had to be liquidated. And you did it with his brass candlestick."

His mouth worked, perspiration bathing his ashen face.

I said, "You tried to lay a false trail by implicating Knebel. Writing an anonymous letter, making an air reservation in Knebel's name, planting that mustache in his car. All for nothing, Sam. Because you made a fatal mistake. You failed to notice that small flaw in one of my typewriter keys. Oh, they'll nail you all right. They'll get an identification from somebody—the manager of the Sutton Towers, an employee at the bank, a neighbor of Braun's. And they know how to search. They'll take your place apart, board by board. Don't think for a moment they can't find that one million dollars."

Blake looked at me in despair, then he bent over and covered his face with his hands. His ragged breathing was the only sound in the room.

ALL IN THE WAY YOU READ IT

by *Isaac Asimov*

In which the members of the Black Widowers Club are challenged to solve one of the most baffling and ingenious problems ever brought to their postprandial attention. And yet—the quintessence of a truly baffling and ingenious puzzle—the answer was so simple! . . .

WHEN Tom Trumbull arrived—late, of course—at the Black Widowers banquet and called for his Scotch and soda, he was met by James Drake, the organic chemist, who was wearing a rather hangdog expression on his face.

Drake's head made a gentle gesture to one side.

Trumbull followed him, unpeeling his coat as he went, his tanned and furrowed face asking the question before his voice did. "What's up?" he said.

Drake held his cigarette so that the smoke curled bluely upward. "Tom, I've brought a physicist as my guest."

"So?"

"Well, he has a problem and I think it's up your alley."

"A code?"

"Something like that. Numbers, anyway. I don't have all the details. I suppose we'll get those after the dinner. But that's not the point. Will you help me if it becomes necessary to hold down Jeff Avalon?"

Trumbull looked across the room to where Avalon, the patent attorney, was standing in staid conversation with the man who was clearly the guest of the evening since he was the only stranger present.

"What's wrong with Jeff?" said Trumbull. There didn't seem anything wrong with Avalon, who was standing straight and tall as always, looking as though he might splinter if he relaxed. His graying mustache and small beard were as neat and trim as ever and he wore the careful smile on his face that he insisted on using for strangers. "He looks all right."

Drake said, "You weren't here last time. Jeff has the idea that the meetings of the Black Widowers are becoming too much of a puzzle-session every month."

"What's wrong with that?" asked Trumbull, as he passed his hands over his tightly waved off-white hair to press down the slight disarray that the wind outside had caused.

"Jeff thinks we ought to be a purely social organization— convivial conversation and all that."

"We have that anyway."

"So when the puzzle comes up, help me sit on him if he gets grouchy. You have a loud voice and I don't."

"No problem. Have you talked to Manny?"

"Hell, no. He'd take up the other side just to be contrary."

"You may be right. —Henry!" Trumbull waved his arm. "Henry, do me a favor. This Scotch and soda won't be enough. It's cold outside and it took me a long time to get a taxi."

Henry smiled, his unlined face looking twenty years younger than his actual sixtyishness. "I had assumed that might be so, Mr. Trumbull. Your second is ready."

"Henry, you're a diamond of the first water." —Which, to be sure, was a judgment concurred in by all the Black Widowers.

"I'll give you a demonstration," said Emanuel Rubin, the writer. He had quarreled with the soup which, he maintained, had a shade too much leek in it to make it fit for human consumption, and the fact that he was in a clear minority of one rendered him all the more emphatic in his remaining views. "I'll show you that any language is really a complex of languages. —I'll write a word on each of these two pieces of paper. The same word. I'll give one to you, Mario, and one to you, sir."

The second went to Dr. Samuel Puntsch, who had, as was usually the case with guests of the Black Widowers, maintained a discreet silence during the preliminaries.

Puntsch, who was a small slim man dressed in a funereal color scheme that would have done credit to Avalon, looked at the paper and lifted his eyebrows.

Rubin said, "Now neither of you say anything. Just write down the number of the syllable that carries the stress."

Mario Gonzalo, the Black Widowers' artist member, had just completed a sketch of Dr. Puntsch, and he laid it to one side. He looked at the word on the paper before him, wrote a number without hesitation, and passed it to Rubin. Dr. Puntsch did the same.

Rubin said, with indescribable satisfaction, "I'll spell the word. It's u-n-i-o-n-i-z-e-d, and Mario says it's accented on the first syllable."

"*Yoo*-nionized," said Mario. "Referring to an industry whose working forces have been organized into a labor union."

Dr. Puntsch laughed. "Yes, I see what you mean. I called it un-*eye*-onized—referring to a substance that did not break down into ions in solution. I accent the second syllable."

"Exactly. The same word to the eye, but different to men in different fields. Roger and Jim, being scientists, would agree with Dr. Puntsch, and Tom, Jeff, and Henry would probably agree with Mario. It's like that in a thousand different places. Fugue means different things to a psychiatrist and a musician. The phrase 'to press a suit' means one thing to a nineteenth-century lover and another to a twentieth-century tailor. No two people have exactly the same language."

Roger Halsted, the mathematician, said with the slight hesitation that was almost a stammer, "There's enough overlap so that it doesn't really matter, does it?"

"Most of us can understand each other, yes," said Rubin querulously, "but there's less overlap than there ought to be. Every small segment of the culture develops its own vocabulary for the sake of forming an in-group. There are a million verbal walls behind which fools cower, and it does more to create ill-feeling—"

"That was Shaw's thesis in *Pygmalion*," growled Trumbull.

"No, you're quite wrong, Tom. Shaw thought it was the result of faulty education. I say it's *deliberate* and that this does more to create the proper atmosphere for world collapse than war does." And he tackled his roast beef with a fierce cut of his knife.

"Only Manny could go from unionized to the destruction of civilization in a dozen sentences," said Gonzalo, and passed his sketch to Henry for delivery to Dr. Puntsch.

Puntsch smiled a little shakily at it for it had emphasized his ears more than a purist might have thought consistent with good looks. Henry put it on the wall with the other sketches.

It was perhaps inevitable that the discussion veer from the iniquities of private language to word puzzles and Halsted achieved a certain degree of silence over the dessert by demanding to know the English word whose meaning and pronunciation changed when it was capitalized. Then, when all had given up, Halsted said slowly, "I would say that 'polish' becomes 'Polish,' right?"

Avalon frowned portentously, his luxuriant eyebrows hunching over his eyes. "At least that isn't as offensive as the usual Polish jokes I can't avoid hearing sometimes."

Drake said, his small gray mustache twitching, "We'll try something a little more complicated after the coffee."

Avalon darted a suspicious glance in the direction of Dr. Puntsch and, with a look of melancholy on his face, watched Henry pour the coffee.

Henry said, "Brandy, sir?"

Puntsch looked up, and said, "Why, yes, thank you. That was a very good meal, waiter."

"I am glad you think so," said Henry. "The Black Widowers are a special concern of this establishment."

Drake was striking his water glass with a spoon.

He said, trying to elevate his always fuzzily hoarse voice, "I've asked Sam Puntsch here partly because he once worked for the same firm I work for out in New Jersey, though not in the same department. He doesn't know a damn thing about organic chemistry; I know that because I heard him discuss the subject once. On the other hand, he's a pretty fair-to-middling physicist. I've also asked him here because he's got a problem and I told him to come down and entertain us with it, and I hope, Jeff, you have no objections."

Geoffrey Avalon, twirled his brandy glass gently between two fingers and said grimly, "There are no bylaws in this organization, Jim, so I'll go along with you and try to enjoy myself. But I must say I would like to relax on these evenings; though perhaps it's just the old brain calcifying."

"Well, don't worry, we'll let Tom be griller-in-chief."

Puntsch said, "If Mr. Avalon—"

Drake said at once, "Pay no attention to Mr. Avalon."

And Avalon himself said, "Oh, it's all right, Dr. Puntsch. The group is kind enough to let me pout on occasion."

Trumbull scowled and said, "Will you all let me get on with it? Dr. Puntsch, how do you justify your existence?"

"Justify it? I suppose you could say that trying to have our civilization last for longer than a generation is a sort of justification."

"What does this trying consist of?"

"An attempt to find a permanent, safe, and nonpolluting source of energy."

"What kind?"

"Fusion energy. Are you going to ask me for details?"

Trumbull shook his head. "No, unless they're germane to the problem that's disturbing you."

"Only tangentially; which is good." Puntsch's voice was reedy, and his words were meticulously pronounced as though he had at one time had ambitions to become a radio announcer. He said, "Actually, Mr. Rubin's point was a rather good one earlier in the evening. We all do have our private language, sometimes more so than is necessary, and I would not welcome the chance to have to go into great detail on the matter of fusion."

Gonzalo, who was wearing complementing tones of red and therefore dominated the table visually even more than usual, muttered, "I wish people would stop saying that Rubin is right."

"You want them to lie?" demanded Rubin, head thrown up at once, his sparse beard bristling.

"Shut up, you two," said Trumbull. "Dr. Puntsch, let me tell you what I know about fusion energy and you stop me if I'm too far off base. It's a kind of nuclear energy produced when you force small atoms to combine into larger ones. You use heavy hydrogen out of the ocean, fuse it to helium, and produce energy that will last us for many millions of years."

"Yes, it's roughly as you say."

"But we don't have it yet, do we?"

"As of today, no."

"Why not, Doctor?"

"Ah, Mr. Trumbull, I take it you don't want a two-hour lecture."

"No, sir, how about a two-minute lecture?"

Puntsch laughed. "About two minutes is all anyone will sit still for. The trouble is we have to heat up our fuel to a minimum temperature of forty-five million degrees centigrade, which is about eighty million fahrenheit. Then we have to keep the fusion fuel—heavy hydrogen, as you say, plus tritium which is a particularly heavy variety—at that temperature long enough for it to catch fire, so to speak, and we must keep it all in place with strong magnetic fields while this is happening.

"So far, we can't get the necessary temperature produced quickly enough, or hold the magnetic field in being long enough for the fusion fuel to ignite. Delivering energy by laser may be the best bet but we need stronger lasers than we have so far, plus stronger and better designed magnetic fields than we now have. Once we manage it and *do* ignite the fuel, it will be a breakthrough, but God knows there will remain plenty of engineering problems to solve before we can actually begin to run the Earth by fusion energy."

Trumbull said, "When do you think we'll get to that first breakthrough? When do you think we'll have ignition?"

"It's hard to say. American and Soviet physicists have been inching toward it for a quarter of a century. I think they've almost reached it. Five years more maybe. But there are imponderables. A lucky intuition might bring it this year. Unforeseen difficulties may carry us into the Twenty-first century."

Halsted broke in, "Can we wait till the twenty-first century?"

"Wait?" said Puntsch.

"You say you are trying to have our civilization last more than a generation. That sounds as though you don't think we can wait for the twenty-first century."

"I see. I wish I could be optimistic on this point, sir," said Puntsch gravely, "but I can't. At the rate we're going, our petroleum will be pretty much used up by the year 2000. Going back to coal will present us with a lot of problems and leaning on breeder fission reactors will involve getting rid of enormous quantities of radioactive wastes. I would certainly feel uncomfortable if we don't end up with working fusion reactors by, say, 2010."

"'After us, the deluge,'" said Avalon.

Puntsch said, with a trace of acerbity, "The deluge may well come after our time, Mr. Avalon. Do you have any children?"

Avalon, who had two children and three grandchildren, looked uncomfortable and said, "But fusion energy may stave off the deluge and I take it your feelings about the arrival of fusion are optimistic."

"Yes, there I tend to be optimistic."

Trumbull said, "Well, let's get on with it. You're working at Jim Drake's firm. I always thought of that as a big drug-supply house."

"It's a hell of a lot more than that," said Drake, looking dolefully at what was left of a cigarette package as though wondering whether he ought to light another one or refrain for ten minutes.

Puntsch said, "Jim works in the organic chemistry department, I work in plasma physics."

Rubin said, "I was down there once, visiting Jim, and took a tour of the plant. I didn't see any Tokamaks."

"What's a Tokamak?" asked Gonzalo at once.

Puntsch said, "It's a device within which stable magnetic fields—pretty stable anyway—can be set up to confine the super hot gas. No, we don't have any. We're not doing anything of that sort. We're more or less at the theoretical end of it. When we think up something that looks hopeful, we have arrangements with some of the large installations that will allow it to be tried out."

Gonzalo said, "What's in it for the firm?"

"We're allowed to do some basic research. There's always use for it. The firm produces fluorescent tubes of various sorts and anything we find about the behavior of hot gases—plasma, it's called—and magnetic fields may always help in the production of cheaper and better fluorescents. That's the practical justification of our work."

Trumbull said, "And have you come up with anything that looks hopeful? In fusion, I mean, not in fluorescents."

Puntsch began a smile and let it wipe off slowly. "That's exactly it. I don't know."

Halsted placed his hand on the pink area of baldness in the forepart of his skull and said, "Is that the problem you've brought us?"

"Yes," said Puntsch.

"Well, then, Doctor, suppose you tell us about it."

Puntsch cleared his throat and pursed his lips for a moment, looking around at the men at the banquet table and leaning to one side in order to allow Henry to refill his coffee cup.

"Jim Drake," he said, "has explained that everything said in this room is confidential; that everyone"—his eyes rested briefly on Henry—"is to be trusted. I'll speak freely, then. I have a colleague working at the firm. His name is Matthew Revsof and Drake knows him."

Drake nodded, "Met him at your house once."

Puntsch said, "Revsof is halfway between brilliance and madness, which is sometimes a good thing for a theoretical physicist. It means, though, that he's erratic and difficult to deal with at times. We've been good friends, mostly because our wives have gotten along particularly well. It became one of those family things where the children on both sides use us almost interchangeably as parents, since we have houses on the same block.

"Revsof is now in the hospital. He's been there two months. It's a mental hospital and he had a violent episode that put him into it, but there's no point in going into the details of that. However, the hospital is in no hurry to let him go and that creates a problem.

"I went to visit him about a week after he had been hospitalized. He seemed perfectly normal, perfectly cheerful; I brought him up to date on some of the work going on in the department and he had no trouble following me. But then he wanted to speak to me privately. He insisted the nurse leave and that the door be closed.

"He swore me to secrecy and told me he knew exactly how to design a Tokamak in such a way as to produce a totally stable magnetic field that would contain a plasma of moderate densities indefinitely. He said something like this: 'I worked it out last month. That's why I'm here. Naturally, the Soviets saw to it. The material is in my home safe—the diagrams, the theoretical analysis, everything.'"

Rubin, who had been listening with an indignant frown, interrupted. "Is that possible? Is he the kind of man who could do that? Was the work at the stage where such an advance—"

Putsch smiled wearily. "How can I answer that? The history of science is full of revolutionary advances that required small insights that anyone might have had, but that, in fact, only one person did have. I'll tell you this, though. When someone in a mental hospital tells you he has something that has been eluding the cleverest physicists in the world for nearly thirty years, and that the Russians are after him, you don't have a very great tendency to believe it. All I tried to do was soothe him.

"But my efforts to do that just excited him. He told me he planned to have the credit for it; he wasn't going to have anyone stealing priority while he was in the hospital. I was to stand guard over the home safe and make sure no one broke in. He was sure Russian spies would try to arrange a break-in and he kept saying over and over again that I was the only one he could trust and as soon as he got out of the hospital he would announce the discovery and prepare a paper so that he could protect his priority. He said he would give me coauthorship. Naturally, I agreed to everything just to keep him quiet and got the nurse back in as soon as I could."

Halsted said, "American and Soviet scientists are cooperating in fusion research, aren't they?"

"Yes, of course," said Puntsch. "The Tokamak itself is of Soviet origin. The business of Russian spies is just Revsof's overheated imagination."

Rubin said, "Have you visited him since?"

"Quite a few times. He sticks to his story. It bothers me. I don't believe him. I think he's mad. And yet something inside me says: What if he isn't? What if there's something in his home safe that the whole world would give its collective eyeteeth for?"

Halsted said, "When he gets out—"

Puntsch said, "It's not that easy. Any delay is risky. This is a field in which many minds are eagerly busy. On any particular day someone else may make Revsof's discovery, assuming that Revsof has really made one—and he will then lose priority and credit, and for all I know, a Nobel Prize. And to take the broader view, the firm will lose a considerable amount of reflected credit and the chance at a substantial increase in its prosperity. Every employee of the firm will lose the chance of benefiting from whatever prosperity-increase the firm might have experienced. So you see, gentlemen, I have a personal stake in this, and so has Jim Drake, for that matter.

"But even beyond that. The world is in a race it may not win. Even if we do get the answer to a stable magnetic field, there will be a great deal of engineering to work through, as I said before, and, at the very best, it will be years before fusion energy is really available to the world—years we might not be able to afford. In that case, it isn't safe to lose any time waiting for Revsof to get out."

Gonzalo said, "If he's getting out soon—"

"But he isn't. That's the worst of it," said Puntsch. "He may never come out. He's deteriorating fast."

Avalon said in his deep solemn voice, "I take it, sir, that you have explained the advantages of prompt action to your friend."

"Yes, I have," said Puntsch. "I've explained it as carefully as I could. I said we would open the safe before legal witnesses and bring everything to him for his personal signature. We would leave the originals after making copies. I explained what he himself might possibly lose by delay. All that happened was that he well, in the end he attacked me. I've been asked not to visit him again till further notice."

Gonzalo said, "What about his wife? Does she know anything about this? You said she was a good friend of your wife's."

"So she is. She's a wonderful girl and she understands perfectly the difficulty of the situation. She agrees that the safe should be opened."

"Has she talked to her husband?" asked Gonzalo.

Puntsch hesitated. "Well, no. She hasn't been allowed to see him. He—he . . . This is ridiculous, but I can't help it. He claims Barbara, his wife, is in the pay of the Soviet Union. Frankly, it was Barbara whom he—when he was put in the hospital—"

"All right," said Trumbull gruffly, "but can't you get Revsof declared incompetent and have the control of the safe transferred to his wife?"

"First, that's a complicated thing. Barbara would have to testify to a number of things she doesn't want to testify to. She—she loves the man."

Gonzalo said, "I don't want to sound ghoulish, but you said that Revsof is deteriorating fast. If he does—"

"Deteriorating mentally, not physically. He's only thirty-eight years old and could live thirty more years and be mad every day of it."

"Eventually, won't his wife be forced to request that he be declared incompetent?"

Puntsch said, "But when will that be? And besides, all this still isn't the problem I want to present. I had explained to Barbara exactly how I would go about protecting Matthew's priority. I would open the safe and Barbara would initial and date every piece of paper in it. I would photocopy it all and give her a notarized statement to the effect that I had done this and that I acknowledged that everything I removed was

Revsof's work, and his alone. The originals and the notarized statement would be returned to the safe and I would work with the copies.

"You see, she had told me at the very start that she had the combination. It was a matter of first overcoming my own feeling that I was betraying a trust, and secondly, overcoming her scruples. I didn't like it but I felt I was serving a higher cause and in the end Barbara agreed. We decided that if Revsof was ever sane enough to come home, he would agree we had done the right thing. And his priority *would* be protected."

Trumbull said, "I take it you opened the safe, then."

"No," said Puntsch, "I didn't. I tried the combination Barbara gave me and it didn't work. The safe is still locked."

Halsted said, "You could blow it open."

Puntsch said, "I can't bring myself to do that. It's one thing to be given the combination by the man's wife. It's another to—"

Halsted shook his head. "I mean, can't Mrs. Revsof ask that it be blown open?"

Puntsch said, "I don't think she would ask that. It would mean bringing in outsiders, and it might destroy the contents. But why doesn't the combination work? *That's* the problem."

Trumbull put his hands on the table and leaned forward. "Dr. Puntsch, are you asking us to answer that question? To tell you how to use the combination you have?"

"Yes."

"Do you have the combination with you?"

"You mean the actual slip of paper that has the combination written on it? No. Barbara keeps that and I see her point. However, if you want it written down, that's no problem. I remember it well enough." He brought out a little notebook from his inner jacket pocket, tore off a sheet of paper, and wrote rapidly. "There it is."

Trumbull glanced at it solemnly, then passed the paper to Halsted on his left. It made the rounds and came back to him.

Trumbull folded his hands and stared solemnly at the bit of paper. He said, "How do you know this is the combination to the safe?"

"Barbara says it is."

"Doesn't it seem unlikely to you, Dr. Puntsch, that the man you described would leave the combination lying about? With the combination available, he might as well have an unlocked safe. This row of symbols may have nothing to do with the safe."

Puntsch sighed. "That's not the way of it. It isn't as though the safe ever had anything of intrinsic value in it. There's nothing of great intrinsic value in Revsof's house altogether, or in mine, for that matter. We're not rich and we're not very subject to burglary. Revsof got the safe about five years ago and had it installed to keep papers in. He had this fetish about losing priority even then, but it wasn't till recently that it reached the point of paranoia. He simply made a note of the combination for his own use so he wouldn't lock himself out.

"Barbara came across it one day and asked what it was and he said that it was the combination to his safe. She said, 'Well, don't leave it lying around,' and she put it in a little envelope in one of her desk drawers feeling he might need it someday. He never did, apparently, and I'm sure he must have forgotten all about it. But she didn't forget, and she's certain it has never been disturbed."

Rubin said, "But he might have had the combination changed."

"That would have meant a locksmith in the house. Barbara says she's sure it never happened."

Trumbull said, "Is that all that was written on the page—just six numbers and a letter of the alphabet?"

"That's all."

"What about the back of the sheet?"

"Nothing."

Trumbull said, "You understand, Dr. Puntsch, this isn't a

code, and I'm not an expert on combination locks. What does the lock look like?"

"Very ordinary. I'm sure Revsof could not afford a really fancy safe. There's a dial with numbers around it from one to thirty, and a knob with a little pointer in the middle. Barbara has seen Matthew at the safe and there's no great shakes to it. He turns the knob and pulls it open."

"She's never done that herself?"

"No. She says she hasn't."

"She can't tell you why the safe doesn't open when you use the combination?"

"No, she can't. And yet it seems straightforward enough. Most of the combination locks I've dealt with—all of them, in fact—have knobs that you turn first in one direction, then in the other, then back in the first direction again. It seems clear to me that according to the combination, I should turn the knob to the right till the pointer is at twelve, then left to twenty- seven, then right again to fifteen."

Trumbull said thoughtfully, "I can't see that it could mean anything else."

"But it doesn't work," said Puntsch. "I turned twelve, twenty-seven, fifteen a dozen times. I did it carefully, making sure the little pointer was exactly centered on each line. I tried making extra turns—you know, right to twelve, then left one full turn and then to twenty-seven, then right one full turn and then to fifteen. I tried making one full turn in one direction and not in the other. I tried every trick I could think of, jiggling the knob, pressing it, everything."

Gonzalo said, grinning, "Did you say 'Open Sesame'?"

"It didn't occur to me to do so," said Puntsch, not grinning, "but if it had, believe me I would have tried it. Barbara says she never noticed him do anything special, but, of course, it could have been something unnoticeable, and for that matter she didn't watch him too closely. It wouldn't occur to her that she'd have to know someday."

Halsted said, "Let me look at that again." He stared at the combination. "This is only a copy, Dr. Puntsch. This can't be exactly the way it looked. You might be copying it as you *thought* it was. Isn't it possible that some of the numbers in the original might be equivocal—so that you could have mistaken a seven for a one, for instance?"

"No, no," said Puntsch, shaking his head vigorously. "There's no chance of a mistake in the numbers, I assure you."

"What about the spaces?" said Halstead. "Was it spaced exactly like that?"

Puntsch reached for the paper and looked at it again. "Oh, I see what you mean. No, as a matter of fact, there were no spaces. I put them in because that was how I think of it. Actually the original is a solid line of symbols. It doesn't matter though, does it? You can't divide it any other way. I'll write it down for you without spaces." He wrote a second time under the first and shoved it across the table to Halsted.

$$12R2715$$

He said, "You can't divide it any other way. You can't have a 271 or 715. The numbers don't go higher than thirty."

"Well now," muttered Halsted. "Never mind the numbers. What about the letter R?" He licked his lips, obviously enjoying the clear atmosphere of suspense now centered on him. "Suppose we divide the combination this way." And he wrote:

$$12 \quad R27 \quad 15$$

He held it up for Puntsch to see, and then for the others. "In this division, it's the twenty-seven which would have the sign for 'right,' so the two other numbers that turn left. In other words, the numbers are twelve, twenty-seven, and fifteen all right, but you turn left, right, left, instead of right, left, right."

Gonzalo protested. "Why put the R there?"

Halsted said, "All he needs is the minimum reminder. He knows what the combination is. If he reminds himself the middle number is right, he knows the other two are left."

Gonzalo said, "But that's no big deal. If he just puts down the three numbers, it's either left, right, left, or else it's right, left, right. If one doesn't work, he tries the other. Maybe the R stands for something else."

"I can't think what," said Dr. Puntsch gloomily.

Halsted said, "The symbol couldn't be something other than an R, could it, Dr. Puntsch?"

"Absolutely not," said Puntsch. "I'll admit I didn't think of associating the R with the second number, but that doesn't matter anyway. When the combination wouldn't work right, left, right, I was desperate enough not only to try it left, right, left; but right, right, right and left, left, left. In every case I tried it with and without complete turns in between. Nothing worked."

Gonzalo said, "Why not try all the combinations? There can only be so many."

Rubin said, "Figure out how many, Mario. The first number can be anything from one to thirty in either direction; so can the second; so can the third. The total number of possible combinations, if any direction is allowed for any number, is sixty times sixty times sixty, or over two hundred thousand. And that doesn't allow for extra turns."

"I think I'd be willing to blow it open before I try them all," said Puntsch.

Trumbull turned to Henry, who had been standing at the sideboard, an intent expression on his face. "Have you been following all this, Henry?"

Henry said, "Yes, sir, but I haven't actually seen the figures."

Trumbull said, "Do you mind, Dr. Puntsch? He's the best man here, actually." He handed over the slip with the numbers written in three different ways.

Henry studied them gravely and shook his head. "I'm sorry. I had had a thought, but I see I'm wrong."

"What was the thought?" asked Trumbull.

"It had occurred to me that the letter R might have been in the small form. I see it's a capital."

Puntsch looked astonished. "Wait, wait. Henry, does it matter?"

"It might, sir. We don't often think it does, but Mr. Halsted explained earlier in the evening that 'polish' becomes 'Polish,' changing the meaning and pronunciation simply because of the capitalization."

Puntsch said slowly, "But you know, it *is* a small letter in the original. It never occurred to me to reproduce it that way. I always use capitals when I print. How odd."

There was a faint smile on Henry's face. He said, "Would you write the combination with a small letter, sir?"

Puntsch, flushing slightly, wrote:

$$l2r2715$$

Henry looked at it and said, "As long as it is a small 'r,' I can now ask another question. Are there any other differences between this and the original?"

"No," said Puntsch. Then, defensively, "No significant differences. The matter of the spacing and the capitalization hasn't changed anything, has it? Of course, the original isn't in my handwriting."

Henry said quietly, "Is it in anyone's handwriting, sir?"

"What?"

"I mean, is the original typewritten, Dr. Puntsch?"

Dr. Puntsch's flush deepened. "Yes, now that you ask, it *was* typewritten. That doesn't mean anything, either. If there were a typewriter here I would typewrite it for you, though, of course, it might not be the same make of typewriter that typed out the original."

Henry said, "There's a typewriter in the office on this floor. Would you care to type it, Dr. Puntsch?"

"Certainly," said Puntsch. He was back in three minutes, during which time not one word was said by anyone at the table. He presented the paper to Henry, with the typewritten line under the four lines of handwritten ones:

l2r2715

Henry said, "Is this the way it looked? The typewriter that did the original did not have a particularly unusual typeface?"

"No, it didn't. What I have typed looks just like the original."

Henry passed the paper to Trumbull, who looked at it and passed it on.

Henry said, "If you open the safe, you are very likely to find nothing of importance, I suppose."

"I suppose it, too," snapped Puntsch. "I'm almost sure of it. It will be disappointing but much better than to keep on wondering."

"In that case, sir," said Henry, "I would like to remind you that Mr. Rubin spoke of private languages early in the evening. The typewriter has a private language, too. The standard typewriter uses the same symbol for the numeral one and the small form of the twelfth letter of the alphabet.

"If you wanted, in handwriting, to abbreviate 'left' and 'right' by the initial letters, there would be no problem, since neither form of the handwritten letter is confusing. If you used a typewriter and abbreviated it in capitals, it would also be clear. Using small letters, it is possible to read the combination as 12 right, 27, 15; or possibly 12, right 27, 15; or, as *left* 2, right 27, *left* 5. The 1 in 12 and 15 is not the numeral 1, but the small version of the letter L and it stands for left. Revsof knew what he was typing and it didn't confuse him. But it could confuse others. It's all in the way you read it."

Puntsch looked at the symbols open-mouthed. "How did I miss that?"

Henry said, "You spoke, earlier, of insights that anyone might have, but that only one actually does have. It was Mr. Gonzalo who had the key."

"I?" said Gonzalo, puzzled.

"Mr. Gonzalo wondered why there should be only one letter," said Henry, "and it seemed to me he was right. Revsof would surely indicate the letters for both directions, or for neither. Since one direction was unquestionably present, I wondered if the other might not be also. And I simply looked for it."

DAY OF RECKONING
by Patricia Highsmith

Do you like horror stories? If you don't, we suggest that you skip this one. If you do like an occasional tale of horror, Patricia Highsmith's "Day of Reckoning" will be your saucer of crime. And if you do read this story, we doubt if you will ever lose the image in your mind's eye of that predawn scene in front of the long gray barn when "it looked as if snow had fallen on the land." Except that it wasn't snow. . . .

JOHN took a taxi from the station, as his uncle had told him to do in case they weren't there to meet him. It was less than two miles to Hanshaw Chickens, Inc., as his Uncle Ernie Hanshaw now called his farm. John knew the white two-story house well, but the long gray barn was new to him. It was huge, covering the whole area where the cow barn and the pigpens had been.

"Plenty of wishbones in that place!" the taxi driver said cheerfully as John paid him.

John smiled. "Yes, and I was just thinking—not a chicken in sight!"

John carried his suitcase toward the house. "Anybody home?" he called, thinking his Aunt Helen would probably be in the kitchen now, getting lunch.

Then he saw the flattened cat. No, it was a kitten. Was it real or made of paper? John set his suitcase down and bent

265

closer. It was real. It lay on its side, almost level with the damp reddish earth, in the wide track of a tire. Its skull had been crushed and there was blood. The kitten was white with patches of orange and black.

John heard a hum of machinery from the barn. He put his suitcase on the front porch, and hearing nothing from the house, set off at a trot for the new barn. He found the big front doors locked and went round to the back, again at a trot, because the barn seemed to be a quarter of a mile long. Besides the machine hum, John heard a high-pitched sound, a din of cries and peeps from inside.

"Ernie?" John yelled. Then he saw Helen. "Hello, Helen!"

"John! Welcome! You took a taxi! We didn't hear any car."

She gave him a kiss on the cheek. "Why, you've grown another three inches."

His uncle climbed down from a ladder and shook John's hand. "How're you, boy?"

"Okay, Ernie. What's going on here?" John looked up at moving belts which disappeared somewhere inside the barn. A rectangular metal container, nearly as big as a boxcar, rested on the ground.

Ernie pulled John closer and shouted that the grain, a special mixture, had just been delivered and was being stored in the factory, as he called the barn. This afternoon a man would take back the container.

"Lights shouldn't go on now, according to schedule, but we'll make an exception so you can see. Look!" Ernie pulled a switch inside the barn door and the semidarkness changed to glaring light, bright as full sun.

The cackles and screams of the chickens augmented like a siren, like a thousand sirens, and John instinctively covered his ears. Ernie's lips moved, but John could not hear him. John swung around to see Helen. She was standing farther back, and waved a hand, shook her head and smiled, as if to say she couldn't bear the racket. Ernie drew John farther into the barn, but he had given up talking and merely pointed.

The chickens were smallish and mostly white, and they all shuffled constantly. John saw that this was because the platforms on which they stood slanted forward, inclining them toward the slowly moving feed troughs. But not all of them were eating. Some were trying to peck the chickens next to them.

Each chicken had its own little wire coop. There must have been forty rows of chickens on the ground floor, and eight or ten tiers of chickens went up to the ceiling. Between the double rows of back-to-back chickens were aisles wide enough for a man to pass and sweep the floor, John supposed, and just as he thought this, Ernie turned a wheel, and water began to shoot over the floor. The floor slanted toward various drain holes.

"All automatic! Somethin', eh?"

John recognized the words from Ernie's lips and nodded appreciatively. "Terrific!" But he was ready to get away from the noise.

Ernie shut off the water.

John noticed that the chickens had worn their beaks down to blunt nubs. What else could they do but eat? John had read a little about battery chicken farming. These hens of Ernie's, like the hens he had read about, couldn't turn around in their coops. Much of the general flurry in the barn was caused by chickens trying to fly upward.

Ernie cut the lights. The doors closed after them, also automatically.

"Machine farming has really got me over the hump," Ernie said, still talking loudly. "I'm making good money now. And just imagine, one man—me—can run the whole show!"

John grinned. "You mean you won't have anything for me to do?"

"Oh, there's plenty to do. You'll see. How about some lunch first? Tell Helen I'll be in in about fifteen minutes."

John walked toward Helen. "Fabulous."

"Yes. Ernie's in love with it."

They went on toward the house, Helen looking down at her feet because the ground was muddy in spots. She wore old tennis shoes, black corduroy pants, and a rust-colored sweater. John purposely walked between her and where the dead kitten lay, not wanting to mention it now.

He carried his suitcase up to the sunny corner room in which he had slept since he was a boy of ten, when Helen and

Ernie had bought the farm. He changed into blue jeans and went down to join Helen in the kitchen.

"Would you like an old-fashioned? We've got to celebrate your arrival," Helen said. She was making two drinks at the wooden table.

"Fine. Where's Susan?" Susan was their eight-year-old daughter.

"She's at a—well, sort of summer school. They'll bring her back around four-thirty. Helps fill in the summer holidays. They make awful clay ashtrays and fringed money purses— you know. Then you've got to praise them."

John laughed. He gazed at his aunt-by-marriage, thinking she was still very attractive at—what was it? Thirty-one, he thought. She was about five feet four, slender, with reddish blonde curly hair, and eyes that sometimes looked green, sometimes blue. And she had a very pleasant voice. "Oh, thank you." John accepted his drink. There were slices of fruit in it, topped with a cherry.

"Awfully good to see you, John. How's college? And how're your folks?"

Both those items were all right. John would graduate from Ohio State next year when he would be 20, then he was going to take a postgraduate course in government. He was an only child, and his parents lived in Dayton, 120 miles away.

Then John mentioned the kitten. "I hope it's not yours," he said, and realized at once that it must have been, because Helen put her glass down and stood up. Who else could the kitten have belonged to, John thought, since there was no other house around?

"Oh, Lord! Susan's going to be—" Helen rushed out the back door.

John ran after her, straight for the kitten which Helen now saw from a distance.

"It was that big truck this morning," Helen said. "The driver sits so high up he can't see what's—"

"I'll help you," John said, looking around for a spade or a trowel. He found a shovel and returned, and pried the body up gently, as if it were still alive. He held it in both his hands. "We ought to bury it."

"Of course. Susan mustn't see it, but I've got to tell her."

John dug where Helen suggested, a spot near an apple tree behind the house. He covered the grave over and put some tufts of grass back so it would not catch the eye.

"The times I've brought that kitten in the house when the damned truck came!" Helen said. "She was barely four months, wasn't afraid of anything, just went trotting up to cars as if they were something to play with, you know?" She gave a nervous laugh. "And this morning the truck came at eleven, and I was about to take a pie out of the oven."

John didn't know what to say. "Maybe you should get another kitten for Susan as soon as you can."

"What're you two doing?" Ernie walked toward them from the back door of the house.

"We just buried Beansy," Helen said. "The truck got her this morning."

"Oh." Ernie's smile disappeared. "That's too bad. That's really too bad, Helen."

But at lunch Ernie was cheerful enough, talking of vitamins and antibiotics in his chicken feed and the production of one and one-quarter eggs per day per hen. Though it was July, Ernie was lengthening the chickens' "day" by artificial light.

"All birds are geared to spring," Ernie said. "They lay more when they think spring is coming. The ones I've got are at peak. In October they'll be under a year old, and I'll sell them and take on a new batch."

John listened attentively. He was to be here a month and wanted to be helpful. "They really do eat, don't they? A lot of them have worn off their beaks, I noticed."

Ernie laughed. "They're debeaked. They'd peck each other through the wire if they weren't. Two of 'em got loose in my first batch and nearly killed each other. Well, one did kill the other. Believe me, I de-beak 'em now, according to instructions."

"And one chicken went on eating the other," Helen said. "Cannibalism." She laughed uneasily. "Ever hear of cannibalism among chickens, John?"

"No."

"Our chickens are insane," Helen said.

Insane. John smiled a little. Maybe Helen was right. Their noises had sounded pretty crazy.

"Helen doesn't much like battery farming," Ernie said apologetically to John. "She's always thinking about the old days. But we weren't doing so well then."

That afternoon John helped his uncle draw the conveyor belts back into the barn. He began learning the levers and switches that worked things. Belts removed eggs and deposited them gently into plastic containers. It was nearly 5:00 P.M. before John could get away. He wanted to say hello to his cousin Susan, a lively little girl with hair like her mother's.

As John crossed the front porch he heard a child's weeping, and he remembered the kitten. He decided to go ahead anyway and speak to Susan.

Susan and her mother were in the living room—a front room with flowered print curtains and cherrywood furniture. Some additions, such as a bigger television set, had been made since John had seen the room last. Helen was on her knees beside the sofa on which Susan lay, her face buried in one arm.

"Hello, Susan," John said. "I'm sorry about your kitten."

Susan lifted a round wet face. A bubble started at her lips and broke. "Beansy—"

John embraced her impulsively. "We'll find another kitten. I promise. Maybe tomorrow. Yes?" He looked at Helen.

Helen nodded and smiled a little. "Yes, we will."

The next afternoon, as soon as the lunch dishes had been washed, John and Helen set out in the station wagon for a farm eight miles away that belonged to some people named Ferguson. The Fergusons had two female cats that frequently had kittens, Helen said. And they were in luck this time. One of the cats had a litter of five—one black, one white, three mixed—and the other cat was pregnant.

"White?" John suggested. The Fergusons had given them a choice.

"Mixed," Helen said. "White is all good and black is—maybe unlucky."

They chose a black and white female with white feet.

"I can see this one being called Bootsy," Helen laughed.

The Fergusons were simple people, getting on in years, and very hospitable. Mrs. Ferguson insisted they partake of a freshly baked coconut cake along with some rather powerful homemade wine. The kitten romped around the kitchen, playing with gray rolls of dust that she dragged out from under a big cupboard.

"That ain't no battery kitten!" Frank Ferguson remarked, and drank deep.

"Can we see your chickens, Frank?" Helen asked. She slapped John's knee suddenly. "Frank has the most *wonderful* chickens, almost a hundred!"

"What's wonderful about 'em?" Frank said, getting up on a stiff leg. He opened the back screen door. "You know where they are, Helen."

John's head was buzzing pleasantly from the wine as he walked with Helen out to the chicken yard. Here were Rhode Island Reds, big white Leghorns, roosters strutting and tossing their combs, half-grown speckled chickens, and lots of little chicks about six inches high. The ground was covered with claw-scored watermelon rinds, tin bowls of grain and mush, and there was much chicken dung. A wheelless wreck of a car seemed to be a favorite laying spot: three hens sat on the back of the front seat with their eyes half closed, ready to drop eggs which would surely break on the floor behind them.

"It's such a wonderful *mess!*" John shouted, laughing.

Helen hung by her fingers in the wire fence, rapt. "Like the chickens I knew when I was a kid. Well, Ernie and I had them too, till about—" She smiled at John. "You know—a year ago. Let's go in!"

John found the gate, a limp thing made of wire that fastened with a wooden bar. They went in and closed it behind them.

Several hens drew back and regarded them with curiosity, making throaty, skeptical noises.

"They're such stupid darlings!" Helen watched a hen fly up and perch herself in a peach tree. "They can see the sun! They can fly!"

"And scratch for worms—and eat watermelon!" John said.

"When I was little, I used to dig worms for them at my

grandmother's farm. With a hoe. And sometimes I'd step on
their droppings and Grandma always made me wash my feet
under the garden hose before I came in the house." She
laughed. A chicken evaded her outstretched hand with an
Urrr-rrk! "Grandma's chickens were·so tame, I could touch
them. All bony and warm with the sun, their feathers. Sometimes I want to open all the coops in our barn and open the
doors and let all our chickens loose, just to see them walking
on the grass for a few minutes."

"Say, Helen, want to buy one of these to take home? Just
for fun? Maybe a couple of 'em?"

"No."

"How much did the kitten cost? Anything?"

"No, nothing."

Susan took the kitten into her arms, and John could see
that the tragedy of Beansy would soon be forgotten. To
John's disappointment, Helen lost her gaiety during dinner.
Maybe it was because Ernie was droning on about his profit
and loss—not loss really, but outlay. Ernie was obsessed,
John realized. That was why Helen was bored.

Ernie worked hard now, regardless of what he said about
machinery doing everything. There were creases on both
sides of his mouth, and they were not from laughing. He was
starting to get a paunch. Helen had told John that last year
Ernie had dismissed their handyman Sam, who'd been with
them seven years.

"Say," Ernie said, demanding John's attention. "What
d'you think of the idea? Start a battery chicken farm when
you finish school, and hire *one man* to run it. You could take
another job in Chicago or Washington or wherever, and
you'd have a steady *separate* income for life."

John was silent. He couldn't imagine having a battery
chicken farm.

"Any bank would finance you—with a word from Clive, of
course."

Clive was John's father.

Helen was looking down at her plate.

"Not really my lifestyle, I think," John answered finally. "I
know it's profitable."

After dinner Ernie went into the living room to do his reckoning, as he called it. He did some reckoning almost every night. John helped Helen with the dishes. She put a Mozart symphony on the record player. The music was nice, but John would have liked to talk with Helen.

On the other hand, what would he have said, exactly? *I understand why you're bored. I think you'd prefer pouring slop for pigs and tossing grain to real chickens, the way you used to.* John had a desire to put his arms around Helen as she bent over the sink, to turn her face to his and kiss her. What would Helen think if he did? That night, lying in bed, John dutifully read the brochures on battery chicken farming that Ernie had given him.

". . . The chickens are bred small so that they do not eat so much, and they rarely reach more than 3½ pounds . . . Young chickens are subjected to a light routine which tricks them into thinking that a day is 6 hours long. The objective of the factory farmer is to increase the original 6-hour day by leaving the lights on for a longer period each week. Artificial Spring Period is maintained for the hen's whole lifetime of 10 months . . . There is no real falling off of egg-laying in the natural sense, though the hen won't lay quite so many eggs toward the end . . ." (Why? John wondered. And wasn't "not quite so many" the same as "falling off"?) "At 10 months the hen is sold for about 30c a pound, depending on the market. . . ."

And below:

"Richard K. Schultz of Poon's Cross, Pa., writes: 'I am more than pleased and so is my wife with the modernization of my farm into a battery chicken farm operated with Muskeego-Ryan electric equipment. Profits have quadrupled in a year and a half and we have even bigger hopes for the future. . . .'

"Writes Henry Vliess of Farnham, Kentucky: 'My old farm was barely breaking even. I had chickens, pigs, cows, the usual. My friends used to laugh at my hard work combined with all my tough luck. Then I. . . .'"

John had a dream. He was flying like Superman in Ernie's chicken barn, and the lights were all blazing brightly. Many of the imprisoned chickens looked up at him, their eyes flashed silver, and they were struck blind. The noise they made was fantastic. They wanted to escape, but could no longer see, and the whole barn heaved with their efforts to fly upward. John flew about frantically, trying to find the lever to open the coops, the doors, anything, but he couldn't.

Then he woke up suddenly, startled to find himself in bed, propped on one elbow. His forehead and chest were damp with sweat. Moonlight came strong through the window. In the night's silence he could hear the steady high-pitched din of the hundreds of chickens in the barn, though Ernie had said the barn was absolutely soundproofed. Maybe it was "daytime" for the chickens now. Ernie said they had three more months to live.

In a short time John became more adept with the barn's machinery and the fast artificial clocks, but since the dream he no longer looked at the chickens as he had the first day. He did not look at them at all if he could help it. Once Ernie pointed out a dead one, and John removed it. Its breast, creased from the coop's barrier, was so distended it might have eaten itself to death.

Susan had named her kitten Bibsy, because it had a white oval on its chest like a bib.

"Beansy and now Bibsy," Helen said to John. "You'd think all Susan thinks about is food!"

Helen and John drove to town one Saturday morning. It was alternately sunny and showery, and they walked close together under an umbrella when the showers came. They bought meat, potatoes, washing powder, white paint for a kitchen shelf, and Helen bought a pink-and-white-striped blouse for herself. At a pet shop John acquired a basket with a pillow to give Susan for Bibsy.

When they got home there was a long dark gray car in front of the house.

"Why, that's the doctor's car!" Helen said.

"Does he come by just to visit?" John asked, and at once felt stupid, because something might have happened to Ernie. A grain delivery had been due that morning, and Ernie was always climbing about to see that everything was going right.

There was another car, dark green, which Helen didn't recognize. Helen and John went into the house.

It was Susan. She lay on the living-room floor beneath a plaid blanket, only one sandaled foot and yellow sock visible under the fringed edge. Dr. Geller was there, and a man Helen didn't know. Ernie stood rigid and panicked beside his daughter.

Dr. Geller came toward Helen and said, "I'm sorry, Helen. Susan was dead by the time the ambulance got here. I sent for the coroner."

"What *happened?*" Helen started to touch Susan, and instinctively John caught her.

"Honey, I didn't see her in time," Ernie said. "She was chasing under that damned container after the kitten just as it was lowering."

"Yeah, it bumped her on the head," said a husky man in tan workclothes, one of the delivery men. "She was running out from under it, like Ernie said. My *gosh,* I'm sorry, Mrs. Hanshaw!"

Helen gasped, then she covered her face.

"You'll need a sedative, Helen," Dr. Geller said.

The doctor gave Helen a needle in her arm. Helen said nothing. Her mouth was slightly open, and her eyes stared straight ahead. Another car came and took the body away on a stretcher.

With a shaky hand Ernie poured whiskies.

Bibsy leaped about the room and sniffed at the red splotch on the carpet. John went to the kitchen to get a sponge. It was best to try to clean it up, John thought, while the others were in the kitchen. He went back to the kitchen for a saucepan of water, then scrubbed at the abundant red.

His head was ringing, and he had difficulty keeping his balance. Back in the kitchen, he drank off another whiskey at a gulp and at once it burned his ears.

"Ernie, I think I'd better take off," the delivery man said solemnly. "You know where to find me."

Helen went up to the bedroom she shared with Ernie and did not come down when it was time for dinner. From his room John heard floorboards creaking faintly and knew that

Helen was walking about in the room. He wanted to go in and speak to her, but he was afraid he would not be capable of saying the right thing. Ernie should be with her, John thought.

John and Ernie gloomily scrambled some eggs, and John went to ask Helen if she would come down or would she prefer to have him bring her something. He knocked on the door.

"Come in," Helen said.

He loved her voice, and was somehow surprised to find that it wasn't any different since her child had died. She was lying on the double bed, still in the same clothes, smoking a cigarette.

"I don't care to eat, thanks, but I'd like a whiskey."

John rushed down, eager to get something she wanted. He brought ice, a glass, and the bottle on a tray. "Do you just want to go to sleep?" John asked.

"Yes."

She had not turned on a light. John kissed her cheek, and for an instant she slipped her arm around his neck and kissed his cheek also. Then he left the room.

Downstairs the eggs tasted dry and John could hardly swallow even with sips of milk.

"My God," Ernie said. "My God." He was evidently trying to say more as he looked at John with an effort at politeness, or closeness.

And John, like Ernie, found himself looking down at his plate, wordless. Finally, miserable in the silence, John got up with his plate and patted Ernie awkwardly on the shoulder. "I'm sorry, Ernie."

They opened another bottle of whiskey, one of the two bottles left in the living-room cabinet.

"If I'd known this would happen I'd never have started this damned chicken farm. You know that. I meant to earn something for my family—not go limping along year after year."

John saw that the kitten had found the new basket and gone to sleep in it on the living-room floor. "Ernie, you probably want to talk to Helen. I'll be up at the usual time tomorrow to give you a hand." That meant 7:00 A.M.

"Okay. I'm in a daze tonight. Forgive me, John."

John lay for nearly an hour in his bed without sleeping. He heard Ernie go quietly into the bedroom across the hall, but he heard no voices or even a murmur after that. Ernie was not much like Clive, John thought. John's father might have given way to tears for a minute, might have cursed. Then with his father it would have been all over, except for comforting his wife.

A raucous noise, rising and falling, woke John up. The chickens, of course. What the hell was it now? They were louder than he'd ever heard them. He looked out the front window. In the predawn light he could see that the barn's front doors were open. Then the lights in the barn came on, blazing out onto the grass. John pulled on his shoes without tying them and rushed into the hall.

"Ernie! Helen!" he yelled at their closed door.

John ran out of the house. A white tide of chickens was now oozing through the wide front doors of the barn. What on earth had happened? "Get *back!*" he yelled at the chickens, flailing his arms.

The little hens might have been blind or might not have heard him at all through their own squawks. They kept on flowing from the barn, some fluttering over the others, and sinking again in the white sea.

John cupped his hands to his mouth. "Ernie! The *doors!*" He was shouting into the barn, because Ernie must be there.

John plunged into the hens and made another effort to shoo them back. It was hopeless. Unused to walking, the chickens teetered like drunks, lurched against each other, stumbled forward, fell back on their tails, but they kept pouring out, many borne on the backs of those that walked. They were pecking at John's ankles.

John kicked some aside and moved toward the barn doors again, but the pain of the blunt beaks on his ankles and lower legs made him stop. Some chickens tried to fly up to attack him, but had no strength in their wings. *They are insane,* John remembered. Suddenly frightened, John ran toward the clearer area at the side of the barn, then on toward the back door. He knew how to open the back door. It had a combination lock.

Helen was standing at the corner of the barn in her bathrobe, where John had first seen her when he arrived. The back door was closed.

"What's *happening?*" John shouted.

"I opened the coops," Helen said.

"Opened them? Why? Where's Ernie?"

"He's in there." Helen was oddly calm, as if she were standing and talking in her sleep.

"Well, what's he *doing?* Why doesn't he close the place?" John was shaking Helen by the shoulders, trying to wake her up. He released her and ran to the back door.

"I've locked it again," Helen said.

John worked the combination as fast as he could, but he could hardly see it.

"Don't open it! Do you want them coming *this* way?" Helen was suddenly alert, dragging John's hands from the lock.

Then John understood. Ernie was in there. Even if Ernie were screaming, they couldn't have heard him.

A smile came over Helen's face. "Yes, he's in there. I think they'll finish him."

John, not quite hearing over the noise of chickens, had read her lips. His heart was beating fast.

Then Helen slumped and John caught her. John knew it was too late to save Ernie. He also thought that Ernie was no longer screaming.

Helen straightened up. "Come with me. Let's watch them," she said, and drew John feebly, yet with determination, along the side of the barn toward the front doors.

Their slow walk seemed to take four times longer than it should have. He gripped Helen's arm. "Ernie *in* there?" John asked, feeling as if he were dreaming, or perhaps about to faint.

"In there." Helen smiled at him again, with her eyes half closed. "I came down and opened the back door, you see— and then I went up and woke Ernie. I said, 'Ernie, something's wrong in the factory, you'd better come down.' He came down and went in the back door—and I opened the coops with the lever. And then—I pulled the lever that opens the front doors. He was in the middle of the barn then, because I started a fire on the floor."

"A fire?" Then John noticed a pale curl of smoke rising over the front door.

"Not much to burn in there—just the grain," Helen said. "And there's enough for them to eat outdoors, don't you think?" She gave a laugh, and John shuddered. John pulled her faster toward the front of the barn. There seemed to be not much smoke. Now the whole lawn was covered with chickens and they were spreading through the white rail fence onto the road, pecking, cackling, screaming, a slow army without direction. It looked as if snow had fallen on the land.

"Head for the house!" John said, kicking at some chickens that were attacking Helen's ankles.

They went up to John's room. Helen knelt at the front window, watching. The sun was rising on their left, and now it touched the reddish roof of the metal barn. Gray smoke was curling upward from the horizontal lintel of the front doors. Chickens paused, stood stupidly in the doorway until they were bumped by others from behind.

The chickens seemed not so much dazzled by the rising sun—the light was brighter in the barn—as by the openness around them and above them. John had never before seen chickens stretch their necks just to look up at the sky. He knelt beside Helen, his arm around her waist.

"They're all going to—go away," John said. He felt curiously paralyzed.

"Let them."

The fire would not spread to the house. There was no wind, and the barn was at least thirty yards away. John felt quite mad, like Helen, or the chickens, and was astonished by the reasonableness of his thought about the fire's not spreading.

"It's all over," Helen said, as nearly the last of the chickens wobbled out of the barn. She drew John closer by the front of his pajama top.

John kissed her gently, then more firmly on the lips. It was strange, stronger than any kiss he had ever known with a girl, yet curiously without further desire. The kiss seemed only an affirmation that they were both alive. They knelt facing each other and embracing tightly.

The cries of the hens had ceased to sound ugly, and now sounded only excited and puzzled. It was like an orchestra playing, some members stopping, others resuming their instruments, making a continuous chord but without a tempo.

John did not know how long they knelt like that, but at last his knees hurt, and he stood up, pulling Helen up, too. He looked out the window and said, "They must be all out. And the fire isn't any bigger. Shouldn't we—shouldn't we—"

But the obligation to look for Ernie seemed far away, not at all pressing. It was as if he had dreamed this night or this dawn, and Helen's kiss, the way he had dreamed about flying like Superman in the barn. Were they really Helen's hands in his now?

She slumped again, and plainly she wanted to sit on the carpet. So he left her and pulled on his jeans over his pajama pants. He went down and entered the barn cautiously by the front door. The smoke made the interior hazy, but when he bent low he could see fifty or more chickens pecking at something on the floor. Bodies of chickens overcome by smoke lay all around, like little white puffs of smoke themselves, and some live chickens were pecking at these.

John moved toward Ernie. He thought he had braced himself, but he hadn't braced himself enough for what he saw. He ran out again, very fast, because he had breathed once, and the smoke had nearly got him.

In his room Helen was humming and drumming on the window sill, gazing out at the chickens left on the lawn. The hens were trying to scratch in the grass, and were staggering, falling on their sides, but mostly falling backward, because they were used to shuffling to prevent themselves from falling forward.

"Look!" Helen said, laughing so hard there were tears in her eyes. "They don't know what grass is! But they like it!"

John cleared his throat and said, "What're you going to say? What'll we say?"

"Oh—say." Helen seemed not at all disturbed by the question. "Well—that Ernie heard something and went down and—he wasn't completely sober, you know. And—maybe he pulled a couple of wrong levers—Don't you think so?"

THE BIG STORY
by Dick Francis

Dick Francis brought a seldom used milieu to the mystery novel—horseracing in all its fascinating forms. His stories are the most authentic of their kind—and with good reason. Dick Francis knows what he is writing about—he's a former professional jockey, he became Britain's champion steeplechase rider, and for four years was the jockey for the Queen mother.

This story has the Kentucky Derby as its backdrop. But even more important than the racing atmosphere, the fixing and the bookmaking and the pickpocketing, even the Derby run itself, is Mr. Francis' insight into a very human being, a washed-up, chiseling turfwriter who got the biggest break in his news career at Churchill Downs. . . .

WHEN the breakfast-time Astrojet from La Guardia was still twenty minutes short of Louisville, Fred Collyer took out a block of printed forms and began to write his expenses.

Cab fare to airport, $15.

No matter that a neighbor, working out on Long Island, had given him a free ride door to door; a little imagination in the expense department earned him half as much again (untaxed), as the *Manhattan Star* paid him for the facts he came up with every week in his Monday racing column.

Refreshments on journey, he wrote, *$5.*

281

Entertaining for the purpose of obtaining information, $6.50.

To justify that little lot he ordered a second double bourbon from the air hostess and lifted it in a silent good-luck gesture to a man sleeping across the aisle, the owner of a third-rate filly that had bucked her shins two weeks ago.

Another Kentucky Derby. His mind flickered like a scratched print of an old movie over the days ahead. The same old slog out to the barns in the mornings, the same endless raking over of past form, searching for a hint of the future. The same inconclusive workouts on the track, the same slanderous rumors, same gossip, same stupid jocks, same stupid trainers shooting their damn stupid mouths off.

The bright burning enthusiasm which had carved out his syndicated by-line was long gone. The lift of the spirit to the big occasion, the flair for sensing a story where no one else did, the sharp instinct which sorted truth from camouflage, all these he had had. All had left him. In their place lay plains of boredom and perpetual cynical tiredness. Instead of exclusives he nowadays gave his paper rehashes of other turf-writers' ideas, and a couple of times recently he had failed to do even that.

He was 46.

He drank.

Back in his functional New York office the Sports Editor of the *Manhattan Star* pursed his lips over Fred Collyer's account of the Everglades at Hialeah and wondered if he had been wise to send him down as usual to the Derby.

That guy, he thought regretfully, was all washed up. Too bad. Too bad he couldn't stay off the liquor. No one could drink and write, not at one and the same time. Write first, drink after; sure. Drink to excess, to stupor, maybe. But *after.*

He thought that before long he would have to let Fred go, that probably he should have started looking around for a replacement that day months back when Fred first turned up in the office too fuddled to hit the right keys on his typewriter. But that bum had had everything, he thought. A true journalist's nose for a story, and a gift for putting it across so vividly that the words jumped right off the page and kicked you in the brain.

Nowadays all that was left was a reputation and an echo;

the technique still marched shakily on, but the personality behind it was drowning.

The Sports Editor shook his head over the Hialeah clipping and laid it aside. Twice in the past six weeks Fred had been incapable of writing a story at all. Each time when he had not phoned through they had fudged up a column in the office and stuck the Collyer name on it, but two missed deadlines were one more than forgivable. Three, and it would be all over. The management were grumbling louder than ever over the inflated expense accounts, and if they found out that in return they had twice received only sodden silence, no amount of for-old-times'-sake would save him.

I did warn him, thought the Sports Editor uneasily. I told him to be sure to turn in a good one this time. A sizzler, like he used to. I told him to make this Derby one of his greats.

Fred Collyer checked into the motel room the newspaper had reserved for him and sank three quick midmorning stiffeners from the bottle he had brought along in his briefcase. He shoved the Sports Editor's warning to the back of his mind because he was still sure that drunk or sober he could outwrite any other commentator in the business, given a story that was worth the trouble. There just weren't any good stories around any more.

He took a taxi out to Churchill Downs. (*Cab fare, $4.50,* he wrote on the way; and paid the driver $2.75.)

With three days to go to the Derby the track looked clean, fresh, and expectant. Bright red tulips in tidy columns pointed their petals uniformly to the blue sky, and patches of green grass glowed like shampooed rugs. Without noticing them Fred Collyer took the elevator to the roof and trudged up the last windy steps to the huge glass-fronted press room which ran along the top of the stands.

Inside, a few men sat at the rows of typewriters knocking out the next day's news, and a few more stood outside on the balcony actually watching the first race, but most were engaged on the day's serious business, which was chat.

Fred Collyer bought himself a can of beer at the simple bar and carried it over to his named place, exchanging hi-yahs with the faces he saw on the circuit from Saratoga to Hollywood Park. Living on the move in hotels, and altogether rootless since Sylvie got fed up with his absence and his drinking and took the kids back to Mom in Nebraska, he looked on racetrack press boxes as his only real home. He felt relaxed there, assured of respect. He was unaware that the admiration he had once inspired was slowly fading into tolerant pity.

He sat easily in his chair reading one of the day's duplicated news releases.

"Trainer Harbourne Cressie reports no heat in Pincer Movement's near fore after breezing four furlongs on the track this morning."

"No truth in rumor that Salad Bowl was running a temperature last evening, insists veterinarian John Brewer on behalf of owner Mrs. L. (Loretta) Hicks."

Marvelous, he thought sarcastically. Negative news was no news, Derby runners included.

He stayed up in the press box all afternoon, drinking beer, discussing this, that, and nothing with writers, photographers, publicists, and radio newsmen, keeping an inattentive eye on the racing on the closed-circuit television, and occasionally going out onto the balcony to look down on the anthill crowd far beneath. There was no need to struggle around down there as he used to, he thought. No need to try to see people, to interview them privately. Everything and everyone of interest came up to the press box sometime, ladling out info in spoonfed dollops.

At the end of the day he accepted a ride back to town in a colleague's Hertz car *(cab fare, $4.50)*, and in the evening having laid substantial bourbon foundations in his own room before setting out, he attended the annual dinner of the Turfwriters' Association. The throng in the big reception room was pleased enough to see him, and he moved among the assortment of newsmen, trainers, jockeys, breeders, owners and wives and girl friends like a fish in his own home pond. Automatically before dinner he put away four doubles on the rocks, and through the food and the lengthy speeches afterward kept up a steady intake. At half-past eleven, when he tried to leave the table, he couldn't control his legs.

It surprised him. Sitting down, he had not been aware of being drunk. His tongue still worked as well as most around him, and to himself his thoughts seemed perfectly well organized. But his legs buckled as he put his weight on them, and he returned to his seat with a thump. It was considerably later, when the huge room had almost emptied as the guests went home, that he managed to summon enough strength to stand up.

"Guess I took a skinful," he murmured, smiling to himself in self-excuse.

Holding onto the backs of chairs and at intervals leaning against the wall, he weaved his way to the door. From there he blundered out into the passage and forward to the lobby, and from there, looking as if he were climbing imaginary steps, out into the night through the swinging glass doors.

The cool May evening air made things much worse. The earth seemed literally to be turning beneath his feet. He listed sideways into a half circle and, instead of moving forward to the parked cars and waiting taxis, staggered head-on into the dark brick front of the wall flanking the entrance. The impact hurt him and confused him further. He put both his hands flat on the rough surface in front of him and laid his face on it, and couldn't work out where he was.

Marius Tollman and Piper Boles had not seen Fred Collyer leave ahead of them. They strolled together along the same route making the ordinary social phrases and gestures of people who had just come together by chance at the end of an evening, and gave no impression at all that they had been eyeing each other meaningfully across the room for hours, and thinking almost exclusively about the conversation which lay ahead.

In a country with legalized bookmaking Marius Tollman might have grown up a respectable law-abiding citizen. As it was, his natural aptitude and only talent had led him into a lifetime of quick footwork which would have done credit to Muhammad Ali. Through the simple expedient of standing bets for the future racing authorities while they were still young enough to be foolish, he remained unpersecuted by them once they reached status and power; and the one sort of winner old crafty Marius could spot better even than horses was the colt heading for the boardroom.

The two men went through the glass doors and stopped just outside with the light from the lobby shining full upon them. Marius never drew people into corners, believing it looked too suspicious.

"Did you get the boys to go along, then?" he asked, standing on his heels with his hands in his pockets and his paunch oozing over his belt.

Piper Boles slowly lit a cigarette, glanced around casually at the star dotted sky, and sucked comforting smoke into his lungs.

"Yeah," he said.

"So who's elected?"

"Amberezzio."

"No," Marius protested. "He's not good enough."

Piper Boles drew deep on his cigarette. He was hungry. One hundred and eleven pounds to make tomorrow, and only a five-ounce steak in his belly. He resented fat people, particularly rich fat people. He was putting away his own small store of fat in real estate and growth bonds, but at 38 the physical struggle was near to defeating him. He couldn't face many more years of starvation, finding it worse as his body aged. A sense of urgency had lately led him to consider ways of making a quick $10,000 that once he would have sneered at.

He said, "He's straight. It'll have to be him."

Marius thought it over, not liking it, but finally nodded.

"All right, then. Amberezzio."

Piper Boles nodded, and prepared to move away. It didn't do for a jockey to be seen too long with Marius Tollman, not if he wanted to go on riding second string for the prestigious Somerset Farms, which he most assuredly did.

Marius saw the impulse and said smoothly, "Did you give any thought to a diversion on Crinkle Cut?"

"It'll cost you," he said.

"Sure," Marius agreed easily. "How about another thousand, on top?"

"Used bills. Half before."

"Sure."

Piper Boles shrugged off his conscience, tossed out the last of his integrity.

"Okay," he said, and sauntered away to his car as if all his nerves weren't stretched and screaming.

Fred Collyer had heard every word, and he knew, without having to look, that one of the voices was Marius Tollman's. Impossible for anyone long in the racing game not to recognize that wheezy Boston accent. He understood that Marius had been fixing up a swindle and also that a good little swindle would fill his column nicely. He thought fuzzily that it was necessary to know who Marius had been talking to, and that as the voices had been behind him he had better turn round and find out.

Time however was disjointed for him, and when he pushed himself off the wall and made an effort to focus in the right direction, both men had gone.

"Damn," he said aloud to the empty night, and another late homegoer, leaving the hotel, took him compassionately by the elbow and led him to a taxi. He made it safely back to his own room before he passed out.

Since leaving La Guardia that morning he had drunk six beers, four brandies, one double Scotch (by mistake), and nearly three fifths of bourbon.

He woke at eleven the next morning, and couldn't believe it. He stared at the bedside clock.

Eleven.

He had missed the barns and the whole morning merry-go-round on the track. A shiver chilled him at that first realization, but there was worse to come.

When he tried to sit up, the room whirled and his head thumped like a piledriver. When he stripped back the sheet, he found he had been sleeping in bed fully clothed with his shoes on. When he tried to remember how he had returned the previous evening, he could not do so.

He tottered into the bathroom. His face looked back at him like a nightmare from the mirror, wrinkled and red-eyed, ten years older overnight. Hungover he had been any

number of times, but this felt like no ordinary morning-
after. A sense of irretrievable disaster hovered somewhere
behind the acute physical misery of his head and stomach,
but it was not until he had taken off his coat and shirt and
pants, and scraped off his shoes, and lain down again weakly
on the crumpled bed, that he discovered its nature.

Then he realized with a jolt that not only had he no recollection of the journey back to his motel, he could recall practically nothing of the entire evening. Snatches of conversation from the first hour came back to him, and he remembered sitting at table between a cross old writer from the *Bal-
timore Sun* and an earnest woman breeder from Lexington,
neither of whom he liked; but an uninterrupted blank started from halfway through the fried chicken.

He had heard of alcoholic blackouts, but supposed they
only happened to alcoholics; and he, Fred Collyer, was not
one of those. Of course, he would concede that he did drink
a little. Well, a lot, then. But he could stop any time he liked.
Naturally he could.

He lay on the bed and sweated, facing the stark thought
that one blackout might lead to another, until blackouts gave
way to pink panthers climbing the walls. The Sports Editor's
warning came back with a bang, and for the first time, uncomfortably remembering the two times he had missed his
column, he felt a shade of anxiety about his job.

Within five minutes he had reassured himself that they
would never fire Fred Collyer, but all the same he would for
the paper's sake lay off the drink until after he had written
his piece on the Derby. This resolve gave him a glowing feeling of selfless virtue, which at least helped him through the
shivering fits and pulsating headaches of an extremely
wretched day.

Out at Churchill Downs three other men were just as worried. Piper Boles kicked his horse forward into the starting
stalls and worried about what George Highbury, the Somerset Farms' trainer, had said when he went to scale at two
pounds overweight. George Highbury thought himself
superior to all jocks and spoke to them curtly, win or lose.

"Don't give me that rot," he said to Boles's excuses. "You

went to the Turfwriters' Dinner last night, what do you expect?"

Piper Boles looked bleakly back over his hungry evening with its single martini and said he'd had a session in the sweat box that morning.

Highbury scowled. "You keep your fat backside away from the table tonight and tomorrow if you want to make Crinkle Cut in the Derby."

Piper Boles badly needed to ride Crinkle Cut in the Derby. He nodded meekly to Highbury with downcast eyes, and swung unhappily into the saddle.

Instead of bracing him, the threat of losing the ride on Crinkle Cut took the edge off his concentration, so that he came out of the stalls slowly, streaked the first quarter too fast to reach third place, swung wide at the end and lost his stride straightening out. He finished sixth. He was a totally experienced jockey of above average ability. It was not one of his days.

In the grandstand Marius Tollman put down his binoculars, shaking his head and clicking his tongue. If Piper Boles couldn't ride a better race than that when he was supposed to be trying to win, what sort of damn hash would he make of losing on Crinkle Cut?

Marius thought about the $10,000 he was staking on Saturday's little caper. He had not yet decided whether to tip off certain guys in organized crime, in which case they would cover the stake at no risk to himself, or to gamble on the bigger profit of going it alone. He lowered his wheezy bulk onto his seat and worried about the ease with which a fixed race could unfix itself.

Blisters Schultz worried about the state of his trade, which was suffering a severe recession.

Blisters Schultz picked pockets for a living, and was fed up with credit cards. In the old days, when he'd learned the skill at his grandfather's knee, men carried their billfolds in their rear pants' pockets, neatly outlined for all the world to see. Nowadays all these smash-and-grab muggers had ruined the market; few people carried more than a handful of dollars around with them, and those that did tended to divide it into

two portions, with the heavy dough hidden away beneath
zippers.

Fifty-three years Blisters had survived, 45 of them by stealing. Several shortish sessions behind bars had been regarded
as bad luck, but not as a good reason for not nicking the first
wallet he saw when he got out. He had tried to go straight
once, but he hadn't liked it—couldn't face the regular hours
and the awful feeling of working. After six weeks he had left
his well paid job and gone back thankfully to insecurity. He
felt happier stealing $2 than earning ten.

For the best haul at the races you either had to spot the big
wads before they were gambled away, or follow a big winner
away from the payout window. In either case, it meant hanging around the pari-mutuel with your eyes open. The trouble was, too many racetrack cops had cottoned to this *modus·
op,* and were apt to stand around looking at people who were
just standing there looking.

Blisters had had a bad week. The most promisingly fat wallet had proved, after half an hour's careful stalking, to contain little money but a lot in pornography. Blisters, having a
weak sex drive, was disgusted on both counts.

For his first two days' labor he had only $23 to show, and
five of these he had found on a stairway. His meager room in
Louisville was costing him $8 a night, and with transporta-
tion and eating to take into account, he reckoned he'd have
to clear $300 to make the trip worthwhile.

Always an optimist, he brightened at the thought of Derby
Day. The pickings would certainly be easier once the real
crowd arrived.

Fred Collyer's private Prohibition lasted intact through
Friday. Feeling better when he woke, he cabbed out to Churchill Downs at 7:30, writing his expenses on the way. They
included many mythical items for the previous day, on the
basis that it was better for the office not to know he had been
a paralytic on Wednesday night. He upped the inflated total
a few more dollars; after all, bourbon was expensive, and he
would be off the wagon by Sunday.

The initial shock of the blackout had worn off, because
during his day in bed he had remembered bits and pieces

which he was certain were later in time than the fried chicken. The journey from dinner to bed was still a blank, but the blank had stopped frightening him. At times he felt there was something vital about it he ought to remember, but he persuaded himself that if it had been really important, he wouldn't have forgotten.

Out by the barns the groups of reporters had already formed round the trainers of the most fancied Derby runners. Fred Collyer sauntered to the outskirts of Harbourne Cressie, and his colleagues made room for him with no reference to his previous day's absence. It reassured him: whatever he had done on Wednesday night, it couldn't have been scandalous.

The notebooks were out. Harbourne Cressie, long practiced and fond of publicity, paused between every sentence to give time for all to be written down.

"Pincer Movement ate well last evening and is calm and cool this A.M. On the book we should hold Salad Bowl, unless the track is sloppy by Saturday."

Smiles all round. The sky blue, the forecast fair.

Fred Collyer listened without attention. He'd heard it all before. They'd all heard it all before. And who the hell cared?

In a rival group two barns away the trainer of Salad Bowl was saying his colt had the beating of Pincer Movement on the Hialeah form, and could run on any going, sloppy or not.

George Highbury attracted fewer newsmen, as he hadn't much to say about Crinkle Cut. The three-year-old had been beaten by both Pincer Movement and Salad Bowl on separate occasions, and was not expected to reverse things.

On Friday afternoon Fred Collyer spent his time up in the press room and manfully refused a couple of free beers. (*Entertaining various owners at track, $22.*)

Piper Boles rode a hard finish in the sixth race, lost by a short head, and almost passed out from hunger-induced weakness in the jocks' room afterward. George Highbury, unaware of this, merely noted sourly that Boles had made the weight and confirmed that he would ride Crinkle Cut in the big race tomorrow.

Various friends of Piper Boles, supporting him toward a daybed, asked anxiously in his ear whether tomorrow's scheme was still on. Piper Boles nodded. "Sure," he said faintly. "All the way."

Marius Tollman was relieved to see Boles riding better, but decided anyway to hedge his bet by letting the syndicate in on the action.

Blisters Schultz lifted two billfolds, containing respectively $14 and $22. He lost ten of them backing a certainty in the last race.

Pincer Movement, Salad Bowl, and Crinkle Cut, guarded by uniformed men with guns at their waists, looked over the stable doors and with small quivers in their tuned-up muscles watched other horses go out to the track. All three could have chosen to go too. All three knew well enough what the trumpet was sounding for, on the other side.

Saturday morning, fine and clear.

Crowds in their thousands converged on Churchill Downs. Eager, expectant, chattering, dressed in bright colors and buying mint juleps in takeaway souvenir glasses, they poured through the gates and over the infield, reading the latest sports columns on Pincer Movement versus Salad Bowl, and dreaming of picking outsiders that came up at 50 to 1.

Blisters Schultz had scraped together just enough to pay his motel bill, but self-esteem depended on better luck with the hoists. His small lined face with its busy eyes wore a look near to desperation, and the long predatory fingers clenched and unclenched convulsively in his pockets.

Piper Boles, with 126 to do on Crinkle Cut, allowed himself an egg for breakfast and decided to buy property bonds with the five hundred in used notes which had been delivered by hand the previous evening, and with the gains (both legal and illegal) he should add to them that day. If he cleaned up safely that afternoon, he thought, there was no obvious reason why he shouldn't set up the same scheme again, even after he had retired from riding. He hardly noticed the shift in his mind from reluctant dishonesty to habitual fraud.

Marius Tollman spent the morning telephoning to various

acquaintances, offering profit. His offers were accepted. Marius Tollman felt a load lift from his spirits and with a spring in his step took his 260 pounds downtown where a careful gentleman counted out $10,000 in untraceable notes. Marius Tollman gave him a receipt, properly signed. Business was business.

Fred Collyer wanted a drink. One, he thought, wouldn't hurt. It would pep him up a bit, put him on his toes. One little drink in the morning would certainly not stop him writing a punchy piece that evening. *The Star* couldn't possibly frown on just *one* drink before he went to the races, especially not as he had managed to keep clear of the bar the previous evening by going to bed at nine. His abstinence had involved a great effort of will; it would be right to reward such virtue with just one drink.

He had, however, finished on Wednesday night the bottle he had brought with him to Louisville. He fished out his wallet to check how much he had in it: $53, plenty after expenses to cover a fresh bottle for later as well as a quick one in the bar before he left.

He went downstairs. In the lobby his colleague Clay Petrovitch again offered a free ride in his Hertz car to Churchill Downs, so he decided he could postpone his one drink for half an hour. He gave himself little mental pats on the back all the way to the racetrack.

Blisters Schultz, circulating among the clusters of people at the rear of the grandstand, saw Marius Tollman going by in the sunshine, leaning backward to support the weight in front and wheezing in the growing heat.

Blisters Schultz licked his lips. He knew the fat man by sight, knew that somewhere around that gross body might be stacked enough bread to see him through the summer. Marius Tollman would never come to the Derby with empty pockets.

Two thoughts made Blisters hesitate as he slid like an eel in the fat man's wake. The first was that Tollman was too old a hand to let himself be robbed. The second, that he was known to have friends in organized places, and if Tollman was carrying organization money Blisters wasn't going to

burn his fingers by stealing it, which was how he got his nickname in the first place.

Regretfully Blisters peeled off from the quarry, and returned to the throng in the comforting shadows under the
grandstand.

At 12:17 he infiltrated a close-packed bunch of people
waiting for an elevator.

At 12:18 he stole Fred Collyer's wallet.

Marius Tollman carried his money in cunning underarm
pockets which he clamped to his sides in a crowd, for fear of
pickpockets. When the time was due he would visit as many
different selling windows as possible, inconspicuously dis-
tributing the stake. He would give Piper Boles almost half of
the tickets (along with the second $500 in used notes), and
keep the other half for himself.

A nice tidy little killing, he thought complacently. And no
reason why he shouldn't set it up some time again.

He bought a mint julep and smiled kindly at a girl showing
more bosom than bashfulness.

The sun stoked up the day. The preliminaries rolled over
one by one with waves of cheering, each hard-ridden finish
merely a sideshow attending on the big one—the Derby, the
roses, the climax, the ninth race.

In the jocks' room Piper Boles had changed into the silks
for Crinkle Cut and began to sweat. The nearer he came to
the race the more he wished it was an ordinary Derby Day
like any other. He steadied his nerves by reading the *Financial Times.*

Fred Collyer discovered the loss of his wallet upstairs in
the press box when he tried to pay for a beer. He cursed,
searched all his pockets, turned the press box upside down,
got the keys of the Hertz car from Clay Petrovitch and trailed
all the way back to the car park.

After a fruitless search there he strode furiously back to
the grandstands, violently throttling in his mind the stinking
bum who had stolen his money. He guessed it had been an
old hand, an old man, even. The new vicious young lot relied
on muscle, not skill.

His practical problems were not too great. He needed little

cash. Clay Petrovitch was taking him back to town, the motel bill was going direct to the *Manhattan Star,* and his plane ticket was safely lying on the chest of drawers in his bedroom. He could borrow twenty bucks or so, maybe, from Clay or others in the press box, to cover essentials.

Going up in the elevator he thought that the loss of his money was like a sign from heaven; no money, no drink.

Blisters Schultz kept Fred Collyer sober the whole afternoon.

Pincer Movement, Salad Bowl, and Crinkle Cut were led from their barns, into the tunnel under the cars and crowds, and out again onto the track in front of the grandstands. They walked loosely, casually, used to the limelight but knowing from experience that this was only a foretaste. The first sight of the day's princes galvanized the crowds toward the pari-mutuel window like shoals of multicolored fish.

Piper Boles walked out with the other jockeys toward the wire-meshed enclosure where horses, trainers, and owners stood in a group in each stall. He had begun to suffer from a feeling of detachment and unreality; he could not believe that he, a basically honest jockey, was about to make a hash of the Kentucky Derby.

George Highbury repeated for about the fortieth time the tactics they had agreed on. Piper Boles nodded seriously, as if he had every intention of carrying them out. He actually heard scarcely a word; and he was deaf also to the massed bands and the singing when the Derby runners were led out to the track. *My Old Kentucky Home* swelled the emotions of a multitude and brought out a flutter of eye-wiping handkerchiefs, but in Piper Boles they raised not a blink.

Through the parade, the canter down, the circling round, and even into the starting stalls, the detachment persisted. Only then, with the tension showing plain on the faces of the other riders, did he click back to realization. His heart rate nearly doubled and energy flooded into his brain.

Now, he thought. It is now, in the next half minute, that I earn myself $1,000 and after that, the rest.

He pulled down his goggles and gathered his reins and his whip. He had Pincer Movement on his right and Salad Bowl on his left, and when the stalls sprang open he went out between them in a rush, tipping his weight instantly forward over the withers and standing in the stirrups with his head almost as far forward as Crinkle Cut's.

All along past the stands the first time he concentrated on staying in the center of the main bunch, as unnoticeable as possible, and round the top bend he was still there, sitting quiet and doing nothing very much. But down the backstretch, lying about tenth in a field of 26, he earned his $10,000.

No one except Piper Boles ever knew what really happened; only he knew that he'd shortened his left rein with a sharp turn of his wrist and squeezed Crinkle Cut's ribs with his right foot. The fast galloping horse obeyed these directions, veered abruptly left, and crashed into the horse beside him.

The horse beside him was still Salad Bowl. Under the impact Salad Bowl cannoned into the horse on his own left, rocked back, stumbled, lost his footing entirely, and fell. The two horses on his tail fell over him.

Piper Boles didn't look back. The swerve and collision had lost him several places which Crinkle Cut at the best of times would have been unable to make up. He rode the rest of the race strictly according to his instructions, finishing flat out in twelfth place.

Of the 140,000 spectators at Churchill Downs only a handful had had a clear view of the disaster on the far side of the track. The buildings in the infield, and the milling crowds filling all its farthest areas, had hidden the crash from nearly all standing at ground level and from most in the grandstands. Only the press, high up, had seen. They sent out urgent fact-finders and buzzed like a stirred-up beehive.

Fred Collyer, out on the balcony, watched the photographers running to immortalize Pincer Movement and reflected sourly that none of them would take closeup pictures of the second favorite, Salad Bowl, down on the dirt. He watched the horseshoe of dark red roses being draped over the winner and the triumphal presentation of the trophies, and then went inside for the rerun of the race on television. They showed the Salad Bowl incident forward, backward, and sideways, and then jerked it through slowly in a series of stills.

"See that," said Clay Petrovitch, pointing at the screen over Fred Collyer's shoulder. "It was Crinkle Cut caused it. You can see him crash into Salad Bowl . . . there! . . . Crinkle Cut, that's the joker in the pack."

Fred Collyer strolled over to his place, sat down, and stared at his typewriter. Crinkle Cut. He knew something about Crinkle Cut. He thought intensely for five minutes, but he couldn't remember what he knew.

Details and quotes came up to the press box. All fallen jocks shaken but unhurt, all horses ditto; stewards in a tizzy, making instant enquiries and rerunning the patrol camera film over and over. Suspension for Piper Boles considered unlikely, as blind eye usually turned to rough riding in the Derby. Piper Boles had gone on record as saying "Crinkle Cut just suddenly swerved. I didn't expect it and couldn't prevent him bumping Salad Bowl." Large numbers of people believed him.

Fred Collyer thought he might as well get a few pars down on paper; it would bring the first drink nearer, and boy how he needed that drink! With an ear open for fresher information he tapped out a blow-by-blow I-was-there account of an incident he had hardly seen. When he began to read it through, he saw that the first words he had written were: "The diversion on Crinkle Cut stole the post-race scene . . ."

Diversion on Crinkle Cut? He hadn't meant to write that . . . or not exactly. He frowned. And there were other words in his mind, just as stupid. He put his hands on the keys and tapped them out.

"It'll cost you . . . a thousand in used notes . . . half before."

He stared at what he had written. He had made it up, he must have. Or dreamed it. One or the other.

A dream. That was it. He remembered. He had had a dream about two men planning a fixed race, and one of them had been Marius Tollman, wheezing away about a diversion on Crinkle Cut.

Fred Collyer relaxed and smiled at the thought, and the

next minute knew quite suddenly that it hadn't been a dream
at all. He had heard Marius Tollman and Piper Boles planning a diversion on Crinkle Cut, and he had forgotten because he'd been drunk. Well, he reassured himself uneasily,
no harm done; he had remembered now, hadn't he?

No, he hadn't. If Crinkle Cut was a diversion, what was he
a diversion *from?* Perhaps if he waited a bit, he would find he
knew that too . . .

Blisters Schultz spent Fred Collyer's money on two hot
dogs, one mint julep, and five losing bets. On the winning
side he had harvested three more billfolds and a woman's
purse: total haul, $94. Gloomily he decided to call it a day
and not come back next year.

Marius Tollman lumbered busily from window to window
of the pari-mutuel and the stewards asked to see the jockeys
involved in the Salad Bowl pile-up.

The crowds, hot, tired, and frayed at the edges, began to
leave in the yellowing sunshine. The bands marched away.
The stalls which sold souvenirs packed up their wares. Pincer
Movement had his picture taken for the thousandth time,
and the runners for the tenth, last, and least interesting race
of the day walked over from the barns.

Piper Boles was waiting outside the stewards' room for a
summons inside, but Marius Tollman used the highest class
messengers, and the package he entrusted was safely delivered. Piper Boles nodded, slipped it into his pocket, and gave
the stewards a performance worthy of Hollywood.

Fred Collyer put his head in his hands, trying to remember. A drink, he thought, might help. Diversion. Crinkle Cut.
Amberezzio.

He sat up sharply. Amberezzio. And what the hell did that
mean? *It has to be Amberezzio.*

"Clay," he said, leaning back over his chair. "Do you know
of a horse called Amberezzio?"

Clay Petrovitch shook his bald head. "Never heard of it."

Fred Collyer called to several others through the hubbub,
"Know of a horse called Amberezzio?" And finally he got an
answer. "Amberezzio isn't a horse, he's an apprentice."

"It has to be Amberezzio. He's straight."

Fred Collyer knocked his chair over as he stood up. They had already called one minute to post time on the last race.

"Lend me twenty bucks, there's a pal," he said to Clay.

Clay, knowing about the lost wallet, amiably agreed and slowly began to bring out his money.

"Hurry," Fred Collyer said urgently.

"Okay, okay." He handed over $20 and turned back to his own typewriter.

Fred Collyer grabbed his racecard and pushed through the post-Derby chatter to the pari-mutuel window farther along the press floor. He flipped the pages . . . Tenth race, Homeward Bound, claiming race, eight runners . . . His eye skimmed down the list and found what he sought.

Philip Amberezzio, riding a horse Fred Collyer had never heard of.

"Twenty on the nose, number six," he said quickly, and received his ticket seconds before the window shut. Trembling slightly, he pushed back through the crowd, out onto the balcony. He was the only reporter watching the race.

Those jocks did it beautifully, he thought in admiration. Artistic. You wouldn't have known if you hadn't known. They bunched him in and shepherded him along, and then at the perfect moment gave him a suddenly clear opening. Amberezzio won by half a length, with all the others waving their whips as if beating the last inch out of their mounts.

Fred Collyer laughed. That poor little so-and-so probably thought he was a hell of a fellow, bringing home a complete outsider with all the big boys baying at his heels.

He went back inside the press box and found everyone's attention directed toward Harbourne Cressie, who had brought with him the owner and jockey of Pincer Movement. Fred Collyer dutifully took down enough quotes to cover the subject, but his mind was on the other story, the big one, the gift.

It would need careful handling, he thought. It would need the very best he could do, as he would have to be careful not to make direct accusations while leaving it perfectly clear that an investigation was necessary. His old instincts partially reawoke. He was even excited. He would write his piece in the quiet and privacy of his own room in the motel. Couldn't do

it here on the track with every turfwriter in the world looking
over his shoulder.

Down in the jockeys' changing room Piper Boles quietly
distributed the pari-mutuel tickets which Marius Tollman
had delivered: $500 worth to each of the seven "unsuccess-
ful" riders in the tenth race, and $1,000 worth to himself.
Each jockey subsequently asked a wife or girl friend to collect
the winnings and several of these would have made easy prey
for Blisters Schultz, had he not already started home.

Marius Tollman's money had shortened the odds on Amberezzio, but he was still returned at 12 to 1. Marius Tollman
wheezed and puffed from payout window to payout window,
collecting his winnings bit by bit. He hadn't room for all the
cash in the underarm pockets and finally stowed some casually in more accessible spots. Too bad for Blisters Schultz.

Fred Collyer collected a fistful of winnings and repaid the
$20 to Clay Petrovitch.

"If you had a hot tip, you might have passed it on," grumbled Petrovitch, thinking of all the expenses old Fred would
undoubtedly claim for his free rides to the track.

"It wasn't a tip, just a hunch." He couldn't tell Clay what
the hunch was, as he wrote for a rival paper. "I'll buy you a
drink on the way home."

"I should damn well think so."

Fred Collyer immediately regretted his offer, which had
been instinctive. He remembered that he had not intended
to drink until after he had written. Still, perhaps
one. . . . And he did need a drink very badly. It seemed a
century since his last, on Wednesday night.

They left together, walking out with the remains of the
crowd. The track looked battered and bedraggled at the end
of the day; the scarlet petals of the tulips lay on the ground,
leaving rows of naked pistils sticking forlornly up, and the
bright rugs of grass were dusty gray and covered with litter.
Fred Collyer thought only of the dough in his pocket and the
story in his head, and both of them gave him a nice warm
glow.

A drink to celebrate, he thought. Buy Clay a thank-you

drink, and maybe perhaps just one more to celebrate. It wasn't often, after all, that things fell his way so miraculously.

They stopped for the drink. The first double swept through Fred Collyer's veins like fire through a parched forest. The second made him feel great.

"Time to go," he said to Clay. "I've got my piece to write."

"Just one more," Clay said. "This one's on me."

"Better not."

He felt virtuous.

"Oh, come on," Clay said, and ordered. With the faintest of misgivings Fred Collyer sank his third; but couldn't he still outwrite every racing man in the business? Of course he could.

They left after the third. Fred Collyer bought a fifth of bourbon for later, when he had finished his story. Back in his own room he took just the merest swig from it before he sat down to write.

The words wouldn't come. He screwed up six attempts and poured some bourbon into a glass.

Marius Tollman, Crinkle Cut, Piper Boles, Amberezzio . . . It wasn't all that simple.

He took a drink. He didn't seem to be able to help it.

The Sports Editor would give him a raise for a story like this, or at least there would be no more quibbling about expenses.

He took a drink.

Piper Boles had earned himself $1,000 for crashing into Salad Bowl. Now how the hell did you write that without being sued for libel?

He took a drink.

The jockeys in the tenth race had conspired to let the only straight one among them win. How in hell could you say that?

He took a drink.

The stewards and the press had had all their attention channeled toward the crash in the Derby and had virtually ignored the tenth race. The stewards wouldn't thank him for pointing it out.

He took another drink. And another. And more.

His deadline for telephoning his story to the office was ten o'clock the following morning. When that hour struck he was asleep and snoring, fully dressed, on his bed. The empty bourbon bottle lay on the floor beside him, and his winnings, which he had tried to count, lay scattered over his chest.

WHO HAS SEEN THE WIND?

by Michael Gilbert

Welcome back, Petrella, in a tale of heart and human understanding—and police work, in the days when Petrella was still a Detective Constable. "Most police work," Petrella believed, "was knowledge—knowledge of an infinity of small everyday facts, unimportant by themselves, deadly when taken together." . . .

TO SUPERINTENDENT Haxtell, education was something you dodged at school and picked up afterward as you went along.

"All I need in my job," he would say, "I learned in the street."

And he would glare down at Detective Petrella, whom he had once found improving his mind with Dr. Bentley's *Dissertation on Fallacies* at a time when he should have been thumbing his way through the current number of *Hue & Cry*.

Petrella was, of course, an unusual Detective Constable. He spoke three languages—one of them was Arabic, for he had been brought up in Egypt; he knew about subjects like viniculture and the theory of the five-lever lock; and he had an endlessly inquiring mind.

The Superintendent approved of that. "Curiosity," he said. "Know your people. If you don't know, ask questions. Find out. It's better than book learning."

Petrella accepted the rebuke in good part. There was a lot of truth in it. Most police work was knowledge—knowledge

303

of an infinity of small everyday facts, unimportant by themselves, deadly when taken together.

Nevertheless, and in spite of the Superintendent, Petrella
retained an obstinate conviction that there were other things
as well, deeper things and finer things: colors, shapes, and
sounds of absolute beauty, unconnected with the world of
small people in small houses in gray streets. And while in one
pocket of his old raincoat he might carry Moriarty's *Police
Law,* in the other would lie, dog-eared with use, the *Golden
Treasury* of Palgrave.

*"She walks in beauty, like the night Of cloudless climes and starry
skies,"* said Petrella, and, "That car's been there a long time.
If it's still there when I come back it might be worth looking
into."

He was on his way to Lavender Alley to see a man called
Parkoff about a missing bicycle. It was as he was walking
down Barnaby Passage that he forgot poetry and remembered he was a policeman.

For something was missing. Something as closely connected with Barnaby Passage as mild with bitter or bacon with
eggs. The noise of the Harrington children at play.

There were six of them, and Barnaby Passage, which ran
alongside their back garden, was their stamping ground. On
the last occasion that Petrella had walked through it, a well-
aimed potato had carried away his hat, and he had turned in
time to see the elfin face of Mickey Harrington disappear behind a row of dustbins. He had done nothing about it, first
because it did not befit the dignity of a plainclothes detective
to chase a small boy, and secondly because he would not have
had the smallest chance of catching him.

Even when not making themselves felt, the Harrington
family could always be heard. Were they at school? No, too
late. In bed? Much too early. Away somewhere? The Harrington family rarely went away. And if by any chance they
had moved, that was something he ought to know about, for
they were part of his charge.

Six months ago he had helped to arrest Tim Harrington.
It had taken three of them to do it. Tim had fought because
he knew what was coming to him. It was third time unlucky
and he was due for a full stretch.

Mrs. Harrington had shown only token resentment at this sudden removal of her husband for a certain nine and a possible twelve years. He was a man who took a belt to his children and a boot to his women. Not only when he was drunk, which would have been natural, if not forgivable, but with cold ferocity when sober.

Petrella paused at the corner where the blank walls of Barnaby Passage opened out into Barnaby Row. It was at that moment that a line of Rossetti came into his head. *Who has seen the wind?* he murmured to himself. *Neither you nor I.*

A casement rattled up and an old woman pushed out her head. "Lookin' for someone?"

"Er, good evening, Mrs. Minter," said Petrella politely. "I wasn't going to—that's to say, I wondered what had happened to Mrs. Harrington. You can usually hear her family."

"Noisy little beggars," said Mrs. Minter. But she said it without feeling. Children and flies, hope and despair and dirt and love and death: she had seen them all from her little window.

"I wondered if they'd gone away."

"They're home," said Mrs. Minter. "And Mrs. Harrington." Her eyes were button-bright.

"Well, thank you," said Petrella. His mouth felt dry now that he found his suspicions suddenly confirmed.

"You're welcome," said Mrs. Minter.

As Petrella turned away he heard the window slamming down and the click of the catch.

He climbed the steps. Signs of calamity were all about him: the brass dolphin knocker unpolished, the steps unwhited. A lace curtain twitched in the front window, and behind the curtain something stirred.

Petrella knocked. He had lifted the knocker a second time when it was snatched out of his hand by the sudden opening of the door, and Mrs. Harrington stood there.

She was still the ghost of the pretty girl Tim Harrington had married ten years before, but life and rough usage had sandpapered her down to something finer and smaller than nature had ever intended. Her fair hair was drawn tightly over her head and all her girl's curves were turning into planes and angles.

Usually she managed a smile for Petrella, but today there was nothing behind her eyes but emptiness.

"Can I come in?" he asked.

"Well—yes, all right."

She made no move. Only when Petrella actually stepped toward her did she half turn to let him past her, up the dark narrow hall.

"How are the children?" he asked—and saw for himself. The six Harrington children were all in the front room, and all silent. The oldest boy and girl were making a pretense of reading books, but the four younger ones were just sitting and staring.

"You're very quiet," he said. "Has the scissor man come along and cut all your tongues out?"

The oldest boy tried out a grin. It wasn't a very convincing grin, but it lasted long enough for Petrella to see some freshly dried blood inside the lip.

I can smell tiger, he thought. The brute's here all right. He must have made his break this afternoon. If it had been any earlier, the news would have reached the station before I left it.

"I'd like a word with you," he said. "Perhaps you could ask the children to clear out for a moment." He looked at the door which led, as he knew, into the kitchen.

"Not in there," she said quickly. "Out into the hall."

Now that he knew, it was obvious. The smallest boy had his eyes glued to the kitchen door in a sort of dumb horror.

They shuffled out into the hall. Petrella said softly, "I'm not sure you shouldn't go too. There's going to be trouble."

She looked at him with sudden understanding. Then she said, in a loud rough voice, "I don't know what you're talking about. If you've got anything to say, say it and get out. I got my work to do."

"All right," said Petrella. "If you want to play it that way."

He was moving as he spoke. The door to the kitchen was a fragile thing. He ran at it, at the last moment swinging his foot up so that the sole of his heavy shoe landed flat and hard, an inch below the handle.

The door jumped backward, hit something that was behind it, and checked. Petrella slid through the opening.

Tim Harrington was on his knees on the floor. The door

edge had cut open his head, and on his stupid face he had the look of a boxer when the ring gets up and hits him.

Petrella fell on top of him. He was giving away too much in weight and strength and fighting experience for any sort of finesse. Under his weight Harrington flattened for a moment, then braced himself, and bucked.

Petrella had his right arm in a lock round the man's neck, and hung on. Steel fingers tore at his arm, plucked it away, and the lumpy body jerked again, and straightened. Next moment they were both on their feet, glaring at each other.

In the front room the woman was screaming steadily, and a growing clamor showed that the street was astir. But in the tiny kitchen it was still a private fight.

Harrington swung on his heel and made for the window into the garden. For a moment Petrella was tempted. Then he jumped for the big man's legs, and they were down on the floor again, squirming and fighting and groping.

There was only one end to that. The bigger man carried all the guns. First he got Petrella by the hair and thumped his head on the linoleum. Then he shambled to his feet and, as Petrella turned onto his knees, swung a boot.

If it had landed squarely, that would have been the end of Petrella as a policeman, and maybe as a man as well; but he saw it coming and rolled to avoid it. And in the moment that it missed him, he plucked at the other foot. Harrington came down and in his fall brought the kitchen table with him. A bowl of drippings rolled onto the floor, spilling its brown contents in a slow and loving circle. Petrella, on his knees, watched it, fascinated.

Then he realized that he was alone.

His mind was working well enough to bring him to his feet but his legs seemed to have an existence of their own. They took him out into the front room, which was empty, and then into the hall.

He was dimly aware of the children, all staring at him, all silent. The door was open. In the street footsteps, running.

"You won't catch him now," said Mrs. Harrington.

He turned his head to look at her, and the sudden movement seemed to clear his brain. "I'm going after him," he said. "Ring the police."

Then he was out in the street, and running. Mrs. Minter

shouted, "Down there, mister," and pointed. He stumbled, and righted himself. Harrington was already disappearing round the corner. Petrella shambled after him.

When he got to the corner there was one car in the road ahead of him and no one in sight. The car was moving, accelerating, a big blue four-door sedan. Too far away to see the license number.

"Gone away!"

A second car drew up behind him, and a voice said politely, "Is there anything wrong?"

Petrella became aware that he was standing, swaying, in the middle of the road. Behind him, its hood inches from his back, was a neat little sports car in two shades of green, driven by a fat young man with fair hair and a Brigade-of-Guards mustache.

"Police," said Petrella. "Got to get that car. It's stolen."

The blue sedan was turning into High Street now. "Move over. I'll drive."

"Hop in," said the young man. "You don't look too fit. I'd better do the driving. It's a tricky little bus, this, till you get the hang of it."

"All right," muttered Petrella. "But quick."

The young man took him at his word. The little car jumped forward like a horse at the touch of a spur. They cornered into High Street, under the nose of a bus, and shot down the middle of the crowded road.

The young man hardly seemed to have moved in his seat. He handled his car like a craftsman, insolently exact, both careful and careless at the same time.

"Right fork ahead. He's going up to the Heath, I think."

"His neck'll be for sale if he does much more of *that*," said the young man calmly. The blue sedan had pulled out, charged past a bus, and only just got back again ahead of the oncoming truck.

"I say," said Petrella, "you can drive."

"Done a good deal of it," said the man. "Rally stuff mostly, a bit on the track. Name of Blech."

Petrella placed him then.

Time came, and time went, and they were off the Heath and making for the maze of small streets which fills the triangle between Hampstead, Regent's Park, and Camden Town.

"I'm a bit too light to ram him," said Blech. "No need, really. All we have to do is keep in sight. He'll do himself soon."

It happened as he was speaking. The road went up in a hump over the Canal. The blue sedan hit the rise so fast that it almost took off, came down threshing and screaming, went into a long sideways skid, hit the low parapet, and toppled over.

Blech came neatly to a halt, and Petrella was out, and running again.

The blue car was standing on its nose in three feet of water and mud, sinking ponderously. Petrella got the rear door open, and pulled. Behind him, Blech pulled. As the car fell away, the bulk of Tim Harrington tumbled back on top of them.

Petrella seized him by the hair and hammered his head on the towpath.

He felt a restraining hand on his arm, and the mists cleared again for a moment. "I think," said Blech, "that you're being rather too—er—vigorous with him. What he wants is first aid, really."

"Sorry," said Petrella. "Not thinking very straight. Fact is, I think I'm a bit concussed myself."

"That makes two of you. If you helped, we might get him into my car."

They did this, between them. The street slept in a timeless summer's evening doze. From first to last no other person appeared on the scene.

"Where to now?"

Petrella tried to think. Harrington was out cold. There was a big purple bruise on one side of his forehead, and an occasional bubble formed in the corner of his open mouth. He was a hospital case. But no hospital would take him in without explanations. Nor would any other police station.

"Home," he said. "The way we came. It'll be quicker in the long run."

They drove home decorously, back up onto the Heath, and west, with the setting sun in their eyes. For a few seconds Petrella dozed. That wouldn't do. No time to sleep. Job not finished. Better talk and keep awake.

"It's very good of you," he said, "to take all this trouble."

"Enjoyed it," said Blech. "What is he?"

"He's an escaped convict," said Petrella. "Named Harring-ton. Not exactly a pleasant character."

"How did you cotton on to him?"

How had he? It was so many years ago. A great gale was singing through his head, a mighty diapason of sound that came and went. "It was Rossetti put me on to him," he said, as the gale dropped for a moment.

"Rossetti? *The Blessed Damozel*—"

"Not Dante Gabriel, Christina. *Who has seen the wind? Neither you nor I: But when the trees bow down their heads The wind is passing by.* Fork left here."

"That's nice," said Blech. "Is there any more of it?"

"Who has seen the wind? Neither I nor you: But when the leaves hang trembling The wind is passing through." That was it. Hang trembling. It was the children that had made him certain. Sitting there like drugged mice.

"I must remember that," said Blech. "Here we are, I think. You'd better get some help to carry out our passenger. And then you ought to lie down, I think."

Superintendent Haxtell reckoned that he was beyond surprise, but the events of that evening tried him hard. First, there came two stalwart constables, supporting the drooping figure of a convict of whose escape in transit from one prison to another he had only just been notified; secondly, a diffident figure, whose face he vaguely recognized from the columns of the popular press; and, bringing up the rear, his shirt torn open to the waist, his face rimmed with blood and dried dripping, Detective Petrella.

When he had sorted things out a bit, he sat down to make his report.

Plainly it was a case that reflected the greatest credit on all concerned. And a lot of it must, and should go to Petrella. And, according to Petrella, Blech had behaved very well. A foreigner, but a good chap. So far so good.

But what the Superintendent couldn't make out was exactly what credit was to be given to a person named Rossetti. Sounded like some sort of Italian. Some further inquiries needed there. His pen scratched busily . . .

A FOOL ABOUT MONEY

by Ngaio Marsh

A chuckling (and in its own way, chilling) cocktail party story that could easily become a legend in its own time—and a new and unexpected facet of Dame Ngaio's talent. . . .

"WHERE money is concerned," Harold Hancock told his audience at the enormous cocktail party, "my poor Hersey—and she won't mind my saying so, will you, darling?—is the original dumbbell. Did I ever tell you about her trip to Dunedin?"

Did he ever tell them? Hersey thought. Wherever two or three were gathered did he ever fail to tell them? The predictable laugh, the lovingly coddled pause, and the punchline led into and delivered like an act of God—did he, for pity's sake, ever tell them!

Away he went, mock-serious, empurpled, expansive, and Hersey put on the comic baby face he expected of her. Poor Hersey, they would say, such a goose about money. It's a shame to laugh.

"It was like this—" Harold began. . . .

It had happened twelve years ago when they were first in New Zealand. Harold was occupied with a conference in Christchurch and Hersey was to stay with a friend in Dunedin. He had arranged that she would draw on his firm's Dunedin branch for money and take in her handbag no

311

more than what she needed for the journey. "You know how you are," Harold said.

He arranged for her taxi, made her check that she had her ticket and reservation for the train, and reminded her that if on the journey she wanted cups of tea or synthetic coffee or a cooked lunch, she would have to take to her heels at the appropriate stations and vie with the competitive male. At this point her taxi was announced and Harold was summoned to a long-distance call from London.

"You push off," he said. "Don't forget that fiver on the dressing table. You won't need it but you'd better have it. Keep your wits about you. 'Bye, dear."

He was still shouting into the telephone when she left.

She had enjoyed the adventurous feeling of being on her own. Although Harold had said you didn't in New Zealand, she tipped the taxi driver and he carried her suitcase to the train and found her seat, a single one just inside the door of a Pullman car.

A lady was occupying the seat facing hers and next to the window.

She was well-dressed, middle-aged and of a sandy complexion with noticeably light eyes. She had put a snakeskin dressing case on the empty seat beside her.

"It doesn't seem to be taken," she said, smiling at Hersey.

They socialized—tentatively at first and, as the journey progressed, more freely. The lady (in his version Harold always called her Mrs. X) confided that she was going all the way to Dunedin to visit her daughter. Hersey offered reciprocative information. In the world outside, plains and mountains performed a grandiose kind of measure and telegraph wires leaped and looped with frantic precision.

An hour passed. The lady extracted a novel from her dressing case and Hersey, impressed by the handsome appointments and immaculate order, had a good look inside the case.

The conductor came through the car intoning, "Ten minutes for refreshments at Ashburton."

"Shall you join in the onslaught?" asked the lady. "It's a free-for-all."

"Shall you?"

"Well—I might. When I travel with my daughter we take turns. I get the morning coffee and she gets the afternoon. I'm a bit slow on my pins, actually."

She made very free use of the word "actually."

Hersey instantly offered to get their coffee at Ashburton and her companion, after a proper show of diffidence, gaily agreed. They explored their handbags for the correct amount. The train uttered a warning scream and everybody crowded into the corridor as it drew up to the platform.

Hersey left her handbag with the lady (an indiscretion heavily emphasized by Harold) and sprinted to the refreshment counter where she was blocked off by a phalanx of men. Train fever was running high by the time she was served and her return trip with brimming cups was hazardous indeed.

The lady was holding both their handbags as if she hadn't stirred an inch.

Between Ashburton and Oamaru, a long stretch, they developed their acquaintanceship further, discovered many tastes in common, and exchanged confidences and names. The lady was called Mrs. Fortescue. Sometimes they dozed. Together, at Oamaru, they joined in an assault on the dining room and together they returned to the carriage where Hersey scuffled in her stuffed handbag for a powder-compact. As usual it was in a muddle.

Suddenly a thought struck her like a blow in the wind and a lump of ice ran down her gullet into her stomach. She made an exhaustive search but there was no doubt about it.

Harold's fiver was gone.

Hersey let the handbag fall in her lap, raised her head, and found that her companion was staring at her with a very curious expression on her face. Hersey had been about to confide her awful intelligence but the lump of ice was exchanged for a coal of fire. She was racked by a terrible suspicion.

"Anything wrong?" asked Mrs. Fortescue in an artificial voice.

Hersey heard herself say, "No. Why?"

"Oh, nothing," she said rather hurriedly. "I thought—perhaps—like me, actually, you have bag trouble."

"I do, rather," Hersey said.

They laughed uncomfortably.

The next hour passed in mounting tension. Both ladies affected to read their novels. Occasionally one of them would look up to find the other one staring at her. Hersey's suspicions increased rampantly.

"Ten minutes for refreshments at Palmerston South," said the conductor, lurching through the car.

Hersey had made up her mind. "Your turn!" she cried brightly.

"Is it? Oh. Yes."

"I think I'll have tea. The coffee was awful."

"So's the tea actually. Always. Do we," Mrs. Fortescue swallowed, "do we really want anything?"

"I do," said Hersey very firmly and opened her handbag. She fished out her purse and took out the correct amount. "And a bun," she said. There was no gainsaying her. "I've got a headache," she lied. "I'll be glad of a cuppa."

When they arrived at Palmerston South, Hersey said, "Shall I?" and reached for Mrs. Fortescue's handbag. But Mrs. Fortescue muttered something about requiring it for change and almost literally bolted. "All that for nothing!" thought Hersey in despair. And then, seeing the elegant dressing case still on the square seat, she suddenly reached out and opened it.

On top of the neatly arranged contents lay a crumpled five-pound note.

At the beginning of the journey when Mrs. Fortescue had opened the case, there had, positively, been no fiver stuffed in it. Hersey snatched the banknote, stuffed it into her handbag, shut the dressing case, and leaned back, breathing short with her eyes shut.

When Mrs. Fortescue returned she was scarlet in the face and trembling. She looked continuously at her dressing case and seemed to be in two minds whether or not to open it. Hersey died a thousand deaths.

The remainder of the journey was a nightmare. Both ladies pretended to read and to sleep. If ever Hersey had read guilt in a human countenance it was in Mrs. Fortescue's.

"I ought to challenge her," Hersey thought. "But I won't. I'm a moral coward and I've got back my fiver."

The train was already drawing into Dunedin station and Hersey had gathered herself and her belongings when Mrs. Fortescue suddenly opened her dressing case. For a second or two she stared into it. Then she stared at Hersey. She opened and shut her mouth three times. The train jerked to a halt and Hersey fled.

Her friend greeted her warmly. When they were in the car she said, "Oh, before I forget! There's a telegram for you."

It was from Harold.

It said: YOU FORGOT YOUR FIVER, YOU DUMBBELL. LOVE HAROLD.

Harold had delivered the punchline. His listeners had broken into predictable guffaws. He had added the customary coda: "And she didn't know Mrs. X's address, so she couldn't do a thing about it. So of course to this day Mrs. X thinks Hersey pinched her fiver."

Hersey, inwardly seething, had reacted in the sheepish manner Harold expected of her when from somewhere at the back of the group a wailing broke out.

A lady erupted as if from a football scrimmage. She looked wildly about her, spotted Hersey, and made for her.

"At last, at last!" cried the lady. "After all these years!"

It was Mrs. Fortescue.

"It *was* your fiver!" she gabbled. "It happened at Ashburton when I minded your bag. It was, it was!"

She turned on Harold. "It's all your fault," she amazingly announced. "And mine of course." She returned to Hersey. "I'm dreadfully inquisitive. It's a compulsion. I—I—couldn't resist. I looked at your passport. I looked at everything. And my own handbag was open on my lap. And the train gave one of those recoupling jerks and both our handbags were upset. And I could see you," she chattered breathlessly to Hersey, "coming back with that ghastly coffee.

"So I shoveled things back and there was the fiver on the floor. Well, I had one and I thought it was mine and there wasn't time to put it in my bag, so I slapped it into my dressing case. And then, when I paid my luncheon bill at Oamaru, I found my own fiver in a pocket of my bag."

"Oh, my God!" said Hersey.

"Yes. And I couldn't bring myself to confess. I thought you might leave your bag with me if you went to the loo and I could put it back. But you didn't. And then, at Dunedin, I looked in my dressing case and the fiver was gone. So I thought you knew I knew." She turned on Harold.

"You must have left *two* fivers on the dressing table," she accused.

"Yes!" Hersey shouted. "You did, you did! There were two. You put a second one out to get change."

"Why the hell didn't you say so!" Harold roared.

"I'd forgotten. You know yourself," Hersey said with the glint of victory in her eye, "it's like you always say, darling, I'm such a fool about money."

THE CABIN IN THE HOLLOW
by Joyce Harrington

Joyce Harrington's fourth story shows her talent, her very real gift, in perhaps its finest light—a "regional" story, deeply observed and deeply felt, with a filigree of detail that is always precisely right, a story that is meaningful and moving and splendid. . . .

THE DREAM came again last night. It seems like it came almost before I was asleep and lasted all night, even a few seconds after I woke up. Although I know that can't be true. I read in a magazine once about the scientists who measure dreams, and make lines on charts, and they all say that dreams only last a few seconds. They hook people up to machines while they're sleeping, and the machines can tell when they're dreaming and when not. I'd surely like to find out if my dream really lasts all night. But I wouldn't like to be hooked up to any machine. No sirree.

It's always summer in the dream. That's how I knew it was a dream the first time it came. It was full summer and the air was all hazy and lazy with the smell of hot dirt and piney woods. It seemed so real that when I woke up I almost thought I'd left the real world behind and was waking into a nightmare of coming to the city and living through the winter in three cold rooms high up in a rat-trap building without even a dirt yard and no real job after five months of walking the hard pavements.

317

In the dream I was standing in a dirt road that went uphill and around a bend. I knew I'd been climbing that road for a spell because I felt sweaty and just a mite tired, but a good kind of tired. On one side of the road was a big patch of horse nettles. Just beyond them and going on up the hillside was a clump of spindly pitch pines. On the other side of the road were some more horse nettles and then a grassy place with some boulders and a scramble of jack oaks going on down the hill.

I dreamed I just went over and sat down in the grassy place with my back against a boulder and looked out over the hills and hollows and let the sun beat down on me. I set there for a long time. Maybe it was just a few seconds like the dream scientists say, but I watched the sun cross over the sky and listened to the click beetles and the bees buzzing around where there was a pipe vine crawling all over a dead tree trunk.

That's all there was that first time, except for some red squirrels carrying on in amongst the jack oaks, and my hand itching for my shotgun.

The dream came several times after that, maybe five or six. And it's always the same—the road and the horse nettles and the trees with the squirrels frisking in amongst them. But each time I have the dream something else is added on at the end. The second time of the dream I was setting there in the grassy place watching the squirrels and wishing for my shotgun, and I started to feel hungry like it was getting to be dinnertime. I got up from the grassy place and commenced walking on up the road. By and by I came to a big huckleberry bush hanging right out over the road. I stopped and ate some. Ate a lot, but there were plenty, and then I took off my hat and filled it to take some home to Glenna. That was the end that time.

Each time the dream came it would be the same, and each time at the end I would be a little further along that road and the sun would be a little further down the sky. Until finally, the way it was last night, I came to a bend in the road and I stood there with my hat full of huckleberries, knowing, just knowing, that when I got around that bend there would be a cabin with wood smoke coming from the chimney, and Glen-

na would be there with dinner on the table and the kids playing around in the dooryard. That was when I woke up, right
there at the bend in the road with home just a few steps
away.

I got up then. Gray winter light was coming in the window,
and there was dirty gray snow on the window ledge. It was
cold under the quilt even though I had my long johns on. I
jumped out of bed. Well, call it a bed, but it's just a mattress
on the floor. Got dressed in a hurry because I wanted to get
down to the unemployment office early so I wouldn't have to
wait so long in line.

Glenna had a pot of coffee going and she had the gas oven
on full blast with the door open so it was warmer in the kitch-
en. She was crumbling dry biscuits into bowls for the kids.
She doused the crumbs with hot coffee and carefully mea-
sured a spoonful of condensed milk into each of the four
bowls. Her hand shook a little over Calvin's bowl so he got a
little extra.

"I'll just have some coffee," I said, before she could start
crumbling up some biscuit for me. I wanted her to save some
for herself. She was wearing the dress she always wore when
she was in her last months and couldn't get into anything
else. Not that she had much else to get into, but she loved
that faded old calico dress with its lace-trimmed collar and its
tiny buttons at the throat and the careful smocking across the
front. Her mother had made it for her while she was waiting
on Calvin to be born, and she'd worn it for each and every
child after him.

The kids ate quietly and fast. Too quiet. It wasn't natural
for kids to be that quiet. Glenna's raised them up to be polite
and respectful to their elders, but this quiet was something
else. Something lost and not right.

For maybe the hundredth time I thought about mornings
back home with everyone hustling around doing their chores
and the old cow yelling her head off for somebody to come
and milk her. Calvin had taken on that chore when he was
ten. Denzil fed the chickens and slopped the hogs, and Vergil hauled in wood for the stove. Even LaDonna did her part,
setting out plates on the table just so, like a little five-year-old

mother, while Glenna fried sausage and cut thick slices of homemade bread.

It would be warm and smoky inside the house. The dogs would come in and lie beside the stove, and everybody would be bright-eyed and laughing and telling what they'd seen outside that morning. Could be a possum sleeping in the woodpile or a fog rolling in over the hill or a deer come down to drink from the pond. It was all good news, better than what we heard on the portable radio when it was working. Then the school bus would come beeping around the bend and the boys would moan and groan and trudge off with their books and lunch buckets, unless it was planting or harvest or just time to go after squirrel.

Whenever I got to thinking like that I'd have to stop and remember it wasn't always that good.

I made myself think about the times when there was too much rain or not enough rain and the corn didn't do so good. The time the cow sickened and had to be put down, and Glenna cried so to see her old friend go like that. Or the time that the lightning struck the big old mockernut tree and it fell on the barn and caved in the roof.

But worst of all was the time the man came in a big Chrysler car with a paper in his pocket and said he owned everything that was underneath of our land. Not he himself, but the Company he worked for and that amounted to the same thing. He showed me the paper and there was my Daddy's signature at the bottom plain as if I saw him put it there myself. My Daddy learned to sign his name after he was a grown man and many's the night I'd seen him practicing to get it just right, so I'd recognize it anywhere. It was Daddy who'd insisted that I learn how to read and figure and study about the world outside our hills so when the time came I could make up my own mind whether to stay or go. But he'd never told me anything about this paper.

The Company man puffed himself up inside his sharp plaid city suit and made ready to read the paper out loud. Well, "Excuse me," I said, "I'd like to read that paper myself." I was polite and all, but I did want him to know that hillbilly though I might be, I was not ignorant.

A lot of good my pride did me, because that paper said exactly what he said it did, in amongst the whereases and the aforesaids. It said that my Daddy had sold the mineral rights under our land to the Company for $200, and the Company could come in any time they liked and take out whatever they could find there. Only they couldn't touch the cabin or the outbuildings.

"Do you understand what the paper says?" he asked, reaching for it with a soft white hand.

"Means you're planning to do a little digging," I answered. We were standing on the porch all this time, and Glenna was standing just inside the door with LaDonna hiding behind her skirt.

The Company man laughed a fat jolly ha-ha-ha and said, "That's exactly right. We've got to do a little digging and get that coal out. I'm glad you understand, sir. Saves time that way. And trouble. Now, we'll give you a chance to get your crops in before we start." He pulled another piece of paper from his pocket. "Now, let's see. We've got the shovels and the crew scheduled to start in about three weeks. Okay? See you then."

He stepped down off the porch, moving smartly for a short fat man.

"Corn won't be ready in three weeks," I called after him.

I guess he didn't hear me. He just went straight to his big black car and got in. The car was a bit dusty on top of its polish and I wondered how many country roads he'd traveled and how many pieces of paper he'd brought into the hills and hollows. He nosed the car on up the road, and I guessed that Avery Spencer, over the hill and down the next hollow, would be in line to get some good news too. I turned to Glenna and saw the fear in her brown eyes and in her white pinched lips.

I don't know how long I was lost in remembering, but my back was starting to feel blistered. I'd been standing in front of the open oven door to soak up some heat. It's funny how that oven heat doesn't warm your bones. It just makes your skin hot. Nothing like the sun heat in the dream that seemed to warm from the inside out. Only that heat didn't last past waking up. Wish I could carry that dream sun inside me all through the day, walking through the gray snow and the icy puddles with the wind coming around the corners of buildings sudden-like and blasting right through my old hunting jacket.

I had a swallow of coffee left in my cup. It was pretty light in color and tasted weak. Glenna must be trying to make the coffee go farther than it's supposed to. She was clearing off the table now and the kids were putting on their jackets to go to school. At least they got the free hot lunch along with their letters. Calvin, being in junior high school, minded a lot having to line up for the free lunch tickets in full sight of all the other kids. I think if it was only for himself he wouldn't do it. Would rather go hungry. But he always managed to carry something home in his pocket, some bread or an apple, or sometimes a piece of meat wrapped up in a sheet of notebook paper.

The kids left quietly, only Calvin stopping to say, "Goodbye, Dad. 'Bye, Ma." I'd have to be leaving soon myself if I was going to pick up on any jobs that might be offered today. Glenna was washing up the breakfast bowls in cold water. She looked tired and her belly made it awkward for her at the sink. Her soft brown hair that used to be curly and bouncy hung limp on her shoulders. She said it was because she lacked rainwater to wash it with.

"I best be going now," I said.

"Yes."

"I'll surely get something today."

"Yes."

"We can always get the welfare."

"Yes." Her dull eyes flashed for just a moment. "No. No, we can't do that."

But the sparkle had flared and was gone, and I knew it would be gone forever if we once took the welfare. It hurt my heart something fierce to see my pretty Glenna, who used to laugh and sing, who knew all the old songs and could play the zither till it brought tears of pleasure to your eyes, to see my lady-wife brought so low and downhearted. Maybe she'd perk up after the baby came.

"How are you feeling?" I asked her.

"All right. A little tired."

"Will it be soon?"

"Next week, maybe. Maybe sooner. Or later. I wish. . . ."

Her voice trailed off, but I knew she was wishing she didn't have to have this baby in the city hospital where the doctors raced around from one to the next and the nurses didn't have time to hold her hand and say a few words of comfort. I knew she was wishing for her own bedstead with the carved posts that she'd clung to when the pains came fast, for the granny-woman who'd caught each and every one of the other babies, for her mother and her own kind of womenfolk clustering around holding her hand and giving her encouraging words and sips of honey-sweetened ginger tea to ease her time.

"Got to go now," I said. There was no way to say anything else.

All the way down to the unemployment office I kept trying to get back inside the dream, to be walking that dirt road instead of these chilly, slopped-over, crowded city sidewalks, feeling the sun on my back instead of the eyes of the hundreds of people walking behind me or riding in cars or buses if they were lucky. Oh, I know they weren't looking at me. Like as not, they didn't even see me or know I was there. It was just that there was no peace in feeling that hurrying multitude all around me, not like the peace of country roads where a man could be alone and feel right with himself.

But the more I tried to remember the dream, the more my remembering turned to the old home and how it was when the bulldozers came. They started in on the trees first. Cut the trees down and blasted out the stumps. They had trucks going up and down the road hauling those logs away. It was like seeing dear friends cut down in their prime and carted away in a never-ending funeral procession.

Glenna wouldn't step foot outside the cabin once they started their chopping and blasting. She tried to keep the kids inside too. But the boys just wouldn't be kept. To Denzil and Vergil it was better than a revival meeting, but I could see Calvin turning thoughtful and silent as he watched them gouging away at the hillside.

I was no better. I'd gotten in what corn was ready for pick-

ing, but there was a lot left still in the ear that I'd never see
the benefit of. But once the 'dozers and the power shovels
started tearing chunks out of the land it seemed like I got
paralyzed. Could do nothing but listen to the hungry grinding and wait and watch while the face of the hillside changed
like the face of a beautiful woman turned haggard and old
before her time by a great sorrow. The animals couldn't take
it any better than we could. Both dogs disappeared one night
and we never saw them again. The sow littered early and ate
her farrow. The chickens ran around pecking at each other
and the hens almost stopped laying entirely.

I'd seen strip-mined land once before. It was in the south-
ern part of the state where we'd gone once to visit with some
of Glenna's kin. There was a place where there'd once been a
hill, covered with trees older than the oldest person around
those parts. When we saw it, the shovels had finished their
work and gone away. There was no sign of any hill, just
blackened holes and trenches and scattered rocks like bones
sticking out of a half-rotted corpse. Round and about there
were heaps of earth just shoved aside with the life gone out
of it. As far as we could see there was no growing thing.

The people there said that in dry weather when the wind
blew, the gritty dust rose in great clouds and covered everything for miles around, and when it rained the black mud
crept into the hollows smothering everything in its path. In
one place there'd been a mud avalanche that covered a whole
cabin, and a baby was crushed to death when the walls caved
in. Those people hadn't been able to stop the shovels from
coming, and now that it was all over and the land was dead,
they didn't know what to do. They just hung on.

Before the shovels started in on our hillside I went to see
the preacher, hoping he could give me some advice on how
to stop them and maybe help me get together with some of
the others whose land was threatened. I told him about the
paper with my Daddy's signature on it, and what I'd seen of
land that had been worked over by those shovels. He said I
should hold fast and pray to God. He said I should render
unto Caesar, and I should have faith in God and in our President to see the right thing done. He said it was possible that
the Government would make the Company put everything

back the way it was before. I said I didn't see how they could do that since it took a while to grow a tree.

Later on I heard that the Company had given the preacher a donation for his Bible study school, but I don't know if that was true.

We hung on. We watched the shovels take huge bites out of the hill, chew them up and spit them out at the edge of the cornfield. We watched the trucks come up the road empty and go down full, and we ate their dust. The day the bulldozer flattened Glenna's kitchen garden I spoke what was on my mind.

"Glenna," I said after supper that night, "it's time to go."

"I guess so," she answered. "Where can we go?"

"I've thought about that some." I was trying to sound very calm and sensible, but truth of the matter was that I was scared by what I was going to say. "I don't see how we can start up another place, even if I knew of another place to start. We haven't got the money to buy land. Anyway, I'd just be setting on it waiting for the shovels to come over the hill and start in again."

"Then what can we do?"

I think Glenna knew what I had in mind. There wasn't much that we kept secret from each other, and although she never said much it seemed she could almost read my thoughts sometimes. I was just filling in words to keep from getting to the point.

"I'm still a young man, Glenna, and I've got my health and my strength. I can read and write and figure. But most of all I'm willing to work. And I do believe that any man, he's willing to work, can find a job to do."

"You mean we're going to the city."

"Well, yes." We were sitting at the plank table, and Glenna got up to stack the supper dishes and heat the water in the big tin dishpan.

"Oh, I fear it. I don't like it and I fear it," she whispered.

"It'll be all right, Glenna," I told her. "There are lots and lots of people who do okay in cities. Maybe there are some bad ones there, but so are there anywhere. And along of the bad ones I'll bet there are ten times as many good folk, helping and kind. Only we don't ever get to hear of them. And the kids'll get to go to good schools and make something of themselves and not be poor dirty farmers like their Daddy." I was telling all this to Glenna, but I was telling it to myself as well, bolstering up my plan every way I could.

"I recollect the time Acey Doolittle went to Indianapolis and had his car stolen and all his money and had to hitchhike back home."

"Aw, Glenna, he was drunk at the same time and you know it."

I'd done an awful lot of talking for one time and I was afraid that any more and I'd start losing faith in my decision.

"Guess I'll go to bed now," I said. "We'll be pretty busy from tomorrow, selling off the hogs and chickens and deciding what we can carry along with us in the car."

I reached the unemployment office in record time—twenty minutes of fast walking. Running more like. Running in front of the memory of the little house in the hollow with its shutters closed up so it couldn't look out at the creeping deadness all around it, and us driving away in the old Chevy with every mortal thing we could carry packed inside and tied on top. Now the old Chevy sat out in the street with its wheels gone and its seats and engine gone and all the glass smashed out. Nobody even wanted to haul its carcass away for junk.

I gave in my name to the lady at the front desk. She ought to know it by heart by this time since she heard it darn near every morning. But somehow she never seemed to remember. I knew her name all right. She had it on a little metal plate on her desk. Miss I. Fonseca. She had stiff bright yellow hair and blue on her eyelids and a lot of red lipstick on her mouth. Her voice was hard and loud, but more than that it was disconnected some way, as if the things she had to say had nothing to do with Miss I. Fonseca.

I went and found a plastic chair to sit on and wait and the back section of a newspaper to read while I was waiting. I was about halfway through the Help Wanted ads, wondering how on earth I was ever going to get the experience that everybody seemed to want even for a job of janitoring, when Miss I. Fonseca called my name.

"Mr. Powell will see you now," she said in that loud and distant way of hers.

I'd seen Mr. Powell before and he'd given me a few jobs of casual labor over the months. I never thought to see the day when I would be beholden to a colored man for a job of work. But Mr. Powell was kind and polite and seemed to understand the hardships of a country person in the city. He told me once that his own people had come up from the South years ago when he was a kid, so I guess he remembered the way of it.

I walked over to his cubicle lined around with green metal walls halfway up and frosted glass the rest of the way.

"Morning, Mr. Mayhew," he said. "Have a seat. How's it going?"

"Morning, sir. Okay, I guess." I set down and waited.

He shuffled through a stack of cards on his desk and pulled one out.

"It says here on your card that you can read and write and do arithmetic."

"Yes, sir."

"Well, I just had a call from Mossbacker's Warehouse. Seems a forklift tipped over and landed on their checker. They need a replacement right away. Think you can handle it?"

"Yes, sir." I had no notion of what a checker was supposed to do, but I wasn't about to tell that to Mr. Powell, decent as he was.

"It's easy work," he said. "All you have to do is mark off on a check list whatever goes in or comes out of the warehouse and add it up at the end. And if you work out all right, the job might last until the regular man gets out of the hospital. If you get over there right away you'll be able to get in a good seven hours. Here's the address." He scribbled on a slip of paper. "And the directions how to get there."

I stood up. "Thank you, Mr. Powell. I'll sure do my best." He held out his hand and I took it. I'd never shaken the hand of a colored man before, but this was a man who was helping me to stand tall and not looking down on me for a dumb redneck. Sometimes the old ways of thinking and doing need to be shook up a little. I turned to leave.

"Ah . . . Mr. Mayhew. . . ."

I turned back in the doorway.

"The warehouse is about three miles from here. Have you got bus fare?"

I hesitated, then started to say "yes" although all I had was enough to buy a cup of coffee for my lunch, and that wasn't enough for bus fare. But before I could say anything, Mr. Powell was around his desk and pressing some coins into my hand.

"It's just a loan. You can pay me back." He clapped me on the shoulder. "Good luck. I'll call and tell them you're on the way."

I ran out of the unemployment office and all the way to the bus stop, no room in my head or my heart now for memories. I was a man with a job of work to do and impatient to get at it and prove myself. The bus came within a few minutes and I took that as a good omen. I was on my way. We'd be all right now.

I scarcely noticed the dreary city landscape as the bus rolled along. I kept thinking of all the things we needed and how we could get some of them in just a few hours. We could all go down to the store after I got home from work and have a good time deciding what we needed most. Maybe I could keep enough back for a little present for Glenna, a growing plant or a shiny hair clip, something to cheer her up. Before I finished thinking about all the ham hocks and beans we'd be able to buy, the bus reached my stop and I jumped off happy as a kid diving off a barn rafter into a pile of hay.

The job was easy, just like Mr. Powell said. But it was cold. I stood out on the loading dock all morning checking in a shipment of automobile parts. The crates were all marked with what was inside them, and all I had to do was find the right place on the check list and make a mark against it. Then the forklift went on inside the warehouse.

I worked slowly at first, to be sure I got everything right, but I soon got the hang of it and speeded up. My hands got numb but I tried not to let that slow me down. I would have worked right through lunchtime, but everybody else knocked off so there was nothing for me to check. A canteen wagon came around and I borrowed fifty cents against my day's pay and bought some hot soup and coffee.

We all sat around an oil stove just inside the warehouse and warmed ourselves against the afternoon's work. There were about eight other men working there. I didn't say very much, just made myself known, and listened while they discussed the accident that had brought me such good luck. The regular checker had suffered two broken ribs and a dislocated shoulder. No one knew when he'd be able to come back to work. I was sorry for his pain, but grateful for my chance to work a few days and get some of that experience I didn't seem to have.

We finished unloading the automobile parts during the afternoon and started working on an outgoing shipment of machine tools. Five o'clock came and I was ready to go on working all night if need be, but I went to the office and collected my day's pay, less the fifty cents lunch money. The boss asked me if I could come back next day and I said that wild horses couldn't keep me away if he wanted me there. He laughed and said I was a good worker all right, and he'd see me in the morning.

With $13.50 in my pocket I felt like a millionaire. Even so, I decided to walk home because the bus fare would just buy a quart of milk for the kids. I walked back along the bus route, looking in the shop windows along the way. I came to a dime store and went into its bright lights and warm thick popcorn-and-candy smell. They had some plants way in the back of the store, but they looked so sad and droopy it would only make Glenna more downhearted to set eyes on one of them. I could have got her a goldfish in a bowl for ninety-nine cents, but I was afraid it would freeze to death before I got it home. So I settled for a bright green plastic hair barrette with yellow daisies on it for forty-nine cents plus tax.

I practically ran the rest of the way and was on our block before it really got dark. I passed the old Chevy where it sat ringed round with street filth and gray slush. Some kids were jumping on top of it. The rear license plate was gone and I thought that was a good thing so nobody could find out it was

mine and give me parking tickets. The front plate, the one
that said *West Virginia—Almost Heaven,* was still in place. I
guess nobody wanted that, or believed it was true.

The hallway was dark, as always. The super hardly ever
bothered to put new light bulbs in. They always got stolen after a few days. But I knew my way by feel and by smell.
There were always the same number of steps going up and
coming down, and I ran up those four flights and around
those dark landings like I was running up to Salvation John-
ny's camp meeting to be saved. I couldn't wait to lay my day's
earnings before Glenna and tell her that I might be working
steady for a while.

The door of the apartment was locked and I was glad of
that. Glenna often forgot to keep the door locked. We'd never had a lock on the door back home. In the city it was best to
keep your door locked. I banged on the door and yelled for
her to open up. There was no sound from inside. I thought
maybe she and the kids had gone out or maybe her time had
come and they'd all gone to the hospital. I got out my key
and unlocked the door.

It was dark in the apartment, but what came out at me and
almost bowled me over was the smell. The gas smell came bil-
lowing out of there into my face like a suffocating demon. I
must have yelled because I got a lungful of it that made me
dizzy. I know that I reached inside the door and flicked on
the overhead light. I know that I ran into the kitchen and
threw a chair at the window.

After that things are a little mixed up, but I know what I
saw. I saw my old shotgun lying on the kitchen table with a
piece of paper propped up against it. I saw Glenna setting on
a kitchen chair with her head lying on the open oven door.
LaDonna was lying at her feet. I think I turned the gas off
then.

I went into the next room where the kids slept and I saw
Denzil and Vergil clutching at each other on the floor in a
corner, and the dried blood on their faces. I saw where Calvin had tried to crawl out of the room in spite of the terrible
wound in his chest and hadn't been able to make it. I went
back to the kitchen.

Cold air was coming in the broken window. The gas smell

was less, but I was still dizzy and there was a distant clanging sound in my head. I felt like I was moving through thick layers of clutching invisible fog. I raised Glenna up. Her face was so flushed she looked like she had a terrible consuming fever. But when I put my lips on her forehead she was cold. I laid her head back down.

I remembered the piece of paper on the table. I went over and picked it up. It was a piece of Calvin's notebook paper. I felt it in my hands, the dry rustle of it, and I smelled the schoolroom smell of it, but it was a long time before I could bring myself to read it. It was written in pencil, in Glenna's careful schoolgirl handwriting, all the letters formed as though the teacher were standing over her with a paddle ready to swat if she did it wrong.

It said, "I can't bear to birth my baby in this place. I'm going Home, and I'm taking the children with me. Sweet Jesus forgive me." That was all.

I put the paper back on the table and I went over and closed the apartment door. And locked it. I went and picked Glenna up off the chair and carried her into the bedroom. She was heavy, but I made it all right. I laid her on the mattress, straight and neat. Then I put each of the children in their own beds and covered them up. I cleaned the shotgun as best I could and put it away. And then I went to bed.

I lay down beside Glenna and pulled the quilt over both of us. I closed my eyes, and the dream came right away. I was standing in the dirt road, but this time I had my shotgun in my hand. I sat in the grassy place, and when the squirrels started carrying on I was ready for them, and I got five. I tied them together and hung them over my gun barrel. When I got to the huckleberry bush I laid the gun and the squirrels in the road, and picked my hat full of berries.

I went on up the road and at the bend I could already smell wood smoke and hear the kids shouting and laughing. I rounded the bend and it was all just as I knew it would be. I left the squirrels on the porch and took the berries inside to Glenna. She was setting in her old rocker nursing a tiny new girl baby. Calvin helped me skin the squirrels, and Denzil and Vergil each begged for a tail to hang on their belts. Everything was the way it was supposed to be.

But sometimes, after I go to bed in that cabin in the hollow, after the kids are all quietened down, and maybe Glenna's sitting up late doing some mending, sometimes when I go to sleep I'll have a dream of people trying to talk to me, of being in ice cold water up to my neck, of being struck by lightning and the shock of it passing through my whole body. But it's never very real. It's not a real place and nothing you could even call a nightmare. And it doesn't happen very often, just once in a while.

Life just goes on in that cabin in the woods. The seasons come and go. The trees stand tall. Glenna grows her runner beans and her squash and tomatoes. The boys and I go hunting, and the girls will learn to make butter and bake bread. And somehow I know that no power shovel is ever going to come over this hill.

EDITORIAL POSTSCRIPT

The story you have just read was nominated by MWA (Mystery Writers of America) as one of the six best new mystery short stories published in American magazines and books during 1974.

THE PROBLEM OF THE COVERED BRIDGE

by Edward D. Hoch

For some time now, as readers of Ellery Queen's Mystery Magazine *have observed, Edward D. Hoch has had a story in every issue of* EQMM—*occasionally two stories in the same issue, one signed by a pseudonym (R. L. Stevens— there, the cat is out of the bag!). The simple truth is, Mr. Hoch is probably the most prolific writer of consistently interesting short stories in the mystery field today, and it is a pleasure and a privilege to offer you his varied series with such regularity. And if Mr. Hoch maintains his standard of quality—and we have every confidence he will, indeed every confidence he will even raise the quality level in terms of texture and substance—he will surely achieve a niche in the Mystery Hall of Fame.*

Here is the short-story box score for Edward D. Hoch as of February 22, 1974 (note the date): more than forty stories about Captain Leopold, the straightforward procedural cop whose cases are anything but straightforward; thirty stories about Rand, the code-and-cipher counterspy-detective; twenty-five stories about Nick Velvet, the unique thief who steals only the valueless; five stories about Sebastian Blue and Laura Charme, Interpol investigators; and assorted stories about Ulysses S. Byrd, con man, and the Lollipop Cop, and at least four other characters.

Up to February 22, 1974, Mr. Hoch had published more than 350 short stories—repeat, 350 short stories—and at that date he was only 44 years old!

We pay this tribute to Mr. Hoch on his 44th birthday,

*and to celebrate the event we are happy to offer the first of a
new Hoch series—the first story about Dr. Sam Hawthorne,
a retired New England doctor, now in his seventies, who
looks back to some of the miracle problems in his past. . . .*

"YOU'RE always hearin' that things were better in the good ol'
days. Well, I don't know about that. Certainly medical treat-
ment wasn't better. I speak from experience, because I started my practice as a country doctor up in New England way
back in 1922. That seems a lifetime ago now, don't it? Heck,
it *is* a lifetime ago!

"I'll tell you one thing that was better, though—the mysteries. The real honest-to-goodness mysteries that happened to
ordinary folks like you an' me. I've read lots of mystery stories in my time, but there's never been anything to compare
with some of the things I experienced personally.

"Take, for instance, the first winter I was up there. A man
drove his horse and buggy through the snow into a covered
bridge and never came out t'other end. All three vanished off
the face o' the earth, as if they'd never existed!

"You want to hear about it? Heck, it won't take too long to
tell. Pull up your chair while I get us—ah—a small libation."

I'd started my practice in Northmont on January 22, 1922
(the old man began). I'll always remember the date, 'cause it
was the very day Pope Benedict XV died. Now I'm not Catholic myself, but in that part of New England a lot of the people are. The death of the Pope was a lot bigger news that day
than the openin' of Dr. Sam Hawthorne's office. Nevertheless, I hired a pudgy woman named April for a nurse,
bought some second-hand furniture, and settled in.

Only a year out of medical school, I was pretty new at the
game. But I made friends easily, 'specially with the farm families out along the creek. I'd driven into town in my 1921
Pierce-Arrow Runabout, a blazin' yellow extravagance that
set my folks back nearly $7,000 when they gave it to me as a
graduation gift. It took me only one day to realize that families in rural New England didn't drive Pierce-Arrow Run-
abouts. Fact is, they'd never even seen one before.

The problem of the car was solved quickly enough for the winter months when I found out that people in this area lucky enough to own automobiles cared for them during the cold weather by drainin' the gas tanks and puttin' the cars up on blocks till spring arrived. It was back to the horse an' buggy for the trips through the snow, an' I figured that was okay by me. In a way it made me one of them.

When the snow got too deep they got out the sleighs. This winter, though, was provin' unusually mild. The cold weather had froze over the ice on Snake Creek for skatin', but there was surprisin' little snow on the ground and the roads were clear.

On this Tuesday mornin' in the first week of March I'd driven my horse an' buggy up the North Road to the farm of Jacob an' Sara Bringlow. It had snowed a couple of inches overnight, but nothin' to speak of, and I was anxious to make my weekly call on Sara. She'd been ailin' since I first come to town and my Tuesday visits to the farm were already somethin' of a routine.

This day, as usual, the place seemed full o' people. Besides Jacob and his wife there were the three children—Hank, the handsome 25-year-old son who helped his pa work the farm, and Susan an' Sally, the 16-year-old twin daughters. Hank's intended, Millie O'Brian, was there too, as she often was those days. Millie was a year younger than Hank, an' they sure were in love. The wedding was already scheduled for May, and it would be a big affair. Even the rumblings 'bout Millie marryin' into a non-Catholic family had pretty much died down as the big day grew nearer.

"'Lo, Dr. Sam," Sally greeted me as I entered the kitchen.

I welcomed the warmth of the stove after the long cold drive. "Hello, Sally. How's your ma today?"

"She's up in bed, but she seems pretty good."

"Fine. We'll have her on her feet in no time."

Jacob Bringlow and his son entered through the shed door, stampin' the snow from their boots. "Good day, Dr. Sam," Jacob said. He was a large man, full of thunder like an Old Testament prophet. Beside him, his son Hank seemed small and slim and a bit underfed.

"Good day to you," I said. "A cold mornin'!"

"'Tis that. Sally, git Dr. Sam a cup o' coffee—can't you see the man's freezin'?"

I nodded to Hank. "Out cuttin' firewood?"

"There's always some to cut."

Hank Bringlow was a likable young chap about my own age. It seemed to me he was out of place on his pa's farm, and I was happy that the wedding would soon take him away from there. The only books an' magazines in the house belonged to Hank, and his manner was more that of a fun-lovin' scholar than a hard-workin' farmer. I knew he and Millie planned to move into town after their marriage, and I 'spected it would be a good thing for both of 'em.

Millie always seemed to be workin' in the kitchen when I made my calls. Maybe she was tryin' to convince the family she could make Hank a good wife. By the town's standards she was a pretty girl, though I'd known prettier ones at college.

She carefully took the coffee cup from young Sally an' brought it to me as I found a place to sit. "Just move those magazines, Dr. Sam," she said.

"Two issues of *Hearst's International?*" It wasn't a magazine frequently found in farmhouses.

"February and March. Hank was readin' the new two-part Sherlock Holmes story."

"They're great fun," I admitted. "I read them a lot in medical school."

Her smile glowed at me. "Mebbe you'll be a writer like Dr. Conan Doyle," she said.

"I doubt that." The coffee was good, warming me after the cold drive. "I really should see Mrs. Bringlow an' finish this later."

"You'll find her in good spirits."

Sara Bringlow's room was at the top of the stairs. The first time I went in, back in January, I found a weak, pale woman in her fifties with a thickened skin and dulled senses, who might have been very close to death. Now the scene was different. Even the room seemed more cheerful, an' certainly Sara Bringlow was more vividly alive than I'd ever seen her. Sittin' up in bed, with a bright pink shawl thrown over her shoulders, she welcomed me with a smile. "See, I'm almost all better! Do you think I can git up this week?"

Her illness today would probably be classed as a form of thyroid condition called myxedema, but we didn't use such fancy words back then. I'd treated her, an' she was better, an' that was all I cared about. "Tell you what, Sara, you stay in bed till Friday an' then you can get up if you feel like it." I winked at her 'cause I knew she liked me to. "If truth be known, I'll bet you been sneakin' out of that bed already!"

"Now how would you know that, Doctor?"

"When Sally met me at the door I asked how you were and she said you were up in bed but seemed pretty good. Well now, where else would you be? The only reason for her sayin' it like that was if you'd been up and about sometime recently."

"Land sakes, you should be a detective, Dr. Sam!"

"I have enough to do bein' a doctor." I took her pulse and blood pressure as I talked. "I see we had some more snow this mornin'."

"Yes indeed! The children will have to shovel off the ice before they go skatin' again."

"The wedding's gettin' mighty close now, isn't it?" I suspected the forthcomin' nuptials were playin' a big part in her recovery.

"Yep, just two months away. It'll be a happy day in my life. I s'pose it'll be hard on Jacob, losin' Hank's help around the farm, but he'll manage. I told him, the boy's twenty-five now—got to lead his own life."

"Millie seems like a fine girl."

"Best there is! Catholic, of course, but we don't hold that agin' her. 'Course her folks would rather she married Walt Rumsey on the next farm, now that he owns it an' all, but Walt's over thirty—too old for a girl like Millie. I 'spect she knowed that too, when she broke off with him."

There was a gentle knock on the door and Susan, the other twin, came in. "Momma, Hank's gettin' ready to go. He wants to know about that applesauce for Millie's ma."

"Land sakes, I near forgot! Tell him to take a jar off the shelf in the cellar."

After she'd gone I said, "Your daughters are lovely girls."

"They are, aren't they? Tall like their father. Can you tell them apart?"

I nodded. "They're at an age where they want to be individuals. Sally's wearin' her hair a mite different now."

"When they were younger, Hank was always puttin' them up to foolin' us, changin' places and such." Then, as she saw me close my bag, her eyes grew serious for a minute. "Dr. Sam, I *am* better, aren't I?"

"Much better. The thickenin' of your skin is goin' away, and you're much more alert."

I left some more of the pills she'd been takin' and went back downstairs. Hank Bringlow was bundled into a fur-collared coat, ready for the trip to Millie's house. It was about two miles down the windin' road, past the Rumsey farm and across the covered bridge.

Hank picked up the quart jar of applesauce and said, "Dr. Sam, why don't you ride along with us? Millie's pa hurt his foot last week. He'd never call a doctor for it, but since you're so close maybe you should take a look."

Millie seemed surprised by his request, but I had no objection. "Glad to. I'll follow you in my buggy."

Outside, Hank said, "Millie, you ride with Dr. Sam so he doesn't get lost."

She snorted at that. "The road doesn't go anywhere else, Hank!"

But she climbed into my buggy an' I took the reins. "I hear tell you've got yourself a fancy yellow car, Dr. Sam."

"It's up on blocks till spring. This buggy is good enough for me." Mine was almost the same as Hank's—a four-wheeled carriage with a single seat for two people, pulled by one horse. The fabric top helped keep out the sun and rain, but not the cold. And ridin' in a buggy during a New England winter could be mighty cold!

The road ahead was windin', with woods on both sides. Though it was nearly noon, the tracks of Hank's horse an' buggy were the only ones ahead of us in the fresh snow. Not many people came up that way in the winter. Before we'd gone far, Hank speeded up and disappeared from sight round a bend in the road.

"Hank seems so unlike his pa," I said, making conversation.

"That's because Jacob is his stepfather," Millie explained. "Sara's first husband—Hank's real father—died of typhoid when he was a baby. She remarried and then the twins were born."

"That explains the gap."

"Gap?"

"Nine years between Hank and his sisters. Farm families usually have their children closer together."

Hank's buggy was still far enough ahead to be out of sight, but now the Rumsey farm came into view. We had to pause a minute as Walt Rumsey blocked the road with a herd of cows returnin' to the barn. He waved and said, "Hank just passed."

"I know," Millie called back. "He goes so fast we can't keep up with him."

When the cows were gone I speeded up, still following the track of Hank's buggy in the snow. As we rounded the next corner I thought we'd see him 'cause the road was now straight and the woods on both sides had ended. But there was only the covered bridge ahead, and the empty road runnin' beyond it to the O'Brian farm.

"Where is he?" Millie asked, puzzled.

"He must be waitin' for us inside the bridge." From our angle we couldn't yet see through it all the way.

"Prob'ly," she agreed with a chuckle. "He always says that covered bridges are kissin' bridges, but that's not true at all."

"Where I come from—" I began, and then paused. The interior of the bridge could be seen now, and no horse an' buggy were waitin' inside. "Well, he certainly went in. You can see the tracks in the snow."

"But—" Millie was half standing now in her seat. "Something's there on the floor of the bridge. What is it?"

We rode up to the bridge entrance and I stopped the horse. There were no windows cut into the sides of this covered bridge, but the light from the ends and from between the boards was enough to see by. I got down from the buggy. "It's his jar of applesauce," I said. "It smashed when it fell from the buggy."

But Millie wasn't lookin' at the applesauce. She was starin' straight ahead at the unmarked snow beyond the other end of the fifty-foot bridge. "Dr. Sam!"

"What is it?"

"There are no tracks goin' off the bridge! He came into it, but he didn't leave it! Dr. Sam, *where is he?*"

She was right, by gum! The tracks of Hank's horse an' buggy led into the bridge. Fact is, the damp imprint of the meltin' snow could be seen for several feet before it gradually faded away.

But there was no horse, no buggy, no Hank Bringlow.

Only the broken jar of applesauce he'd been carrying.

But if he hadn't disturbed the snow at the far end of the bridge, he must be—he *had* to be—still here! My eyes went up to the patterned wooden trusses that held the bridge together. There was nothing—nothing but the crossbeams and the roof itself. The bridge was in remarkably good shape, protected from weathering by its roof. Even the sides were sturdy and unbroken. Nothin' bigger than a squirrel could've fit between the boards.

"It's some sort of trick," I said to Millie. "He's got to be here!"

"But *where?*"

I walked to the other end of the bridge and examined the unmarked snow. I peered around the corner o' the bridge at the frozen surface of Snake Creek. The skaters had not yet shoveled off the snow, and it was as unmarked as the rest. Even if the horse an' buggy had passed somehow through the wooden floor or the sides o' the bridge, there was no place they could've gone without leavin' a mark. Hank had driven his buggy into the bridge with Millie an' me less than a minute behind him, dropped his quart jar o' applesauce, and vanished.

"We've got to get help," I said. Instinct told me I shouldn't disturb the snow beyond the bridge by goin' forward to Millie's house. "Wait here an' I'll run back to Rumsey's farm."

I found Walt Rumsey in the barn with his cows, forkin' hay out of the loft. "'Lo, Doc," he called down to me. "What's up?"

"Hank Bringlow seems to have disappeared. Darnedest thing I ever saw. You got a telephone here?"

"Sure have, Doc." He hopped down to the ground. "Come on in the house."

As I followed him through the snow I asked, "Did Hank seem odd in any way when he went past you?"

"Odd? No. He was bundled up against the cold, but I knew it was him. I kept my cows to the side o' the road till he passed."

"Did he say anything?"

"No, just waved."

"Then you didn't actually see his face or hear his voice?"

Walt Rumsey turned to me. "Wa-el, no. But hell, I've known Hank mosta my life! It was him, all right."

An' I s'pose it had to be. No substitution o' drivers could've been made anywhere along the road, and even if a substitution had been made, how did the substitute disappear?

I took the phone that Walt Rumsey offered, cranked it up, and asked for the Bringlow farm. One of the twins answered. "This is Dr. Sam. We seem to have lost your brother. He didn't come back there, did he?"

"No. Isn't he with you?"

"Not right now. Your pa around?"

"He's out in the field somewhere. You want Momma?"

"No. She should stay in bed." No need to bother her yet. I hung up an' called the O'Brian farm with the same results. Millie's brother Larry answered the phone. He'd seen nothin' of Hank, but he promised to start out on foot toward the bridge at once, searchin' for buggy tracks or footprints.

"Any luck?" Rumsey asked when I'd finished.

"Not yet. You didn't happen to watch him after he passed, did you?"

Rumsey shook his head. "I was busy with the cows."

I went back outside and headed for the bridge, with Rumsey taggin' along. Millie was standin' by my horse an' buggy, lookin' concerned. "Did you find him?" she asked.

I shook my head. "Your brother's on his way over."

While Rumsey and I went over every inch of the covered bridge, Millie simply stood at the far end, watchin' for her brother. I guess she needed him to cling to just then. Larry

O'Brian was young, handsome, an' likable—a close friend of both Hank Bringlow an' Walt Rumsey. My nurse April told me that when Walt inherited the farm after his folks' death, both Larry and Hank helped him with the first season's planting. She'd also told me that despite their friendship Larry was against Hank marryin' his sister. P'raps, like some brothers, he viewed no man as worthy of the honor.

When Larry arrived he had nothing new to tell us. "No tracks between here an' the farm," he confirmed.

I had a thought. "Wait a minute! If there aren't any tracks, how in heck did you get over here this mornin', Millie?"

"I was with Hank at his place last night. When the snow started, the family insisted I stay over. We only got a couple of inches, though." She seemed to sense an unasked question, and she added, "I slept with the twins in their big bed."

Larry looked at me. "What d'you think?"

I stared down at the smashed quart of applesauce which everyone had carefully avoided. "I think we better call Sheriff Lens."

Sheriff Lens was a fat man who moved slowly and thought slowly (Doctor Sam continued). He'd prob'ly never been confronted with any crime bigger than buggy stealin'—certainly nothin' like the disappearance from the covered bridge. He grunted and rasped as he listened to the story, then threw up his hands in dismay. "It couldn'ta happened the way you say. The whole thing's impossible, an' the impossible jest don't make sense. I think you're all foolin' me—maybe havin' an April Fool joke three weeks early."

It was about then that the strain finally got to Millie. She collapsed in tears, and Larry and I took her home. Their pa, Vincent O'Brian, met us at the door. "What is this?" he asked Larry. "What's happened to her?"

"Hank's disappeared."

"Disappeared? You mean run off with another woman?"

"No, nothin' like that."

While Larry helped Millie to her room, I followed Vincent into the kitchen. He wasn't the hulkin' ox of a man that Jacob Bringlow was, but he still had the muscles of a lifetime spent in the field. "Hank wanted me to come along," I explained. "Said you'd hurt your foot."

"It's nothin'. Twisted my ankle choppin' wood."

"Can I see it?"

"No need." But he pulled up his pants leg reluctantly and I stooped to examine it. Swellin' and bruisin' were pronounced, but the worst was over.

"Not too bad," I agreed. "But you should be soakin' it." Glancing around to be sure we weren't overheard, I lowered my voice and added, "Your first thought was that Hank Bringlow had run off with another woman. Who did you have in mind?"

He looked uneasy. "Nobody special."

"This may be serious, Mr. O'Brian."

He thought about it and finally said, "I won't pretend I'm happy about my daughter marryin' a non-Catholic. Larry feels the same way. Besides, Hank fools around with the girls in town."

"For instance?"

"For instance Gert Page at the bank. Wouldn't be surprised he run off with her."

I saw Millie comin' back downstairs and I raised my voice a bit. "You soak that ankle now, in good hot water."

"Has there been any word?" Millie asked. She'd recovered her composure, though her face still lacked color.

"No word, but I'm sure he'll turn up. Was he in the habit of playin' tricks?"

"Sometimes he'd fool people with Susan an' Sally. Is that what you mean?"

"Don't know what I mean," I admitted. "But he seemed anxious for you to ride with me. Maybe there was a reason."

I stayed for lunch, and when no word came I headed back to town alone. The Sheriff an' some others were still at the covered bridge when I rode through it, but I didn't stop. I could see they'd gotten nowhere toward solvin' the mystery, and I was anxious to get to the bank before it closed.

Gert Page was a hard-eyed blonde girl of the sort who'd never be happy in a small New England town. She answered my questions 'bout Hank Bringlow with a sullen distrust she might have felt towards all men.

"Do you know where he is, Gert?"

"How would I know where he is?"

"Were you plannin' to run off with him before his marriage?"

"Ha! Me run off with him? Listen, if Millie O'Brian wants him that bad, she can have him!" The bank was closin' and she went back to countin' the cash in her drawer. "B'sides, I hear tell men get tired of married life after a bit. I just might see him in town again. But I sure won't run off with him and be tied to one man!"

I saw Roberts, the bank's manager, watchin' us and I wondered why they kept a girl like Gert on the payroll. I 'spected she was most unpopular with the bank's lady customers.

As I left the bank I saw Sheriff Lens enterin' the general store across the street. I followed and caught him at the pickle barrel. "Anything new, Sheriff?"

"I give it up, Doc. Wherever he is, he ain't out by the bridge."

The general store, which was right next to my office, was a cozy place with great wheels of cheese, buckets o' flour, an' jars o' taffy kisses. The owner's name was Max, and his big collie dog always slept on the floor near the potbellied stove. Max came around the counter to join us and said, "Everyone's talkin' about young Hank. What do you think happened?"

"No idea," I admitted.

"Couldn't an aeroplane have come over an' picked up the whole shebang?"

"I was right behind him in my buggy. There was no aeroplane." I glanced out the window and saw Gert Page leavin' the bank with the manager, Roberts. "I hear some gossip that Hank was friendly with Gert Page. Any truth to it?"

Max scratched the stubble on his chin and laughed. "Everybody in town is friendly with Gert, includin' ol' Roberts there. It don't mean nothin'."

"I guess not," I agreed. But if it hadn't meant anything to

Hank Bringlow, had it meant somethin' to Millie's pa an' brother?

Sheriff Lens and I left the general store together. He promised to keep me informed, and I went next door to my office. My nurse April was waitin' for all the details. "My God, you're famous, Dr. Sam! The telephone ain't stopped ringin'!"

"Hell of a thing to be famous for. I didn't see a thing out there."

"That's the point! Anyone else they wouldn't believe—but you're somethin' special."

I sighed and kicked off my damp boots. "I'm just another country doctor, April."

She was a plump jolly woman in her thirties, and I'd never regretted hirin' her my first day in town. "They think you're smarter'n most, Dr. Sam."

"Well, I'm not."

"They think you can solve this mystery."

Who else had called me a detective that day? Sara Bringlow? "Why do they think that?"

"I guess because you're the first doctor in town ever drove a Pierce-Arrow car."

I swore at her but she was laughin' and I laughed too. There were some patients waitin' in the outer office and I went to tend to them. It was far from an ordinary day, but I still had my practice to see to. Towards evening, by the time I'd finished, the weather had turned warmer. The temperature hovered near 40 and a gentle rain began to fall.

"It'll git rid o' the snow," April said as I left for the day.

"Ayah, it'll do that."

"Mebbe it'll uncover a clue."

I nodded, but I didn't believe it. Hank Bringlow had gone far away, and the meltin' snow wasn't about to bring him back.

The telephone woke me at four the next mornin'. "This is Sheriff Lens, Doc," the voice greeted me. "Sorry to wake you, but I gotta bad job for you."

"What's that?"

"We found Hank Bringlow."

"Where?"

"On the Post Road, about ten miles south o' town. He's sittin' in his buggy like he jest stopped for a rest."

"Is he—?"

"Dead, Doc. That's what I need you for. Somebody shot him in the back o' the head."

It took me near an hour (Doctor Sam went on) to reach the scene, drivin' the horse an' buggy fast as I could over the slushy country roads. Though the night was mild, the rain chilled me to the bone as I rode through the darkness on that terrible mission. I kept thinkin' about Millie O'Brian, and Hank's ma only just recoverin' from her lengthy illness. What would the news do to them?

Sheriff Lens had some lanterns out in the road, and I could see their eerie glow as I drove up. He helped me down from the buggy an' I walked over to the small circle of men standin' by the other rig. Two of them were deputies, another was a farmer from a nearby house. They hadn't disturbed the body—Hank still sat slumped in a corner o' the seat, his feet wedged against the front o' the buggy.

I drew a sharp breath when I saw the back of his head. "Shotgun," I said curtly.

"Can you tell if it happened here, Doc?"

"Doubtful." I turned to the farmer. "Did you find him?"

The man nodded and repeated a story he'd obviously told 'em already. "My wife heard the horse. We don't git nobody along this road in the middle o' the night, so I come out to look around. I found him like this."

In the flare of lantern light I noticed somethin'—a round mark on the horse's flank that was sensitive to my touch. "Look here, Sheriff."

"What is it?"

"A burn. The killer loaded Hank into the buggy an' then tied the reins. He singed the horse with a cigar or somethin' to make it run. Could've run miles before it stopped from exhaustion."

Lens motioned to his deputies. "Let's take him into town. We won't find nothin' else out here." He turned back to me. "At least he's not missin' any more."

"No, he's not missin'. But we still don't know what happened on that bridge. We only know it wasn't any joke."

The funeral was held two days later, on Friday mornin', with a bleak winter sun breakin' through the overcast to throw long March shadows across the tombstones of the little town cemetery. The Bringlows were all there, 'course, and Millie's folks, and many from town. Afterwards many of us went back to the Bringlow farm. It was a country custom, however sad the occasion, and many neighbors brought food for the family.

I was sittin' in the parlor, away from the others, when the bank manager, Roberts, came up to me.

"Has the Sheriff found any clues yet?" he asked.

"Nothin' I know of."

"It's a real baffler. Not just the *how*, but the *why*."

"The *why?*"

He nodded. "When you're goin' to kill someone you just do it. You don't rig up some fantastic scheme for them to disappear first. What's the point?"

I thought about that, and I didn't have a ready answer. When Roberts drifted away I went over to Sara Bringlow and asked how she was feelin'. She looked at me with tired eyes and said, "My first day outta bed. To bury my son."

There was no point arguin' with a mother's grief. I saw Max bringin' in a bag of groceries from his store and I started over to help him. But my eye caught somethin' on the parlor table. It was the March issue of *Hearst's International.* I remembered Hank had been reading the Sherlock Holmes story in the February and March issues. I located the February one under a stack o' newspapers and turned to the Holmes story.

It was in two parts, and called *The Problem of Thor Bridge.*

Bridge?

I found a quiet corner and sat down to read.

It took me only a half hour, and when I finished I sought out Walt Rumsey from the next farm. He was standin' with Larry O'Brian on the side porch, an' when he saw me comin' he said, "Larry's got some good bootleg stuff out in his buggy. Want a shot?"

"No, thanks, Walt. But you can do somethin' else for me. Do you have a good stout rope in your barn?"

He frowned in concentration. "I s'pose so."

"Could we ride over there now? I just read somethin' that gave me an idea about how Hank might've vanished from that bridge."

We got into his buggy an' drove the mile down the windin' road to his farm. The snow was melted by this time, and the cows were clustered around the water trough by the side of the barn. Walt took me inside, past empty stalls an' milk cans an' carriage wheels, to a big shed attached to the rear. Here, among assorted tools, he found a twelve-foot length of worn hemp.

"This do you?"

"Just the thing. Want to come to the bridge with me?"

The ice of the creek was still firm, though the road had turned to mud. I handed one end o' the rope to Rumsey and played out the other end till it reached the edge of the frozen creek. "What's this all about?" he asked.

"I read a story 'bout a gun that vanished off a bridge by bein' pulled into the water."

He looked puzzled. "But Hank's buggy couldn'ta gone into the crick. The ice was unbroken."

"All the same I think it tells me somethin'. Thanks for the use o' the rope."

He took me back to the Bringlow house, puzzled but unquestioning. The mourners were beginning to drift away, and I sought out Sheriff Lens. "I've got an idea about this mystery, Sheriff. But it's sort of crazy."

"In this case, even a crazy idea would be welcome."

Jacob Bringlow, tall and unbent from the ordeal of the funeral, came around the corner o' the house with one of the twins. "What is it, Sheriff?" he asked. "Still searchin' for clues?"

"We may have one," I said. "I got an idea."

He eyed me up an' down, p'raps blamin' me for what happened to his stepson. "You stick to your doctorin'," he said with a slur, and I knew he'd been samplin' Larry's bottle. "Go look at my wife. She don't seem right to me."

I went inside and found Sara pale and tired-looking. I ordered her up to bed and she went without argument. Max was leavin', and so was the O'Brian family. The banker had already gone. But when I went back on the porch, Jacob Bringlow was still waitin' for me. He was lookin' for trouble. Maybe it was a mixture of grief and bootleg whiskey.

"Sheriff says you know who killed Hank."

"I didn't say that. I just got an idea."

"Tell me. Tell us all!"

He spoke loudly, and Larry O'Brian paused with Millie to listen. Walt Rumsey came over too. In the distance, near the buggies, I saw Gert Page from the bank. I hadn't seen her at the funeral, but she'd come to pay some sort of last respects to Hank.

"We can talk about it inside," I replied, keepin' my voice down.

"You're bluffin'! You don't know a thing!"

I drew a deep breath. "All right, if you want it like this. Hank was reading a Sherlock Holmes story before he died. There's another one he prob'ly read years ago. In it Holmes calls Watson's attention to the curious incident of the dog in the nighttime. I could echo his words."

"But there was no dog in the nighttime," Sheriff Lens pointed out. "There's no dog in this whole danged case!"

"My mistake," I said. "Then let me direct your attention to the curious incident of the cows in the daytime."

It was then that Walt Rumsey broke from the group and ran towards his buggy. "Grab him, Sheriff!" I shouted. "He's your murderer!"

I had to tell it all to April, back at my office, because she hadn't been there and wouldn't believe it otherwise. "Come on, Dr. Sam! How did the cows tell you Walt was the killer?"

"He was bringin' them back to the barn, across the road, as we passed. But from where? Cows don't graze in the snow, and their waterin' trough is next to the barn, not across the road. The only possible reason for the cows crossin' the road in front of us was to obliterate the tracks of Hank's horse an' buggy.

"Except for those cows, the snow was unbroken by anything but the single buggy track—all the way from the Bringlow farm to the covered bridge. We know Hank left the farm. If he never reached the bridge, whatever happened to him had to happen at the point where those cows crossed the road."

"But the tracks to the bridge! You were only a minute behind him, Dr. Sam. That wasn't long enough for him to fake those tracks!"

I smiled, runnin' over the reasonin' as it first came to me. "Roberts the banker answered that one, along with Sherlock Holmes. Roberts asked *why*—why did the killer go to all that trouble? And the answer was that he didn't. It wasn't the killer but Hank Bringlow who went to all the trouble.

"We already knew he'd fooled people with his twin sisters, confusin' their identities. And we knew he'd recently read *The Problem of Thor Bridge,* which has an impossible suicide of sorts takin' place on a bridge. It's not too far-fetched to imagine him arrangin' the ultimate joke—his own disappearance from that covered bridge."

"But *how,* Dr. Sam?" April wanted to know. "I read that Sherlock Holmes story too, an' there's nothin' in it like what happened here."

"True. But as soon as I realized the purpose o' those noonday cows, I knew somethin' had happened to those tracks at the barn. And only one thing could've happened—Hank's buggy turned off the road and went *into* the barn. The tracks from the road to the bridge were faked."

"How?" she repeated, not yet ready to believe a word of it.

"*When* is the more important question. Since there was no time to fake the tracks in the single minute before we came along, they had to have been done earlier. Hank and Walt Rumsey must've been in cahoots on the scheme. Walt went out that mornin', after the snow had stopped, with a couple o' old carriage wheels linked together by an axle. On his boots he'd fastened blocks o' wood a couple o' inches thick, with horseshoes nailed to the bottoms.

"He simply trotted along the road, through the snow, pushin' the pair o' wheels ahead of him. He went into the bridge far enough to leave traces o' snow, then reversed the blocks o' wood on his boots and pushed the wheels back again. The resultin' tracks looked like a four-footed animal pullin' a four-wheeled buggy."

"But—" April started to object.

"I know, I know! A man doesn't run like a horse. But with practise he could space the prints to look good enough. And I'll bet Hank an' Walt practiced plenty while they waited for the right mornin' when the snow was fresh but not too deep. If anyone had examined the tracks o' the horse carefully, they'd've discovered the truth. Careful as he was, Walt Rumsey's prints comin' back from the bridge woulda been a bit different, hittin' the snow from the opposite direction. But they figured I'd drive my buggy up to the bridge in his tracks, all but obliteratin' them, which is what I did. They couldn't really be examined then."

"You're forgettin' the broken jar o' applesauce," April said. "Don't that prove Hank was *on* the bridge?"

"Nothing of the sort! Hank knew in advance his ma planned to send the applesauce to Mrs. O'Brian. He prob'ly suggested it, and he certainly reminded her of it. He simply gave Walt Rumsey a duplicate jar a day or two earlier, an' it was that jar Walt broke on the bridge. The jar Hank was carrying went with him into Walt's barn."

"What if it hadn't snowed that mornin'? What if someone else came along first to leave other tracks?"

I shrugged. "They would've phoned one another and postponed it, I s'pose. It was only meant as a joke. They'd have tried again some other day, with other witnesses. They didn't really need me an' Millie."

"Then how did it turn from a joke to murder?"

"Walt Rumsey had never given up lovin' Millie, or hatin' Hank for takin' her away from him. After the trick worked so well, he saw the perfect chance to kill Hank and win her back. Once I knew he was in on the trick, he had to be the killer—else why was he keepin' quiet 'bout his part in it?

"Hank had hidden his horse an' buggy in that big shed behind the Rumsey barn. When we all went back to town, an' Hank was ready to reappear an' have a good laugh on everyone, Walt Rumsey killed him. Then he waited till dark to dispose of the body on the Post Road. He drove the buggy part way, turned the horse loose to run, and walked home.

"This mornin' after the funeral I made an excuse of wantin' a piece of rope so I could see the inside of Rumsey's barn again. He had spare carriage wheels there, and the shed was big enough to hold a horse an' buggy. That was all the confirmation I needed."

April leaned back and smiled, convinced at last. "After this they'll probably give you the Sheriff's job, Dr. Sam."

I shook my head. "I'm just a country doctor."

"A country doctor with a Pierce-Arrow car!" . . .

"That's the way it happened, back in '22. I've often thought I should write it up now that I'm retired, but there's just never enough time. Sure, I've got other stories. Lots of 'em! Can I get you another—ah—small libation?"